And then,
I found you

And Then, I Found You – Anthology

A collection of short stories about surviving a negative past and finding your happily ever after.

For information for usage, contact CL Foster at:
InkedPhoenix1@gmail.com

Created and printed in the United States of America.
First Edition – February 2016
ISBN-10: 1523979933
ISBN-13: 978-1523979936

Cover art by: Cover Lust Designs
Cover typography by: White Rabbit Book Design
Formatting by: CL Foster
Editing by: Karla Bostic

Our Charity

All proceeds of the sale of this anthology go to RAINN.

The Rape, Abuse & Incest National Network (RAINN) is the largest American anti-sexual assault organization. They operate the National Sexual Assault Hotline and various programs to prevent sexual assault, help victims, and to ensure that rapists are brought to justice.

For more information about our charity or to become a volunteer:
http://rainn.org/

Dedication

To the happily ever after makers.
Thank you.

Contents

Love's Choice
CL Foster

Chapter One

"You're an absolutely crazy person, Rayna!" she said, throwing herself across the bed to block the suitcase.

Chuckling, I simply tossed the handful of clothes over her into the open bag. A rogue shirt landed on the edge, pinning her blonde locks to the bag. "Yeah, we established that a dozen years ago when I physically signed a paper agreeing to be your best friend. Who does that anyway? Best friend contract? Get out. You're in my way," I scoffed as I continued gathering my clothes.

"Well, it made our friendship stronger. You have clauses and stuff holding you to me. This is like a marriage. 'Til death do us part," she said with a grunt as she tugged her hair away from the bag a moment before I shoved her out of the way. Settling at the top of my bed, she leaned against the headboard and glared at me. "I should have put another clause in there that said you're not allowed to randomly leave and go to a foreign country to meet up with potential serial killers without supervision."

"Jolie, you can't make a turkey sandwich by yourself," I scoffed. "How on Earth would you possibly chaperone or supervise me?"

"It's harder to kill two people at once!" she shouted, kicking the edge of my suitcase as she crossed her arms over her chest.

"Well, good because I won't be alone," I pointed out.

She gave an exasperated huff. "What if *he* is the killer, doofus?"

Shrugging, I asked. "Have you seen me? I'm fluffy and hard to kidnap. You worry too much," I said as I rearranged the clothes in the bag, double checking to make sure I had everything I would need. Because I'd never spent a weekend in Paris during the summer, I wasn't sure what I needed to pack, so I was struggling. "I've had self-defense classes and I know this man. You're tripping out for nothing."

"You're going to go meet a stranger!" she huffed again as she tossed her hands in the air. Her voice was nearing dog-whistle decibel.

"Steven is not a stranger, Jo. Please take a few deep breaths and trust me on this."

Mumbling to herself she stood up and started to pace behind me. "Okay, Ms. Rational Thinker," she started, sarcasm flung from her throat like angry spittle. "How long have you known this *person?*"

The emphasis on person wasn't missed by me, but I rolled my eyes and kept my voice as calm as I possibly could. "I've known *Steven* for a year and ten months," I corrected as I zipped up the suitcase and moved toward the bathroom to get my hairbrush and a few other things.

"How do you know he's an actual person?" she asked, sounding more exasperated by the second.

"I've seen him on video chat at least twice a month for nearly two years. We text each other every day, have shared pictures of our families, and much more. I know he's a person. Will you please try to relax and trust me?"

"What if he doesn't even show up? He could be a weak ass chicken shit and not even meet you there and you'll be all alone," she rationalized.

I chuckled. "Oh no, not an entire weekend in Paris all alone. How will I ever survive?" I pretended to be exasperated. My sarcasm had to be obvious. "Stop stressing out. I'm going to the city of love. Have you seen all of that amazing architecture? Art? Culture? I'm still seeing all of that with or without him. If he doesn't show up, that tells me to let go of this crazy feeling, and if he does, then…" I couldn't finish the thought. If he didn't meet me there, my heart would probably be crushed, but if my past has taught me nothing else, I had learned to stop expecting things from people. I was going with a good attitude and planned to have an amazing time in Paris. If someone joined me on that adventure, amazing. If they didn't, oh well. Life was no longer going to screw me over. I refused to be sad or focus on the negative things ever again.

"But what if he shows up and he isn't the same in person? What if something happens and you never come back? What if he talks you into living there? What if you get hurt and I'm not there to help you?" she screeched suddenly, bursting through the bathroom door to hug me. "You can't live there. What about me?"

Smoothing her hair down, I held my best friend to my chest and let her cry out her feelings. I knew this was coming and I knew it was needed. She didn't understand why I was doing this. It was weird for her that I met someone in the way that I did and that we decided to meet in another country that wasn't our own. Even though she knew my past and understood my pain, she couldn't grasp why I needed a change and why this was the best thing that had gone on in my life in forever.

Just as I had stopped trusting people, she had also. Neither of us had been in a relationship for years because of it. When I met Steven, I was immediately drawn to him. We had common interests, his smile and humor captivated me, and I just knew I needed him in my life in any way I could get him. At the time, I thought it was because

I needed a friend that understood me on the level he did, but I had no idea of the impact he was going to make on my future.

Now, I couldn't imagine my life without him. Even though we lived in different countries and were really tied to our work and lives, we somehow thought there would be a way to make things work. We both knew we were crazy, but it was better to be crazy and happy than alone and sad.

"Jo," I soothed. "I love you. You know that, right?"

"Well, duh. You better," she snorted into my t-shirt.

"Why are you so opposed?" I asked as she straightened herself out and washed her face in the sink. The tears all over her cheeks were cute, but puffy eyes and snot were not. "If you have a damned good reason why I shouldn't chase happiness and at least go meet him, I will listen to you. I really will."

Hanging her head, she paused for two full minutes before she said, "I don't have one."

I sighed and took her hand, dragging her out of the bathroom to get her to sit on the bed with me. We sat facing each other, our legs curled under us, just like we always have.

Taking a deep breath, I said, "If I don't try, I will never know."

She nodded. "I really understand that."

"We truly care for each other and both think it's love," I added.

"I know. I've seen the change in you. In your eyes and how you do things. I know he's good for you, I'm just... I don't know."

"We don't call each other boyfriend, girlfriend, or anything like that. We know how impossible and ridiculous this is. We want this chance to just see. One weekend. We will be together, meet each other, see how we are in person, and just give it one shot. If we only get along as friends, we will have a great time and see the sites and enjoy an amazing weekend. If what we think we feel is truly there, we will have a lot of discussing to do so we can figure out the next steps."

She nodded and looked down at the comforter on the bed. Distracting herself with geometric patterns was always her escape when situations got uncomfortable for her mind.

Seeing she was going to shut down and just listen, I continued. "He's amazing and makes me laugh every single day, Jo. He's brilliant and sweet, and I never have to wonder or worry about what is going on with him. Even though he's time zones away from me, he always says goodnight to me. Every morning, when I wake up, he's the first one to tell me good morning. He's much more than I could ever even dream of for myself, so I have to know." I took a deep breath. "I deserve this and so does he."

She looked up, her eyes clashing with mine. "Oh my goodness, Rayna. I'm so sorry. Of course you deserve happiness. Ugh. I'm such a jackass. Please don't think I'm bitter or don't want you to be happy. Is that what I sound like? Geez, I'm such a bitch!"

Chuckling, I shook my head. "No, you're worried and you have every right to be. If you weren't worried about me, I don't think I could do this, to be honest. I need someone that has my best interest at heart that isn't starry eyed over 'some dude on the internet' as you say. I appreciate your cynicism to a point."

"Well, I'm nothing if not savagely cynical," she said with a laugh.

"You keep me balanced and make sure I don't lose myself, and that's a beautiful thing."

Looking back down at the comforter, she asked, "But what if you get there and you guys fall in love and you never come home?"

"I have to come home, don't be silly. I have too much going on here and making a leap like that really is crazy," I confessed. "This trip isn't for a shotgun wedding or something. It's truly to meet and see where it takes us."

"Okay, but promise me that you will come home on Tuesday and you will tell me all about it and won't hold anything at all back," she said, once again meeting my gaze. Her giant green eyes sparkled for a moment. "Even the dirty details if things get fun."

"Oh, hush your filthy mouth. It's not even like that," I said as I stood up to grab the rest of my things from the bathroom.

"Nope," she said, jumping up to snag my hand. "Promise or I will protest by lying in front of the taxi until you miss your flight. Don't test my limits. I'm crazy as hell."

Laughing much harder than I expected, I almost fell over. As I gripped the arm of the chair by the bathroom, I wiped the tears from my eyes and managed to say, "Okay, geez. I promise. Dirty details and all. Now stop martyring yourself and help me get my stuff together or I'm going to miss my flight and this whole freak out will be for nothing."

~

After a long, drawn out goodbye, Jolie finally peeled herself off of me so my taxi could leave with ample time to get me to the airport for my flight. Superstition and general knowledge of travel made me nervous to check bags unless absolutely necessary, so I only brought enough stuff that would fit into one small bag and a carry-on. That way, all of my stuff could stay with me.

I didn't bring my laptop or any other electronic device besides my cellphone for emergencies and to be able to connect to the internet for calls when possible. I'd downloaded Skype on it and promised to call Jolie when I found access as soon as I landed. I'd brought two paperback books with me to enjoy on the flights and figured I could have a nap the rest of the time or even snag another book during my layover if I needed to.

Getting through security was surprisingly quick and painless, especially since I was about to board an international flight, but as a superstitious woman, I had to smile. Things finally being easy and working in my favor had to mean something good. Right?

Chapter Two

"Ma'am, can I interest you in a beverage?" the flight attendant asked me as we leveled out and started to cruise our way to Paris.

"Wine," I chuckled. "No, I'm totally kidding," I corrected quickly when I saw her reaching for the wine. I'd picked up a large bottle of water in a shop before boarding. Showing her, I added, "If I need something later, I will bug you though."

"Sure, sweetie," she said with a smile as she went on to the next person.

Wine would have mellowed me out far too much and I would have slept the majority of the flight. Amazingly, I wasn't even nervous, I was just anxious to get there. It felt like an eternity before the flight would arrive so I could finally meet Steven. Though, maybe I should have taken the wine so I could stop agonizing over how awkward I was going to be the moment we truly were within hugging distance of each other.

I knew I was going to screw it up somehow and fumble around or fall on my face or something equally as embarrassing. I'd dreamt about the meeting so many times and it was always perfect, so I knew real life wasn't going to work out as well. My luck with things was awful, at best. Though, if I were being honest, since meeting Steven, my mind and heart had changed so much, it was starting to be difficult to think negatively or wait for bad. It was sheer fear.

Starting almost a year before, we planned our trip together. We decided to split the cost of the trip evenly. As I was traveling from the states and he was within driving distance of Paris, my flight there was the bulk of the expense, but he refused to allow me to pay it alone. Being burned so many times in the past made us both independent, wary, and stubborn. Our pasts also made us cautious, but more than anything, we were appreciative. The balance was kind of comical, but truly was the grounds for our entire friendship. Everything was about duality and being equal.

After months of friendship, chats, and random fun, something within us just shifted. One day, he just blurted out "I love you" during a phone call. Though I already knew how I felt for him, I was too scared to say so before because I knew all of the obstacles between us. If I was honest, at that moment, I didn't even see myself as good enough for him. And though I could tell how he felt by how he treated me, it was shocking to hear it straight from his mouth. How could someone so incredible love me? After how everyone else had treated me in my life, this beautiful, intelligent, amazing person loved me? It felt unreal, but amazing at the same time.

Having gone through what we did before we knew each other made us love fiercely and know we deserved it in return. Trusting in love was the hard part.

I stumbled over my words, but didn't waste another moment before I let him know that the feeling was mutual. We didn't dwell on it or make a big deal out of it, nor did we rush to do anything about that revelation after. We continued to build our friendship, enjoy each other's company, and live life, while including the other as much as possible. After just a few months, my friendship with him was more fulfilling than any other relationship in my past.

One night, we started chatting about random places in the world. My persistent wanderlust always had me daydreaming about my next big adventure. The one place we had both seen with friends or family, but never truly explored as an adult, was Paris. I suggested we meet there for a visit. It started as a half-hearted joke, but as soon as we both realized how amazing it would be to see it together, we got serious about the planning.

We booked a suite with two bedrooms in it so we wouldn't be presumptuous enough to think we were going to actually sleep together. Because we wanted to spend time together and be close enough to do as many things as possible with each other, we chose that option. The suite had a kitchenette, couch, television, dvd player, and other cozy amenities. We technically could spend the entire weekend in the room and never need to venture out, but that wasn't our plan.

After deciding that Paris was the place, we started researching the amazing things in the area and made up a loose itinerary to make sure we experienced as much as possible together while getting to know each other in person. It was going to be beautiful and awesome.

I'd decided even before paying for my ticket that it was going to change how I saw the world. Regardless of what happened, this trip was a turning point in my life. I was doing something crazy for once. I was living for myself and putting myself out there without reservation.

"Business or pleasure?" the gentleman to my right asked, snatching me from my thoughts. His distinguished good looks and disposition made me smile. Sitting with his legs crossed and a cup of tea on a flight just made me giggle. He reminded me of an older British actor that I admired.

"Pleasure," I answered with a smile. "And you?"

"Business," he chuckled, then sighed. "Always business."

"Such is life," I agreed with a shrug. I typically would think traveling is strictly for pleasure, but if I needed to travel to amazing cities for my job, that would be awesome, so I couldn't really complain too much. "Business must be doing well, if you're having to travel to such a lovely city for it."

He nodded. "Meeting your love in Paris, that's beautiful and romantic," he said, his voice full of whimsy.

Surprised at his guess, I paused for a moment before answering. "We are friends, but yes, something like that."

"Your eyes don't say he is your friend," the man pointed out.

Nodding, I had to agree. "Rayna," I said, giving him my hand to shake.

"Charles," he answered, lightly shaking my hand. "If your friend sees your eyes in person, he will be a fool not to fall desperately in love. Men die wishing they had someone to love them that much." His voice made him sound sad, as if he knew from experience.

"Ladies do, too," I said honestly. "I've been through almost every sort of hell there is and had just about given up on thinking love was even a real thing. I'm still holding on to the notion that he is some sort of magical being luring me to take a vacation for myself and won't even be there." Laughter could mask my fear, couldn't it?

"But you're so young," he chastised.

"I'm not a whippersnapper, that's for sure," I said with a giggle. "But, yeah, I have a lot of miles left on me. Lots of roads and heartaches have been traveled in this weary body, sir."

Chuckling, he said, "Well, I think the people that go through the worst stuff are the ones most deserving of a second or third or hundredth chance. However you find your blessing is worth it." He punctuated his sentence by raising his tea in a "toast" to me. I joined and took a drink of my water.

At least a hundred times in the last few months, I wondered what I had done to deserve him. I'd been abandoned, abused, mistreated, injured, poor, cheated on, put through hell in every way I could imagine, and still my heart sought out and saw love. Jolie always said my heart was a love-detector and anywhere that love could happen, I would find it. Though it was usually for others, I had a knack for finding good souls.

Frowning, he added, "Whoever hurt you never deserved you."

Stunned, I just looked at him. This complete stranger could see wounds I knew I covered with years of practice. "No, none of them ever did," I agreed. "They didn't deserve my time or heart at all."

"But this one does," he said with certainty.

"He does, yes. Even if it isn't with me, he deserves the world," I said, my voice softening.

"His name?"

"Steven," I answered, my lips curving into the silly smile I couldn't stop from happening when I spoke his name.

Smiling, Charles reached over and patted my hand, "I will say a prayer that your other half realizes what he has with you when you get there." Finishing his tea, he handed his cup to the flight attendant as she passed by. "It's going to be great." Leaning his head back, he closed his eyes to rest.

What a lovely gesture from a stranger. I knew how I felt was obvious, but for someone else to be so encouraging when my own best friend was all spikes and napalm was unusual, but comforting.

I decided to try to have a nap also. The flight was long and I had plenty of time to read, snack, and rest more if I needed to.

~

The rest of the flight was uneventful. I read an entire novel, played some puzzle games on my phone, and took a few cat naps. I couldn't stay asleep for anything in the world. My nervous energy made me want to pace the floor. I tried my best to keep my cool and funnel the energy into good things, but tight quarters on a plane left me with skimpy options.

As we landed, my stomach erupted with the ever-familiar butterflies that always started their dance the second I heard Steven's name or voice. Even after over a year, it was ever-present. Though he wasn't due to arrive until a few hours after me, just the fact that I was where we planned to meet made my excitement level skyrocket.

My life-long wanderlust gave me a multitude of opportunities to brush up on my traveling habits and perfect my routine. Getting through customs and out of the airport was a breeze. I didn't even have to wait for a taxi to take me to the hotel as many were waiting at the curb already prepared for the inbound flight from the states.

In awful French, I let the driver know which hotel I needed to get to.

Chuckling, the driver said, "Sure thing, mademoiselle."

"I should have known you would speak English," I said, shaking my head. "Thank you."

"It helps to understand where people are going if I am to make money," he added with a smile.

The sun was just about to peak over the horizon as we exited the airport to start the short drive to the hotel. "Great point," I answered as I lost myself out of the window.

I was so enchanted with the scenery being illuminated by the sun that I didn't even realize we were already at the hotel when the taxi stopped.

"Mademoiselle? Are you alright?" the taxi driver asked me through the crack in my rolled down window, his brown eyes cloudy with concern. He'd stopped, exited the taxi, and got my bags out of the trunk before I realized we had arrived. He was waiting to open the door, but I was leaning against it.

Shaking myself from my stupor, I chuckled. "Yes, I'm so sorry. I think I was daydreaming."

"That happens to many," he said as I sat up in the seat, allowing him to open the door for me.

I glanced at the meter and pulled the cash from my pocket to pay him before exiting the vehicle. "Thank you very much," I said as I handed him the fare and a too-large tip.

"You're welcome," he said, shoving the money in his pocket. He didn't even count it. "Do you need help with your bags?"

"Not at all." Grabbing my bags, I scurried into the hotel after gawking at its external beauty for a full minute. "I wonder if I'm actually going to see anything here or if I'm going to stare at everything in awe and then wake up back in the states on Tuesday confused," I said to myself as I walked toward the front desk to check in. I knew it was too early to check in, but as other things seemed to fall into place, I thought it best to at least see if I could get the key to the room early.

"Perhaps a nice shower and some breakfast will help your jet lag, miss?" the young lady at the desk suggested.

"I'm sorry?" I asked as I sat my bag down.

"You were speaking to yourself, I'm sure, but I thought to answer your query with a suggestion. It happens to guests all the time, miss. Coming to a new place, you might be overwhelmed, but food and a bath normally fixes most ailments, in my opinion," the girl said with a smile. Her bright blue eyes radiated happiness.

"Oh. I'm losing my mind. Thank you. That's a wonderful suggestion and I think I will do just that if I can go to my room?" I asked with hope lacing my words. I gave her my information and she confirmed that our room was ready and I was able to go ahead up.

"Would you like the second key or would you like for the other person to collect their key upon arrival, miss?"

Taking a minute to ponder, I decided to leave the key for him to collect.

The girl handed me the key and gave me a little advice about her favorite breakfast available nearby. I decided to go up for a shower so I could wash the feel of airplane off of me and change my clothes before heading back out on a mini-adventure alone.

Chapter Three

The shower was amazing and just what I needed to knock myself out of my strange mind-haze. The excitement of meeting Steven coupled with the strange short dreams I was having on the way to Paris had made me a walking disaster. However, after the shower, the time until his arrival seemed like decades.

Glancing at my cell phone screen, I saw that there were two more hours until his bus would arrive. The bus would be dropping him off in the center of the city, which was walking distance from the hotel. I compared the map on my phone to the list of great places the clerk had given me to find one close to where I needed to meet Steven.

Before leaving, I decided to connect to the Wi-Fi and save lives. If I didn't check in soon with Jo, international havoc could certainly occur.

On the second ring, Jolie answered, "I won't pay the ransom until I have proof of life."

Chuckling to myself for a moment, I debated playing along, but decided not to rile her. "I miss you, too?" I asked.

"Well, you just blew a fine chance to play Taken: Paris with me. Good job. Now I will have to go there next just to mess with you," she huffed into the phone.

"See, if that was someone actually holding me for ransom, you would feel like a jerk right now," I reasoned.

"Okay, yeah, good point. But who has your Skype log-in information anyway? Who else calls that way? Losers."

"Gee, thanks?" I asked as I pulled on my favorite flats.

"No, I mean a kidnapper, weirdo. They would call from a blocked satellite number and all that good stuff, you know?" she tried to reason back.

"You're so well versed in this. Maybe we should go into international kidnapping when I come home," I suggested.

"Shut up. Is he there yet? Did you kiss him? How's the food? What time is it? I haven't slept yet. Am I talking too much?"

"No. No. I don't know. About nine in the morning. Yes," I answered her questions in succession. After a slight pause, realizing she was reloading her answer cannon, I added, "I arrived before him, remember? I came up to the room, took a shower, and now I'm heading out for breakfast."

"Nice. Eat lots of pastry before he gets there so he doesn't think you're some sort of weirdo," she suggested. "You're in Paris. Oh my goodness, the food. I would ask you to bring me something back, but I know you and baked goods. I won't even go there."

I chuckled. "I will be happy to, if I remember. Don't hold me to that, you know my brain."

"I do," she said with a laugh. "Well, I won't hold you on the phone. Thank you for checking in and all that. I guess I can finally sleep."

"Dude. It's like three in the morning for you. Why are you awake?" I asked, sounding flustered.

"Because my friend is globetrotting and I need to make sure she's going to make it home in one piece?" she asked, sounding exacerbated. "Plus, I was working on this really amazing thing for work. I'm going to get a raise or start my own company, or just become a superhero. Something. I'm not sure, but go. I will tell you all about it later."

Giggling, I said, "Okay, that sounds amazing. Can't wait!"

"I love you more than chocolate," she said.

"I love you more than pastry," I responded as I quickly ended the call. We could banter on and on for hours, but I had things to do.

~

The walk to the diner was quick and gorgeous. I admired the buildings on the way and indulged in the sights and sounds of Paris in the morning. I have this theory that every city is really two cities. The daytime version of itself that is beautiful, sweet, and interesting, and the nighttime version that is full of adventure, danger, and spice. Thus far, my theory held with a multitude of other cities.

When I arrived at the diner, the waitress took my order and hustled away only to return seconds later with my tea. I'd decided to wait on food as Steven would be arriving within the hour and sharing a meal was on the list of my most sought after moments with him.

I sipped my tea and watched people for what felt like only minutes, but apparently was far longer. My tea was empty and the bus pulled up across the street. I waved for the waitress to bring my check and she shook her head. "No charge," she said as she looked across the street and smiled. "Go."

Crossing the street, I had to force myself to slow down when I realized I was nearly running to the bus. When I rounded the back of the bus, I decided to stand off to the side to allow people to get off and meet up with their loved ones or head to their new destinations in peace.

I watched each face come down the steps, and each new one that appeared in the door made my heart skip a beat. The anticipation was moments away from killing me when I saw him. The familiar butterflies swarmed in my belly and my cheeks became flushed. He was almost within pouncing distance!

Taking a few deep breaths in a really loose attempt to calm myself I looked down at my hands, which were in front of me with my fingers laced. I slowly counted to five to give my nerves just a moment of peace before I walked over to the bus.

"Are your hands that interesting, baby?" he asked me before I could even look up.

Jerking my head up fast enough to make myself dizzy, my eyes clashed with his and I immediately pulled him into a hug. He dropped his bag and wrapped his arms around me so tightly, I was sure I had no breath left. I was further sure I didn't need that breath anyway and silently begged him to never let go. My face was nestled in his neck and I wanted nothing more in the world than to stay right there forever.

I melted into the hug and held it for much longer than I probably would have planned if I had thought it through. Releasing him, I said, "Oh, sorry. I couldn't not hug you. I've wanted to do that for far too long." I knew I sounded awkward.

"No complaints here," he said with a smile. "But if that's the case then, I really have to tell you something."

"Wait, if you're going to say something bad, can it wait until later? I'm really sort of buzzing in this euphoric bubble of awesome that I've had built up in my head since last year when we started to plan this whole thing and I'm just-"

Before I could finish my sentence, he kissed me. The most tender, sweet kiss of my life. One hand went to my waist to pull me closer to him and the other looped gently behind my neck to keep my lips pressed against his. "I love you," he whispered when his lips parted from mine.

"I love you, too, but-"

"Nope. No 'but'. That's it. I just needed to tell you that in person and I needed to kiss you. I've also waited to do that for far too long. You know, since we are getting things out of the way and all," he chuckled.

The grin on my face nearly hurt my cheeks.

"I refuse to let things get awkward with us. I will not start off being weird with you. We came here to be together, so let's be together. We know each other better than anyone else knows us. Why be strange or awkward? You never let me feel awkward and I won't let you feel like that, okay?"

He had a point.

"Okay," I agreed.

Stepping back, he picked up his bag from the sidewalk and laughed. "And now, I'm starving. Shall we?" he offered me his elbow.

"Oh, I know a place," I said.

"Of course you do. I would be shocked if you don't know of every place on this whole city block by now."

"Oh hush. I just had tea earlier here while I waited for you," I said as I pointed to the cute little diner. "They have pastries and things. Or we can go to this Café that is only a few streets over. I hear they have delicious things."

Tilting his head, he said, "Can we get something to go? We can take it to the room and talk. I don't really want to cart this bag around forever."

"Are you just trying to get me alone?" I asked with suspicion.

"Of course I am," he said offhandedly before adding, "I lured you to Paris to have my nefarious way with you." Giving a low, evil chuckle, he winked at me.

"Well, that sounds like fun and all, but you are way too sweet for that. So pastries or real food?" I asked.

He sighed. "Fine. Real food."

I led the way to the Café while never letting go of his arm.

~

After a delicious meal full of laughs, sweet moments, stories, and smiles, we headed to the hotel so he could drop his bag off and prepare for the rest of our day.

Completely forgetting to stop at the front desk on the way up, I made a mental note for us to swing by later to get his key.

When we walked into the suite, he tossed his bag on the chair next to the door and kicked off his shoes. "Whoa, fancy."

"Right? This place is bigger than my house," I said in agreement.

"Seriously! Mine, too," he said as he pounced over the back of the couch and sat on it. "Come on. Let's snuggle," he suggested.

"It's noon," I scoffed.

"There's a time for snuggling in America? So glad I don't live there. Also, we aren't there, we're in Paris and I think all moments are snuggle-moments. Now come here, woman," he said with force before laughing. "I can't even pretend to be angry or rough. Stop making me be savage."

I kicked off my shoes and padded around the couch.

He sat up on the edge of the couch when he saw me. "Oh, I don't want to force you or anything like that. If you're nervous, I mean-"

Standing up to walk away, he turned and I grabbed his hand. "Don't be silly. I'd love to snuggle with you. I'm just nervous if I do that, we might not get back up. Ever."

"I think I'm really nervous that I'm going to mess something up, baby," he confessed softly.

"Me too!" I nearly shouted.

Chuckling at my weirdness, he hugged me. "Aren't we just a pair?"

"Of weirdos? Yes. We are," I said, trying not to melt into the hug he was giving me.

He released me and sat on the couch, picking the remote to the television up on his way down. "You had a long flight and I was on the bus for a bit. How about, before we go out, we watch something mindless, chat, and snuggle. I would prefer to look at and listen to you than see anything out there," he gestured toward the window.

"We had a plan. Don't mess it up," I said as I lowered myself onto the couch next to him.

"The only way this trip will be messed up is if you decide you hate me and never want to see me again after this," he murmured.

Scoffing, I turned to make a joke, but the look on his face shocked me. He was serious. "What? Never."

"Fair warning, I'm about to make things really weird," he said as he scooted back a bit and grabbed my hand.

I chuckled. "So, you'll be yourself and I will swoon all over the place? Got it. I'm prepared to love you extra."

Smiling at me, he said, "You are really good at disarming me. Thanks, baby."

"Well, go ahead and make it weird. Get it over with, but after this, don't drop any more weird faces or bomb shells on me, okay? My poor heart cannot take it. I'm really nervous now," I confessed.

"I was nervous you wouldn't like me anymore once you met me." He had to pause because I burst into laughter, but shut up when I realized he was still serious. "I came here fully thinking that we would meet, go for lunch, and that you would be like 'okay, buddy. See ya next time' or something and then leave without having any moments of truly connecting. I was petrified that would happen, to be honest."

"Yeah, me too." I didn't want to admit it, but now it felt simply silly. After that amazing kiss and our lunch together, it was even silly of me to feel weird about snuggling. "I think the first day is just strange because of the nerves."

He nodded.

"But okay, so I love you, you love me-"

"If you start singing big purple dinosaur songs, I will be forced to forget your name in public," he threatened with a laugh.

"Shut up," I commanded, joining in the laughter. "What I was going to say was, it's silly for either of us to feel nervous. We know each other. We might not physically know each other, but emotionally and mentally, we do. It might take some time to not feel strange about the physical part because we've been without each other this whole time, but from what I can see, we both truly crave that connection, so let's let go of all the ideas and thoughts we came into this agreement with and just enjoy ourselves, okay?"

Looking stunned, he nodded.

"Do you have nothing to say?" I asked, giggling.

"I was going to suggest that, but as the guy, I didn't want to sound like I was trying to get into your pants." His eyes widened and we simultaneously burst into laughter.

"We're adults. If you are trying to get into my pants, chances are that I was somehow requesting you do that anyway," I said as I shrugged and leaned into him. "Now, what are we going to watch?" I asked as I stole the remote to turn the television on.

Chapter Four

Hours later, after having twenty random conversations and giving commentary on strange French television shows, we looked out the window and realized it was almost dark.

"Oh," he said, his hand going to his stomach. "I think we forgot to have dinner."

"I think we also forgot to have a day out together," I chuckled. "Maybe we should at least fix one of these issues."

"Well, the night is young and if you remember, we didn't have big plans for the first day," he said as we stood up to stretch. "What would you like for dinner?"

"I don't know, love," I answered honestly before it suddenly came to me. "Oh! I know!"

"What?" he asked, looking around as if I was warning him that a wild animal was going to decapitate him.

"Sorry, I got excited," I said with a chuckle. "Let's leave and wherever we end up, we will have dinner there," I suggested.

"Spontaneous and scary, I like it," he agreed. "Should I change my clothes?"

"Why? Do you have someone you need to impress?" I asked. He was wearing jeans and a cute t-shirt. I thought he looked great. I had on a simple pair of slacks and a top also. Neither of us was "fancy" by any definition.

"Well, you, of course."

"Oh, good. You're already doing that. No need to change," I said honestly. "Are we trying to go somewhere nicer? I have an outfit for that. One. I seriously brought one because I don't do fancy, as you know," I chuckled.

"We can do that Sunday night if you'd like. Tonight we can just see what happens. Maybe we'll end up at some crazy treasure that isn't even on tourist maps," he said, sounding excited.

"Yep, that's why I like to just go and see what happens. We can be in an RPG and hunt for quests," I laughed at my own joke.

The smirk on his face made me want to kiss him, but I decided not to hold him hostage with an overage of affection. I sat back down to put my shoes on to leave for our adventure and when I stood up, he wrapped his arms around me.

With his lips only a breath away, he said, "It looked like you wanted to kiss me."

I wrapped my arms around him also and breathlessly answered. "I did, but I didn't want to be in your face all day."

"Why not? You were the one that said we crave the connection and suggested we just go with it," he reminded.

"Yeah, I guess I did," I said, staring into his eyes. In photos and on videos, his eyes always captivated me. They spoke volumes of the man he was and made me love him more every time I saw them, but in person, I was lost in them. Some say a picture tells a thousand words, but that beautiful man's eyes spoke a lifetime. I could see joy, pain, fear, power, and every other thing life handed a person with one look in his eyes. He could send me a photo of himself and I would instantly know if he was tired, upset, or in an amazing mood. That window to the soul was always open and I loved to look into it.

The corners of his mouth pulled into the adorable grin I had adored for what felt like forever. Apparently he didn't disapprove of my staring.

A moment later, he leaned his head down the fraction I needed to effectively reach his lips. Our kiss was tender, warm, and encompassing. His lips felt better than I ever imagined as they slowly danced and collided with mine over and over. Each passing second, the kiss intensified until he pulled his head back, almost panting.

"Whoa," he managed.

Smiling, I rested my face on his chest and hugged him a moment longer, not wanting the moment to completely end.

"If we don't leave this room right now, I fear that we might never see Paris at all until we leave Tuesday," he mumbled into my ear, his breath caressed my ear and neck and made knowing how to properly answer impossible.

Knowing he was right, I kissed him on the cheek and said, "Okay, get your shoes on. I will meet you downstairs."

"Are you going to just leave me here?" he asked, astonished.

"Yes and no," I answered. "I saw a cool map thing in the lobby and I wanted to scout ahead."

"You want to plan our adventure?" he chuckled.

"No, I just need to take a peek at a real map because I'm not taking my phone and I want to get my bearings. Stop harassing me, it's for our safety," I chastised.

"Well, don't leave the lobby. I don't want to have to go psycho if someone tries to kidnap you."

Laughing, I quickly told him about my conversation with Jolie earlier and how funny it was that they made the same joke. He agreed they would get along in real life and promised to be down in a few minutes.

I made a beeline for the lobby to view the gorgeous map of Paris I saw on the wall as I was coming in. I saw key places that all people travel to Paris to see. The Louvre, the Eiffel Tower, the Arc de Triomphe, and Notre Dame were all beautiful and definitely things I would love to experience with him. Many were even close to our hotel, but I was more interested in the streets and landmarks to make sure we could find our way back later.

"Mademoiselle?" a male clerk at the counter called to me.

"Yes?" I asked, turning around.

"Is there something I can help you find?" he asked, smiling friendly.

"No, thank you. I'm planning a little evening adventure," I said, returning the smile.

"If you are to go out alone, may I suggest the main streets?" He looked genuinely worried for me. How sweet.

"She's not alone," Steven said, coming out of the elevator with a wide grin on his face. He'd changed his t-shirt.

"Oh, love, you should pick up your key while we're here. I only picked up my key when I got here," I suggested.

"Do you plan to leave me somewhere?" he asked with a chuckle.

"No, but what if I lose my key or something? You never know with me," I answered honestly.

"You're right," he said, kissing me on the cheek before he walked to the desk to get his key.

A moment later, the clerk said, "You and your lady have a wonderful evening. Monsieur."

"We will," Steven said over his shoulder before taking my hand and guiding me out of the hotel. The doorman nodded to us as we left.

With our fingers laced, I asked, "So? Which way do you want to go?"

Looking both ways, he said, "Ladies choice."

Without thinking another moment, I tugged him right as we headed into the unknown dusk of Paris.

~

I was pleased to find out that my theory about nights being full of adventure, danger, and spice in all cities was correct. We saw amazing artists performing on the street, some alleys looked far less than savory, and we'd found one awesome place after another. One played amazing music and had really interesting people flowing from every window and door possible. Another had beautiful women dancing topless on a stage. Steven quickly declined my offer for us to stay for that show.

When the sun set completely, we decided to stop at "the next awesome looking place" we came to for a bite to eat. Both of us felt close to ravenous at that point, but we'd been enjoying our exploration of the city so much that we kept finding excuses not to stop at places.

The next place we saw was a small tavern on a corner. It was what some would call a "hole in the wall" and looked, from the outside, to only be big enough to hold a small handful of people.

"Here we are," I said, stepping toward the entrance.

"Are you sure you want to go here?" he asked, tugging me back and away from the door.

"We said the next place, love. We're both hungry and it looks cozy. Plus, in my experience, the little places are the best ones. I guarantee we wouldn't see this on some tourist map," I rationalized.

"I feel that I should take you somewhere nicer," he said, looking almost sad.

I pointed to a sign. "Look, they have crazy drinks we can try and I bet the owner makes the food. Come on, it will be fun." When he didn't budge, I smiled at him. "Love, this place looks neat and different. Plus, I'm here with you. I don't need or want fancy. I just want to be with you. Okay?"

He nodded.

"If you have somewhere you'd rather go, we can go there. I promise I don't care where we go," I reassured. "I just want to be with you."

"No, I'm just being weird. Sorry, let's go," he said, stepping forward to open the door for me to enter. He looked inside before he let me through, as if to check the safety of the place.

When we walked in a sweet girl came around the bar and offered us a small table in the corner and handed us menus.

"Oops, you're up," I announced to him. "It's all in French."

"Does that give me permission to order for you?" he asked with a laugh, knowing not being in control of what happened to me usually would freak me out.

I inspected him for a moment and nodded. "Yep. Go for it. I trust you."

After coming out of his stunned silence a few moments later, he waved the girl down to return to the table. He quickly ordered and she left.

"Wanna tell me what I'm going to have?" I asked, almost nervous.

"Nope. You will love it though," he said, confidently. Our hundreds of conversations on our meals, likes, and dislikes made me completely trust him. He knew what I liked and didn't like.

The girl returned a few minutes later with some beers, saying something to him in French before scurrying away again.

Before I had a chance to ask, he said, "She says it will be fifteen minutes or so."

"Ooh, fast!"

⁓

We laughed and enjoyed another meal together. Each chance he could, he would touch my hand and share a story. The time flew by so quickly, by the time we were finished eating, we'd polished off our meals and a few beers each.

"Should we call for a taxi or walk off this buzz?" he asked as we left the tavern.

"We're honestly only a few blocks from the hotel," I said, looking up and to the left. Turning back toward the tavern, I pointed right. "That way, actually."

"Really? Cool. Maybe we should just walk it off, then."

"Or, we could walk this way and see the Eiffel Tower. I'm sure it will look really neat while my eyes are all blurry," I said with a giggle. Stepping away from the tavern and to the left, I walked slightly into the street and pointed. "See?"

"Oh yeah, it's right there, isn't it?" he said. "I've seen it before, but how gorgeous is it at night?"

"Incredible," I said as he wrapped his arm around my waist and pulled me closer to him. He kissed my cheek. "Not better than that, though," I said softly. "I bet people who live here take this view for granted."

He nodded. "People never truly understand what they have until it's no longer with them," he muttered, sounding sad.

"Well, now that we've seen that, shall we head back to the hotel?" I suggested.

"Sounds like a plan," he quickly agreed, taking my hand and nearly running back toward the hotel.

~

Our walk back was nearly silent with the exception of a few offhanded comments on the scenery and nice temperature.

We made it back to the hotel in minutes and went up to the room silently. When we walked in, things felt tense and awkward and I wasn't sure why, but hoped it was simply because we were both tired from the long, eventful day.

Looking down at the carpet, I released his hand and said, "I'm going to have a shower and get ready for bed."

"Oh, okay," he said simply.

Not wanting to upset him or guess what was bothering him, I leaned forward to kiss his cheek and rushed off to my room. I assumed he would figure out the room on the other side of the suite was his, though we hadn't discussed it earlier in the day. Luckily, both rooms had their own bathroom so I was able to shower and change without having to bother him or go back into the main area.

Once I finished my night time routine, I decided I needed something to drink, so I ventured out into the open area toward the kitchenette. Steven was nowhere to be seen and the door to the other room was closed.

Earlier, the clerk said there was juice and a few other things in the fridge for us that were complimentary. I grabbed a glass from the cabinet and poured myself a glass of grape juice and went to sit on the couch. Without turning the television on, I simply curled my feet under myself and picked up my cellphone off of the table.

My thumb hovered over the button to dial Jolie. After an amazing day, it was always my instinct to call her and tell her about it, but really all I wanted to do was curl up with Steven and talk or sleep or anything. I put the phone back down and decided against making the call. After a few minutes of sitting in silence, I finished my juice. I went back to the kitchen, washed my cup, and put it in the dish rack to dry.

Stepping from the kitchenette, I looked at Steven's door, still closed. Something had upset him and I had a sinking feeling it was me, though I couldn't put my finger on what I could have done. Instead of making a big deal out of it or bothering him, I decided to go to bed.

On the table by the door was a pad of paper and a pen. I jotted a short note to him and left it on the counter in the kitchenette in case he came out and wasn't sure if I wanted to talk to him. I waited for another minute and then shuffled to my room, leaving the door open slightly.

I got in bed and stared at the ceiling in the darkness. He was within the same breathing space as I, it felt odd to sleep without saying goodnight. In a year and ten months, we'd never gone to bed without saying goodnight. It was usually a few minute to hour-long process each night. Tonight, when he could truly hug me and kiss me goodnight, he chose not to for whatever reason. Though I had a feeling something was going on with him, it hurt much more than I thought it would.

I came into the visit with an open mind, but our first day made me feel connected to him in ways I couldn't explain. We were in love with each other. It was obvious in how we treated each other. No kisses like those were between "just friends." Maybe he realized it was a mistake and wanted to take a step back and took our buzzed evening as the way out.

Not knowing what to do and having no way to find answers even if I wanted them, I decided to sleep. Though the bed felt strangely empty without him, I knew we'd never planned to sleep together. I shook my head at my crazy-girl brain, held my pillow to my chest, and allowed the exhaustion of the flight, the day, and my emotions to take me off to dreamland.

Chapter Five

Dreams plagued me off and on for hours. I tossed and turned, without being able to truly relax. Something was wrong and I was basically in the same room as the man I loved and needed to know that he was okay. Even if he had changed his mind about me or anything with us, I wanted him to know that if he was upset, he could talk to me. I needed him to be okay. I'd said before that I wanted a happy life for him no matter what and I meant that with all of my heart.

Just as I rolled over to get out of bed, the mattress dipped slightly.

"Please don't leave," he whispered in the darkness.

Stunned, I couldn't move.

"I'm sorry," he continued as he laid next to me, looping his arm around my waist as he pulled me closer to him.

Laying my head on his chest, I tried not to cry. "Never be sorry to me."

"I should have kissed you goodnight. I should have spoken to you. I should have done things very differently, but I want to fix that right now. For letting you down on our first night together, I really am sorry. I know sorry means nothing, but I want to try to at least right the wrongs I've created." His voice was angry, but not at me.

I brought my hand up to his chest and gently caressed where his heart was. "You're here now and you didn't owe me anything, though I did want to kiss you goodnight."

He brought his hand to my cheek and guided my face up. Capturing my lips with his, his other hand tightened at my waist, holding me closely to him.

Under my palm, his heart started to pound as his breath quickened.

"I... I," he started, releasing my lips. "I don't want to seem forward or be inappropriate to you," he husked.

"I wanted you here with me. It felt strange not to say goodnight to you or for you to snuggle with me," I said honestly. "We always speak of snuggling and can for just this small amount of time. I really want to take advantage of these moments and not let them pass us by. You know?"

"I do. I haven't slept yet or anything," he confessed.

"Why?" I asked, trying to sit up in the bed so I could speak to him face to face.

His grip tightened on my waist again. "Please stay here, baby. Please."

"Okay, love. I'm not leaving."

"You will leave me," he said flatly.

"No, love. I want nothing more than to be here with you right now," I reassured him. How he would think I would want to be anywhere else but there was unfathomable to me.

"No, I mean on Tuesday. You will leave. I will go home. Things will go back to how they were." The sheer sadness in his voice broke my heart. "We both know it's coming. We planned this knowing what the next thing was. We were greedy and selfish and needed time together, but what about after? What about after I've tasted your lips all weekend and felt the warmth of your breath on my chest and neck? What about when I smell your shampoo or eat something that we had together and my heart breaks again because you aren't there to share it with? What about then?"

Tears flooded my eyes and the dam immediately broke. All of those "what ifs" were in my heart, too.

He continued. "What happens when someone asks me how my girlfriend is and I say that I don't have one when I know damned well that I am hopelessly in love with you?"

My breath hitched, but I didn't speak. We never used labels with each other. We purposefully never used official titles. We didn't get overly serious or make things a big deal that would eventually hurt us.

"What am I supposed to do when I want to come home to you, celebrate things, live, and just be with you and you aren't there?" He didn't move, but his breath was becoming shallow and pained. "Why do you live there and I live here? Why isn't life fair?"

"I don't know, love. I really don't know," I finally answered, unable to control my tears or his pain.

"How can you make me fall in love with you with one kiss?" he murmured.

"You kissed me first," I chuckled around my tears.

"I did and I loved you then, but when you looked at me like I was everything in the whole world to you and you kissed me, it's like you infected me or something," he said, the anger returning to his voice despite his half-hearted joke.

Leaning up on an elbow, I looked at him in the darkness. "Steven, you didn't know you are everything in the world to me before now?"

"I heard your words. I knew they were true," he said. "But, when you looked at me like that, I felt flooded with it and couldn't deny it any longer."

"I'm sorry," I said, sadness filling me. He loved me, but didn't want to.

He chuckled. "You're sorry for making me feel loved?"

"No, I'm sorry that I'm there and you're here and that it hurts you." I wiped my tears off of my face with the back of my hand and laid my head back on his chest. "So, what now?"

"Now, we sleep. I think all we needed to be comfortable was each other," he suggested.

"You will sleep here with me?" I asked, sounding shocked.

"Is that okay?" Always a gentleman.

I wrapped my arm around his waist and snuggled him as close as I could. "Best news ever," I mumbled into his chest.

"Hey," he whispered.

"Yeah?"

He kissed my forehead. "I love you, baby. Sweet dreams."

"I love you too. My dreams are coming true, but I'm sure I can come up with something else," I said with a giggle. I kissed his chest and snuggled back close to him and was asleep within seconds.

~

The next morning, I woke up to a cold, empty bed. Fear nearly strangled me as I shot up and panicked. I knew that I wasn't hallucinating. I knew Steven came to my room the night before. I knew for sure. I could smell him on my hands and pillow still.

In my tank top and shorts, I shot out of the bedroom and into the main area to find a note on the counter next to mine from the night before.

"I promised you that I would make you an epic meal one day. Just in case this is the only time I ever get to cook for my girlfriend, I'm going to take the chance. I'm running to the market and will be back soon. I love you, Steven

P.S. Your hair looks awesome in the morning."

Laughing, I put the note down and padded back to my room to brush my obviously-wicked hair and put real clothes on before he got back.

By the time I brushed my hair and teeth and washed my face, I heard the front door click closed. Foregoing real clothes, I peeked around the corner to see Steven putting down a few bags on the counter. When his hands were clear, I dashed from the room and pounced on him, wrapping my arms around his waist from behind him.

"Good morning, love," I announced.

"Well, good morning, baby," he said, smiling like a fool as he turned around to see his attacker face-to-face.

I grabbed his face and kissed him fiercely before he could speak another word. "If you ever leave me in bed by myself in a foreign country again, I will be forced to torture you when you return."

"What would this torture entail exactly?" he asked me cautiously.

Pretending to think, I paused. "No kisses forever and also no cheese. And no beer. And maybe no snuggles, I'm not sure how drastic I think this torture needs to be."

Throwing his hands in the air, he said, "I surrender. I promise to never do that again, without just cause."

"Wait, you tried to throw in stipulations. Not cool."

"I think cooking you a wonderful breakfast is an amazing reason to leave. Though, I confess, it was nearly impossible to get out of bed with you lying next to me," he said before kissing me sweetly. "Now, I have things to make unless you'd like to starve?"

I looked down at my stomach and laughed. "Dude. You were snuggled up with all this. You know I will never die of starvation."

"Well, good. I think you're wonderful like that, so I should get to making breakfast before that changes and I lose all the good snuggles," he said with a wink as he walked around me toward the kitchenette.

Pulling a barstool out from the counter, I sat on the other side to watch him work. My eyes met with the note and a playful smirk crossed my lips.

"So… this note…" I lead.

"Yes?" he asked as he busied himself with the breakfast preparation.

"Well, I'm just curious how you thought I would miss being called your girlfriend," I said, the amount of sass in my voice could have possibly stopped a tank in motion.

Without skipping a beat, he said, "You're probably the most observant person on the planet. I didn't expect you to miss it and wanted you to have it in writing for future reference, just in case you decided to try to forget your title in my life."

My heart flat lined for a moment. Shaking my head, all I could manage was, "Say what now?"

Chuckling, he rounded the counter and kissed me. "Rayna, will you be my girlfriend?"

"Well, of course, but… the upset and the what ifs and everything?" I questioned. After our talk the night before, I was sure he would never honestly want to put a title on us because of all of the fears and questions.

"Baby, look. We are in love, right?" he asked, sincerity ripping through each word.

I nodded, unable to think of where it was going.

"Then, that's it. We are in love. We've spent time together. We know it's real. We will figure it out. *We. Us.* However you want to say it," he said with a grin. "I know we've gone through some stuff and have roadblocks. I really do know that it's not going to be easy, but," he paused and waited until my eyes met his, "you are worth it. Okay? We are great together."

"We really are," I gushed in agreement.

"Okay, so is that a yes then?" he asked.

"I've been yours in my heart for a year and ten months. This is sort of just a formality, really," I chuckled.

"One that I wanted to do properly and in person if ever possible." His eyes drilled into mine. "I want you to know that I chose you all those months ago and every day since, and I always will."

"That's what love is, isn't it? A choice."

He nodded. "Yes, baby. It really is."

"My answer is definitely 'yes', by the way."

"Oh, I know," he said, sounding smug as he walked back into the kitchen. "Now stop giving me a hard time, I have to feed my beautiful girlfriend before we go out on our adventure today."

"Sounds like a plan!"

Epilogue

Luckily, our weekend together didn't fly by. It was spent with long, amazing days filled with adventure, art, beauty, amazing food, snuggles, talking, and kisses.

Steven never spent a single night in his room and stayed by my side the entire time. Each night we would discuss the day and what we loved about it and would end the night with a kiss. Each morning we would discuss the future before heading out on our adventures. By Tuesday, we had a plan in place about how we would make our relationship work. Though both of us felt tied to our country, job, and life, the truth was, none of that even mattered in the grand scheme of things. At the end of the day, we just wanted each other and a life together. Whatever that took, we were willing to do it.

My goodbye to my love was the most painful thing I had endured in years. Fear almost crippled me the morning I was leaving. Fear that it was the last time I would see or touch him. Fear that he would get home and suddenly be over me. Fear that I was actually crazy and hadn't even left home and this had all been some crazy dream. But, that fear was washed away the second he held me to his chest and said, "Stop worrying. This is our life. Us. We are going to be okay. I love you." His unwavering faith in us gave me strength.

We aren't perfect. We will have good days and bad days like everyone else. But our love is true and came from somewhere we weren't expecting. It built from a friendship and grew into adoration and shifted into love.

So, thank you Steven. Without you, I wouldn't be who I am right now. For one moment to know this kind of love, I would have endured even more than I did. I was so lost... and then, I found you.

Every Day
Jessica Surgett

1

Life is messy. I get that. I know that nobody is perfect, people make mistakes, and forgiveness is a virtue. But as I stare at my boyfriend's bare ass laying passed out drunk on our bed once again, I begin to see the gray areas in these statements. People make mistakes, but how many times do we have to forgive the same mistake? My normal mantras are no longer working. The more I try to grasp at them, the more they slip through my fingers and float away. I want to float away with them.

I peel my eyes from his prone figure, and they settle on the vomit covered clothing sitting in a pile on the floor. The ones I wrestled him out of before he collapsed into his blissful darkness. Life is messy, but I'm sick of being his maid.

Very carefully, I pick up the soiled clothes and make my way to the washing machine in the hallway. I pour in the detergent and watch as the water rises, slowly covering all evidence of his latest "setback." He'll wake in the morning and tell me how sorry he is; how he didn't mean it. He'll use sweet words and those big blue eyes to convince me not only that he is fine, but that part of this is my fault, too. He'll tell me how I can help prevent this from happening again; how it was something I said that set him off. He'll nurse my wounds so sweetly, covering every bruise with kisses and every insult with proclamations of love. He'll lay out each word so carefully that I won't be able to see them twisting until the noose is already wrapped around my neck, choking out the last of my arguments.

Except this time will be different. This time he'll wake in the morning to nothing but an empty house and clean clothes. This time I'll be gone before he has a chance to change my mind.

I return to the bedroom and take one last look at his sleeping form. He's completely naked, one leg hangs off the bed, and there's a rather large puddle of drool gathering on the navy bedspread. He looks so innocent in this moment; so helpless. I quickly turn and head for the living room before the guilt can set in. I've made my decision. No turning back.

As I grab the duffel bag I packed earlier from the couch, my sleeve moves up and my eyes catch on his fingerprints painted in purple on my wrist. The violet blooms are almost beautiful, much prettier than the ugly yellow-green color they'll become. I pull down my sleeve and shake the thought from my head. It's not beautiful. It's a bruise. A physical reminder of his rage and my fear, and my reason for leaving. I squeeze my eyes shut. This is not beautiful.

Throwing the bag over my shoulder, I'm surprised by it's weightlessness. This bag holds everything I own, do I really have so little to my name? It's so light, yet it feels heavy with the weight of my decision as I carry it out the door. I imagine my guilt and confusion tucked inside next to my socks and underwear.

The steps are slick with ice, and I worry for a moment that my beat up hatchback won't start. Saying a prayer, I climb into the car, close my eyes, and turn the ignition. It takes three cranks and a moment of panic, but the engine starts. I release the breath I was holding and realize I'm shaking. It's cold, but that's not the cause. My heart pounds in my chest, and even though my breath swirls from my lips in little white puffs, I'm sweating. I feel terrified and exhilarated all at once. I'm really doing this--finally doing this.

Taking deep breaths, I wait for the car to heat up and focus on the trailer in front of me. This is the last time I will ever see this place.

Sitting safely in my car, I stare harshly at my former prison. The screen door is more holes than screen, and the bug zapper on the porch casts a green hue through the multitude of bug carcasses. I relate so much to those damn dead bugs. Lured in by beauty and extinguished by the same light. They're trapped in there, but I refuse to stay trapped.

I feel my anger rise, and suddenly it's as if all the emotions I've been burying for the past eight months are screaming to be released. Tears fall freely from my eyes and my shaking becomes almost violent. I want to scream, but he's still too close for that. I'm not far enough away from the fear yet. So I bite my lip until I taste copper and sob as quietly as I can, letting out some of the anger and sorrow I've been hoarding. I calm down enough to put the car in gear and give one last glare to the trailer before backing out onto the gravel road.

2

I walk into the gymnasium and smile. The room is freezing and smells like feet, but this has become my happy place. I chose Minnesota because of it's cold climate and hospitable reputation, and was not disappointed on either front. I've lived here less than a year and already this feels more like home to me than anywhere I've ever lived. The thought makes me want to weep with joy and relief.

There's a good turn out tonight. Four women graze the cookie table while two more sit awkwardly in the circle of chairs set up a few feet away, sipping water and waiting for the meeting to start. Our group leader waves at me from the bleachers, and I make my way toward her, untangling my long blond hair with my fingers as I go. *I love you, Minnesota, but the wind I could do without.*

I climb past two men sitting in the front row, joining Laura who is seated a few rows up. She and I have become close this past year. The first thing I did upon arriving in Northfield was find this group. I knew I needed to talk to someone about the mess I'd left behind, and that if I didn't keep up my momentum, be proactive, I'd sink quickly. And I had no one to dig me out if that happened. That's how I discovered *Blue Skies Therapy* and ended up at my first group counseling session.

Laura grabs my hands and rubs heat into them as I sit beside her. "Jen, I'm so glad you're here."

I raise my eyebrows, and we both grin because I'm always here.

"I was hoping you would share some of your story tonight." Her face sobers and she continues in a conspiratorial whisper, "I suspect Abigail is going through a similar situation."

We both casually glance at Abigail. I note the way she favors her right leg as she stands, and how her eyes are downcast as Emily chats with her lightheartedly. It could be nothing, but we're all here for a reason after all.

Laura and I share a worried look, and I nod, "Of course. Whatever I can do to help."

When I first discovered this group, I thought I'd have trouble opening up about my time with Charlie. I thought I'd come to these meetings, sit quietly off to the side, and listen to everyone else's stories all while keeping mine boxed up nicely in my chest. I imagined their heartache would throw mine in sharp relief. That when compared with true hurt, mine would appear feeble and contrived. Deep down I held onto the fear that Charlie had been right--that I had overreacted to everything. I assumed hearing about people who had been through much worse than me would do nothing but devalue my own grief. I was so wrong.

I spent my first few meetings as an observer, but something happened during my fourth visit. Laura sat us all down and said simply, "You own your pain. It belongs to you and no one else. That is your right." She spoke each word forcefully, and their impact was like a blow to the chest. My story leaked out of my eyes first, then my mouth. I told them everything. The fear that my pain wasn't good enough. That I wasn't worthy of it. That I didn't deserve to grieve and recover because I hadn't suffered deeply enough. Hearing those words freed me. Instead of receiving judgment from the group, I received love and understanding. That was the day I realized I was allowed to get better.

As Laura descends the bleachers to get her notes, my eyes catch on the men sitting below me. Evan, a regular in his late forties, has brought a friend tonight. The new guy appears to be about my age, and is not completely unpleasant to look at. His tanned skin and dark features are similar to Evan's, and I wonder if they are related. As the two stand and walk to the circle, my theory is further cemented. They walk with the same confident swagger.

I find myself smiling. Evan is a sweet man, and I'm glad to see he has family who cares enough about him to be here. My smile fades though as the mystery guest sits in a chair facing me and our eyes meet. His eyes are so dark they appear black at this distance, but it isn't their color that strikes me, it's the hate I see simmering inside them. This man is furious down to his core. Evan says something to him, and the man throws him a quick smirk, but that spark of anger still flickers. He can smile all he wants, but I still see it. I'd recognize that spark anywhere; I used to see it in the mirror everyday. After I left Charlie, I had a lot of rage to deal with.

It isn't until Laura calls my name that I realize I'm the last to join the group. Heat rushes to my face as I awkwardly make my way down the bleachers. I force my curiosity down and compose myself. I have a story to share and this is important. I try hard not to glance at Abigail too much as Laura introduces me and gives me the floor.

Unfortunately, I end up standing directly across from Mystery Guest. With his height and ramrod straight spine, and my petiteness, I find myself at eye level with him. And those midnight eyes never leave my face as I speak. His intense, dark orbs bore into me. Stealing my thoughts, my words. I can't stop myself from staring right back as I stumble through my story. I should be able to handle his stare; he's supposed to be watching me and listening. I, however, should not be caught in his gaze this way. I'm supposed to be addressing the whole group, not speaking only to him.

Somehow I manage to fumble through. Abigail leaves afterward without a word, but I see the war waging in her eyes as she smiles politely when people wish her a goodnight. All I can do is plant the seed. It's up to her to water it. I really hope she does. The rest of the group begins trickling out, and I start stacking chairs with Laura.

"Um, care to explain what happened tonight?" Her brows are halfway up her forehead and I can tell she's barely suppressing laughter.

"Oh, shut up." I grumble.

Laura doesn't comment further, but she waggles her eyebrows suggestively. I smack her and hurry to my car, flustered.

3

As I wait for the car to warm up, I watch my breath clouding in the air and contemplate what the hell just happened. The meeting has ended and most everyone has left, but my heart still races in my chest. I've been having trouble controlling it ever since I locked eyes with Mystery Guest, aka Max. Max is Evan's nephew, and from what I've heard in past meetings, that spark of rage I saw makes sense. Evan comes from a long line of alcoholics, his older brother--Max's father, included. This should make Max off-limits for me. I have enough of my own baggage. I don't know how I could handle someone else's. I don't know why I'm even thinking this way; being with Max would be bad for us both. He deserves someone untainted, someone who can focus on helping him without adding to his burden. I don't want to be anyone's burden.

My traitorous heart, however, seems intent on ignoring my brain. As the frost melts from the windshield, I see the object of my musings sitting alone on a bench outside the gymnasium. His black hair lays slicked back from his hands repeatedly running through it, and his right leg bounces rapidly. It's glaringly obvious he wants to be anywhere but here. The stubborn organ in my chest tightens, and I groan in frustration. My resolve to stay away weakens and is replaced with empathy. What kind of person would I be if I left him there alone? I slowly lower my head onto the steering wheel. *Et tu, brain?* I'm out of the car and heading toward him before I can think better of it.

"Hi," is my brilliant opening line. I cling to my coat so he can't see my hands shake as I try to smile.

He doesn't say anything at first, just looks up at me blank faced. The white clouds of breath coming from him are the only indication he is alive, but they tell me nothing. He takes a deep breath and lets it out slowly. I imagine the cloud of steam transforming into letters, spelling out the thoughts in his head. That one looked like "Hello." I smile to myself at the silly thought, and he finally smiles back. I want to see him smile again.

"Would you like to join me on the swings?" I ask, nodding toward the playground in the lot next to us.

His brows knit in confusion. "You want me to... swing with you?"

He's really not making this easy on me. "Yes," I state simply. "It's Max, right?" We went around the circle and introduced ourselves during the meeting, but we never spoke personally.

He nods, brows still knit, but curiosity tilting his head now.

"Well you see, Max, I have an intense love of swings, and that blue one over there is calling my name. Care to join me?"

He's still for another couple of beats, but then he surprises me by standing and bending slightly at the waist, offering me his elbow in a gentlemanly fashion, "M'lady." There's a glint in his eye and a smirk on his lips. My stomach flips.

I slip into the act, gracefully laying my hand on his arm, "Thank you, Maximus. Let us adjourn to the swing set."

He nods as if this is completely normal behavior, and we crunch through the gravel parking lot with our heads held high. By the time we take our seats next to each other on the cracked plastic, my mood has shifted from trepidation to excitement. I grasp the chains and lean back as far as my arms will allow, legs straight out in front of me, and gaze at the stars. It's a beautiful night. The air is crisp and almost completely covers the smell of the cows. My breath looks like hope. Max shifts in his swing, and I look over and smile. He returns it, and I feel our friendship click into place.

"So," I say, sitting up, "your uncle's still in there talking to Laura. Mind if I ask if everything's okay?"

Max becomes fascinated with a weed that has grown tall near the base of the swing set and doesn't answer immediately. I'm tempted to take it back, apologize for prying and leave it alone, but I wait for his response instead. I have a gut feeling he needs to talk about something. His baggage matches mine, and I suddenly feel the intense need to help him carry it.

He clears his throat and opens his mouth, but all that comes out is another cloud of breath. This one looks like exhaustion.

"It's a long story," he manages.

I give him a sad smile, "It always is."

"He brought me here tonight to talk about my dad. He has... some anger issues." He throws a sideways glance at me. I only nod. I don't miss the fact that he didn't speak during the meeting, but choose not to comment on it.

"Oh, I understand that." I laugh humorlessly. He heard my story tonight. I don't think any elaboration is necessary.

He's deep in thought now, his brows creased and lips pursed. I resume my stargazing for a few minutes before I feel his eyes on me again. His face has softened, and his next breath looks like vulnerability. I raise my brows in question.

"About all that," he says, "do you mind if I ask you a question?"

I twist in my swing a little, enjoying the lazy movement. "I'm an open book."

He licks his bottom lip and asks, "How do you do it?"

I stop the gentle sway of my swing and sit up straight, giving him my full attention, "Do what?"

"How are you so… happy?" He emits a strangled laugh. I see so much sorrow in that breath, and my heart cracks at the sight.

The question is difficult for him. He's not merely asking how I've achieved this, after everything I've been through. He wants to know why he can't be happy too. My heart cracks wider at his revelation.

I study the same weed Max examined, and think hard about his question. "I just… decided to be."

I look up and see Max beginning to build the walls back up around himself.

I rush on, desperate to halt construction. "I don't mean that it was easy, only that it was intentional. One morning I woke up, and decided that I didn't want to live the rest of my life this way: so full of anger and resentment. I could still remember the old me; the me that was full of joy and optimism." I smile. "I missed her."

Max only nods, brows lowered in contemplation.

I share one more thing, because I think he needs to hear it. "I thought it would be impossible. I never imagined that I could let go of all that pain, but I had to try. I woke up every morning, and made the conscious decision to be happy that day. Some days were better than others, but I did it, no matter what. Eventually, it got a little easier." I smile at Max. His eyes look damp, and I give him the courtesy of pretending not to notice.

"I still have to remind myself sometimes," I say. Then my lips curl into a wicked smile, "but it helps to remember that every time I have a good day, they lose, and I win."

Max meets my eyes and smiles back, but I call its bluff. The spark is gone for now, but it's replaced by an overwhelming sorrow. I'm not sure which is worse. I say no more, only stare right back, willing him to see as deeply into me as he's allowing me to see into him. Somehow I recognize that this is not something he normally permits, and I cherish the moment for as long as I can. He breaks the connection first and I instantly feel the loss. There's a hole in my chest where he's already made a place for himself. It scares me how easily he fit inside. Evan's voice calls out for Max, and he walks away without a word.

4

I wake slowly, the ringing of my phone interrupting my date with *Aladdin*. My addled brain is slow on the uptake, and I manage to find my phone purely by muscle memory.

"'Lo?" I mumble incoherently.

"Jenna?"

"Satan?" I retort without thinking.

"Um, I'm sorry. Did I wake you?" It is at this point that I recognize Max's voice and immediately regret every decision I've made so far today.

I sit up so fast I lose my phone in the tangle of blankets around me. I search frantically for it, but my hair is in my face, impeding my vision, and my legs are so wrapped up in blankets I can barely move. Through my flailing I can faintly hear Max calling my name. I momentarily considering yelling "Marco!" at my phone, but decide against giving him any more proof that I'm insane. Eventually I manage to Houdini out of the bed, locate my phone, and attempt to apologize.

"Max? Oh my God, I am so sorry. I didn't know it was you."

"No, you thought it was Satan," he teases, "Common mistake."

"You mistaken for the devil often, then?"

"It's the horns and tail."

"You should probably stop carrying around that pitchfork, too."

The easy flow of our banter has me grinning from ear to ear. I'm so relieved he finds my awkwardness funny; I can't remember ever clicking so well with someone. Did we really meet only two nights ago?

Max clears his throat, "So, I'm sure you're wondering how I got your number."

No, actually. The thought hadn't even crossed my mind.

He forges on, "I asked my uncle to ask Laura for it. I hope that's okay. I realize how weird that is. It's just… I enjoyed hanging out with you the other night. I wanted to see if we could get together again."

My cheeks might not survive this phone call. "Of course! I'd love to see you again."

"Great! I mean, okay. Are you busy tonight?"

I'm scheduled at five tomorrow morning at the Piggly Wiggly, so going out tonight is probably not smart, but I can't seem to make myself care. "Nope. Free as a bird."

"Great, Can I take you to dinner? Say around seven?" The excitement in his voice is palpable, and it puts me at ease that whatever this is between us, it's mutual.

"Seven is perfect."

The doorbell rings at seven on the dot. I try to take my time walking to the door. I want to run to it and fling it open, but I'm pretending I have some control over myself. My pounding heart seems to laugh at me in my chest. I smooth my hands over my peasant blouse one more time and adjust my already perfect long blond hair, sweeping it over one shoulder before opening the door. Nervous hello's are exchanged as my eyes take him in. I attempt to be covert. I fail miserably. It's hard not to gawk at him. He's wearing a gray pea coat over a dark green button-down shirt and black denim pants that fit him stupendously. It's nothing fancy, but I can tell he put extra effort into his appearance. His hair is slicked back just like it was the last time I saw him, but there's some kind of product in it now. I have to check that my mouth isn't hanging open.

When I finally meet his gaze, I'm pleased to find that I was not caught staring, as he is still busy examining me. His eyes hold none of the perverse or predatory qualities I'm used to receiving, and I am amazed to discover that I quite like Max raking his eyes over me. I have always been supremely uncomfortable with the attentions of men. In Max though, I see nothing but awe and wonder. I feel weightless under his gaze. His eyes fill me like a balloon; I worry I might float away.

Is this what it's supposed to feel like? I've never had someone want me for anything other than what I can do for them. I'm used to being used, but Max is looking at me with reverence. Is this what it would feel like to be loved? *Did I just use the "L" word?* It's exciting and terrifying. By the time his eyes work their way to mine his cheeks betray a small blush, and the butterflies in my stomach start a rave.

"Please, come in." I find my manners and usher him into my tiny apartment. It's not much, but I love my little home and refuse to be ashamed of it. I'm proud of this life I've carved out for myself.

"Nice place," he says taking a cursory glance of the living room and attached kitchen. He looks back at me and smiles.

"It's small, I know," I reply, "but it's all I need."

"It's cozy," he says with a smirk, "and it suits you."

I give him a questioning look.

"It feels happy."

It's the the best compliment he could've given me.

5

Max takes me to the only Italian restaurant in town. *Luigi's* is practically empty. Aside from an adorable older couple and a man in a suit dining with his laptop, we have the place to ourselves. We cover all the generic first date trivia. His favorite color is green, he likes classic rock, his favorite book is *The Catcher in the Rye*, and he works for his dad's company as an accountant.

We eat by candlelight, and our chemistry continues to amaze me. I have to keep reminding myself that we just met, because I feel as if I've known him my whole life. It might be the bread sticks talking, but by the time we leave the restaurant, I'm almost convinced we're soul mates. I try to be wary, but the hope refuses to sink. It's like a buoy bobbing up and down in my chest. I'm either falling in love or getting seasick. There's that word sneaking into my thoughts again. Love? There's no way. That is completely crazy. *Calm yourself, Jenna!*

Neither one of us has any desire to end the night, so Max drives around while we talk and watch the scenery pass us by. Everything is so beautiful this time of year. The trees are a kaleidoscope of colors, and they've begun hanging the twinkle lights on Main Street. I look out from my warm seat in the truck and think about the possibility of magic. The glittering landscape makes me feel as if anything were possible. Even this. Even us. The hope in my chest bounces higher.

It's freezing, but I've always loved cold weather best. Winter is like the beginning of Mother Nature's regeneration process. It's her death before resurrection. Before she can start fresh in the spring, everything from the past year must fade away. And she does it with beauty and grace. I look out at the glittering landscape and take courage. If she can do it, so can I.

We come upon a park, and Max begins slowing down. He doesn't say a word as he parks near the swing set, and I reply with a huge grin. As we round the front of the truck, I take off running. I look back once to make sure he's participating in my impromptu race. The smile on his face is heart-stopping. Max's normal countenance is pretty somber, so seeing him so happy and carefree is even more satisfying.

I reach the swings first, grabbing a chain to help slow myself as I flip around and face him, giggling like a little girl. He slows to a jog as he reaches me, still grinning, and stops on the other side of the swing. A laugh escapes him, and our heavy breathing fills the space between us. Our mingled breaths rise up into the cold night air and my heart goes along for the ride. I grab the other chain of the swing and Max follows suit, covering my hands with his own. Our smiles fade, and as he leans over the swing toward me, I try to pause time. I know this is a pivotal moment. I feel it deep in my bones. From now on, the rest of my life will be broken into two parts: before this kiss and after it.

I take in Max's glittering eyes. His pink nose. His mussed hair. His lips, slightly parted.

And then they're on mine, and everything is oblivion. Sweet oblivion.

We don't stay at the park long, but we do sit on the swings for a few minutes. Holding hands and grinning like the fools we probably are. Eventually, snow begins falling lightly. Max pulls me toward his truck, attempting to keep the flakes from me by wrapping his arm around my shoulders. Before we reach the truck I stop, pulling away from him. He looks confused, but waits to see what I'll do. It's such a simple thing, but the fact that he allows me to do as I please instead of forcing me into the truck is monumental to me. My heart squeezes in my chest.

I close my eyes, throw my arms wide and stick out my tongue. The icy flakes melt on impact and I giggle at the sensation. I look back at Max and see that wonder in his eyes again. My face is wet with snow, and the numbness I feel makes me sure it is splotched pink and red as well, yet he looks at me like I'm beautiful. I feel myself falling further, like *Alice* down the rabbit hole. Then there is a slight shift, like a light being flicked off in a house. His face stays the same, but his eyes lose their smile. The sorrow has returned, and I wonder what called it back.

We get into the truck, and Max turns up the heat. I take my gloves off and attempt to wipe my face with them. He laughs at me and removes his gloves too.

"Here." He takes my cold face in his warm hands and I close my eyes, melting into them with a contented sigh.

His lips brush mine again, and we get lost for a little while in the warmth of the truck and each other. We sit together, hands clasped, and talk about our hopes and dreams. The conversation is much deeper now than it was at dinner. We've crossed a bridge. No going back.

I talk about my childhood, and how I ended up with someone like Charlie. He opens up a little about his father. How tough he's always been on him and how he hates working for him, but doesn't feel like he can leave. I manage to crack open the door just a little bit, but I know there's a lot more behind it. There's more hidden in the dark corners of Max. There's a reason for that spark. I hope one day he'll trust me with all his secrets, but today is not that day. I don't push on the door, and we move on to other topics. The cab fills with our hopes and dreams as we soak each other up. Tonight is about happiness and new beginnings. Tonight is about us.

6

It's been over a week since I've heard from Max. I tell myself over and over again that it's not a big deal. We went on one date, so what? Maybe he didn't have a good time, maybe the crazy connection I felt was, in fact, crazy. Maybe his grandmother died and I'm going to feel really bad in a few days when he calls to apologize, and I've been sitting here, seething over nothing. The more I obsess over his silence, the more frustrated I become. I haven't even considered dating anyone since I left Charlie, and I finally take a risk only to be tossed aside.

I tell myself to calm down. That I'm overreacting. But I can't help feeling betrayed. Because whether or not Max is feeling what I'm feeling, he knows my past. He has to have some idea what his silence is doing to me. I at least deserve a "sorry, not interested" call. Mostly though, I am frustrated with myself. I let myself be sucked in way too easily, and that was something I had sworn never to do again.

I keep busy, focus on work, and don't let myself wallow. I am stronger than I used to be. Ultimately, I decide to be proud of myself. I took a leap, put myself out there. I have no control over other people's actions, only my own, and I have done nothing wrong.

I smile as I recognize Laura's voice in my head. She noticed I was off at the last meeting, but I assured her I was fine. She apologized sheepishly for giving Evan my number for Max, but insisted she did it as a friend who was trying to "hook a sister up." I could tell she desperately wanted to ask about Max, but aside from a good humored lecture about handing out my phone number, I refused to say a word. I wasn't up for that just yet. I was still holding out hope he'd call. After nine days of unanswered calls and one unreturned message, I'm ready to put that to bed. Sleep tight hopes and dreams, maybe one day you'll get the chance to be real.

I'm walking to my car after work when I see a familiar truck at the gas station across the street. It's eleven at night, and I'm exhausted after a nine-hour shift, but my legs carry me across the street anyway. Evan looks up from the pump and spots me as I jog over. He immediately averts his eyes. My suspicion spikes. I land heavily in front of him and prop both fists on my hips.

"Evan." My eyes are slits as he glances up at me sheepishly.

"Jenna! I almost didn't see ya there, Darlin'. How you doin'?" His efforts to appear nonchalant do not fool me.

"Evan," I say with force. "Spill."

He sighs heavily, running a hand down his face. "Hell, Sugar. How much time ya got?"

My stance wavers as I take in Evan's weary face. He looks like he's aged a decade, and his clothes are wrinkled. I drop my arms. "Seriously, Evan. What is going on?" I place a hand on his arm, and he smiles at me sadly.

He studies my face closely as he asks, "How much did Max tell ya about his father?"

"Not much. I know he works for him, and that his name is Michael."

Evan nods, but still looks uncertain. He's trying to decide how much to divulge.

"I know he was hard on him," I hedge, "and I suspect there's a lot more to it than that."

He huffs and mumbles, "A bit more, yeah. You could say that."

I give Evan my best puppy eyes and he relents with a groan. "Alright. He'll kill me for tellin' ya, but they got into it real good a few days ago."

I nod. "Okay. And?"

Evan deflates, "And he's been at the hospital for three straight days."

I immediately panic. It feels as if he's just poured ice into my veins.

"I can't get him to leave!" Evan continues, running his hand through his hair just like Max does when he's anxious.

Wait. What? "Evan, why is he at the hospital?"

He hitches up his pants and tells the ground, "Because he put his dad there."

Oh. Oh no. "I need to see him."

I climb into the cab of the truck and Evan follows me, shaking his head. "Oh no you don't..."

"Please, Evan. I care about him." My eyes fill with tears unexpectedly, and I look at the ground to try and hide them. "I just want to help. If I can."

I look back up and Evan's eyes look a little watery too. "I think, just maybe, ya can." We both smile a bit, and he adds, "I hope ya can."

Why on earth did I insist on coming here? When he told me Max was at the hospital with his father, I hadn't really thought it through. I just got in Evan's truck and told him to drive. Now that I'm here, I have time to doubt my actions. I force myself to take a moment and think about the facts. Max is here because he violently attacked someone, and I have a habit of attracting abusive men. My heart riots against my brain at the thought, but I force a truce. I'm smarter than I used to be. I will only give my heart to Max if my brain agrees to it.

I stand awkwardly next to Evan in the waiting room and twist my hair around and around my index finger.

Twist. Should I leave?

Twist. Should I stay?

A nurse in magenta scrubs makes her way toward us. Her brown hair is pulled back in a severe bun, but her face is kind. She smiles and stage whispers to Evan, "Is this her?" then winks at me.

I smile back nervously and continue the assault on my hair.

"That's her, alright," he says crossing his arms.

I raise my eyebrows at Evan and he explains, "Gretta here has seen a lot of Max and I the past few days."

Is he... blushing? *Interesting.*

"I may have told her a little about you." He scratches the back of his neck, and Gretta winks again.

I'm shocked to say the least. Sure, I've known Evan for a while now, but we've never been exceedingly close.

"Oh, he's told me *all* about you and that nephew of his." Gretta places her hands over her heart and swoons dramatically.

I blush fiercely. What did Max say about me? Does this mean I wasn't the only one having crazy notions of love?

Gretta goes on, seemingly oblivious to the fact that my brain is exploding in my head. "That boy is head over heels for you, Darlin'." She sighs and flutters her eyelashes. Gretta certainly has a flair for the dramatics. "Oh to be young and in love."

I don't even have time to process this before Max is suddenly rounding the corner. He sees me first, and freezes in his tracks. Evan and Gretta stay quiet as he stares me down. There's a bruise on his left cheekbone. It's dark yellow, so I assume it's from when this all began. I'm pretty good at estimating the age of a bruise. It's not the injury that makes me go cold, though. It's not his dirty, wrinkled clothes, or his greasy hair either. What freezes my insides is that spark. It's back, and it's not a spark anymore. It's an inferno. The anger inside him has flared to life since I last saw him, and it scares me. I want to cry for him. Try to extinguish the flame with my tears.

"What is she doing here?"

Max doesn't come any closer, and he doesn't address me at all. He's glaring at Evan. I can see the accusation there, and I wonder if they've fought about me before.

Gretta scoffs and rolls her eyes like Max is a petulant child. Evan holds up his hands in surrender. "Now don't you look at me like that, boy. I was mindin' my own business when she came up to me. She hopped in my damn truck and refused to budge. What was I supposed to do?"

Max lowers his head and grips his hair tightly in both hands.

Evan speaks softly, as if he's talking to a spooked animal. "You're not him, son. It was an accident."

Max stiffens, then turns his ire on me. "Why would you do that? This isn't any of your business! You need to leave." His lips press into a hard line, and he adds for good measure, "I don't want you."

Not, *"I don't want you here."* No. He doesn't want me at all. My heart breaks in two and I feel my chest for blood. I don't know what I was expecting, but not this. I didn't think Max would ever remind me of Charlie.

Gretta storms up to Max, finger wagging. "How dare you speak to her like that! She came here to take care of you, and you go and brush her off like day old toast!"

Max surprises us all by raising his voice right back at the nurse. "You have no idea what you're meddling in!" The room goes silent.

Evan doesn't allow things to escalate any further. He grabs Max's arm and leads him back down the hallway. "That's enough of that, boy. You need to cool off." Evan is forceful, but steady. He pushes Max back into whatever room he came from, and I'm grateful for his quiet strength.

Gretta and I stand silently, staring at the empty hall. Her mouth is hanging open in shock. She wasn't expecting that either. She looks at me and her jaw snaps shut. I don't know exactly when I started crying, but my tears push Gretta back into nurse mode.

She takes my hand gently. "Here, Sweetie, just take a seat right over here." She ushers me to a chair that was vacated during our argument. Gretta rubs my trembling arms up and down vigorously and shakes her head. Her brows are drawn together and I know she sees how deep his reaction has cut me. My initial reaction to rage is to disassociate, so after a minute or two, my emotions catch up and everything gets much worse. Gretta holds me as I cry.

Evan returns a little while later. I've managed to pull myself together, but he's not blind. As he and Gretta hold a whispered conversation against the far wall, I see him frowning at my red eyes and puffy face. There is a television directly across from me, but I don't know what I'm watching. My mind is full of Max. I picture him saying the words to me over and over again. *I don't want you.*

I should leave. I told myself I was going to be smart about this, and Max just gave me my answer. I lower my head into my hands and grip my hair so tightly it hurts. I want to pull the answers out. I don't understand what is happening to him. Why would he treat me this way? I take a deep breath, rub my sore scalp, and think.

Evan gave me a quick summary of what happened on the drive over. Max's father has a habit of showing up at his house in the middle of the night, drunk, and looking for a fight. Usually, Max lets him wear himself out, banging on the door and yelling a bit, then drives him home. This time was different. His patience finally snapped, and he gave his father the fight he'd been looking for. It only took two punches to turn him into a bloody heap of booze and regret. I remember Evan's comment from earlier, *"You're not him, son."*

That's when it all clicks into place. The reason he refuses to leave his father's side. The reason he was cruel to me. The reason he is so angry. He's angry with himself. He wants me to leave him for my own protection. He put his father in the hospital, and now he thinks he's dangerous. Just like Charlie. My heart and brain race side by side, connecting the dots. Charlie never would have pushed me away. He wanted me around to take the hits and the blame. I imagine Max grouping himself with him and my stomach churns. I think I understand now. And I need to talk to him, because I have more faith in him than he does. Charlie never made me feel loved the way Max has in just this short time we've had together. He's not like him at all. I know it. My heart and brain agree. Now I just need to convince him. I stand up and walk toward Evan and Gretta, fists clenched and jaw set. I've cried about it, now I'm ready to fight. He doesn't want me? *Bullshit.*

8

Evan's eyebrows hit his hairline when I told him I was staying. Well, not so much told him as yelled it at him. He tried to talk me out of it, but Gretta took my side. She saw my determination and told Evan not to worry about me; that I was "Made of tough stuff." Either I made her proud with my stubbornness, or she wants to see me tear Max a new one. Either way, she checks on me often as I sit and wait for Max to agree to see me. There's no excuse for the way he spoke to me, but as hurt as I am, he needs me right now. He's at a crossroads, and if I don't grab his hand now, I'm afraid he'll take a path I can't follow him down. He needs me for guidance. And I need him, too. This may be my one big shot at happiness. I refuse to let him ruin it for us.

I've been the damsel in distress. I spent my whole life bending to the will of others. I won't be that person anymore. I am strong, and I deserve to make my own decisions. I will not be dismissed by someone I care about simply because they are hurting and are afraid to let me see it. So no matter what Max says to try and push me away, I won't leave until he's listened to what I have to say. Then he can decide whether he's going to run, or stand with me.

Three hours. That's how long it takes Evan to convince him to talk to me. I stopped looking up every time I heard a door open hours ago, so I don't notice him until the toes of his shoes poke into my line of sight. I take my time, studying the scuffed toe of one black shoe for a moment before raising my eyes to meet his. I've been waiting three hours, but now I want more time. This could end with me walking out the door, never to see him again. I'm suddenly in no rush.

"I can't believe you waited this long."

"I can't believe you made me wait this long."

We each test out a smile. He looks much better now--more like himself. I look for the spark, but see only hollowness. His anger is gone, but so is everything else. He seems so lost. I stand, take one of his hands, and lead him out to the lobby. The only other person out here is a nurse on night duty, and she is sitting with her feet up on the desk, watching something on her phone.

I position him against a wall and he leans back with a sigh. He looks exhausted. The deep kind of exhaustion that comes from the heart. I try to collect all the arguments flying around in my head as I walk back and forth a few times. He softly grasps my hand and stops my pacing.

"I know you're full of it," is what pops out first.

He doesn't deny it, only lets his head fall back against the wall and talks to the ceiling. "Yes. I am."

"You know, for a second, you made me think I was crazy." I shake my head and he lowers his to look at me as I continue. "For one moment I considered that everything I felt for you was delusion. That I had fallen for someone who didn't give a rat's ass about me." His eyes fill with tears, but they don't fall. "Again." Mine do.

He reaches for me, but I take a step back, holding up a hand. "No. You listen to me first."

I take a deep breath and prepare myself. "I know that you're hurting. I know there's a deep pain inside you. I see it in your eyes. I can see your anger, always simmering under everything else. I may not know all the dirty details, but I recognize a kindred spirit."

His laugh interrupts my speech and I shoot him a glare.

He stands up straight. "You are nothing like me." He spits it out like it burns. A tear falls, and he swipes it away angrily before going on. "You want to know why I never called?"

In all the excitement, it hadn't occurred to me that this all happened three days ago, but he hasn't called me in nine.

"I wanted to call the very next morning after our date. Hell, I wanted to call from my cell phone the second you closed your door and I couldn't see you anymore!" He takes a shaky breath, and I stand completely still, waiting with bated breath for him to finish his thought.

"It was the snowflakes." He says in a softer voice. "I watched you catching snowflakes on your tongue, and I thought- I'll ruin her." His eyes bore into me, begging me to understand. "You're so much better than me, Jenna. You've been through all I have and more, and yet you've overcome everything. You're happy and whole." He deflates against the wall, "I can't do that." His voice breaks along with my heart. Then his hands turn to fists as he clenches his jaw. "I won't bring you down with me."

There he goes again, trying to make my decisions for me. My blood begins to boil as I get in his face. "I get to make my own choices, Max. And do you really have so little faith in yourself? In me? You think I would *let* you bring me down?"

His mouth opens and closes in confusion.

"You think I'm so weak I couldn't handle being with you?" I'm picking up steam now, and forge on before he can respond. "Because I've got news for you, Max: I am strong. And you know what else? So are you. You have the same strength inside you that I have. You just need help finding it. And guess what? I'm an excellent detective." He chews on his bottom lip as I soften my tone. "I never thought I'd find someone, Max. I thought I was tainted." He lowers his brows and I continue before he can argue. "And then, I found you." I smile wistfully. "I want to help you. And I want you by my side to help me, too. I still have bad days. Contrary to what you might think, I am not perfect. Don't you see how well we fit?"

I take his hands and step into his space. He's propped up against the wall so that I'm standing between his legs. I do my best to fill the emptiness I see in his eyes. I remember how I felt him nestle into my heart that first night, and try to do the same to him. I want to fill the void and make him whole again.

"Remember when you asked me how I was happy?" I whisper.

He nods, just a tiny movement, so as not to break this spell.

"I told you it was a decision I made every day. A decision I still make every day." My heart is racing with adrenaline. This is it. He's about to decide which way our future will go.

His lids are slightly hooded as he nods again.

"So," I lick my lips, "what's your decision? Are you going to stay alone, wallowing in your pain? Or are you going to let me help you out of the hole?"

He leans in slow, allowing our foreheads to touch. My whole body relaxes at the contact. As my hands loosen their death grip on his, he lets go to slide his fingers into my hair. He holds me there for a long moment. Eyes closed, breaths deep. Then he finally presses his lips to mine and whispers, "I'm going to be happy."

As he wraps me in his arms I hear clapping from behind us. We pull apart and look to find Gretta and the other nurse standing behind the desk. Gretta is crying and clutching her hands together, a huge grin on her face. The nurse I don't know is less emotional, but just as interested in us.

"Should I make popcorn?" I call over.

Gretta laughs and scurries off. To tell Evan, I assume.

The other woman shrugs and plops down into her chair.

I turn back around in Max's arms and take his face in my hands.

Grinning, he says, "I love you, you know."

They're the sweetest words I've ever heard. Because I believe them. "I know."

Inevitably Yours
Jennifer Rose

I couldn't believe the weather. It was a brutally cold, stormy night, with no signs of letting up until there was at least a foot of snow on the ground. The only thing worth doing on a night like this was climbing into bed and burrowing under the covers.

I knew I should have moved to Florida when Felix died, but no, I had decided to stay put surrounded with all things familiar. I was never one who enjoyed change. I liked the same things, was caught up in my routine shuffle, my humdrum boring life. I was happy like this even if I had to put up with New York snow.

"Good evening, Mrs. Long," Henry, the doorman greeted me. "Evening."

Henry held open the door, tipping the brim of his hat to avoid a sudden gust of snow from blowing into his face. I walked into the lobby and removed my gloves, the tips of my fingers bright red and aching from the cold. I searched my purse for my keys.

"That's some night out there," he laughed. "Not even sure a penguin would appreciate it."

"I was just thinking how nice Florida would be about now," I chuckled, walking over to the wall of brass mailboxes and inserted my key.

"Planning a vacation this year, Mrs. Long?"

"No, I'm not the vacation type, Henry," I confessed.

Since Felix left me, I didn't do holidays, nor did I ever expect to in the future. I made no plans other than going to work, coming home, and spending the evening puttering around my empty apartment. Then I'd go to bed early, so I could wake and do it all over again.

"I think I'll do Cuba this year, the wife was talking about going to see family in Ireland, but I think tropical is the way to go what do you think?"

The squish between my toes was an icy-cold reminder that I needed to buy new boots. Another pair of shoes was ruined in the name of vanity. Boots were sloppy and did nothing for my legs, yet I wouldn't be standing with my teeth chattering, envisioning my toes turning black, and falling off, if I gave in and purchased a pair.

The mailman had stuffed so many letters into my mailbox, I wondered how the hinges held. I looped the handle of my purse over the small brass door and proceeded to dump the lot inside.

"Ireland is much nicer in the spring," I told Henry. "I spent my honeymoon there. It's such a lovely country, depending on which part you visit, of course. If I went to Cuba, I would make sure it was one of those all-inclusive resorts. I think it's safer."

"Cuba it is," Henry laughed. "Oh, I almost forget. I signed for a letter that arrived by courier a few hours ago. Let me get it for you."

Henry handed me a bulky manila envelope. It was addressed to Felix & Roberta Long. I still couldn't get used to the idea that Felix was gone. Five years seemed to fly past as if he were killed yesterday when he was killed by a drunk driver coming home from a business trip. I suppose what bothered me most was never getting to say goodbye.

"Thank you, Henry," I stuffed the letter into my bag with the rest of the mail and pressed the elevator button. "Have a nice evening, don't work too hard."

"Never," Henry promised with a smile, as the elevator door started to close. "Enjoy your evening, Mrs. Long."

Barely inside my apartment for two minutes and the phone started ringing. I quickly shrugged out of my coat, hanging it on the rack beside the door and kicked off my sopping wet shoes. I raced to the phone, tapping the caller display because it wasn't working.

"Hello?"

"Bobby. I'm not bothering you, am I?" Roman asked. His voice always managed to send a delightful shiver up my spine.

"Just got in the door, actually," I held back a giggle. Roman had this strange effect on me, made me often giggle uncontrollably like a schoolgirl. "Can I change and call you back?"

"Okay. I'll be waiting with bated breath until you do."

"Just don't hold it," I joked, he was always so easy to talk to. "Give me five."

"Five it is," he chuckled and hung up.

Roman Welch was my dearly departed husband's best friend since childhood, now mine. Actually, from the day Felix introduced us, I think the three of us became inseparable. After Felix's funeral, Roman in a way filled the space in my heart that Felix left behind. I love him, I just didn't want to love him. I liked to refer to Roman as my unique, one of a kind friend. I wanted to keep him that way, it was for the best.

I jumped into a hot shower. My feet were thankful for the heat. I pulled on a pair of warm fleece pajamas, heavy work socks and my favorite pair of fuzzy, seen-better-days slippers. Then I poured myself a large glass of wine.

It was easier to dump the contents of my purse onto the dining table, than try to remove everything in an orderly fashion. As I sorted through the junk and important things, the manila envelope caught my eye. It had no return address and no markings to give me a clue as to where it came from. It must have been important though, why else would Henry be prompted to sign for it?

I unlatched the metal clasp and peeked inside before taking it, the phone and my wine glass over to the sofa. Shoving a few books and magazines aside on the coffee table, I pulled out the envelopes contents as I dialed Roman's number.

"Hey beautiful," Roman said, in a naughty tone that I loved. "What are you wearing?"

"Nothing," I giggled. "I decided to give the neighbors a thrill."

"Lucky neighbors," he laughed. I adored that laugh. "What are your plans for tonight?"

"Wine, wine and more wine," I giggled, as I opened a smaller white envelope containing a letter. The letter head belonged to a cruise line of all things.

"Bobby?" Roman yelled. "Did I lose you?"

Felix had always called me Roberta. In fact, I couldn't remember him calling me anything else. Roman was the only one that called me Bobby, and secretly I liked hearing him say it.

"No, I'm sorry. I was distracted for a moment. What did you say?"

"I said, I feel like pepperoni pizza," he chuckled. "But I can't eat a whole one by myself."

Roman was attempting to lure me in with food. He knew I couldn't resist the offer of pizza, nor could I turn down some much needed time spent with a good friend.

"But I'm already in my jammies," I whined, knowing he didn't want me out in the cold. "And it's a bitch outside."

"Colder than a witch's tit," Roman agreed. "How about I order the pizza for delivery and meet it in the lobby? That is, unless you'd rather have an evening to yourself."

"An evening alone?" I pretended to ponder. "Or free pepperoni pizza, specially delivered by a tall, sexy man? Really, you don't want to come out in this shit."

"I live a block away," Roman rationalized. "Besides, I'd risk a little frostbite to see my favorite lady…and eat pepperoni pizza."

"I'm filling your wine glass as we speak," I told him.

"See you soon," Roman said, and I hung up.

I didn't do goodbyes since Felix died, so I never said it.

Celebration Cruises, the letterhead said. It didn't ring a bell. I took a mouthful of wine and read on.

Dear Mr. & Mrs. Long,

Your names were entered in the Give a Heart Charity Auction some time ago. Due to an unfortunate mix-up, some prizes were not awarded to date, your prize being one of them.

It is my extreme pleasure to congratulate you both on winning the grand prize 'Lover's Package' from Celebration Cruises…

"Holy shit." My voice echoed back at me in the quiet apartment. "I won a cruise?"

The letter went into great detail, basically saying it was a nine-night Mediterranean couple's cruise, all-inclusive, including airfare. How exciting. I was kind of warming up to the idea of taking a vacation after all.

Why not? Single women went on cruises alone all the time. I could, too. Then I read the disclaimer nearing the bottom of the page and let out a disheartened sigh.

Couples Only

Not only was it highlighted, it was underlined to add extra emphasis. Well, if that didn't feel like the air being released from my happy balloon. I tossed the letter aside and sipped my wine.

I ran to the door when the buzzer made two sharp beeps.

"Yes," I said, speaking close to the antiquated intercom.

"Mr. Welch is here to see you, Mrs. Long," Henry announced.

"Send him up please, Henry."

"Will do, Mrs. Long."

For some crazy reason, I ran into the washroom and made sure my hair looked nice. I leaned closer to the mirror, baring my teeth and using my index finger like a toothbrush. Nothing between my teeth and just in case, I checked for boogers. Don't judge, you know you've done it.

Roman knocked on the door as he opened it. There was no need for formality between us. We've known each other too long for that shit. I came out of the washroom and smiled when I caught sight of him, resembling a bundled up, partially-frozen Eskimo.

"You have one hell of an addiction to pizza to come out in the middle of a storm."

I helped him out of his Parka and draped it over one of the dining room chairs to dry. I watched as he toed off his boots and set them on the rubber boot tray at the door. He turned to me and smiled, rubbing his hands together as if in anticipation of something a touch spicier than pizza.

If ever a man could be called beautiful, Roman was that man. He had premature gray hair like Richard Geer and the most striking blue eyes I'd ever seen. They reminded me of the pool at a spa, sparkling and inviting. And his lips, oh his lips, they had only ever kissed my cheeks, but in my fantasies they were warm and soft.

Yeah, I fantasized about Roman. I was a woman with desires and a heartbeat. I was certain ninety percent of the woman that saw him on a daily basis, no doubt daydreamed about being with him. Felix once told me that Roman thought I was hot. I remember slapping his arm and giggling, it was weeks before I could make eye contact with Roman after that.

"You might want to warm it up," Roman said, picking up the pizza box from the chair beside the door and handing it to me.

"I'm on it," I said, taking it into the kitchen and setting the oven to warm. "I put your wine on the coffee table."

"Thanks," he called out. "So, how was your day?"

I transferred the pizza from the box onto a baking sheet and put it in the oven, setting the timer for ten minutes. I grabbed our bottle of wine from the counter and walked into the living room.

"Like every other day, it basically sucked," I told him, not really interested in talking about my work. "And how was yours?"

Since Felix had no life insurance when he was killed, and the bills had to be paid, I had no choice but to work. Luckily, Roman was a self-made millionaire and could choose to do as he pleased. If he didn't want to go into work, he simply stayed in bed. To look at Roman, you'd never know it though; he was easygoing and down to earth. He only dressed in a suit when and if he went to work, the rest of the time it was either jeans or sweats. Tonight, he was dressed casually in dark gray sweats, a t-shirt, and black hoodie.

"Teleconference," he huffed. "I sat in front of my laptop for four hours, in a shirt, suit jacket, and a pair of boxers. Good thing Yamamoto didn't get a load of me from the waist down."

We laughed as I topped off our glasses, while fighting images of just how sexy he must have looked.

"What's this?" Roman picked up the cruise ship magazine that came in the package and fanned through it.

"I... won a cruise," I answered, just as the timer on the oven started its annoying shrill. "But I'm not going."

"How come?" Roman asked, from behind me. I turned to face him, slipping my hands into a pair of oven mitts.

"Because it was Felix and I who won," I raised my brows, then leaned into the oven and pulled out the pizza. "Grab us plates?"

"Bobby, you can go yourself ,you know?" Roman gently scolded, as he fetched two plates from the cupboard and tore a few sheets of paper towel from the roll. "It's about time you got out of this apartment and had some fun. I miss Felix, too, but he's gone Bobby, and life goes on."

"I know," I assured him. "I really do. That's not the reason."

"Then what?" he egged me on, as he placed two slices of Pizza onto each plate, handing me one. "Is the hot sauce still in the same place?"

"Yep," I answered, leaving him to find the hot sauce and went into the living room, still talking, "It's a couple's only cruise, meaning two people in a relationship. In case you haven't noticed, I'm a single unit now. I'd look pretty stupid going on a couple's cruise alone, wouldn't I? Besides, the fine print says it has to be a couple."

"So, find someone to go with you, one of the girls from work," Roman suggested, sitting on the sofa beside me, shaking hot sauce onto his pizza slices.

"I'm the boss, who'd go with me?" I asked, taking a bite of my pizza and chewing. "Next idea?"

The pizza tasted so good. There was nothing better than pepperoni and stringy, greasy, hot cheese to make me feel better. As well as a glass of cheap wine and good company.

"I'd go with you," Roman blindsided me with a grin and a wink.

"I'm being serious," I chastised, lightly thumped my fist against his arm.

"Why not me?" Roman asked, lifting his glass to his lips and taking a sip of wine before going on. "It's not like I can't take the time off work to go. I can be packed at a moment's notice. And who do you know that's more fun to take on a cruise than yours truly? That's right, no one."

I started seriously considering his suggestion. It could work. Actually the thought was ideal. Me and my best friend, no sticky, awkward romantic notions to worry about. I could be myself and have a good time. Why the hell not?

"Okay," I conceded. "Looks like we're going on a cruise."

Luckily the red tape involved to change the documents from Felix's name to Roman's, wasn't too lengthy a process. In the matter of a few weeks, new documentation was sent with the appropriate changes in place, as well as my up to date passport.

Roman and I had agreed to forgo a plan. We decided to find our stateroom, get unpacked, and wing the rest of the trip. Playing it by ear sounded, as Roman put it, adventurous.

"Doesn't quite look the same as the brochure, does it?" Roman laughed, holding the door while I went in ahead of him.

"I think they may have fabricated a few things," I giggled awkwardly. "Like the fact that there's one bed and my closet at home may be larger."

"It's just a place to rest our heads." Roman tossed our suitcases onto the bed. "It's not like we'll be spending a lot of time in here. I'll arrange for a cot or I can sleep on the floor."

"I'm not letting you sleep on the floor for nine nights," I protested. "It'll be a great cruise for you with a sore back the entire time."

"Then I'll call for a cot," he said, tracing his finger along the ship's directory located by the phone.

"You'll do nothing of the sort," I told him, taking the directory from his hand. "We're grownups, there's no reason we can't share a bed."

What was I saying? Had I popped my cork? Was gray matter oozing from my brain, rendering me a freaking lunatic? Sure we were adults, but Roman was my best friend, someone I fantasized about often.

"I'm okay with it, but what about you?" he gave me a sideways scowl. "I don't know if you could control yourself?"

"Oh, it'll be tough, but I'll try my hardest," I joked, unzipping my suitcase and flipping it open. "What do you want to do first?"

I was ready for a quick change of subject. Almost positive my face was red enough already, by the heat warming my cheeks. Roman took off his shirt and rummaged in his bag, while I avoided looking at him, for fear I'd combust. He put on a t-shirt and tossed his dress shirt on the bed beside me. The breeze his shirt created caused a puff of his cologne to move past my face. Spicy like nutmeg mixed with bergamot and lavender. I missed the scent of a man… among other things.

"How about a walk?" Roman suggested. "We'll nose around the ship for a while and then hit one of the bars. Are you hungry?"

"Not really, but I could go for a drink."

A few hours later, with margaritas in hand, we were resting in loungers on the Lido deck, enjoying the sun.

"Tell me something, Bobby," Roman said, his head back and eyes closed.

"Yes," I answered, as I studied Roman's handsome profile.

"When are you going to start dating again?"

His question came clear out of left field, catching me completely off guard. I looked out at the ocean, not able to wrap my head around the question. It had been five years since Felix died and I'd never thought about dating. For the longest time, just looking at another man felt dirty and cheap, as if I was cheating. Though it was never like that with Roman. I had all kinds of fantasies about him, and many moments filled with dirty thoughts. But those thoughts never felt wrong, they felt natural, like he was part of me. It only made sense that Roman filled the void Felix left behind. If I was to date again, the only man I could see myself with was Roman and that wasn't going to happen anytime soon.

"I don't know," I answered truthfully. "Why do you ask?"

"Making conversation," he shrugged.

"I've never heard you mention dating before," I said, knowing that Roman, when I wasn't working, spent most of his time with me. "When was the last time you went on a date?"

"A few months ago, I guess," his answer was blasé.

For a second, I swore my stomach turned with jealousy. I shook the thought away.

"You never got married, why?" I asked the question I often wondered, but was too afraid to ask, in case I was treading into places I had no business being.

Roman opened his eyes and turned his head to face me, his pretty blue eyes sparkling like diamonds in the sun. He smiled. I loved that smile, it always warmed my heart when I needed it most.

"She got away," he said, with a wink.

"I'm sorry," I offered. "Can I ask what happened?"

There was a long pause, like the kind straight out of a suspense film. The anticipation filled my head with more suspect than necessary.

"She married my best friend," he said, before taking his eyes off of me, resting his head back and closing them again. "And they lived happily ever after."

Oh my God! Oh my God! Oh my God!

Roman was talking about me. No, it couldn't be. I wasn't hearing right, he couldn't have meant me. That was crazy, but if it was true, what did it mean? That he had feelings hidden away for me all this time?

"Roman?"

"I'm starving, let's get something to eat." Roman jumped to his feet.

"All right," I answered, holding out my hand for him to help me up. "Should we change?"

"Nah, I don't feel like going to the dining room," he scrunched his nose. "How about going to that Irish pub we saw? We'll eat a ton of wings and have a few beers."

"Only if you agree to see a movie afterwards," I insisted, happy the awkwardness was dissipating.

"Only if I get to pick what we see," he countered, hip checking me as we walked, causing me to tip off balance. He grabbed my hand to steady me and a spark shot straight to my belly.

I wasn't sure what was happening, but something had changed in the chemistry between us, in a short period of time. It was as if a light had burned out and the bulb to replace it seemed to be a whole lot brighter. That strange exciting sensation that I hadn't felt in such a long time, had a grip on me and it was giving me one hell of a shake. No, I couldn't let this happen. What was the worst way to lose a friend? Fall in love with him.

"Want to sit at the bar?" Roman asked, placing his hand at the small of my back, the heat from his palm burning through the thin fabric of my top.

"Whatever you like," I said, allowing myself to be directed to the far end of the bar.

Most tables were occupied, only a handful of people sat at the bar. As my eyes adjusted to the darkness, I took a look around. This was most definitely a couple's cruise, everyone seemed to be buddied up with that special someone. Many of them snuggled close together, whispering and sharing kisses, the room was flooding over with romance. I felt so out of place, as the bartender came over to take our drink order.

"I'll have whatever's on tap," Roman ordered, standing and leaning into my ear. "I'll be right back."

Beer sounded good, but I changed my mind when I looked over the drink chart on the wall. I ordered a Tom Collins. I hadn't had one in years. It used to be my drink of choice way back when.

"Will you or your husband be ordering anything to eat, this evening?" the bartender asked, as he set down the drinks.

Me or my husband, I giggled, thinking Roman would get a laugh out being referred to as my husband. Roman's words from earlier suddenly haunted me 'She married my best friend, and lived happily ever after'.

"Ma'am?"

I jumped back from my thoughts. "Yes, we will. Thank you."

"I'll get you a menu, be right back."

These crazy thoughts had to stop, before I ended up making a total ass of myself.

I closed my eyes and whispered to myself, "Roman doesn't love, he doesn't love you."

"Hey," Roman said, slipping back into his seat. "Talking to yourself?"

"Sometimes it's the only way to get the answers you want to hear," I joked, the bartender handing us a single menu.

"I'll give you and your wife a moment to decide." He walked away.

"Well, wife," Roman joked, holding one side of the menu, while I held the other. "What looks good to you?"

You, I thought, hoping I didn't say it out loud.

"I don't know, I thought you wanted wings," I reminded him.

"I wouldn't say no to the steak on a Kaiser," he said, pointing it out on the plastic coated menu. "The Fish and chips sounds good too."

"Order me the buffalo shrimp?" I asked him, placing my hand on his forearm as I stood. "Going to visit the little girl's room."

"Fries?"

"No, I'm not all that hungry."

"You okay?" he asked, his concern was sweet.

"Fine," I squeezed his shoulder before walking away.

In the washroom, I flushed my face with cool water, while reiterating Roman's declaration in my head, one last time.

Felix, my love, I spoke in my head, looking at my reflection in the mirror. If my heart is free to love again, give me some kind of a sign. If Roman is my future, then guide my heart where it belongs.

After eating and discussing all that the ship had to offer without making any firm plans, we enjoyed a few more drinks and then went for a walk. It was dark. The stars were putting on an impressive show and the wind had picked up, bringing with it the salty scent of the ocean. Without asking, Roman draped his arm casually over my shoulders. There was a nip in the air and he was probably concerned that I was cold. Sweet as always.

The four Tom Collins I drank at the bar were affecting me with a happy fuzzy feeling. I yawned and blinked my eyes. I was tired, but it was such a beautiful night, I just wanted to enjoy every minute.

"Tired?" Roman asked.

"No," I lied. "I wonder how far out we are."

"Can't be that far," Roman said, pointing to his right. "I can still see lights on the shore over there."

"I'm really happy you convinced me to come on the cruise," I said.

We walked over to the rail and stood, but it was too dark to see much beyond the glow of the ship's lights.

"I'm happy that I convinced you to bring me," he laughed. I rested my head on his shoulder. "Still up for a movie?"

"Yeah, let's go."

Since I had agreed to Roman making the movie choice, we were sitting in our seats watching the ship's agenda for the next eight days on the huge screen, while waiting for The Perfect Day to begin. I didn't put up a stink when he suggested all action movies, mainly because it starred Benicio Del Toro, who I wouldn't kick out of bed for eating crackers, or anything else for that matter. I giggled to myself and Roman looked at me like I'd taken leave of my senses.

When the action kicked into gear, the surround sound was so loud in the small theatre, I flinched each time something crashed or blew up. And when Roman raised his arm and wrapped it around my shoulders, giving me a comforting squeeze, my insides turned to jelly.

Damn it all, if I didn't have to go to the washroom part way into the movie. I excused myself and ran to the ladies room. I didn't want to miss the movie, so I hurried. Too bad they didn't have a pause button. I ran into the closest available stall and closed the door, unzipped and sat.

My jaw dropped open when I read the passage someone had written on the back of the door, in black magic marker.

Don't use your past as an excuse to miss out on your future
This message was left for you

"Holy shit!"

"Everything okay in there?" a voice asked, from the next stall. "Is the toilet roll empty?"

I looked to make sure before answering with a laugh, "Brand new roll, thanks."

Was this it? The sign I had I asked for? I read it repeatedly, the words scoring deeper and deeper into my memory each time. Was this Felix's way of telling me that he approved of Roman and I? I caressed my fingers over the words and smiled.

"Hey you, I was about to send in a search party," Roman whispered, snuggling me closer into his side. "What took you so long?"

"Something caught my attention," I said. "It's not important."

"If you say so."

"I say so, now shut up so I can watch the movie," I giggled, and Roman squeezed me in response.

We waited while the majority of people emptied the theatre and then made our way out and onto the moonlit deck. I couldn't believe the amount of people that were still strolling along hand in hand. It was windy and surprisingly cool for being the Mediterranean. I supposed it had to do with ocean tides, or something far more scientific than my brain could get a grasp around.

"I'm getting tired, would you mind if we went back to the room?"

"Not at all," I agreed, Roman's arm still draped around me. "Tomorrow's another day. We can gamble, eat, swim, eat, have a few drinks, eat."

"Whatever you want to do, Bobby," Roman pressed his lips to my temple. "I shall follow... that is, unless you don't want me to."

"Don't be silly, we're a couple," I playfully scolded, poking him in the ribs and watching him dance around. "Where I go, you go, and vice versa."

Being the gentleman that he was, Roman insisted I shower first. I didn't want to take forever by blow drying my hair, so elected to towel dry it instead. Roman was tired, he clearly needed to sleep by the amount of yawns he tried to hide since we got back to the room. I sat on the end of the bed and bent over, rubbing my hair briskly with the towel. I thought I heard Roman's voice.

"Sorry," he said, "forgot my gear."

I sat up, the towel I was using falling to the floor when I caught sight of Roman, holding a towel around his hips with one hand and his shaving kit with the other. What a beautiful sight to behold. The amount of times I had seen Roman shirtless I could count on one hand, but each time I did, it sent a wonderful warm wave flushing over me.

For a man in his mid-forties, Roman was in remarkable shape. Not that I wasn't. I had a rocking little body for a woman of thirty-six.

I took care of myself and watched what I ate, most of the time. I exercised regularly and never smoked a day in my life.

I'm not saintly, but damned close to it, I giggled.

"Should I be insulted?" he asked, looking over his shoulder and disappearing into the washroom, the door closing behind him.

I laughed loud enough for him to hear me.

Brushing out my hair, I kept visiting images of Roman in that towel. The man was heating up the room and he wasn't even in it. I forced in a deep breath, holding it for a count of ten, and then blowing it out slowly. My body was relaxed, the images had all but evaporated into thin air and my breathing was under control. I had this.

"So, I was thinking," Roman's voice pulled me from my Zen-like state. To my disappointment, he was dressed in shorts and a loose fitting t-shirt. "We should sign up for a dance class, what do you think? After, we can dress up, have dinner in the dining room and then dance until the sun comes up."

"Well," I said, tossing my towel and hair brush onto the bathroom counter, trying to avoid making eye contact. "It would be a very dangerous undertaking on your part, seeing as I have two left feet. My father tried for years to teach me, his toes paid a heavy price."

"That's why I suggested lessons," Roman laughed, seizing me around the waist and tugging me to his chest. He took my hand in his and spun us in a circle. "Besides, they don't call me Fred for nothing. Come on, Bobby. Do it for me, baby."

Baby.

He called me baby and I nearly collapsed in his arms. My heart was beating in my chest like a conga drum, my palms sweaty and the heat in my cheeks rising. How was it that just one word, a silly little term of endearment, could mean more to me than winning the lottery? It couldn't, I was acting childish.

"Ask me again in the morning," I said. "You're clearly sleep deprived."

"The morning it is," he swept me off of my feet, and transported me to the end of the bed. "But I'll warn you, Bobby Long, I have a memory like an elephant, I forget nothing."

He tossed me onto the bed. I laughed so hard my ribs hurt, from him jumping up and down, hopping around on all fours, causing my entire body to shake.

"Stop," I begged, my voice quivering, causing me to laugh harder. "Roman, stop. I'll pee my pants."

"That will be your side of the bed, then."

"Roman, please," I reached up and tickled his ribs, he rolled onto his back and we continued to laugh while we caught our breath.

"You fight dirty, baby," he huffed and puffed. "No fair tickling."

"You're just like a kid," I closed my eyes, tossing my arms over my head.

"My mother always said I'd never grow up," he tittered, rolling onto his side to face me. "I guess she was right."

"Don't grow up," I warned. "I like you just the way you are, don't ever change."

"You like the child in me, don't you?" he threw his leg and arm over me, pinning me in place and proceeded to poke me gently in the ribs, making me squirm to get out of his hold.

"Roman Welch," I giggled. "If you don't stop…"

In a flash, he was on top of me straddling my hips and holding my hands over my head. Silence filled the room, not even the sound of our rapid breathing registered as we stared at each other. Our faces inches apart, Roman's nostrils flared, the blue in his eyes darkening, and his face grew closer.

"I think I'm going to kiss you," he whispered, his minty breath hot on my face. "A simple no and I'll go back to being a gentleman."

"And if I say nothing?" I goaded.

Roman gave me a knowing smile and then touched his lips to mine. His kiss was soft and gentle, the taste of his warm lips finer than the best champagne.

"Did that really happen?" I asked, my mind swimming in a fog when he pulled away.

"It wasn't that bad was it?"

"No."

Suddenly I felt strangely shy with Roman still holding my arms above my head. Roman let out a sigh, releasing my hands and rolling onto his back. Holy tongue-tied moments, we just laid there frozen and speechless, neither knowing what to do.

"For some reason," Roman spoke so softly, I had to strain to hear him. "I pictured the first time we kissed to be… different."

"Oh," I felt my heart tearing from my chest. It wasn't the magic moment for him that it was for me. "Just pretend it never happened."

"That's not what I'm saying," Roman sat up on one elbow, leaning into me. He brushed back a lock of my hair. "This isn't what I wanted."

A tear trickled from the corner of my eye and Roman brushed it away with his thumb.

"It could have been a little more… special, that's all."

"To me it was," I daringly admitted.

Studying me as if I were a piece of art hanging in a gallery, his face took on a wistful gaze.

"For eleven years, I have sat in the back seat and watched while another man, who was my dearest friend, made a life with the only woman I ever loved. And after helping you grieve for the loss of your husband, I think I've bided my time long enough," Roman's eyes met mine, as he lifted my hand to his lips and tenderly took his time kissing each knuckle. "It's taken five years for me to build up the courage to tell you how I feel…Bobby, I love you. I love you with all my heart."

"Roman," I said, as his fingers came to my face and covered my mouth.

"Don't say anything, Bobby," he warned. "I didn't tell you to force you into saying something you're not ready for. I told you because I think it's time we became more than just friends. I'd like us to be so much more. I want to take you on a date."

Roman, my best friend, wanted us to date. All I had to do was say one word and my dreams, my fantasies, could become reality. It wouldn't be a bad thing. We knew each other better than two strangers meeting ever could. He knew all of my quirks, my bad habits, and he'd been privy to some of my moodiest moments. He knew when I needed space and when I needed to be held. I would even risk saying, Roman knew me better than I knew myself.

"Yes," I bit into my bottom lip. "It's time I started dating, and I want it to be you."

"Really?" Roman sat up, with a brilliant smile spread over his face. "Holy shit! I was expecting a fight. I was sure you'd tell me a few cogs had slipped in my brain. I need to hold you, can I hold you?"

Roman was absolutely adorable. Like a big kid set free in a jelly bean factory. You'd have thought he'd won a million dollars, when in fact I was the one that was feeling pretty damned lucky.

"You're sure about this?" I asked, because I wanted there to be no doubts, no trepidation and absolutely no regrets. "Not that I don't... never mind, just hold me."

Pulling me into his arms and plunking me onto his lap, he wrapped his arms around me, tight like he was never letting go. Roman held me before, but never like this and not with this kind of intensity. This was new. His heart was beating with such fierceness, I could feel it against my chest, though mine was beating just as hard.

"Bobby," he said, I loved to hear him say my name. "Kiss me?"

He didn't need to ask twice. I held his face in my hands and stared into his eyes, like seeing them for the very first time. The blue so bright, it was like looking into clear ocean waters. I brought my lips near, but not touching, feeling the emotions transfer between us. I closed the gap pressing my lips delicately to his, his hands splaying across my back, crushing me against him until my ribs ached.

I set my hands on his shoulder and shoved back, breaking the kiss and smiled to reassure him that it was all good.

"We need to take this slow," I told him, though I was ready to feel more than his hands through layers of fabric. "Please understand, it's been a long time since... well, it's just been a long time."

"Anything you want," Roman stood, lifting me with him. "I don't want to rush a minute with you, I'm willing to give this all the time it takes. It's bed time though. What side do you want?"

"The left?" I giggled, as I held on tight and he walked around the bed, lowering me enough to pull back the sheets. Then he dumped me on the bed, chuckling when I let out a sharp squeal.

Roman turned off the overhead light and climbed under the covers, my eyes following his every move. We were going to share a bed, but not sleep together. I couldn't stop myself from giggling. Damn I had to learn how to get over doing that, it annoyed me, how Roman felt about it, I'd find out on time.

Once he turned out the bedside light, the room took on a relaxing glow from the LED light on the alarm clock. Our feet touched under the sheets, his warm from the socks he was wearing, mine cold as always. I swear I had the circulation of an eighty-year-old. My toes went in search of heat, touching his leg.

"Your feet are like ice," Roman balked, before linking our feet together. "Cold feet, warm heart."

"Shouldn't that be hands?"

"Good god woman, they're cold too?" he joked, using the excuse to situate me until I was cocooned in his arms, our legs tangled together, with my head resting happily on his shoulder. "Better?"

"Nice and cozy, thank you," I smiled, though he couldn't see me, placing my hand over his heart. "Good night."

"Sleep tight."

As awkward as I had imagined the morning to be, it felt as if nothing had changed between us. The bond of friendship was still hugely prevalent, my heart held tight to that continued union. I wasn't about to lose what we had built over the years.

While I brushed my hair and swirled it into a French knot, I thought hard regarding my true feelings for Roman. I loved him, I did. But was it the kind of love that could stand the test of time? He was still here. I would think that was a good sign, being that I wasn't exactly a Greek goddess in the light of the morning.

Breakfast was served on deck or in the dining room. We chose to partake on the deck, since it was such a fabulously sunny morning, and there was the slightest breeze coming off of the water.

Afterwards, we enjoyed wasted time in the casino. Where I managed to lose every dime I had allotted and Roman broke even. We toured the ship and did some mindless shopping. I decided to treat myself to a new cocktail dress for our date and found the perfect boutique, sending Roman on his way so he didn't see.

The satiny black fabric clung nicely in all the right places, accentuating my small waist and the curve of my hips. It felt velvety against my skin and plunged perfectly between my breasts where the fabric crisscrossed. It was simply sexy. And the finishing touches were the black lace bra and matching thong, lace trimmed thigh highs and the fuck me stilettos, the sales lady insisted completed the look.

Dance classes were fun, although I couldn't see me doing the tango again anytime soon. I'd only managed to do minor damage to Roman's poor toes, at least from what I could see, I hadn't made him bleed.

We sat on the pools edge, dangling our feet in the cool water, talking about our expectations in life. Mine were basic, I wanted us to be a couple, anything added would just be icing on the cake. Most of all, I wanted nothing to change. Roman assured me it could only get better, stronger, he was so confident in his convictions. Doubt didn't play a role in what Roman expected. I liked his positive outlook. I could take a page from his book.

"I'm going to get dressed first, if that's okay with you," Roman said, grabbing his suit from the end of the bed. "I have something I need to do while you get ready."

"Fine by me," I agreed, sitting down at the table by the window to apply my makeup. "I'll sit here and put my face on."

In view of the fact that I wasn't one to get dolled up on a regular basis, I kept my makeup to a minimum, choosing a dark almost blood red lipstick to give me a splash of color. I wore a pair of tiny diamond studs and my favorite silver bangle bracelet.

Roman came out of the washroom as short time later and stood with his hands held out to his sides, ready for inspection. He looked handsome in his black suit, crisp white dress shirt and dark red tie. His tie matched my lips and I smiled thinking what a fluke it was. Maybe it was a sign that our compatibility stretched beyond the physical. There were forces at work, perhaps an angel working his magic.

"Thank you, Felix," I whispered.

"I have something for you," Roman said, twirling his finger in the air. "Turn around."

Happily I turned my back to Roman and waited in anticipation. I loved surprises. I had since I was a small girl.

Roman's lips touched the tender flesh behind my ear, sending a spark of electricity racing from my head to my toes. Then my eyes caught the sparkle of something silver lowering in front of my face, the cool metal touching my chest. It was a necklace.

"Three diamonds," Roman whispered in my ear, his hot breath caressing my skin. "One for the past, so that you never forget… one for the present, to remind you to live for the moment … and one for the future, which I intend to be a huge part of, if you'll allow me."

I spun to face him, fingering the tiny pendant, the row of stones graduating in size. I threw my other arm around his neck and gave him an appreciative kiss. His arms wrapped around my body tugging me closer as the kiss intensified.

"I love it, thank you. At this rate, you're never going to see me in my new dress," I wiggled free from his hold, enjoying Roman's attempt to make me feel bad by pouting. "And pouting isn't going to work either. Now let me get dressed or we'll be late."

I took the garment bag that my dress was hidden in and ran into the washroom, closing the door. I proceeded to get dressed, starting with the lingerie and looked at myself in the full length mirror on the back of the door. Talk about scantily clad.

Ten minutes later, there was a gentle knock.

"I shall return," Roman called through the door.

"I promise I won't be long."

"Take your time," he said. "Do me a favor and tap on the outer door when you're ready?"

"What are you up to?" I laughed.

"Don't ask questions, you'll find out soon enough."

"Okay," I agreed, but the curiosity was going to make me nuts. I never dressed so fast in my life.

I slipped my feet into my new stilettos and walked back and forth a few times, for a test drive. They were higher than I was used to, but what they did for my legs made them so worth the exorbitant price I paid for them. I snuck one last look in the dresser mirror and inhaled a deep breath before giving a light tap on the door and standing back.

I expected the door to open and when it didn't I wondered how long he was going to keep me waiting. I jumped when there was a loud knock at the door. I opened it enough to see Roman standing holding a single red rose with an amazing smile on his face.

"Roberta," he said.

"I'm sorry, you must have the wrong room, there's no one named Roberta here." I closed the door in his face.

I hoped he understood. I didn't want him calling me Roberta, Felix always called me Roberta. Just like the pendant he gifted me, I wanted my first date with Roman to be in the present, not the past. He knocked again.

"Bobby," he presented the rose, and looked me up and down, before extending his bended elbow. "Would you do me the honor of allowing me to escort you to dinner this fine evening?"

"Mr. Welch," I took the offered rose, held it to my nose and then slipped my hand into the crook of Roman's arm. "It would be my pleasure."

Dinner consisted of prime rib for Roman and Cornish game hen for myself. We each had a slice of layered crème brulee cheesecake, which was beyond decadent that we enjoyed with hot coffee. While we let the food settle, we talked.

"I think I forgot to mention how beautiful you look tonight," Roman's eyes glazed over, when they settled on my cleavage, made all the more spectacular by my dresses neckline.

"Thank you," I said, enjoying the effect I was having on Roman. "You're not looking too shabby yourself."

"This old thing?" he joked, taking a mouthful of coffee and setting his cup down, pushing it aside and leaning forward on his crossed arms. "Do you remember when we met?"

"Of course I remember." And I did. "I had just gotten home from the university. My mom was so furious when Felix came to the house to pick me up. I thought she was going kill him. You were sitting in the back seat of his puke green Chevy Nova, and Felix tore you a new one when you called me Bobby… I secretly loved when you called me that."

"I knew," Roman said. "Your beautiful green eyes always gave you away."

"Anyway," I felt my cheeks warming. "You were wearing a beat up, old, leather jacket, it made you look badass. But I knew as soon as you smiled at me, there wasn't a bad bone in your body."

"Bobby," Roman lifted my hand, resting it in his palm, fingering the plain gold band. "Now that we're dating, don't you think… I mean maybe it's time… not that it's up to me and seriously I shouldn't ask, but as long as you're wearing Felix's ring, I'm going to feel like we're doing something wrong."

"I know you're right," I looked at my wedding band. "I just don't know if I'm ready to…"

"I'm sorry," Roman kissed the back of my hand and then gave it a squeeze. "Let's go dancing. I need to work that cheesecake off before it goes to my hips and ruins this cougar-like physique."

We were laughing from the moment Roman helped me to my feet, to the minute we stepped out onto the dance floor. We danced to nearly every song, slow or fast, opting out when tango music started, having a glass of wine instead.

Excusing myself to the little girls room, Roman said he'd order us one last drink and gave me a sweet peck on the cheek. I pursed my lips together, trying to freshen up my lipstick and used a tissue to blot my forehead and cheeks. An older lady came out from a stall, giving me a smile as she washed her hands.

"You and your husband look very happy," she said. "Celebrating something special this evening?"

I giggled as I tossed the tissue into a trashcan. "We're not married."

"Oh, I'm sorry," she said, embarrassed. "You're wearing a wedding band, I just assumed… I am sorry."

"It's quite alright, no harm done," I assured her, as I held up my hand and spun my wedding band on my finger. "Have a nice evening."

As I walked across the dance floor, the gold band on my finger seemed to grow heavier with each step. The logical side of my brain warning me that it was weighing me down. At that very minute, Starting Over by John Lennon blared from the room's speakers. Roman met me in the center of the dance floor, he pulled me to his chest and spun us, stopping and looking at me with a frown.

"Bobby?"

"Roman, come with me," I grabbed hold of his hand and dragged him behind me. "There's something I have to do and I have to do it now."

"Okay, Bobby, but slow down, you'll break your neck in those heels."

Roman's words stopped me in my tracks, he was right. I held onto his arm while I kicked off my shoes. I picked them up and resumed my quest, tearing along the hall until we got to a set of doors leading out to the upper most deck. We walked out and over to the railing. I leaned against it looking down into the white foamy waves, created by the ship breaking through the still waters.

Roman grabbed hold of my arm, turning me to face him, he looked worried and I smiled as I gently touched his cheek with my hand.

"I haven't lost my mind," I promised. "In fact, I think if anything, I've come to a realization."

"And what would that be?" he asked.

"Five years is long enough," I smiled, taking a small step back as I wiggled off my wedding band and we both stared at it. "You spoke of the past and I understand cherishing the memories, but I've been holding onto the past so tightly, that I forgot to move forward."

"Does this mean that the ring's staying off?" Roman asked cautiously.

"It means, the memories are here," I placed my hand over my heart and held up the ring with the other. "I don't need this to remind me of what I had, but I do need closure."

"Are you certain you want to do this?" he obviously knew my plan. "You could tuck it away in a drawer or the back of your jewelry box."

"No, I can't," I shook my head, determined to do this. "It would be like a constant reminder that I didn't entirely let go. It would be like a dangling thread I was never secure enough to cut. No, I need to do this."

Roman moved back, but didn't step away. He was as much there to support me, as I was determined to get it over with. I wondered if I should say something special, recite a poem or something sappy, and then locked the notion from my mind, there was only one thing to say.

"Goodbye, Felix," I whispered, kissing the ring and then throwing it into the ocean. A tear trickled down my cheek. I wiped it away and turned to Roman with a smile. "Hello, Roman."

"I love you," I said, once we were back in the room and Roman had shrugged off his suit jacket, draping it over the back of a chair.

He looked at me shocked at first, standing at my feet the next second. He took my face in his hands, devouring my mouth.

"Roman," I clasped onto his wrists, whispering against his lips. "Make love to me."

His lips locked to mine, his fingers searching the back of my dress until he found the zipper and slowly lowered it. Roman's hands swept the fabric off my shoulders until it slithered down my body, over my legs, puddling at me feet. He stepped back to peruse the length of my body with an approving smile.

"I've died and gone to heaven," he said, in a husky tone, his fingers tracing along the lace of my bra at the heavy swell of my breast. "Gorgeous."

Loosening Roman's tie, I strategically worked his collar free and unbuttoned his shirt, pushing it off of his shoulders while I used my other hand to open his belt. Clearly, things were moving too slowly for Roman's liking, as he removed my hand and slipped out of his pants and underwear, kicking them across the room. He toed off his socks and looked at me with an impish grin. He was standing in nothing but his tie, his thick cock standing proudly at attention. I bent forward sliding my thong to my ankles and stepping out of it, then stared into his dark heated eyes as I unhooked my bra and tossed it in the air.

"All these years," Roman panted. "I've dreamt of this moment. My images failed to compare. Your beauty is like looking at a fine piece of art."

Gently, he lifted me into his arms, kissing me as he walked over to the bed and lowered me, lying at my side.

"I dreamed of this, too," I confessed.

Roman's hand cradled my breast, his thumb leisurely stroking my nipple, causing a moan to escape my mouth. I clasped hold of his hand and directed it down over my belly, to the apex of my thighs. I spread open my legs, bringing his fingers to my wet opening and inching them into me.

"I need you," I whispered, taking him into my hand and stroking. "We've waited long enough for this. I want you inside me. Make me feel loved again."

"Oh, you're loved," he told me, as he rose, hovering over me, and I spread my legs wider for him. "I'll make you feel things you've never felt before."

Taking the head of his cock in hand, he smoothed it along my wet folds, teasingly several times. His mouth covered mine, our tongues exploring each other's mouths, as he pushed his cock into my waiting sex and his mouth swallowed my euphoric groan. He filled me thoroughly.

Sliding in and out, using a slow tormenting rhythm, his weight resting on me, my fingernails tore into the flesh on his back. There would be marks, but I didn't care, I couldn't get enough of him. The sweat on our flesh mingled, our hectic breathing and moaning filling the small room, as Roman showed me his love.

My legs locked around his waist, my hands scrubbing up and down his abs, as he rose onto his outstretched arms and rammed into me. My eyes widened, a tingle deep inside racing to my very core, forcing my orgasm to come for me. Waves of sinful ecstasy rolled over me, leaving me breathless, as Roman found his own release.

"Oh, Bobby!" Roman called out, dropping on top of me, roughly clasping his hands onto my ass cheeks, as he pumped his seed deep inside of me.

Roman's body relaxed, he rolled onto his back, pulling me with him, my head resting on his shoulder as his fingers stroked along my arm.

"Next time," he kissed the top of my head. "I promise it will last longer, I think after waiting for so long, I lost control."

"It was wonderful," I reassured him, noting how fast his heart was beating under my palm. "I've never had an orgasm during sex before," I giggled. "You could promise me more of those."

"I promise you many, many more."

"I, Captain Arthur St. Clair do, off the record, announce you united at sea. You may kiss your bride."

On the spur of the moment, we purchased rings from a street vendor in Nice, then went to the Captain and asked him to marry us. Contrary to popular belief, we were told that a Captain cannot legally perform a marriage ceremony, though Captain St. Clair was happy to offer us his unauthorized version. So, we quickly changed into suitable attire and purchased flowers from the gift shop before meeting the Captain and a handful of crew, as well as a few dozen curious passengers, on the Lido deck.

The weather was ideal, the sun was shining, the wind blowing just enough to keep us cool, and Calypso, the steel drum band, was playing over by the pool.

I don't remember exactly what the Captain said. I was too busy watching Roman restlessly tugging at the cuffs of his shirt. His hair was being tousled by the breeze and his tongue kept swiping across his lips nervously. He was adorable as usual.

We vowed to love and support each other all the days of our lives, and most of all, remain best friends until the last breaths of life passed our lips. It was short and sweet and I was happier than I'd ever been.

"I'd like to wish you both the best of everything," Captain St. Clair offered, with a handshake. "Remember, the minute you get back to New York, make it official."

"Aye, aye, Captain," Roman joked, and he gave the Captain a salute as he walked away.

"Happy?" Roman asked, caging me against the ship's railing. "Mrs. Unofficially Welch?"

"Over the moon, Mr. Welch."

"What would you like to do now?" Roman asked, brushing the hair off my shoulder, his lips making contact with the nape of my neck.

"I want to dance," I turned in his arm, giving him an adoring kiss.

"It's eleven o'clock in the morning, I don't think dancing starts this early."

"Who needs a dance floor?" I asked, taking his hands and placing them on my hips and resting my hands on his shoulders. "The world is our dance floor."

"I'd rather go back to our room and show my unofficial wife a few private dance moves," he wiggled his brow, pressing his erection against my stomach."

"Who would have guessed a week ago, we'd be unofficially married?" I asked.

"Who knew?" Roman laughed, humming as we danced in place.

"Back home tomorrow," I announced.

"Yeah, to the cold, dreary city," Roman said, lifting me off my feet and spinning us in circles.

"I can't wait, because we're going back as a couple," I smiled into Roman's face, "To our happily ever after."

The end

Safe Haven
Hannah Thorley

"Steven's married now."

"Oh. How lovely." I tried to sound pleased, but I felt the world-bending sensation that meant the blood was draining from my face. I shifted so my hair fell down, shielding me from Mum's eyes. "When was that?"

"Just last week. His mum's still not come down from the high."

I searched for something appropriate to say. "They had good weather for it then." That set her off on a ramble about the unseasonable warmth we were having. I took a big gulp of coffee and steered the conversation even further from my ex.

It lasted until we got outside and went our separate ways. I had just breathed a sigh of relief when Mum called back to me, "You should send them a card."

"What?"

"Steven and Mel. You should send them a congratulations card."

"I will," I said. *Like hell*, I thought.

Without Mum there, my tears started running freely. I told myself all the reasons I shouldn't cry. They had been together for four years; it was hardly shocking that they'd got married. They were already living together before; it wasn't a massive life-change. And it didn't affect me anyway; Steven and I hadn't spoken for ages. But still a hole opened up in my chest that I thought had healed over years ago.

I caught sight of myself in a café window and groaned. I couldn't go home with my face all red and splotchy, and mascara round my eyes. Fred would ask too many questions. I went into the café and waited behind a woman who was ordering something complicated involving soy.

There was a basket on the counter holding some handmade cards for sale. I flicked through them while waiting for the woman to finish ordering, fighting to stop my tears. The last in the pile was a congratulations card; scarlet with two Scottie dogs on the front. One had a top hat and the other a bow on its head.

"Can I help you?" The barista was smiling at me.

"I just wanted to use the bathroom."

Her smile vanished. "Well…it's only for customers, really. You'd have to buy something."

I'd already had coffee with Mum, Fred would go nuts if I bought two in one day. But I couldn't go home like this. I grabbed the Scottie dog card, "How about this?"

"Sure, that's two pounds please."

I tried not to wince as I handed the money over. So much for such a little card.

"Thanks. The bathroom's over there."

I stuffed the card into my bag and trotted over to the bathroom. Looking in the mirror gave me a fright; I was even more dishevelled than I thought. I splashed cold water on my face and scrubbed off the mascara with some paper towels. A smear of foundation, a flick of fresh mascara. I had to be quick.

My eyes were still red, but there was nothing I could do about that. I threw the make up back in my bag and left the café to head home.

~

"Where have you been?"

Every muscle clenched in shock. "You're home early." I tried to smile at Fred, leaning in the kitchen doorway with his arms crossed.

"I said, where have you been?"

"It's Friday, I went for coffee with Mum."

He uncrossed his arms and advanced toward me slowly. "Why did it take so long?"

"I'm sorry, I got held up and -"

"Liar!" His palm slammed onto the door by my ear. "Who were you with?"

"Nobody." I scrabbled in my bag trying to get the card out to show him.

"Who were you with?"

He was so close, my ears rang with his shouting. Tears filled my eyes again and I couldn't stop them falling. I braced, ready for what he would say next. But today was a good day.

The hand that had hit the door gently wiped a tear from my cheek. "I'm sorry, love. Please don't cry. I don't mean to shout." He pulled me into a hug and I relaxed against him. "I just love you so much. I'm so scared that someone will take you away from me. I couldn't live without you."

"You don't have to." I wrapped my arms around his waist and squeezed.

"Say you forgive me?" He pulled back to look into my eyes, looking for all the world like a six-foot tall little boy.

"Of course I forgive you."

~

I didn't tell Fred about the card in the end. He would get jealous again, even though Steven was so over me that he had married someone else, he wouldn't understand.

If I had been smart, I would have thrown it in the bin, but I just couldn't bring myself to do it. So that evening, when Fred went to the pub, I sat down to write in it.

Half an hour later, I was still sitting in front of a completely blank card. How did I even begin?

I should put his name first because he was the one I knew; I had never met Mel. But then that might look like I was just writing to him and she was an afterthought and what kind of message would that send? But then, would putting her name first make it look like I was trying too hard? I dithered back and forth unable to decide. The old clock chimed in the hallway. If I didn't hurry up Fred would be home before I had written one word.

Then I had a flash of inspiration. I grabbed some scrap paper from the hall table and tore it in half. I wrote 'Steven' on one half and 'Mel' on the other, screwed them into tiny balls, and shook them in my cupped hands like dice. I dropped them onto the table, then opened up the one that landed closest to me. 'Steven'.

Dear Steven and Mel...

The rest was easier; congratulations, hope you're happy, resisting the overwhelming urge to use the phrase *'the one that got away'*, signing my name. No kisses.

I leaned back against the hard chair, feeling as though I had run a marathon, and promptly burst into tears. I scooted my chair back quickly. Mustn't cry on the card. That would definitely send the wrong message. Or the correct message. Right then, I honestly didn't know why I was crying. It was becoming a habit.

When I was no longer at risk of leaking on it, I slipped the card into its envelope and licked and sealed it before I could change my mind. I had no idea where they lived, so I wrote out his parents' address from memory and wrote it to *'Mr and Mrs Campbell (the new ones)'*. That almost started me crying again, but then I heard Fred's key in the door and I quickly shoved the card to the back of a drawer.

He came into the kitchen just as I clicked the kettle on. "I'm making a brew," I smiled at him, hoping I didn't look guilty.

He stared at me for a few seconds, and I felt my shoulders tensing. He nodded, slurred "Fanks." And then stumbled into the living room. The roar of some sport program on the TV came through to the kitchen.

I took my time making the tea, and when I tiptoed into the living room Fred was sprawled on the sofa, snoring. I put his tea on the table where he could reach it, but wouldn't knock it over in his sleep, then snuck out again.

This would be my only chance. I took the letter from the drawer and stuck a stamp on it. Crept down the hallway, listening out for the constant snoring. He never remembered to lock the door when he was drunk so at least the sound of the keys turning wouldn't wake him up.

The door opened a crack, and I paused. My heart was pounding painfully against my chest. Up to now I could have just said I was locking it. But once I was outside there would be no excuse. Part of me was screaming to shut the door, throw the card in the bin and forget about it, but I couldn't.

I sucked in a deep breath and opened the door as narrow as possible, so I could just slip through. It closed quietly behind me and I started running. Down the path. Left out the gate. To the post box at the end of the road. I shoved the card in and pushed off the box, using the momentum to run even faster. Stop at the front door. I gripped the handle hard to stop my hands shaking.

Millimetre at a time I pushed it open, holding my breath, straining to hear the sounds from inside. There! A snore! I darted in and closed the door behind me, turning the keys as quietly as possible to lock it.

I wobbled to the kitchen and collapsed into a chair. My whole body was trembling and I was beginning to worry about my heart as it battered at my rib cage. I stirred a heaped spoon of sugar into my mug of tea and drank it in one go, which seemed to help a little.

I'd done it. I'd actually done it. I grinned a shaky smile to myself.

~

It was a good weekend. Fred made breakfast on Saturday and we ate it together in the kitchen. He even took me to the movies on Sunday, pretending to pull out a chair for me, saying "For you, Madame," with his cheeky smile. I remembered why I had fallen in love with him, and vowed to be a better girlfriend.

Even Monday was good. He kissed me before he left for work in the morning, long and slow, and I blushed like a little girl.

But then it was Tuesday.

He always went to the gym before I woke up on Tuesdays, so I didn't see him in the morning. I did my afternoon volunteering in the charity shop at the end of our street, and got several comments on how happy I seemed. I was happy, I realized, as I walked home to prepare dinner. I was planning to cook his favorite; lasagna.

The chopping and frying and stirring were as tedious as ever, but the thought of Fred's reaction kept me going. He would be so pleased with me. I put the dish in the oven and started clearing up the mess I always seem to make in the kitchen.

Then the front door slammed, making me jump. I glanced at the clock, which told me it was later than I thought. A tight knot clenched in my stomach, as I realized Fred was home before his dinner was ready. I quickly filled the kettle and clicked it on. Maybe a cup of tea would tide him over until the lasagna finished cooking.

He called my name and stepped into the kitchen. I held his mug of tea out to him but he ignored it, looking around the kitchen instead.

"Where's dinner?"

The knot squeezed tighter. "It's nearly ready."

"And what the hell have you done to the kitchen?"

"I was cooking. It's lasagna, just for you! I'm just cleaning up."

"You think I want to come home to this mess?"

He was right; it was a mess. I'd got flour all over the floor, and the meat had splattered down the front of the oven. "I'm sorry." I put the mug down and wiped ineffectually at a stain on the table. He stepped toward me and I fought the urge to back away from him.

"I work my arse off all day, every day, for you. To buy you shit. To keep you happy. And what do I get in return? I come home starving, but my food's not ready and the kitchen looks like a pig sty."

"I'm sorry."

"What were you doing that's so much more important than taking care of your man? Than showing me that you love me?"

"I do love you!"

"What were you doing?" His voice was getting louder.

"I just lost track of time, I'm sorry."

"It's that shop isn't it? You met someone there, didn't you?"

"No!"

He grabbed my arm and pulled me closer, digging his fingers in. "I knew it." His voice was quiet now, which somehow made me more frightened. "You're not going there anymore."

I shouldn't have argued, but I was starting to panic. Those few hours in the shop were the highlight of my week. "But they need me; nobody else will work on Tuesdays."

"I said no."

"But- "

"Call them now. Tell them you're not coming back." He took out his phone, hit a button, and pushed it hard against my ear.

"Fred, stop."

"Tell them."

I tried to pull away, but his hand gripped even tighter on my arm.

"Tell them."

"I don't-"

"Tell them!"

"NO!"

I hit the floor. My left cheek was hot and stinging and my eyes were watering. It took me a second to understand. I looked up at Fred. His hand was still raised.

He hit me.

"Now look what you've made me do!" he roared. I instinctively curled into a ball, waiting for another blow, but he turned away and moments later I heard the front door slam again.

I pressed my burning cheek to the cold floor. It was slate, all the way from... somewhere far away. Fred had bought it especially for me the day I told him I'd always dreamed of a slate floor in my kitchen. He was so good to me. He was always so good to me, and I couldn't even cook one meal on time for him.

No wonder he hit me.

The oven timer went off and I pulled myself upright, still trembling. I switched the oven off, took out the lasagna and placed it on the stove top. I stared at it, watching the cheese bubble on top. That was Fred's favorite bit. He was missing it.

I took some paper from the hall and wrote *'I'm sorry. I love you.'*, and placed it on the counter next to the dish. My phone buzzed in my pocket and I grabbed it, hoping it was Fred calling so I could apologize out loud. I was disappointed to see it was a text. But then I recognized the number and my pulse jumped, making my cheek throb.

Hi Soph, it's Steven. I hope this is still ur number. Just wanted to say thanks for the card, that was rly kind of you. How are you doin these days?

Steven still had my number. Something bubbled up inside me and I grinned, but that hurt my sore cheek, so I stopped. I went through to the hallway and looked at myself in the mirror. There was a clear handprint on my cheek. I traced the individual fingers on my reflection in the cold glass. The palm was fainter, and faded to nothing at my nose and mouth.

I deleted Steven's text and put the phone back in my pocket. I didn't know what Fred might do if he found texts from another man on my phone. I really didn't want to find out.

~

Fred didn't come home that night and I slept fitfully waiting for him to appear. I tried to call and sent two texts, but he didn't answer and I didn't want to mother him. I got up when my alarm went off and made breakfast for two, just in case. I wasn't hungry, but I slowly ate my toast anyway. Fred hated waste.

I cleaned the mess I had left in the kitchen yesterday. Sliced the lasagna and put it into tubs in the fridge. Washed up. It was 9am; Fred would be at work. If he had gone to work. I sat at the kitchen table with a cup of tea and laid my phone down on the wood in front of me. I stared at it, willing it to go off, hoping to hear just one word from Fred.

An image popped into my mind, of Steven sitting and staring at his phone the way I was. Hoping to hear from me. It was ridiculous; he would be too busy with his wife to bother about me. But still I found myself picking up my phone, typing in his number, and tapping out a quick text.

Hi Steven. Yes, this is my number. Glad the card arrived :) I'm fine, how are you?

I put it back down and prepared myself to wait for either man to get back to me. But no sooner had I taken a gulp of tea than it pinged with a message. Steven, already.

Oh great, I was worried you might have changed it! Things are good this end. Got a job for a carpenters would you believe! How bout you?

Fred never gets back to me that quickly, I thought, then instantly felt guilty. He was a very busy man. He couldn't just drop everything and text me every five minutes. I deleted the conversation and got on with my housework.

I meant to forget about Steven, leave him to his wife and his dream job, but it was like an itch that just got worse the longer I left it. After an hour, I caved in and told him about my office job. He didn't need to know I'd left that job when I moved in with Fred. The message went off and I felt a thrill when his reply came back less than a minute later.

I lasted twenty minutes that time before the urge to answer got too much for me. Then ten. Then six. Then I couldn't stop myself any more. He told me about their new flat and I balanced the vacuum against my hip while I described Fred's house. He told me what he did at his job and I left the mop dribbling on the kitchen floor to explain the reports I used to run off every day. He mentioned joining the local TA and I went on for several messages about volunteering in the charity shop.

Stick with the volunteer work, it's obviously what you love :)

My stomach dropped. I did love working in the shop, but if Fred didn't want me to go then I would have to give it up. Just like my job.

Better stop. Mel's nearly home. Talk to you tomorrow?

Of course he couldn't talk to me with his wife there. I deleted the whole conversation. Somehow it was over 100 messages. I sighed and wandered through to the kitchen, figuring I had better make some dinner in case Fred came home.

The table was set and I had some of the lasagna warming in the oven when I heard him come in. I rushed out to the hall and threw my arms around his neck.

"Are you okay? I was so worried." I pulled back to examine his face. He looked tired and he hadn't shaved.

"I'm sorry, love." He kissed my forehead. "I'm sorry for worrying you and I'm sorry for…" he reached up and traced a finger lightly over my cheek. "I want to make it up to you." He stepped back and I realized he had one arm behind his back. He brought it forward holding a bunch of flowers. Deep purple tulips; my favourite.

"Oh, Fred. They're gorgeous." I took the flowers from him and ran a thumb up one of the waxy petals. "I love them. Let me get them in some water."

He followed me into the kitchen and, as I sorted the flowers out, he came up behind me and wrapped his arms around my waist. I relaxed back into him with a happy sigh. "I am sorry, love." He spoke into my neck, right at the sensitive part that made me shiver. "Say you forgive me?"

"Of course I forgive you. Let's put these on the table." He released me and I set the vase in the middle of the table. "They're so beautiful. Dinner's ready now."

"Can't wait, I'm starving." He sat on his side of the table and smiled at me. I smiled back, ignoring the dull ache in my cheek. He was happy. Everything was okay when he was happy.

~

I didn't count the days since Fred hit me; it was just a one-off because I pushed him too far. It wouldn't happen again.

But I did know how long it had been since Steven first texted me. I couldn't believe how easy it was to fall back into conversation with him. It was as if the last few years hadn't happened.

We had a routine by then; I texted him as soon as Fred left for work, we spoke all day, until he told me Mel was on her way home. Then I deleted everything and got ready for Fred to come home. Of course, Steven didn't know that bit.

Weekends were different. Steven had texted me once, just as Fred and I were settling down to watch a film.

"Who's that?" he asked, starting to scowl.

I opened the text and quickly deleted it. "Wrong number." I tried to sound uninterested.

"Come on then." He opened his arms and I laid against his chest, shuffling to get comfortable as I breathed a sigh of relief.

We sent odd texts when we could, but between Fred and Mel, we couldn't really maintain proper conversations. Weekends dragged for me.

It was a Wednesday, four weeks and one day since Steven had first texted me. I woke to find the other side of the bed empty and the room much lighter than I was used to.

"Finally she's awake." his sarcastic voice came from the doorway. I looked across but the landing light was bright behind him and I couldn't see his face properly.

"What time is it?" I sat up and checked my phone. 8:30. I jumped out of bed and started pulling on the first clothes I laid my hands on. "I'm sorry, my alarm didn't go off. I'm sure I set it."

"Really?" I registered the tone of his voice and stopped still.

"I definitely set it. I always set it, you know I do."

"Then why am I having to leave for work with no breakfast?"

"Can't you work the toaster?" I clapped a hand over my mouth, wishing I could take the words back, but it was too late.

He charged into the room and grabbed a fistful of my hair, pulling it and bending my head back until I cried out. "Fucking lazy slut! I work my arse off for you, and what do you do? Fuck all, that's what! Is it too much to ask for some breakfast before I go to slave away my life for you?"

"I'm sorry!" I bent my knees to try to relieve the pain in my scalp, but he pulled harder and threw me to the floor. My head banged into the nightstand and I saw white flashes across my vision. When they cleared, I realized I was huddled on the floor, muttering

I'msorryI'msorryI'msorry to an empty room. I crawled up onto the bed and sobbed into the pillows.

I must have dozed off, because I jerked upright when my phone buzzed on the nightstand and for a second I couldn't remember where I was. Groggily, I reached over and saw Steven's number on the screen.

Hey, are you okay? Normally heard from you by now.

For one wild moment I considered telling him everything. But no, he didn't need to deal with my problems. He had already told me Mel was getting wound up about how much I told him, although it never seemed like much when we were talking. I went for a half truth.

Sorry, my alarm didn't go off this morning - I'm running a bit behind!

He answered immediately.

Accidental lie-in, result! :p

I started laughing, but stopped when I felt it turning hysterical. My head hurt and I wished it were as simple as a lie-in. I just couldn't work out how it had happened; My alarm was always set, I didn't even switch it off at the weekend. But when I clicked on to the Alarm page it was set to off. I knew I hadn't done that. Maybe Fred had turned it off, but why would he do that? I couldn't think, my brain felt full of fluff and it occurred to me that I should probably go and get my head checked out. I had hit it pretty hard.

I don't know if I should say this but I just want to tell you. You were in my dream last night.

I rubbed the tears from my eyes and re-read the message. It definitely did say what I thought it said. He was dreaming of me. I found that I was smiling, and I sent back.

I hope it wasn't a nightmare :p

Not at all. It was a VERY good dream.

I felt myself blushing hot. He couldn't mean a sexy dream. Could he? I didn't know how to react, so I threw my phone down on the bed and started tidying up the room. After I had overslept, I would have to hurry to get all the housework done before Fred came home.

While dinner was in the oven that evening, I ran upstairs and picked up my phone from the bed. There was only one text, from Steven.

I'm sorry. I shouldn't have said that.

No worries. Just a busy day.

I waited a few minutes, but he didn't answer me. Mel must have been home. I deleted everything, as usual.

Fred came home this time, with flowers and chocolates and the sorriest face I had ever seen. He ran a hand over my head and I couldn't help wincing when he brushed over the spot that had hit the nightstand.

"I'm so sorry." He lifted my hair and gently kissed the lump that had formed. "Say you forgive me?"

"Of course I forgive you." He let my hair go and I released a breath I didn't realise I had been holding.

That night before going to bed I checked three times to be sure my alarm was set. The third time Fred saw me and he kissed my forehead gently. "I am sorry." I kissed him back and he rolled away with his back to me. We always slept like this, back to back, but tonight I wished he would turn over and hold me.

~

I woke suddenly, gasping and flushed. Had I cried out? I looked across to Fred and saw the slow rise and fall of his chest. Still asleep. I slid out of bed and tiptoed to the bathroom to splash cold water on my face.

I looked in the mirror. My hair was wild and my chest was covered in red splotches. That always happened when Fred and I... The details of my dream flashed through my mind and in the mirror I saw a blush creep up my neck and face. It hadn't been Fred in my dream. It had been Steven. Sighing and calling my name. I splashed more cold water on my burning cheeks. My alarm started ringing and I ran into the bedroom to switch it off.

Fred rolled over and smiled sleepily up at me. "Morning, love."

"Good morning." I leaned over and kissed his forehead.

He laid a hand on my cheek and kissed my mouth, before running the hand down my body. "Come back to bed for a while." He squeezed my bum and I fell onto the bed with a giggle.

I tried very hard not to think of Steven.

As soon as Fred left, with a lingering kiss in the doorway, I snatched my phone up and texted Steven.

Probably shouldn't say this either, but I want to tell you too. You were in my dream last night.

A good dream?

I dithered for a minute. There was a line here that I would cross if I answered him honestly,but he had been honest about his dream. I told myself it was only fair to be honest back.

A VERY good dream.

He sent back a big grinning face and I laughed so loudly it echoed through the house.

No need to be that pleased with yourself :p

You can't stop me :p

I felt quite giddy. So much so, that I decided not to do the housework. It really didn't need to be done every day anyway, Fred wouldn't even notice.

I made myself some tea in the oversized mug I never got to use, took a random book from the shelf in the living room, and settled down on the sofa. But I didn't get much reading done. Steven was on full cheeky form and I found I responded to it, relaxing into the person I used to be. I had missed this, I had missed me.

The line was already crossed by telling him I had a sexy dream, so when he asked what actually happened in it, I didn't hesitate. I relived it as I tapped away, and my skin started warming at the vivid memories. He didn't answer for a few minutes and I started to worry that I'd gone too far, but then a message came through. His dream, in great detail, and it was even hotter than mine. My whole body tingled as I read the words, imagining his hands and lips on me.

Fred had never been further from my mind. Until another message came through.

You don't have to answer this either. Do you ever think about me when you're playing?

My breath felt trapped in my chest. On a wave of guilt I scrambled up off the sofa and grabbed the vacuum. Must make it clean, Fred liked it clean. I did the hallway, the stairs, the living room, even the kitchen. But the clatter of hard plastic on slate was still not enough to drown out my thoughts. It was my secret. The one secret I had never ever admitted to anyone. Even myself.

I always thought of Steven.

But I couldn't tell him that. You don't tell married men that you think about them that way, especially when you live with your own boyfriend. How embarrassing to admit that you still think of someone, while they're happy with their new wife.

As I coiled the power cord of the hoover, my phone went off again.

Because I think of you. Often.

The cord fell to the floor in a heap. I didn't know how to react. I wanted to dance and punch the air, smile so wide it hurt, but also delete everything, block his number, and try never to think of him again. Unbearable. I dithered for a minute, and then typed and hit send before I could think too much about it.

Yes. Yes I think of you.

You don't know how happy it makes me to know that.

I suspected I did, but why would that make him happy? He had a wife to think of him all the time; he didn't need me doing it as well. As if my thought conjured her, he sent the usual cut-off text. I cursed Mel for interrupting us, more vehemently than usual.

My mind was spinning for the rest of the day. Including when Fred came home.

"I said where's the salt?"

I looked up from my plate to see him sitting with his hand held out, scowling. "Sorry." I got the shaker from the cupboard and handed it to him. I sat down and drifted off again.

"What the hell is wrong with you?" He shoved his plate off the table and it shattered on the floor, startling me to my feet.

"What have I done?" I backed against the sideboard, but he followed me and shouted in my face. "I said salt. Salt! This is fucking pepper."

I couldn't work out why he was lifting the shaker so high. Maybe so I could see it better. His arm seemed to come down in slow motion. I realized what was happening a split second before the glass hit my face, and I must have fainted because I never felt the blow.

~

I woke slowly and couldn't work out where I was. I was lying on a bed and Fred was standing over me, but we weren't at home. The room was too big and the lights were too bright. My head ached.

Fred leaned down toward me. I thought he was going to kiss me but instead he hissed in my ear, "You tripped and fell on a glass. If you tell them anything else, I will kill you."

"Tell who?" The skin of my face pulled in a strange way when I spoke. I reached my hand up to touch it just as a woman walked up to the bed.

"Now don't be poking your stitches. The more you poke, the longer they'll take to heal."

"Stitches?"

She was fiddling with a machine at the side of the bed, and I realized I was in hospital. "What happened?"

"You don't remember, dear?"

Fred laced his fingers through mine and squeezed, hard. I shook my head.

"That can happen when you bump your head. You had a fall and got some glass in your cheek, but we got it out. You needed four stitches but don't worry about that; they're awfully small and you shouldn't scar at all."

"When can we go home?" Fred asked. He hadn't released his grip on my hand. My fingers were starting to throb.

"Oh, not tonight, I'm afraid. Well *you* can, obviously, but with a bump to the head, we're keeping Sophie in for observation. Nothing to worry about," She patted my shoulder, "It's just a precaution. Brains are complicated things, we have to be extra careful with them."

I nodded and closed my eyes. It felt like they were only shut for a second, but when I opened them again the room was dark and Fred was gone. With nobody to stop me, I reached up to touch my face. The left side again. I wanted to assess the damage, but it was covered over with something. I couldn't be bothered trying to get it off, so I lowered my hand and quickly fell back to sleep.

It was light when I woke again. My head ached a little less, but my face was still sore under all its wrappings. I grabbed my phone and checked the time. Fred must have gone to work by now. It hurt that he wasn't here for me. My phone started ringing and I hit Answer quickly before it disturbed anyone.

"Hello?"

"Soph?"

"Steven!" My mind flicked through several potential tragedies, "What's wrong?"

"Nothing. Nothing. I just…wanted to hear your voice."

I smiled wide enough to pull my stitches, and didn't even care. "It's good to hear yours."

"Really?"

"Definitely. I didn't realise how much I've missed it," I admitted.

"I know what you mean."

We sat in silence for a few seconds, but it wasn't awkward. I could imagine him holding his phone to his ear and smiling just as I was.

He spoke first. "So, about those texts yesterday."

The texts. With everything that had happened I'd forgotten. "You really think about me? Like that?"

"I always have."

My stomach fizzed, and at the same time I wanted to cry. "But you shouldn't. You're married, you shouldn't be thinking about me."

"I know, but I can't help it."

Everything he said made me feel so much better, and worse. "Of course you can help it. Think about her, not me."

"I can't stop. I love you."

I felt like I'd been electrocuted. But there must be some explanation. "What happened? Did you and Mel fight? You've only been married two months, why do you suddenly want me?"

"Nothing happened. I've always wanted you, Soph. Always. It broke my heart when you moved away."

"But you were with her."

"If…" he sighed.

"If what?" I found I was holding my breath, squeezing the phone against my ear.

"If you'd said something, I would have left her. In a second. I love you."

My words escaped in a whisper, "I love you, too."

More silence, still not awkward, but piercing painful. He loved me. He still loved me, but it was far too late.

"Oh God, what have I done? I should have said something."

"Before you married her? Yeah, that would have been a good idea."

He gave a sad huff of a laugh. "I'm such an idiot."

"I should have said something too, but I thought you didn't want me."

"And I thought *you* didn't want *me*."

A nurse appeared at the end of the ward, and I couldn't remember if you were allowed to use phones in hospital these days. I didn't want to risk being shouted at. "I'm sorry, someone's here for me. I need to go. I'll text you when I can?"

"Okay. I'll be waiting."

We said goodbye and I hung up, quickly tucking the phone under my pillow as the nurse approached. She took the dressing off my face and looked over the stitches. They must have been fine, as she told me I should be free to go once the doctor had seen me.

By the time a doctor arrived, it was late afternoon and while he was checking me over, Fred appeared. He kissed me lightly and then chatted to the doctor as he finished up his examination. I tuned Fred's words out and just watched his mouth move. It was strange to think how many times I had kissed those lips when all I really wanted was Steven.

Fred didn't speak to me until we were in the car on the way home. "What did you tell them?"

"Nothing. Nobody asked."

I expected him to keep asking, not believing me, and I prepared myself for an argument, but he just nodded and the rest of the journey passed in silence.

~

I should have told them. Now he knew he could get away with it, Fred hurt me nearly every day. More carefully now, concentrated, deliberate, and always places where nobody would see.

My life felt like a hyper-real nightmare. Mornings of pain and the fear of it with Fred, then seven hours of talking to Steven, learning each other anew, and then evenings of more violence and shouting. I forgave Fred every time. He was just afraid of losing me, and he was right to be when I spent my days telling Steven how much I loved him.

I didn't want Steven to know what was happening, but one day after I'd ironed his shirt, Fred marked me with the iron; a neat little triangle on my upper arm that burned for hours. Fred left me in tears and I called Steven.

"He did what? Are you okay? Soph, you've got to get out of there."

"No, I'm fine. It's fine. I can't leave, this is my home."

"Where your boyfriend branded you with an iron. You can't stay. Why would you stay? That's not right!"

He was shouting at me, just like Fred did. Instead of cowering, I found I was angry. "Why would you stay with Mel, when you want someone else? That's not right either."

"Mel would never damage me!"

"Is that what you think of me? I'm just damaged goods?"

"Oh, Soph, no. Of course I don't think that. I'm sorry for shouting, I just feel so helpless here. How could he do that to you?"

"It's not his fault. He's afraid that someone will take me away and then he'd be all alone and I hate that. I need to look after him."

"The way he's looking after you?"

I couldn't answer that. I wiped tears from my face, but they wouldn't stop falling.

"You deserve better than this. I would never ever hurt you that way, and that's the kind of love you deserve."

"But I can't have you."

"You will."

"What?" A gentle flutter of hope pushed at my chest.

"I'm not going to leave Mel for you; that's too much to put on you, it's not fair. But we're just not working. At all. I don't know how much longer we can last, we've mentioned the D-word more than once. I won't leave her for you, but the second I'm free I'm coming to find you. I don't know when it will be, but you will have me again."

That stopped my tears.

"You believe me?"

"Yes." And I did. I could picture it. I felt like my heart might crack open. "I believe you."

"I just hope I'm not too late. If he… if something happens to you, I will kill him."

"Please don't. You don't understand."

I could tell he wanted to say more, but he sighed and let it go. "Okay. I'd better get back to work. I can still text though. I love you."

"I love you, too."

Back to the endless housework. Fred had told the charity shop that I couldn't help out anymore, and I was no longer allowed to see Mum, so I had even more time to spend on the house. It still never seemed to be enough for Fred. That day, I used a toothbrush to clean the grout between every tile in the bathroom, and he left a handprint on my thigh because I hadn't noticed some bristles that had fallen to the floor.

I stared down at the red finger marks on my thigh. I traced around them, feeling the heat of my sore skin, while Fred slammed doors downstairs. I wanted to speak to Steven more than anything. I imagined him in the room and for a second saw myself as I would look through his eyes. I couldn't believe it, I had become what I always vowed I never would.

Abused.

A victim.

It was still early, but I crawled into bed, curled into a ball and fell asleep, not even caring what Fred might say. I woke to an empty house and a hard knot of determination and fear in my chest. I was leaving. *Now.*

I dug around under the bed and found my old hiking backpack. I couldn't remember the last time I'd gone hiking. Fred didn't approve.

Trying to be methodical but quick, I worked through my morning routine and shoved things into the bag in that order, but only my things. I left all the jewellery he had given me over the years, all the clothes he had surprised me with. Anything he could lay claim to. The backpack was barely half full. I laid my laptop on top and fastened the buckles tight.

The shaking started as I walked down the stairs with everything I owned slung across my shoulders. Fear was warring with the faint taste of freedom, and I was terrified. I paused by the front door, holding the handle, unable to turn it.

"You can do this." I told myself. "Just think of Steven." I imagined his face when I told him I had left Fred, the relief and the happiness in his voice. That was enough; I opened the door and stepped through. Slammed it behind me, and threw my keys across the tiny front garden. I wouldn't even lock it. Serve him right if he was burgled.

I walked down the road toward the charity shop. I was going to say goodbye to them, but then I imagined Fred going there, asking about me, demanding to know where I was. He would be so angry. They didn't deserve that. Instead, I turned down a different road, stopped at a bus stop and jumped on the first bus that came along.

"How far can I go with this?" I pushed a fiver through the slot.

"That'll get you to Carluke."

I had no idea where that was. Perfect. "Carluke then, please." The machine churned out my ticket and I went to sit down, breathing a massive sigh of relief.

I took three buses, one right after the other, traveling until I was completely lost. Then I got off and wandered around, alternately turning left and right every time I came to a crossroads. Following 'Youth Hostel' signs brought me to a low building, less shabby than I was expecting, with bright yellow letters above the entrance:

SAFE HAVEN

If ever I was looking for a sign, this was it. I went in.

I have news!

I texted Steven as soon as I got into the bedroom, dumping my bag on the floor and flopping onto a bed.

Tell me later? I have to be quiet today.

My stomach dropped. He never had any problem texting me when he was at work; something must have happened. I thought through every possibility. Maybe he was ill. Maybe she was ill. He could be in trouble at work, or busy at work, or not at work at all. Had he left her? Had she left him? Were they arguing? I didn't dare ask.

Okay.

I had been counting on Steven. Without him to speak to, I had all the time in the world to think. I imagined Fred getting in from work, calling out to the empty house, not understanding why there was no answer. He would look for me in every room, then maybe start getting desperate and check in the wardrobe, under the stairs, anywhere big enough that I could be hiding there. Would he be worried, I wondered, picturing something terrible happening to me? Would he think his biggest fear had finally come true and I had run off with someone else? He would be gutted.

"What have I done?" I picked my phone up to call him, but I didn't know what to say, everything I thought of would have made him angry.

Then I couldn't stop myself picturing him in a rage. Remembering the crack of his hand hitting my skin, the white pain of him pulling my hair, the punches and kicks and screaming in my face. I curled into a ball under the thin duvet. I couldn't go back to that. I couldn't. But I was a horrible person for leaving him all on his own. He wouldn't be able to cope without me. The thoughts went round and round in my mind until I finally cried myself into an exhausted sleep.

~

My phone pinged and woke me. For a second, I thought I was in hospital again and I bolted upright, looking around to see if Fred was watching me. Then my memory caught up and I relaxed back down onto the pillow. My pulse was charging, and it just got worse when I saw that the text was from Fred. I opened it, not knowing what to expect.

Hey honey, are u ok? Wher are u? Pls tell me ur alrite?

Guilt crashed down on me. He was worried; he cared about me and I just left without even a note. I should never have left. I threw the duvet off and swung my legs off the bed. I had to get home. My phone rang and I answered without looking.

"I'm so sorry, I can explain."

"Explain what?"

That wasn't Fred. I took the phone from my ear and looked at the screen. "Steven? Isn't Mel home? Has something happened?"

"No, she's not here. What do you need to explain?"

"Nothing. Not to you, anyway. I thought you were Fred."

"What do you need to explain to him?"

"I've…" I had been so looking forward to telling Steven, but I knew he wouldn't be happy that I was going back again.

"Soph. Tell me, please."

"I left him. I'm not sure where I am, I just wanted to get away. But he just texted me, he's really worried. I shouldn't have left him all on his own. I'm going now; I shouldn't get back too late."

"No!"

"He's worrying about me."

"Of course he's worrying; worrying that you'll go to the police or tell his friends or family."

The police. I hadn't thought of that.

"He's obviously capable of sounding like a good guy, otherwise you wouldn't have been with him. But look where you are. You don't even know where you are! You got yourself completely lost to try to get away from him. Why would you go back to someone who made you feel that way?"

"You're right," I admitted.

"And what will he do, when you tell him you ran away? What would he do to you?"

"He never means to hurt me."

Steven sighed. "I'm not arguing with you. Just please don't go back to him."

"What else can I do?"

"Wait for me?"

"For how long? You want me to just put my life on hold on the off chance that your marriage doesn't work out?"

"No. Really no. That's actually why I couldn't talk much today; we've been to the solicitors."

"What? What happened?"

He sighed again, "It's a big mess and it's going to take time. I can't just come and find you tomorrow, but it is happening. Mel's already taken a lot of her stuff and she's staying with her parents until she can find a new place."

"I'm sorry it didn't work out." I wished I could hug him, he sounded so defeated.

"So am I. Yet another thing I've failed at. But once it's all sorted out and I'm free, I will come running. Wherever you are. We will be together."

"I can't wait." I felt like I was floating. If I could have Steven when I thought I had lost him for good, anything was possible. My life stretched out in front of me, full of options and possibilities, and not one of them included Fred.

"I love you, Soph."

"I love you, too."

"I'll see you soon. I love you so very much, and I'll show you one day. One day soon. I promise."

New Beginnings
Stina Rubio

The Beginning

I was told to meet my John at the Motel 6 around the corner from Ramon's house. He usually made me walk the streets at night, alone. He used to go with me, but it looked suspicious. He didn't like the cops stopping us everytime we went out. Ramon didn't trust me. He thought I was going to run the first chance I got and I really wanted to, but where would I go? I had no one, he made sure of that, picking me up off the streets when my mom died. The thought alone was enough to bring tears to my eyes.

I ran a finger under my eyes, wiping away the last traces of tears. I looked over my fingertips, making sure there wasn't any makeup on them. When I was convinced the tears were all removed and my makeup was safe, I tucked my hands inside my jacket pockets.

It was freezing out. I breathed into the night air and watched as the white cloud evaporated. I would feel less like the dead if I wasn't forced to wear this tiny dress. I asked if I could wear pants, but he wouldn't hear it. My question was why I was sporting a black eye tonight. He slapped me so hard, it bruised the whole side of my face.

He didn't care if I went out looking like I was beaten and the "clients" didn't care either. They only cared about one thing; sex.

My phone rang in my pocket. I pulled it out and answered. "Hello," I spoke softly. If I let the phone ring more than once, I would have received more of the same bad treatment when I got home.

"Celia, where are you now?" Ramon husked. No "Hello" or anything that would even resemble caring.

"I'm almost there. I can see the hotel sign right now," I sighed, forgetting who I was talking to.

"Do you have an attitude? I can make it so you can't even talk." He meant it.

"No, Ramon! I was just breathing hard 'cause it's so cold out. I don't have an attitude, I promise. I love everything you do for me. You're the best person I know," I babbled on, stroking his ego as much as possible. It was more out of fear, because I had seen him actually do terrible things to another girl who worked with me. He cut her tongue out and laughed as she bled all over the place. I begged him to let me take her to the emergency room. I even told him I would just drop her off and leave. After an hour, he finally agreed, but only because he was tired of her bleeding all over his house. He acted like the house was nice to begin with. I know people say any place was supposed to be better than the streets, but I wasn't so sure about that now, though.

"That's what I thought." He hung up before I could make an even bigger fool of myself. I let out a breath that I didn't realize I was holding.

I made it to the hotel, looking at the numbers on the door, trying to find the number I was given by Ramon. He told me I had an hour to get this man off and be back in the house. If I wasn't, he would come looking for me. The poor John didn't want to know what would happen to him if Ramon walked over here.

Finally, I found it and knocked lightly. The door swung open, showing a much older man waiting for me on the other side. I wasn't one to complain, I was just here to get the job done and go home so I could eat.

"Come in." He moved out the way as I silently walked past him. The weird thing was he never looked me over, his eyes locked on mine as I passed him. Most Johns just wanted me naked and when I wasn't, they were picturing me naked.

"So, how is your night?" he asked. I stopped cold in my tracks. This guy was definitely a cop. There was no John out there who wondered how my night was going.

"It's fine, but I think I left something at home. I'll be back." I panicked, dropping the phone in my haste as I turned to leave.

"No, don't leave." This time it was a female voice.

"Hey, whatever you two are into is fine, but I don't do buy one, get one free." I snatched my phone off the floor where it fell.

"No, we're not into anything," she said, disgusted.

"Listen, we don't have much time," the man added, moving closer to me.

I quickly put my hands up, to defend myself against him.

"I'm not going to hurt you," he sadly stated, sounding sincere and soothing.

I didn't like that he was judging me. I didn't like that he pitied me. "Stop!" I screamed. They both froze looking at me with wide eyes.

The lady spoke sympathetically to me. "My name is Lauren. We're here to help you, if you want it," she backed away from me slowly, giving me space.

I looked from her to him and laughed. "Help me? With what?" I knew what they were talking about, but I was so scared of Ramon that I was used to lying.

"If you want to get out, this is your chance." The man moved back, too. "My name is Rick. *Pastor* Rick."

"It was nice meeting both of you, but there is no out. There's only death," I stated flatly as I made my way back to the door. They weren't going to stop me and I wasn't going to listen to them if they tried. Before I got to the door, I turned, looking over my shoulder. Both Pastor Rick and Lauren were on their knees facing the wall, praying. I don't know if it was the praying or the fact that I was tired of living the way I did, but something stopped me. I walked over to them and sat on the bed. "How can you guys get me out?" I questioned as I looked at my phone. I had already been gone for thirty minutes, which left thirty more to do whatever it was they were thinking.

"If you want to get out, we will give you everything you need," Lauren smiled at me, hope filling her eyes.

"Let's go then," I rushed. "He'll be here in fifteen minutes to pick me up. He's never late." I helped Lauren up as they gathered their things.

"Is there anything he can track you with?" they asked in unison.

I was sure Ramon wasn't a very smart man, though I would never tell him that to his face. He might be a vicious asshole and great manipulator, but I highly doubted he would use an electronic tracker physically on me without me knowing. The phone on the other hand, could definitely be tracked.

Without a second thought, I threw the phone onto the bed as I walked out of the room. It was like I was saying goodbye to this stupid fucking life. I was never meant for this, I was meant for someone to love me and cherish me. Most of the girls I worked with were good girls, but they were all dealt shitty hands in life. I wanted to cry. I wanted to hug Lauren and Pastor Rick. They didn't know, but they just saved my life.

1

Six months, five days later.

"Celia, how was work today?" Rick asked me through the phone. He and Lauren came to visit me sometimes, but for the most part he checked in with daily calls.

"Good. My feet hurt, but I can't complain." And I honestly couldn't. Six months ago, I was walking the streets in downtown Los Angeles, selling my body to random men. It was nice to have my own place no matter how small it was.

They didn't lie when they told me they would provide me with everything I needed, even though it kind of felt like I was in witness protection. I got a whole new identity, they dyed my hair, and gave me a job. I loved feeling like everything was coming together. I felt safe and stronger than I had in a long time.

"Yes, I'm glad to hear it. Look, I just wanted to call and check in. How are things with church this week?" Of course Rick worried about that the most. We quickly decided I needed to make sure my soul was going to heaven after all the horrible things I'd done in my life. I told him it wasn't like I wanted to do the bad things, but he still felt I needed to get right with the man upstairs.

"Every Sunday, of course," I chuckled into the phone. There wasn't anything about my situation that was funny, but I had to laugh at Rick's constant reminding. He was like the father I didn't have.

"Good, good. Lauren told me to tell you she'll call you later on tonight. She's getting the documents together for the girl that works the 6th and 7th blocks downtown," he exhaled. I knew he was worried about this one, I was too. They told me her pimp was worse than Ramon, if that were even possible.

"Tell her good luck for me. I'm going to hop in the shower."

We said our goodbyes and hung up. There wasn't much he and I talked about. Where Lauren became a good friend to me, Pastor Rick was always business. I didn't blame him because this was his life. The only thing that mattered to Rick was getting the girls out and safe. I suspected that there was a story there, but when I asked Lauren, all she said was that she would tell me one day.

Lauren was Rick's adopted daughter. He took her in when they found her mother half dead in an alley after a John raped and almost killed her. He'd gone in to give Lauren's mother her last rights when he saw the lonely, little girl. To make a long story short, her mother passed away from her injuries and Rick couldn't stand to leave Lauren alone. Maybe that was his true catalyst. Saving the world from creating more Laurens.

Tomorrow was a new day and I had to work. The best part of my day was hopping into the shower and washing away the smell of the grocery store, where I worked. My little studio apartment was small, yet perfect for me. It was located over a laundromat a block from my job. I didn't really go anywhere other than to work and to the library. Work, home, work, go get books. My life was happy here, with all its simpleness. The only thing that kept plaguing me was the dreams. Every night I would dream of Ramon's hands around my neck.

When I stepped out of the shower, a knock sounded on the door. I didn't know anyone in the town, though it didn't stop them from trying to get to know me. It was a small town after all, with just nine-hundred or something residents.

I grabbed a knife off the table and tiptoed to the door. If anything, I was waiting for the day Ramon showed up here. I knew he wouldn't let things go until he had me or one of us was dead.

You can run Celia, but you will never be able to escape me. My head was my worst enemy anymore.

I could still hear his sadistic cackle in my ear. I could still feel the pressure of his fingers as they dug into the tender skin of my throat. He always told me he would kill me.

The knock on the door was harder this time. It rattled all the pictures on the wall; my heartbeat with it. I was terrified to open the door and see who was on the other side. My mind kept telling me to run, but where? I had nothing on but a towel. I really needed to be better prepared.

"Celia, if you don't open this door!" a familiar voice threatened impatiently.

"Lauren?" I asked, feeling relieved immediately.

"Who else would be banging on your door at this time a night?" she asked through the door as I wrestled with undoing the locks to let her in. "I know you don't know anyone in this town or did it change? Please tell me you met a guy? Someone to hold you close at night?" She was laughing and if I didn't get her into the apartment fast, she was going to wake up everyone in the building.

"Lauren, are you crazy? What are you doing here?" I pulled her in by the arm. I looked around the hallway to see if anyone else was out there watching. Thank God no one was there.

"I wanted to surprise you. I know you must be bored here all alone. There is literally nothing to do in this town, I had to come save you," she squeaked as I closed the door solidly behind her.

"Rick told me you were going to call me later tonight. He didn't tell me you were coming," I said.

"I didn't tell him. He wouldn't let me come and I didn't want to feel like a kid tonight. He is always going on about how people wanted to hurt you and if I was with you when they came, they would hurt me too." I knew she didn't think about her words when they came out of her mouth, so I didn't let them bother me. Lauren was Lauren and I loved her as is.

"If they were going to come for me, they would have done it already. Ramon isn't the, *'I'll wait around for you'* type,*" I explained.

She just shrugged her shoulders and plopped down on the couch. "You got anything to eat in this place?" Again this girl had no filter, no wonder I liked her so much.

"I didn't go shopping yet, but now that you're here, I'll go to the store and get us something." Thank goodness the store stayed open twenty-four hours. I hated going alone in the dark, but the way Lauren smelled told me she wasn't going to be going anywhere unless she showered first.

I had gone alone before, mostly in the day, but I would have to get used to it. I had to tell myself *he* wasn't going to come and get me anymore. If he was, he would be here already. "Fine, you take a shower and I'll run out and get us something to eat. If you're not out before I get back I will eat everything alone." I didn't have any siblings, but if I did I hoped it would be like the relationship I had with Lauren.

"Cool, get stuff for tacos," she smiled at me as she entered the bathroom. "Dude, this bathroom is small." Her face contorted into repulsion.

"Sorry it isn't to your liking, Queen Lauren," I bowed and shut the door behind me. I needed to find something to throw on really fast, picking out jeans and a tshirt. Quickly tossing on some clothes, I headed for the door.

When I entered the hall, my heart began to thunder in my chest. I had a mini panic attack every time I stepped foot outside of my door. Gulping down, a lung full of air choked me. I concentrated on placing one foot in front of the other, hoping I would make it out without getting light-headed this time.

I was successful in my quest and made it all the way to the store with no further problems. I cheered myself on with my own little party in my mind. These tiny victories meant I was getting better and the sooner all this was over with, the sooner I would be normal again.

At that time of night, there weren't many people milling around. It was the best time to go shopping, but most people liked to go shopping when they got off work, right around five or six, which is what I normally did, too. I waved to Noreen who was working the register tonight.

"Back so soon?" she asked me as I grabbed a cart.

"Not by choice," I joked. I pushed the cart down the aisle making my way to the meat department. I needed to get ground beef and other things for tacos. I looked over the meat packages wondering why they always put so much in them. I didn't need much to feed Lauren and myself, but my choices were limited to one-pound or five-pound packages of meat. I guess we were going to be eating tacos for the next few days.

"Sarah?" someone called from behind me. In my head, I knew they were referring to me, but even after half of a year, I wasn't used to it yet. Lauren and Rick still called me by my real name and the sound of my issued name still confused me.

I turned in time to see one of my regular customers jogging up to me. "Hi, Able," I smiled oddly.

"I thought that was you," he chuckled softly.

The sound of his voice tightened around my belly. I hadn't been with a man in a long time and I missed the connection, the touch.

"I wanted to stop by and say hi. So, hi," he said, waving at me weirdly.

I giggled at his silliness as he backed into a stack of Cheez-It's. "Hi!" I shouted after him.

It was weird how he made me feel so comfortable. He made me feel like I could open up to him, like I could be his friend. Able distracted me from what I was doing and before I knew it, my co-worker Jane was waving in front of my face. I heard a distinct sound, she was talking to me, but I wasn't hearing anything coming out of her mouth. I was concentrating on the way Able's face lit up when he saw me. My mind kept telling me to stop deluding myself into thinking that a gorgeous man was into me, let alone that he might even be single. He had to be taken, there was no way he wasn't. I would be lying if I said I never thought about him, because I had. There were times I'd entertained the idea of taking him up to my apartment and doing to him what I knew I did best. Thanks to Ramon's perverted ass, I was highly capable of pleasing any man.

Jane gave up trying to talk to me and stomped away. I didn't mean to be rude, but my mind was elsewhere. The thoughts swirled through my head like a nightmare bringing on an anxiety attack. I leaned against the freezer door and inhaled as much as I could, drinking in the air as fast as possible. My doctor told me if this happened I should just breathe and think about something positive and that was what I was going to do.

"You okay?" Able strolled by once more.

"If I didn't know any better, I would think you've been following me," I chuckled to myself as my heart rate slowed.

His face turned from cheerful to fearful in a split second. I immediately felt bad, because my awful joke obviously hit a very sensitive chord. There was something in his expression that made me step back.

He quickly replied to my standoffish ways. "No, I was coming back because I forgot-" he looked around as if he lost something. "Here I needed to get these chicken legs." He stuck them into his cart and rushed off down the aisle.

"Yes," I spouted.

"What?" he asked, pausing halfway down the aisle.

I steadied myself against the cooler before I answered. It wasn't that all men made me nervous, it was the feelings I got around Able that made me question my sanity. You would think I was put off by all men, that I didn't want anything to do with one ever again, but that wasn't the case. Every day Able came here to shop and every day he came to talk to me in my checkout line. "You asked me if I was okay. Yes, I am. Thank you for asking," I pushed off the cooler and looked him in the eyes. He interested me, I wanted to know what he was about.

"Oh, okay," he mumbled as he nervously ran his slim fingers through his jet black hair. Able was different from the type I was used to. He was slimmer, more kept, if that made sense. His tan skin and midnight hair complimented each other nicely. But what got to me were his eyes. They were frighteningly dark. Like the ocean at night, a mystery. One I was willing to solve. "You're welcome, Sarah." He stared at me another moment before he turned down the aisle and disappeared.

Guess that was as good as it was going to get. Able was somewhat of a nerd, always hiding behind his glasses and rarely making eye contact. I sighed and picked out things for breakfast while I was there. If there was one thing I knew was going to remain baffling to me, it was him.

I placed everything on the conveyer belt when I was done. I was happy to say I didn't go over my limit and would be able to take everything to the house in one trip. I thanked Noreen as I took the bags from her and made my way out into the cold night air. There waiting against the wall, to my surprise, was no other than Able.

"I thought I could help you with your bags. It's the least I can do for acting like a weirdo back there." Able reached for the groceries I was holding.

"You sure?" I asked, confused. I didn't want him to feel as if he owed me.

"I'm sure. Plus, it'll give us time to get to know each other." I blushed at his words. My house wasn't too far from where we were. It wasn't going to be a lot of getting to know each other, which was a total bummer.

"Okay then. My house is just over there," I pointed like the knob that I was.

He smiled at me, blinding me with its brilliance. It made me wonder once more how he was single, or if he was. Able was amazingly gorgeous. "Lead the way."

I was having a loss of words. He was right beside me, following me to my crap-tastic apartment. That was, at the moment, occupied by Lauren. There was no way he would be able to go up to the door. That was one of the guidelines when Rick moved me there, no men. No one went into the apartment. I couldn't trust anyone ever again or until they locked Ramon up. Ramon was a slick bastard and he knew how to fly under the radar.

I forgot the company I was in when I heard someone speak. "What was that look for?"

I thought about what he was asking me, I hadn't even noticed I'd made a face. "You know you ask tons of questions." I avoided his inquiry.

The footsteps halted behind me. "Is that a bad thing?" he wondered. I wasn't sure he even meant for me to answer it. It was as if he was talking to himself. He looked as confused as me.

Instead of making a bigger fool of myself than I already was, I decided to respond. "No, I guess it isn't. That is how you get to know someone after all. I'm just not used to such luxuries anymore." I was talking more than I wanted to. Something about him had me feeling at ease, I wasn't sure if I liked that either.

"What brought you here?" He asked, changing the subject.

"I guess the same as everyone else." Though, I didn't know what that was.

He pondered my words. "New start. I get it. I came for the same reasons, years ago."

"Isn't that what everyone wants in the end? A new beginning, one free from our past lives," I noted.

"Yes, that is the goal in the end, isn't it? A place to call home. A place that isn't marred by cruel intentions." He sounded as if he was also running from something he couldn't escape. In the end it would catch up with us, making life as we know it, obsolete.

Before I knew it, we were standing right in front of the building I lived in. "Well, this is me. Thanks for walking me. It was very gentlemanly of you." He handed me the bags and stood there waiting for something. "Thanks again. "I rocked back on my heels waiting for him to say something, anything to make this less uncomfortable.

Finally, he spoke. "I hope to be seeing you around, Sarah."

"Me too," I said as he turned and walked back in the direction we just came.

Shit, I was out of practice and what was it with me? He was everything women dreamt about and here I was making a fool of myself. I slapped my hand to my forehead and backed up into the door to open it since my hands were full. It was past time to feed the mad woman upstairs.

I sighed to myself and realized that I needed to put Able out of my mind, there was no way he would accept me if he knew what I was before anyway.

~

Able

I hated working for this fucker. Ramon was everything I strived to not be like. I owed him and it was killing me. The worst part was that I was starting to like Celia or Sarah. I hated the name Sarah. It didn't match her big, beautiful, cerulean eyes or her deep, wavy, chestnut hair that stopped a little past her shoulders. She was everything my mother told me to look for. It wasn't her looks that attracted me to her, it was the way her smile lit up that whole damn store. It was the way she looked out for everyone around her, without question or expecting anything in return.

And even with all that, I was here to *kill* her.

I would do it just to get out from under Ramon's control. I had to do it to get my family out of harm's way. When Ramon asked me to kill her, I wasn't thinking about the person I was going to be ending. All I heard was him telling me that I would be free of him finally. I jumped at the chance. It wasn't like I hadn't killed someone before, maybe not for money, but growing up where I did, I saw a lot of trouble and participated in it.

The more I watched Celia, the worse I felt. This girl was like me, she'd fell under Ramon's thumb, too. Even worse, I wasn't going to be able to save her, no matter what I tried or wanted. In a different life, I could see Celia and me together. I would protect her from everyone and everything that tried to hurt her. She deserved so much more than she was getting.

And it was coming soon, sadly.

My phone rang in my pocket and before I even looked at it I knew who it was. Ramon.

"What?" I snapped.

He cackled into the phone, leaving gooseflesh all down my arms. "Is that any way to answer the phone? Especially when you know it's me calling. You don't want to end up in a fucking ditch somewhere, do you?" The way he talked wasn't loud or menacing, but you could tell he was all about his business. He spoke into the receiver softly. "Now, where were we? Ah, yes. How is everything going with my sweet, sweet Celia? Or should I call her by the name they're now calling her, Sarah is it?"

"I really couldn't care less about what you call her. To me, she remains nameless," I lied. I clenched my teeth together to stop myself from telling him to go to hell.

"Now, now, don't lie to me. If there is one thing I despise the most, it's liars." He clicked his tongue at me.

I sat on the end of my bed and threw my keys on the night table. I was staying in the shittiest of hotels ever. It had a rancid smell floating through the air and no matter what I sprayed it wouldn't cover it. There were people next door to me who were into the kinkiest sex play ever. I was an open individual, but at times I could swear he was going to murder that poor girl's vagina. "Everything here is fine, I made progress today. She let me walk her to her apartment."

"Isn't that great? Though, I was hoping for the job to be complete already. You are failing me and I hoped I wouldn't have to remind you that failing would be a waste of a good girl." In the background I heard a soft cry.

My sister.

"I'm doing what you asked. I promise. All I need is two more days. Give me that, please," I choked. He told me if I didn't get it done in a timely manner, he was going to start killing people in my family, for each day I was late.

"As you wish, but remember, Able, your sister is sweet and I would love to taste her completely. I'm sure there are even some of my men that would appreciate her lovely little body. Remember my words, Able. I don't give second chances." With those last words he hung up on me.

I threw the phone at the wall and watched the parts clink to the floor. My family's lives were depending on me and here I was finding it difficult to kill this girl, a girl I could see myself with.

What was I going to do?

2

Celia

Lauren was sleeping with her mouth hanging open and her leg draped over the back of my sofa.

"Lauren," I called tapping her softly on the shoulder. Rick called this morning wondering where she was and I couldn't lie to the person I confessed myself to. He was pissed, even though he wouldn't admit to it. He wouldn't say that he didn't like Lauren hanging around me because he thought I was a bad influence. It would go against everything he taught her. I knew though. I knew he didn't want his precious daughter around me and if I were him, I would be the same way.

"What Celia!? What could you want this early in the morning?" She popped up off the couch with mussed hair and an attitude.

She wasn't a morning person either. I didn't want to be a morning person, but waking up was a better alternative to staying asleep and seeing Ramon in my dreams every fucking night. I did get lucky last night and dreamt about Able and his charming smile. The man was taking over my every thought and, for the first time in a long time, I felt the light shining on me.

"Your father knows you're here and he isn't too happy about it," I patted her back and made my way over to the kitchen area.

"I'm grown," she said with a pout. "He can't keep telling me what to do with my life. First, it's all: *You have to stay in school!* and then it's all:*Being around Celia is going to get you hurt!* Why can't he just leave me alone to make up my own mind?"

I poured a cup of tea and brought it to her. "He is right about those two things. School is extremely important and, as for me, we both know I'm a pastor's worst nightmare when it comes to being his daughter's best friend." I moved to her side and sat down with my own cup of tea in hand.

"You know, that's the first time I've heard you calling me your best friend." Tears welled up in her eyes.

"Wow, what just happened? Why are you going to cry?" I asked, genuinely shocked.

She placed her cup down gently and scooted over to me. "Because you are my best friend and it took so long for you to realize that." She pulled me to her, wrapping her long, lanky arms around my shoulders. It was the first hug I'd received since my mother passed away. It was a foreign feeling, but it was warming up my insides.

I brushed off the emotions that were filtering through me like a tidal wave. "Come on, we've got to get you fed and to the bus stop. I wish you could have stayed longer, but your father needs you there."

"What about you? Who's going to take care of you?" Lauren asked me.

"I never needed anyone to take care of me. Life has always been about me floating around and just winging it." I sighed, wishing I really believed I was going to be okay alone.

The rest of the day was spent getting her things together and spending as much time as possible together before her bus came. I didn't know how she managed to fit so much in the tiny bag she brought or how she also was able to fling everything she owned all over the apartment, but she did. I got her to the bus stop a minute before the bus actually got there. I hugged her and told her I'd be out there to visit the first chance I got. She didn't like leaving me there alone, but there wasn't anything we could do about it. Our lives were going in different directions right now and all we could do was wait until they met up again somewhere down the line.

Since today was my day off, I decided to take a walk to the park down the street from my house. I didn't want to go back to my apartment and be alone when Lauren and I were just talking about me and my loneliness. I would be okay, I really would. My only problem was not being able to remember the last time I had a real friend. There were other girls Ramon had me living with in a house. They were all whores like me, selling themselves to the highest bidder just to please Ramon. By pleasing Ramon, you got more things like better food, nicer clothes, he kept you high, and he wouldn't beat you. If you didn't please Ramon, you could end up in a trash can somewhere waiting for the garbage men to pick it up. Ramon would pay them so the bodies of the girls I once knew would never be found.

I strolled over to my favorite bench in the park. The reason for my favoritism was it was dedicated to a little girl who had passed away at the age of seven. It didn't state why she was gone or when it happened, just the inscription, *"In memory of Judy, age 7. When I had you, I learned what life meant."* I sat here on days I couldn't digest my life. It reminded me how precious being here was and how fortunate I was to still be breathing. There were and are some brave little girls facing things they shouldn't have to.

"Sarah?" Again, I knew who it was just from the voice. And again I wondered if he was stalking me, but I let it go because I was on my bench, pondering the meaning of life.

"Able, should I ask how you keep finding me?" I scooted over and patted the seat next to me.

He sat and looked at me for a few seconds. "Would it be so weird to think I just wanted to sit here next to you?"

"Always the questions," I giggled softly.

"I was walking by and thought you might need a friend. You look down today or more so than usual."

He was very perceptive and it made me that much more wary. "I am. I come here when I need time to reflect." I exhaled loudly.

He stood stiffly and began backing away from me with his hands held up. "I didn't mean to intrude on your alone time."

"No, please, come and sit with me. I don't think I need to be alone right now. I've been unaccompanied too long." A tear slid down my cheek and ended at my jaw line. Able took it upon himself to wipe it away, but I doubt he actually knew the significance of what he actually had done. I just really needed to be touched right now. I needed to know I was lovable. I had to feel something again, anything, no matter how short-lived it would be. "Come home with me," I blurted out. If he was smart he would refuse and leave me here to mourn my unfortunate life.

He looked deep into my eyes, holding my stare without reserve. "Okay," he whispered.

Shock rattled my whole body. There were so many positive emotions in that one word. He was sure of himself in that moment. I'd never seen someone so set on what they were saying. "Are you sure? I'm asking you up for more than a cup of tea," I pointed out.

"I got that," he chuckled, holding his hand out to me. "If you want to change your mind, I understand."

"No, I need this," I said simply, placing my hand into his.

He pulled me into his side and slung his arm over my shoulders. "Since this is going faster than I would have liked. I will start the courting now."

I was tickled at his use of the word court. Most men didn't care to date or take care of me. Dating wasn't in their vocabulary let alone courting. I was the woman they used before they went home to lay next to their poor, delusional wives. I was the trash men used up, then discarded.

"Don't look like that or I'll begin to think I'm taking advantage of you," he moved a strand of wayward hair so he could see my face.

I grinned like a lovesick schoolgirl, ducking my head into his shoulder.

"There's that sexy smile, now stop hiding it. I love it when you smile. I love when I make you smile. I can tell from your eyes that you're always sad, always hiding from something." If he knew how on point he was, he would run.

"Come on up," I motioned to my building's door. "It isn't much, but it's where I live." Trying to excuse the mess that I knew was inside waiting for me. Lauren was lucky I loved her. But I couldn't think about them right now. Rick would never forgive me for letting a man into my home or for thinking about the things I was about to do with one.

He let me lead the way into the cubicle sized apartment, where everything but the bathroom was in the main room. "Nice," Able offered as he stepped into the room.

"Thanks, but you don't have to be nice when it clearly is a mess." I started picking up things and flinging them into the basket or putting things where they belonged.

He moved over to me and looked at me funny. "I never say things I don't mean. The sooner we get that out of the way, the sooner we can get to what brought us here," he clasped his hand around my wrist, bringing it behind my back and pinning it there. "What am I going to do with you, Sarah?"

Panic bubbled in my chest. He was taking an aggressive approach. I knew he wasn't going to hurt me, I felt... safe. With my back pinned against the wall and his hands wandering over my womanly curves, I inhaled sharply as he cupped my right breast. "This is what you wanted, right?"

I couldn't speak, so I nodded.

"Good girl. I love how you feel under my hands. Do you like it?"

I nodded again.

"I might seem like I'm gentle, some would call me a geek, but believe me when I tell you I'm far from that," he slipped his glasses off his nose, placing them on the side table. His already intense eyes darkened as he tested and probed parts of my body. I was still silent, not knowing what to say.

"Touch me," a voice came, was that me?

He moved me off the wall, gripping my hips as he lifted me into the air. Out of instinct, I wrapped my body snuggly around his. "Tell me what you want me to do," he murmured.

"Anything," I said before I could stop the words from leaving my mouth.

He smiled devilishly at me before saying, "You might want to rethink your words before you get exactly what you asked for." He sat me down gently at the edge of the bed. I knew he wouldn't hurt me, I felt it with everything in my bones.

This is exactly what I wanted; him. "I have no intention of taking anything back." I laid back onto the bed to prove my point. I meant it to be as sexy as possible, but there were still clothes littering the mattress causing me to bumble about. If Able noticed, he didn't let on and I was thankful for it.

There was something about the way he was taking control, it was doing crazy things to my body. I felt hot one minute and, in the next, I'd shiver from the excitement. He placed his rough hands on my inner thighs and pried them open. It wasn't like I was putting up much of a fight, but a little work wouldn't hurt anyone. After all, I was confused as to why I felt so sure of Able. I didn't want to think about it much, so I placed it in the category of "hey he's hot and I'm horny".

He slid between my legs eagerly. "Hey, stop thinking so much and just let your body respond to me," he directed.

I started to breathe the way the doctor told me to when I would have a panic attack. It would calm me, relaxing me into a state of bliss. After he told me to stop and just feel, that's exactly what I did. I let everything go and started to enjoy this time that we had. He placed soft, delicate kisses up and down my body until I couldn't take anymore. My body convulsed with need. If he didn't penetrate me soon, I would lose it.

"Patience," he said, pulling my stiffened, rosebud tip into his mouth.

I cried out in delight. My body was betraying me as he stripped the last of my clothing off of me. He worked fast, I hadn't noticed when my clothing started disappearing, but it was gone in an instant. "Please," I begged and then froze. That was what Ramon would make me do, when he raped me. It was his way of justifying what he was doing. If I begged him, then I wanted it right? No, that's just what he thought.

"Did I do something wrong?" Able moved away from me, his eyes were still clouded with desire.

I had to get a hold of myself. I couldn't keep thinking of Ramon. How would I ever be able to get on with my life if I kept letting that vile man drag me back into his pit of hell? Moving forward was the only thing I could do and Able was here to help me do just that. "No, nothing. I was just remembering something," I stated and pulled him back to me.

"It didn't look like nothing. If you want to talk—"

I stopped him from going on. "No, there isn't anything I want to talk about. As a matter of fact, I don't want to talk at all."

He took my words of encouragement, placing the swollen head of his cock at my entrance. Like my own clothes, I had no idea when he took his off, but there he was, standing in front of me in all his magnificence. His manhood was long and bulbous. It looked like it was going to explode on impact. I was terrified for a moment. Nothing I had done in my life could have made me prepared for this. He was easily the biggest man I had ever thought about being with.

I licked my lips absently. "Stop doing that or I'm not going to make it into you," he lightly chucked, but it was short lived when he looked down between my legs and saw how soaked I was. "Come here," he whispered, holding out his hand to me.

I took it willingly. He led me to the chair in the corner of the room where Rick would sit when he visited. "This is how it's going to go. I'm going to fuck you against this chair, hard. Then when it's time for me to come I'm going to spill my seed down your throat. If you spit it out or waste any of it I will punish you." Again, this should have terrified me beyond reason, but here I was eagerly waiting for what he was promising.

"Yes," I said, sitting on the edge of the chair taking in all of his beauty. I wished this was a different life where I could love and live freely.

He stalked toward me. "That didn't scare you?" he questioned knowingly.

"No."

He stopped when his cock was throbbing an inch from my face. "Not even a little?" he stroked himself roughly. I was jealous that his hand was touching it. I wanted to be the one bringing him to his peak.

I shook my head, because my throat went dry.

"Good girl, open up. I want to feel your tongue first." I did as I was told. Though I didn't think I was going to be able to fit everything in my mouth, I would try my damnedest.

He pushed in slowly, letting my mouth stretch and become accustomed to the assault he was getting ready to deliver. I moaned around his head, loving the way he tasted on my tongue.

"Not yet. Let go," Able pushed me back. "Place your legs over the arms of the chair. Yes, spread your legs just like that." As he was telling me what to do, he took himself into his hands and stroked vigorously. "You are beautiful," he murmured. It was the first compliment I heard him tell me since we got up here. I was used to dominating men, I just didn't think Able was like that. More surprising was that I loved it on him. "Since you've been here have you fucked anyone else?"

The question was a little off-putting, but I answered anyway. "No." I needed him in me, I was going to cum just looking at him. "Please, take me."

Before he placed his fat head at my entrance he rolled a condom into place, but this time he pushed all the way in. The pressure was wonderful. I didn't know if it was causing me pain or pleasure. Both, maybe. He didn't stop to ask me if I was okay or if I was hurting. He just pumped harder and faster. He never took his eyes off of me, like he was afraid he was going to miss something if he did.

Usually I was left dry and unsatisfied from my past Johns and if I did get to have an orgasm, though they didn't give a damn if I did, it would build in my stomach first. With Able, it was as if we skipped over all that. My orgasm rocked me without warning. I screamed out something incoherent, not wanting the sensation to leave and wanting it to ebb all at once.

"God, if you keep this up, I won't make it to that beautiful mouth of yours," he grunted.

He kept the pace, moving his hips in swirls once in awhile, I felt the signs of another orgasm building. He was a great lover, more that I ever expected. I came undone once more. This time calling out his name. When I was settled and calm, Able pushed me to my knees and told me to open my mouth. I listened willingly and he jammed his cock deep down my throat, fucking my mouth relentlessly. He throbbed in my mouth as he released his hot, salty liquid down my throat. I swallowed greedily, taking every drop he gave me.

When it became too much a drip slid past my lips, collecting at the corner of my mouth. "I told you not to waste anything," he placed his finger over the drop of cum and placed it back on my tongue. "You look good with my dick in your mouth." Where my geek once stood was now a man who knew what he wanted.

"And you look good on me," I commented as I leaned back into the chair. My eyes couldn't stay open. I was sated and exhaustion took over. I drifted off into a restful sleep.

"Sleep, for it is your last," I thought I heard, but I was already out.

It must have been a dream.

Able

I watched her sleep peacefully, her naked body calling out to me in her unrest. I suspected she wasn't used to having anyone this close to her or anyone doing these intimate things to her in a while. Even if it hadn't been a long time since she had sex, this, what we just did, it was different. Even I knew that. I felt everything she was. My body betrayed me, asking my mind if I could kill a woman I was beginning to love. I had studied this woman for months. I might have known her better than she knew herself.

She had a routine before work. She kept it to a T, day in and day out. This woman was anything but ordinary. She was the opposite, really. She was extraordinary and she somehow had let me in.

Only for me to betray her.

There was nothing I could do, I only had one more day at the most. I didn't want to hurt her, she was everything I dreamt about. Her mind was beautiful, her body responsive, and she didn't hold the past over her head. I figured that out when she allowed me to touch her. Anyone who went through what she did wouldn't be able to walk alone or even willingly fornicate with a man. She should think men are the devil. Celia was remarkable because she wasn't letting these things weigh her down.

Staring at her delicate features, her dark hair and caramel skin, she was majestic. And I was deeply falling in love with her. Today was the last day that I would get to end this woman's life. I would get no other. She might have opened up to me and let me in, but tomorrow she would just regret it. I knew she would.

I had to save my family.

I took the syringe out of my pocket and pricked her in the neck with it. This would put her out for a couple of hours. Enough time to move her and get her to the safe location where Ramon told me to take her. A tear slid out of my eye, betraying my emotions. If there was any way I could get this girl out of this and get my family to safety, I would.

Then it hit me, there was a way. I actually could, get her out of this, I just needed to make a call. I searched for Celia's phone finding it on silent under the chair I was just fucking her in. I picked it up and looked for a number. When I found it, I hit dial.

The man on the line was confused as to why I was calling from her phone. He didn't know me and it seemed that Celia didn't tell people about me. It was a good thing for me, but not so much for her. How would they ever know who took her, if she told no one of my existence?

"Look, Rick, this is very important. I'm going to need you to listen to me without interrupting. Can you do that?" I asked.

"Yes."

"I was sent here to kill Celia. Ramon has my family and told me he will be killing them one by one if I don't kill Celia," I stopped, swallowing hard. I might be going to prison for a long time for admitting to this.

"Where is she?" he asked in a straight voice.

"I said no interrupting. I need you to come here. I'm going to take Celia and when I arrive there will be bodyguards and Ramon. All I need you to do is contact the police. You need to give it a minute though or they'll know what's going on. Ramon isn't stupid. Regardless of what everyone thinks of him, he is a business man. And Celia took some of that business when she left. He isn't going to expect me to be there on time. I wouldn't agree to do this until he told me he was holding my sister captive. The only way they're going to put him away is if they catch him in the act." I looked over at Celia."And if I have to die for her to live, I will."

"I've never heard about you, who are you?" he asked.

"Does it matter at this point? Just remember, if I die doing this I'm the one who fell in love with the forbidden girl,." I sighed. I explained to him where the meeting place was. I knew little about his men or how many were going to be there, but if the police had probable cause they could go in there without a warrant. I would already be dead by that point. I planned on going in there armed and if it slowed them down, my life will have meant something. I planned on doing this all after he let my sister go anyway. I didn't doubt that he would have others watching my mom and the rest of the family members. This was the only way I could get her out of this. If I died, it would pay Ramon back for helping me all those years ago when my father died.

"This is the stupidest plan ever. You don't have to die, why would you think that?" Rick shouted.

"It's the only way I can cleanse my family of the mistake I made so many years ago, not to mention what I was thinking about doing to the woman I ended up falling in love with. Please, just take care of Celia and make sure to tell her I loved her. Tell her that the little time I spent with her was the best thing that ever happened to me."

"Why don't you tell her yourself? You're with her, aren't you?" I looked at her unconscious body, still only wrapped in a sheet.

"I am with her, but she's sleeping." I was going to have to put clothes on her before we left. There was no way I would let him see her like this, with an afterglow of the love we made.

Time to right my sins.

I wish there was a reality where I could live and have a family. Maybe make Celia my wife. It might seem ridiculous, but she was it for me. My angel at my darkest times, the love of my life that I just didn't get to know very well. My story had to end sadly for others to have a happy ending, and I was okay with that. My family wouldn't forget the day I laid my life down for others to live.

~

Celia

I was groggy when I woke. I wouldn't have gotten up, but I was so cold I couldn't feel my feet. I peeled my eyes open, expecting to be in my bed with Able by my side, keeping me warm. Yet there I was in a warehouse tied to a fucking chair.

I was wrong to trust him. Able was sitting in front of me, cross-legged looking at me with intent. "Sorry it had to be this way, Celia. I really liked you. I just couldn't let them kill my sister. She would have only been the first and they would have moved on to my mother. When my father died, he left me to take care of them and all I managed to do was get myself into more trouble. I hope you understand," he shrugged like he didn't give a fuck if I understood or not. If I was in his position, I wouldn't give a damn either.

"Wow, how stupid am I?" I asked to no one in particular.

"You're not stupid," Able answered anyway.

"It was a rhetorical fucking question, you idiot!" I shouted. "So, where is he then?"

"Ramon? He told me he would be here in an hour and for me to wait. He's going to bring my sister here." The relief in his eyes boiled my blood, but I couldn't be mad at him for saving his sister. I really was just pissed that Ramon was winning. Able and I were nothing more than pawns in his perverted game.

"Fine. Stop talking to me. I can't stand the sight of you," I said cruelly.

"I had no other option," he said sadly. "If I could save you, if there was a way—" he let his words fall flat.

"Fuck me, then kill me. As first dates go, this one really sucks. It's up there with Hitler giving someone an STD." I couldn't believe my luck. Rick kept telling me that God had a plan for me. If this was his plan, I didn't like him very much. I had been struggling most of my life, when was it my turn to rest? Now, I would never know. This was *my* end. Ramon wasn't going to let me walk out of here alive.

"Look, Celia—"

I stopped him once more. "I take it you know who I am and who I once was."

"Yeah. I know who you are and what that *monster* made you do," he stood and walked over to a little table, picking up a glass of water. "Are you thirsty?"

"No," I snapped. "If you know all that, then you know he never made me do anything. I loved being a whore. I loved fucking random men. I loved when they'd push their cocks into me never pulling out until I was filled to the brim with cum!" I was only screaming the words to piss him off. Something inside of me had to see if he cared at all.

"Stop lying! You didn't like any of it. You couldn't have, you were so young. Too young," he responded.

"You know nothing! You think too much with your heart. I fucked you because I missed the feel of a cock buried deep in me," I spat at him.

"Stop speaking nonsense," he moved to where he was when I woke and sat down.

"You act like you're someone, but deep down you're just a scared little boy. Save your family. I couldn't care less, but stop acting like you give a damn about what they do to me."

"I do care." He looked like he wanted to say more, but at that moment the door opened and in walked Ramon, flanked by two greasy looking behemoths of men.

"Well, isn't this touching? Celia, good to see you, love. How long's it been?" Like he gave a hell about time and where I was. The only thing he cared about was the fact that I left. I didn't say anything because he wasn't worth my words. He wasn't worth anything. I wouldn't even cry when it came time for him to kill me. He was worthless and I wouldn't fall victim in my last moments.

"Where is my sister?" Able questioned, standing stiffly next to my chair.

Ramon's wicked smile glowed in the shadows of the warehouse. "Such spirit, your sister has. It's a shame to see her go," he pouted. Ramon told one of the guards to retrieve her like she was a fucking package. I hated this man with everything I was, but now I wasn't scared. I was going to be me at the end. It was the least I could do for my mother.

"You are going to stay and see this through, right?" Ramon questioned Able. "You aren't going anywhere until she is without breath." The dramatic asshole held his breath to prove his point.

"Yeah, sure. After you lift all restrictions and the contract with me is done. I will never see you again, Ramon."

"Yes. Yes, whatever," he waved his hands and looked over his shoulder as the door opened. In came the Neanderthal of a man and a fragile looking woman, who looked to be in her early twenties. She and Able had striking resemblances.

She fell forward as the giant man pushed her down. "Able, you fool. Why would you do anything for this man?" She looked to me with saddened eyes. "I suppose you are the one all this fuss is about." It wasn't a question more of an accusation.

"I guess," I offered, shrugging.

"Enough already. So glad everyone is reunited and it feels so good!" Ramon cackled at his lyrical joke. "Let's get down to business. You and your lovely sister won't be going anywhere until she is dead." He motioned toward me and looked pointedly at Able.

I was tired of running, tired of being scared of my own shadow. I'd always known Ramon would come for me, but I didn't think it would be like this.

"Get it over with already," I yawned. "I'm sick of this shit and I would rather die than have you touching me with your revolting hands ever again."

"Look at who grew some balls while away," his face transformed in an instant. He went from joyful to sinister in seconds. "I would watch that tongue before I cut it out."

"Do it, old man. I hate you and hope someone shoves a dick in your mouth. Then, I hope you choke to death on your own blood, but alas, that still would be too good for you." I was taking things overboard and I knew it once he began storming toward me.

Able did something funny then, he stood in Ramon's way. "Leave her be. This is my job to finish." Able then turned to me and winked. What the hell was going on?

"Fine, get it over with so I can go home. I have tons of work to catch up on," Ramon remarked as he dug the dirt from under his nails.

"Yes, Able, get on with it," I groaned painfully. I was irritated and I didn't feel like taking shit from anyone right now. The bindings around my wrists were digging into my tender flesh, causing spurts of pain to climb up my arms.

Able was looking everywhere but at me. It seemed as if the mold on the wall was more interesting than me and my impending doom. I was still puzzled as to why he winked at me a moment ago. I prayed hard for forgiveness and I also forgave Able for what he was about to do. Anything that would absolve me from the life of sin I used to live.

I watched as the wheels in Able's head began to spin. "One moment," he held his slim finger up. "I rather my sister didn't see what I'm going to do." He walked her over to the back door and shoved her out. There she was free to run as far and as fast as her legs could go. I envied her at that moment, because there was no one coming to save me, no one knew I was here. I realized in that moment how much I took for granted the few people in my life, even Pastor Rick.

Lauren's delicate features stuck in my mind. I wished I had told her I loved her. I was completely scared of what those words would mean or how they would feel coming from me. "I'll see you on the other side Lauren, hope we meet and we remember each other. I love you," I whispered, knowing she couldn't hear it but needing to say it out loud at least once.

Ramon shook his head at me like I lost my mind. "Who are you talking to?" he wondered, but I wasn't inclined to give him an answer.

"Now that that's done, where were we?" Able stalked toward me with a huge knife, it was the biggest knife I had ever seen.

I was dumbfounded. Panic surged through my body once more. I couldn't believe he was going through with this and worse, he was going to stab me. Was I actually ready to die? He was going to fucking stab me!

"Able, don't do this, please! Remember what we just shared," I cried.

He stopped a foot in front of me. "You know there isn't any way out of this. I explained this all to you. I do like you and I am truly sad that this isn't going to work." He pulled my head onto his stomach and whispered. "When I cut the ties, run. Don't stop, don't look back. Run to the back door, Rick will be there waiting for you." He kissed my cheek softly. "I love you," were his final words before all hell broke loose.

He cut the binds and I dashed around him, making my way to the door. I got out without getting shot, but behind me I could hear guns firing. In the parking lot, I could see Able's sister struggling to get past the policeman that was holding her in place.

"Why would he die for her? He doesn't even know her, she is nothing to him!" she screamed as she kicked the man in his shin. He let her go as he bent over to hold on to his pained leg. She made her way to me and I knew what she was going to do, but I was rooted to the ground.

She slapped me so hard I noted a strong coppery taste burst in my mouth, still, I didn't move. I deserved it all. No, I didn't get him into whatever deal he had going with Ramon, but in the end, I was the one who served him his death certificate.

"I'm so sorry." It was all I could say, there was nothing I could do to bring her brother back.

~

Able

The last few minutes in the warehouse were crazy. Ramon's men began to shoot anything that moved. Meaning, I was a running target. As SWAT descended into the building with their guns all pointed at Ramon and his boys, there was nothing more to do. I wasn't allowed to go out and let the girls know I was okay, because there was tons of questioning going on. For now, I was told they both thought I was dead. I didn't get out unscathed though. I took a bullet to my leg and another in my left lower abdomen.

As I lay there looking up blankly at the ceiling, I was told they were going to fake my death. That way if Ramon got out, which was unlikely, he wouldn't come looking for me. If he saw it, then it must be real, right? They were also going to post a false obituary for Celia for the same reasons.

We were all getting out of this *alive*.

It was days before they allowed me any visitors. I was kept in a hospital that was only for wounded policemen and military. No one knew I was here and they wanted to keep it that way. They told my mother and sister, of course, and they were the first ones who came. They were so happy I was alive, they hit me for it. It was nice knowing I was loved and to know it was finally over.

I asked when the officers were going to let me see Celia, but they told me that might not ever be possible. They didn't know how she was going to react around me. They didn't know if she was scared of me. I told them I understood and that all I could do was wait. I couldn't stay there anymore, so they worked on placing me somewhere else. I didn't want to go and leave my family, but if they were safe, then I would make do.

On the night of my release, my door opened and closed softly in the darkness. I couldn't make out who it was because there was a curtain blocking the view.

"Who's there?" I asked to the feet that stood immobilized at my door.

There was no answer.

Finally, she said something. "I'm beginning to think you followed me here," her soft laugh set my chest on fire.

"Celia?"

"Who else would it be, silly?" she questioned, pulling back the curtain to expose herself.

"The nurse," I offered sarcastically.

"I'm better than a nurse, believe me." She sat at the end of my bed and rubbed my leg. "Heard you get to leave this place soon."

I turned my body away from her just in case there was any residual feelings she was dealing with. "Yep. Once I get my papers, they're going to tell me where I'm going. What about you? I didn't think you were hurt."

"I'm not, they just didn't want anyone seeing me. You know, they killed me too," she smiled as if it were a joke we shared.

"I don't think any of this is funny, Celia. I won't even be able to see my family anymore. Did they even tell Rick and Lauren about you being alive?" I wondered if they were considered her family, because I knew she didn't have anyone.

"No." Sadness covered her face making me regret even asking her the question.

I looked at her as I moved to sit closer. "You know there will be a time where this is all forgotten. People will go on living their lives and we can too," I tried to comfort her.

"I'll be okay," she answered shortly. "So did they tell you where you were going yet?"

"No, I'm still waiting for the paperwork. They told me they would be here any minute with it, but that was an hour ago." She pulled something from her pocket and handed it to me.

"They told me to come and give this to you. I told them I wasn't sure if you wanted to be stuck with me in a town after everything happened, but they were sure you would want just that."

I took the paper she handed me and looked it over. Sure enough the paper held the location they were going to move me to, rather the location they were going to move us to. My mouth hung open a bit. What in the world are these people thinking? I guess my face reflected my confusion because Celia said, "You don't have to go. They said if you didn't like this idea they would move you somewhere else. I can manage on my own. I've been doing it for a while now."

She thought I didn't want to go because of her. I laughed then grabbed my stomach tight because it hurt, causing some blood to seep out of my wound. "Why would you think that? Here I was thinking I would be placed somewhere that I had no one. I was going to be separated from my family... and..." *Get it out.* "And I would be separated from you."

"What?" She looked stunned.

"I told you I loved you. Did you think I was lying? I wouldn't play with *those* words like that."

"But you were hired to kill me." Tears filled her eyes.

"Even more reason to love you. So, Celia, will you have me?"

She took longer than I would have liked her to, but the look on her face told me she was going to say yes. "No."

"No?" I demanded, confused.

"No, I mean yes, but I don't want you to be in this because you feel like you have to. I want you to be with me because you love everything about me. I want you to love me for me, meaning my past and all. So, will *you* have *me*?"

"You were mine from the moment I laid eyes on you. As for your past, I love all of you, I wouldn't want it any other way."

The End

Change of Station
Karla Bostic

1

"Anybody seen Christy this morning?" Julia stuck her head in the door and asked the admin team as she was headed down the hallway.

There was a chorus of "No's" that came from around the room.

"Yeah, actually I did," Renee spoke up. "She was headed into Jay's office with a notepad, when I was coming in the door this morning. Looked like it was serious." Jay Simpson was the Corporate Attorney, who handled all the firm's legal work.

"Oh, good. From what I hear, the attorney meeting went well into the night with the family and I guess there are going to be some major changes around here from now on. I was hoping to get the insider view before she went into lockdown mode this morning. Come find me if you see her before I do, please?"

"You got it, sweetie." Renee piped in. "Hey, don't forget today is y'alls workaversary, and we're all supposed to take a long lunch today to celebrate, even though it's not looking like that is gonna happen."

"I totally agree," Julia replied as she hurried down the hallway toward her desk in front of the accounting division wing of corporate. Jayco, Inc. was a growing law firm specializing in the real estate field. Over the years, they had moved more toward the estate side of things rather than just home purchases.

Sixteen years ago, Christy and Julia had both seen a small ad in the employment section of the local paper. She smiled as she remembered it fondly.

Wanted: Admins for up and coming force to be reckoned with. We are a small company with great potential. Get in on the bottom floor and grow with us.

Julia had always been a sucker for the underdog and it drew her attention right away. Christy was still in the process of getting her degree online and had been looking for a full-time position to pay the bills.

The girls had met in the waiting area of the plush Peachtree Suites Hotel in downtown Atlanta. Looking back, it probably should have concerned her that they were hiring positions for a company that didn't even have offices as of yet. Once again, that love for the underdog had drawn her in.

Two other girls were also waiting to be interviewed for the positions, but both seemed to be aloof and standoffish. Julia and Christy hit it off immediately. It all started as a conversation about the potential of a company that was so new there was no corporate office space yet. From there, it grew into a personal discussion about family, goals, children, and the future of the economy in the Atlanta metropolitan area. The two felt instantly drawn to one another and hated that they were competing for the same position.

Julia was single and just out of college with a degree from Emory University in Business Administration and Marketing. The oldest in a large family of six children. At twenty-years-old, she was very young to have accomplished her degree, which told Christy she had to be very intelligent, right off the bat.

Julia's mother had passed away when she was fifteen.Her father worked for the Sheriff's department and due to strange hours, the burden of cooking, cleaning, and rearing her siblings went to Julia, while she was still attending high school and then later college. She knew the meaning of multitasking at the highest level. Her youngest sibling, Gage, was just two years older than Christy's own daughter, Shelby, so she could relate to the age and challenges that Christy was dealing with on a daily basis.

Christy was a few months behind Julia in college, hoping to graduate the following year if things stayed on course. She had started a bit later in life because she had married young and had her daughter. Now, as a single mother with a six-year-old daughter, she attended college online while looking for a job that would support the two of them. If she was lucky, that job might even feed them and keep them above the poverty line. The idea of any child support was a fictitious dream that she knew wouldn't happen in this lifetime or the next, so she had to find a way to make it on her own.

The girls sat and chatted close to forty-five minutes before either of them were called in for their interview. Things had gone so incredible for Christy that she found herself concerned for Julia, whom she knew also really needed the job. To say that Christy and Mr. Johnson clicked put things mildly. It was as if two minds with one goal were sitting in the same room. Not having completed her degree yet, posed a bit of an issue. She also knew that someone younger than her was coming next in the interview que that had completed her degree, so her nerves were on edge. Trying not to stress over it, she instead focused on what she knew she could accomplish for this company. Interviews were her least favorite thing to do. A person had to essentially convince or sell themselves to any potential employer.

Discovering a challenging way to let them know why they were the better person to hire for the job at hand.

Jace explained his goals for the company. It had been a huge step for his father, the senior Mr. Jace Johnson to invest in his son. His history through college had not shown the best side of him and his sense of privilege had certainly gone to his head. He was the typical only-son of a tycoon. His partying ways were still legend at the UGA campus in Athens.

Jace, Jr. had partied himself through seven of his eight years of college. He knew that it would have continued had there not been that eye-opener homecoming week. He had been out with his buddies painting the town in the UGA school colors black, white, and red. However, their pub crawl ended abruptly when one of his friends was in a terrible accident. Jace had been passed out in the back seat and learned of the accident after the fact, when he was finally awake and lucid later that night.

The trio had been well known around campus for their weekend jaunts and troublemaking with their fraternity brothers. The majority of their house was football stars, so high IQ's didn't matter as much as their high stats on the field or the high dollar bank accounts of their families.

The accident had made the news and was the talk of the campus. Jace felt bad that he had been there in a sense, but didn't know any more than a college freshman stepping on campus for the first time. Apparently, a young couple was on their way to the Athens Regional Hospital on their way to give birth to their first child. They had been hit less than a mile from the hospital and killed on impact.

Since it was at the beginning of winter break, Jace had gone home for the holiday to recover. He was black and blue all over from the seat belt, but nothing was broken. His father constantly harassed him about the stupidity of driving when the campus offered a service to take students home for a small fee. Who was going to leave a beautiful sports car in a dive parking lot for thieves, when they were less than a mile from their destination?

He learned how to dodge his father until the holiday was over and it was time to head back to school. With new classes and mixed up schedules, campus was chaos for the first week back. Though he was still nervous about the problems, all talk of the accident had been put to rest over the break.

It was years later, in the middle of an argument, that Jace learned he had actually been the one driving the car that hit the expectant family. He had been drinking heavily that night and was glad his friend Craig volunteered to be the designated driver. Everything would have been great with that plan, but Craig had been accosted by a group of sorority girls, which left the three guys to fend for themselves.

After tossing his keys to his buds, Craig never gave it another thought as he chased after the beautiful girls. It turned out by some freak of nature that Jace had actually been the lighter drinker of the remaining pack. They called the car service for a ride, but were told it would be at least an hour minimum before they could arrive. Instead of waiting it out, the boys decided to brave the short distance home anyway.

His father had been called by the police captain on duty that night when information about the accident was hitting the air. Jace, Sr. came in and took care of damage control, without pause. Apparently Keith, who was the one actually passed out in the back seat, had a clean record, so the chief said he was the best option and the decision was made to put it all on his Abercrombie-clad shoulders.

The boys really had no memory of what had gone down, but after being slipped a pill by the medics who arrived on site to take care of the situation, they would never know anything except what they were told about the night in question. Jace, Sr. couldn't have his son arrested for the death of miniscule working class citizens. Facts were changed and stories lined up till it was all well and fine.

The family of the young couple was being financially well taken care of and the officers on duty were given the new story of what was to have happened by the chief of police himself. His father covered up his heinous crime.

Thus began an unfathomable rift between the two with resentment on both sides. Jace, Jr. was labeled worthless in his father's eyes and life went forward. Years later, when his father became ill, Jace offered to give part of his liver to save the ailing man. Jace's portion of the liver would regenerate in no time at all, and they would both go on to live a healthy life.

After his selfless act, his father felt obligated to make amends for the years of resentment and began consideration of Jace, Jr. and the family inheritance. Realizing his son had grown up now and would be able to represent his family well at the club as well as in courtrooms, he let go of his animosity. Then a plan was formed to slowly pull him back into the fold and test the waters with the family business.

Jace, Jr. quickly met every requirement and surpassed his father's expectations. It was an impressive turn around. Ten years had passed and the family had grown tighter as a unit and things were looking up. As the only child, there were always high expectations, but Jace was ready to show them who was boss.

His mother, Carol, had always followed the direction of her husband in matters of business. Coming from a wealthy family herself, she never learned to worry herself with matters that were petty. As long as she could continue her lifestyle at the club and with the group of ladies that were her pact, she was happy. Nothing much else mattered.

2

When Carol and Jace, Sr. had first gotten married, she had worried her dreams of the perfect life would all come to a crash. Discovering that she had been unable to produce an heir for her husband threw her life-long plan off track. The Johnson family had ruled the Athens area for more than two hundred years and that was something she wasn't willing to stop, especially due to any fault of hers. Several specialists down the line and thousands of dollars spent on fertility treatments and the same result determined that she was unable to carry a pregnancy to term.

Women of her station simply didn't have that sort of problem. It was their job to further the line and rear the next generation. Afraid her husband would leave her for a better equipped wife, she set to finding a plan to get the heir she needed in order to establish herself in the family.

Gossip shared in the steam room at the club lead to the beginning of her plan. She decided she would simply hire a surrogate. Jace didn't need to know that her eggs were no longer viable, so she would secure her own surrogate and enact her plan. More whispers at the club led to the name of an agency that could provide such services. She met with the agency representative and began the arduous journey of finding the woman who would be the biological mother to her future son.

She wanted a woman with a fair complexion and red hair so that the baby would favor her and not throw question after the birth. After many secret meetings, she and the surrogate came to an arrangement. Angela would provide the eggs and, once fertilized, they would implant two at a time until a pregnancy could come to term. If, for any reason, both eggs were deemed viable male children, then one of the eggs would be aborted in order to give her son the most optimum birth chances.

Thirty-five years ago, such a thing was an extremely cutting edge procedure. The baby would be her child though and, of course, he would be worth of whatever measures she had to take for the pregnancy to come to term and provide her husband with a strong heir.

Carol covered up the fact that the surrogate was donating eggs. She had gone to great pains to make sure he was under the impression his sperm would fertilize his wife's egg and then be implanted into the surrogate to carry to term. He knew it was a difficult situation for Carol, so he let her select the surrogate and handle the first stages as much as possible.

Jace, Sr. felt very comfortable the moment he met Angela. As per the arrangement with Carol, he knew that Angela chose not to be a part of their life after the child was born. Knowing he had little time, he decided to find out as much as he could now while he had the opportunity.

Carol had no idea that Angela had met with her husband at all. Over the course of the next six months, Angela and the senior Jace, developed a bond that later transformed into a relationship. It had grown like a wildfire in the midst of a summer drought.

~

Carol called Angela several times a day once the baby had been implanted. They ran tests to make sure that there was only one viable egg growing to term and that things were going as planned. Angela was healthy and happy. She had the best of everything for the pregnancy.

After a short while, Carol felt the need to move Angela onto the estate with them so she could help to control her diet and see better to her health care. Since Carol was rarely home when she wasn't drinking, it left more opportunity for Angela to find ways to bump into Jace. After a short while, there was no more resisting their affections for one another.

At Angela's last prenatal checkup before the birth, the doctor did an ultrasound to measure the baby's growth progress to assure the baby was growing at the predicted size for the term in the pregnancy. There had been some unexpected news that she wasn't sure how she should handle. Apparently, after the initial tests were run to verify there was one, healthy baby, the egg had divided into twins. During the pregnancy, it appeared that one of the babies had hidden under the other. It was almost as if one twin knew he was a secret gift.

Angela had grown deeply in love with Jace, but she couldn't ask him to leave his wife. She was the surrogate for their child and had signed an agreement. Her job was to bring their child into the world and then disappear from their lives. She knew, however, the truth that the egg was hers and that actually made the twins as much hers as Jace's.

She had been debating what to do about the situation. She considered telling him there was a secret baby and that she wanted to keep that child. But what if he told Carol? She had secretly feared Carol finding out and forcing her to abort the other child and she desperately wanted a child with the man she had grown to love, so she decided to keep it a secret. Even though she was quite far along in the pregnancy, she didn't look too large so she had some time to make her decision.

Carol had mentioned sending Angela to a maternity spa she had heard about. Apparently, one of her friends knew someone who had gone and insisted it was the most relaxing part of gestation. They secluded the patrons away in privacy, so no one could see them when they were at the point of waddle and no longer walking. There was no fear of pictures getting out that they didn't want shared, when the ladies were at their most bloated and felt like beached whales. The spa was supposed to bring the blood pressure down, de-stress the mother, and get her ready for delivery. They even watched the mother's diet, giving her what she was craving the most in moderation.

Secretly, Angela wished Carol would make up her mind. She had come to the decision that if Carol sent her away for the last three months before the birth, that would be her sign that she should keep the baby for herself and raise it. She didn't know if she would tell Jace at that point. She felt the better option for her might be for her to bribe the spa director with some of her more than ample fee for carrying one of these babies to term. Then, there was the side bonus from Carol for donating her eggs for fertilization.

She could actually afford to try to pay her way to peace and silence. The Johnson's had taken care of all her needs since the fertilization process had started, so she didn't have any money going out. She had well over a million dollars just sitting in the bank, waiting for her new life to start. She knew some of the ladies who worked at the spa and felt convinced that they would keep the other baby her secret if that was what she decided. Carol didn't want any contact with her after the birth anyway, so it would work out if that was the decision she came to.

What to do, what to do? It was going to be the hardest decision she had ever made.

As she contemplated her fate, one of the babies decided to play soccer with her ribs. It caught her off guard and took her breath away for a moment. Then, as she rubbed her hand where a tiny foot was kicking, she knew she felt a bond with these babies. She had wanted to have kids of her own, she just hadn't found a good man yet. Now, she was given babies, then the man of her dreams. Even though it was all in the wrong order, she was secretly pleased about things. She wished her parents were there for her to turn to for advice and support. Due to her contract, she wasn't able to tell anyone any of the details, which left her lonely and without a shoulder to cry on when she needed one.

Later that night, Jace peaked his head over the gateway into the guest house where Angela currently resided. From her private little nook, she glowed with a smile that reached from her chubby, swollen toes all the way to her angelic twist of curls over-flowing from her ponytail.

"Cook told me she was sending someone out with your dinner in five minutes, I wondered if you would like to have company? I would love to join you, that is, if you don't mind?" he asked, smoothly.

"Of course," she sighed. "I would love to spend the time with you, Jace. It's your home and you are welcome at my table anytime."

She caught her mind wandering all through dinner. She didn't know how to broach the subject of their relationship or if it even was a relationship to him, as it was to her.

"So, are you gonna tell me what's bothering you, or do I need to tickle it out of you?" his deep voice penetrated her thoughts.

"You should know better than to do that to a pregnant woman, I will wet myself," she laughed.

"You just look so lost and sad. It's breaking my heart. Please, can't you tell me what is bothering you so maybe I can help?" He continued to look deeply into her eyes for any speck of a hint.

She found herself lost in the dark blue pools that were his eyes. How could she ever deny this man anything? She was deeply in love, but at the same time, he wasn't hers.

The time she spent with Jace was something that she would carry with her forever. If she kept the baby, what would her life be like? What if she let them know about the secret twin and they decided to keep it as well? The heir and the spare. She felt that the boys really should have the opportunity to know one another. If not, she would have to move away somewhere so that her secret was never revealed. Her mind waged war with her heart.

3

Six Months Later...

"Does anyone know what time she's gonna get here?" Cheryl squealed.

"Not yet, honey. You must be patient and act mature. If you are to have any hope of getting a job of helping her around the house and with her baby, you will want her to feel like you are trustworthy and dependable, but most of all calm."

"I know, mom. This is just the most exciting news to hit Eleuthera in a very long time. Especially Governor's Harbour," Cheryl bubbled with glee.

"Excuse me, Ms. Chaney," the island slang voice of Deacon interrupted. The Head of Staff at Whel Appointed Estate breezed into the room a moment later. "I just wanted to let you know the ferry is docking now, in case you and Ms. Cheryl wanted to go down and meet the new misses."

"Thank you so much, Deacon. We will be right down in a moment." No more had Deacon cleared the doorway when Louise Chaney turned to her daughter Cheryl and said, "Okay now, quickly go and brush your hair and say a quick prayer. Ask the Lord to help you remember your manners and your station."

Louise took a deep breath and said a prayer herself. They really needed to get the job as governess for the little prince and aide to the rumored heiress who was the new owner of the estate. This had been home as far back as anyone in her family could remember. Rumors had it that when the slave uprising happened in the 1800's, the owner followed the standard set by Lord Rolle on the Exumas Island and gave the land to the slaves who occupied and had run it for generations.

The estate had fallen in disrepair and was all but deserted until the early 1900's when it was purchased by a real estate firm. As the island was in the Bahamas, and at that time under British law, any company worth anything considered it an investment in the future to purchase. It certainly seemed to be paying off finally. Most of the properties were sold and turned into either resorts or rental estates for the wealthy from all over the world.

Governor's Harbour area began to grow in popularity again when most of the estates had been purchased and remodeled inside and out about twenty years ago. Whel Appointed was one of the last to be sold and the renovation had only been completed last year under the very close scrutiny of the Chaney family. Louise's father had instilled in her the love and responsibility of keeping the property as pristine as possible and, most of all, a worth ethic that is simply not known of today. She worked harder most days than many of the slaves did back in the 1800's. However, it was her choice and her love for the property that drove her to such standards. Her husband, Roberto, ran the grounds of the estate and together they worked to make it pristine.

All the hard work seemed to have been noticed when the property was purchased sight unseen three months ago by the very people that had just arrived. They were going only on pictures and the word of those who had worked on the remodel and knew the dignity of the Chaney family. The islands were well-known for detailed carvings and there was no shortage in any direction a person looked, while in the islands.

The home itself was like a warm breeze. It was two stories with wrap around porches that consisted of detailed carvings on the marble balusters that supported a rail that was simply breathtaking. The carvings and inlaid stones formed a mosaic tile look that was only brought down to reality when compared to the home itself. There were ten foot ceilings throughout, wide verandahs that allowed shade on every side of the house, no matter what season was upon them.

Upstairs, there were two large bedroom suites that appeared to be designed for royalty. Only the finest linens were upon the beds which were on pedestals and draped with curtains that gave them the appearance of a royal bedchamber. Heavy, dark mahogany wood made up the furnishings in the first suite. Each piece had carvings that, when placed next to one another, told the story of the property from the late 1400's when it was said Christopher Columbus landed around Cat's Island and discovered the America's.

Rich silks were used to highlight accents around the room. The large suite seemed to be directed toward horse lovers and highlighted the beautiful beasts in several fashions.

The second suite was designed all in cherry and was more designed around the sugar-cane history that ruled the islands for many years. There were pieces that had carvings of workers in the fields toiling away and the large buffet in the sitting room showed a massive gathering of those on the island having a feast that was known to occur each year after the cane season was completed. At the end of the season, a Sugar Cane King was elected from the families who participated in the harvest. There were people of all ages represented in the carvings and many were dancing around the large fire pit in the middle of the island. It was said that whoever was elected King of the harvest that year, would run the planting and schedule the following year. It was a wonderful set of pieces that together told the story of this property.

Great detail went into the restoration and upkeep of the carvings and pieces for historical references. Each suite contained it's own private bath. The size of the room would leave one to wonder if it might have been sleeping quarters for a maid at one time. The bathrooms were located adjacent to the master bedroom, so that someone could always be available for their needs, no matter the hour. After the remodel, it housed white slate floors with a pearl sheen from the pink beaches the area was known for.

A massive, white, marble claw foot tub sat almost in the middle of the bathroom area. The windows were framed on the outside with large overhangs so that there was a sense of privacy with no one being able to see into the room, so whoever chose to soak in the tub could look out to the rolling surf of the beach underneath. There was also a glass encased shower for those inclined for the more traditional form of cleaning themselves, when there was no time to soak. Heated racks kept towels warm whenever reached for. Lit mirrors that ran an entire wall might cause jealousy from anyone who was used to great lighting.

There were plush rugs to step onto when exiting the water. Between the tub and the shower ran a small shelf filled with lotions and oils as well as the essential oils for healing if the need were to arise.

There was a discreet water closet toward the end of the room with a door for privacy.

A large office area was near the entrance to the suite and what Ms. Angela had deemed the nursery. She had sent ahead her wishes and it was ready and waiting for the next would be royal to take up residence. A round white baby bed made of distressed or upcycled wood, was her choice for bedding. It had a white canopy over head with woodland creatures scattered around the baby's area on netting that was more necessary in this part of the world. The linens were of the highest quality and a low changing station was adjacent to a large chest of drawers for his clothing. The lowered changing table had been something she had been adamant about as apparently Angela wasn't very tall and she wanted to be able to reach the baby in comfort.

Cabinets below held diapers, wipes, and all cleaning products necessary. The top of the changing table would lift and shift to the back to reveal an easy to reach baby bath so the little master could have the best available within reach. Ms. Angela nursed the baby so only a few bottles were needed for water and juice. A hutch above held baby foods and cereals. This would be refreshed nightly when the master Prince was down for the night. Cheryl had worked to get everything properly in place that she thought might be needed. She had strived very hard to be sure Ms. Angela would feel she was prepared for whatever need she might have. Shipments of clothing arrived last week and were all properly stored away for easy access.

The other master suite was to be prepared for when the Master of the House was in. Apparently, he came and went at different intervals, but was there with them whenever possible. He had his own quarters so that he might have privacy for business matters or a room for his guest to stay. The sitting room attached to the Master suite had been converted into a business office. There were telecommunication devices arranged so he could speak face to face with whatever department head he needed at a moment of notice. Jace Johnson, Sr. was a business tycoon and a few miles distance was not about to slow him or his business down.

Louise and Cheryl went down together to greet the arriving boat. There was such anticipation on both sides for this meeting. Angela was just reaching the stage where she was comfortable with her money and position. Jace, Sr. was very much in love with her and simply adored the time he could spend with her and their son, Jason. He had been thrilled when he discovered there was a secret twin and agreed with Angela that it was best Carol not be made aware of the situation, unless there was some complication at birth.

Since she had decided to send Angela to the birthing spa, she had not been around for the birth of her son. Things had worked out perfectly with the arrangement Angela made in order to keep the second baby secreted away and kept safe until Carol came and took possession of her son Jace, Jr. The pregnancy had gone without issue and both babies were born healthy.

They were absolutely breathtaking boys from the moment of their first breath. Jace decided that his first born should stay with his mother so he and Angela would always have that bond between them. The second child was given to Carol and with the agreed upon name of Jace Johnson, Jr. went off to live a life of luxury under the public eye and scrutiny. Even though the boys were identical twins, Jason always seemed to thrive and achieve so much more. Jace had been given every privilege, but didn't seem to achieve the same degree of drive as Jason had.

4

Through the years, Jace spent a great deal of time on the estate with Angela and Jason. No one knew any other side of him than the carefree father he presented to the locals when about town with his boy. Jason was a very loving child. He was very much aware of others around him. He went out of his way to assist anyone in need and part of that was from having Cheryl and Louise to help guide in his upbringing.

Jason went to school with the other children on the island. There were excellent teachers brought in by the Johnson estate and the children adored them. Every child in Governor's Harbour grew up with the same privilege of excellent teachers and coaches to aid in their education.

Jace, Sr. felt it was his way of giving back to the island while giving the best to his child. The island of Eleuthera was his oasis. He commuted from the real world of cut throat business to a laid back lifestyle on the island.

Roberto was given the go-ahead and continued to raise sugar cane on the island as had been done for centuries. The profit from the sales went straight to the workers on the land. Workers were given more opportunities than ever before in the island's history. Roberto listened to the worker's ideas to learn better ways and adapt from any historical way of planting or harvesting, which in turn, drove the field hands to work harder for the Johnson family.

Jason had a wonderful family and a great relationship with his father. He had no idea that he had a brother out there living a very different life.

~

Jace, Jr. had been given all the privileges of being the heir of a tycoon. He attended the best private schools and had the most skilled professors to teach at his level of understanding. He was pampered, so he lacked the driving force to push himself toward his goals. He didn't understand why it wasn't just handed to him like everything else in life.

Since there was no competition for his affections, his mother cheered his every achievement. Carol took great pride in the boy. She had two full-time nannies, who tag-teamed to assist his needs when she was not there to see to him. He had a minor affliction with asthma. After the team of doctors ran every test known to man, they determined he would be fine as long as he used his inhaler. He was not quite able to physically assert himself when the weather was humid, but otherwise, he was fine.

Jason, on the other hand, having grown up on the islands and being a very active child, his physical stamina aided his own asthma and never seemed to be an issue.

It truly was amazing how very different two identical twins could be. This certainly gave nod to the nurture over nature side of the arguments. The boys were a classic case to be studied to distinguish the differences.

Over the years, the differences became more apparent in their confidence levels as well as what they did with their free time. Jason looked for ways to aid his teammates and build them all up together as a whole. He searched for ways to make any job easier for the future and more productive on the estate. To put it quite plainly, he was more loving and giving in nature who enjoyed hard work and balance.

Jace, Jr. on the other hand, who was the only known heir to Johnson estate and name, was content to be responsible for the family name continuing into the next generation. His solution was to try to impregnate all beautiful women of childbearing age. He tended to have any problems presented to him along with options for how to solve the crisis, before he made his decisions or put real thought into them.

Jason, on the other hand, did research on any problem at hand and actively sought direction and ways to forego any problems arising again based on the same situation. He didn't mind seeking the aid of those with more knowledge and experience which to him had nothing to do with a degree on paper. Experience meant so much more to him. He often even took it one step further in his research. He gladly gave props where they were due in regards to rewarding those who came up with a solution to any problem at hand.

The two men could not be more different than day is to night. One self-entitled and the other driven to give his best to anything he touched. Jason loved his culture and the history of his home. He actively sought ways to help the less fortunate with skill lessons so that they could better themselves and future generations. He was loved by all who he encountered on a daily basis and he was given respect by those around him because he earned it. He tended to excel at everything he touched and failure wasn't an option.

Sadly, when Jace, Sr. would go to the United States with his other family, he dealt with a spoiled child who had no drive to better himself. His only thoughts were on what else could he be given and what he wanted to do with it. How dare anyone turn down his ideas or cravings for anything he felt necessary in his daily life? He grew to become overbearing and controlling and, when he went to college, felt his father should guarantee him a seat in the fraternity he desired. The one where all the money, and action was going down on any given night.

Jace, Sr. felt a serious disconnect from his namesake. He knew that he and Carol had created a monster in their drive to give him the best of everything. He wondered if there was any way to reach him at that point. He spent most of his time pondering the situation with Carol when he was in country. It wasn't until the accident in college and the realization that he had actually taken a life that he really seemed to wake up. Jace, Sr. reached out to him and felt like it could be a new beginning for him. Thankfully, it had been.

Jace, Jr. saw the life he was leading and where it was headed. He didn't want to be the person he had become. So he set about changing his life from this point forward.

The two became closer from that point forward and Jace seemed to be making strides in becoming the man his father had always wanted him to be. No longer looking just to have a good time, Jace actually cared about his grades and what he was going to do with his degree. How he could use this fortune that would be his one day to change things and help those less fortunate. It was shortly afterward that Jace had come up with the idea to form his own real estate firm.

5

Jace, Jr.'s best grades in law had always been the ones dealing with property issues, those classes had just seemed to come natural to him. The idea of finding a residence for people who were looking, made him feel like he was helping to make homes for families and relieved some of his guilt for taking the one family away. He put together a business plan for his father. Once the go ahead was given, he called and placed an ad in the paper the following day. He was excited to meet the people who would help him reach his dream.

Once he had a staff in place and followed through to see how many employees, he would need would help him determine the size of his offices. He knew money wasn't the issue as his father wouldn't want his name on anything less than spectacular, so sharing the same name was always an added benefit.

Of the four serious candidates that day, he only wanted to hire two. He felt good about working with each and he would follow through on references and once they were verified, he would make his decision. He was determined not to let his attraction to one of the candidates not lead him astray as the best person for the job is what he needed to succeed. His attraction to Julia was immediate, but his business was what had to matter.

Julia and Christy got their calls the morning after their interviews. Each was secretly sad that the other didn't get the position. Both were happy to have the opportunity to get in on the company growing from the ground up. A breakfast meeting at an upscale coffee shop let the players assemble and plan for the offices and what was needed to happen before the doors could open.

Julia was thrilled to see that Christy was hired as well and both girls looked forward to working with one another. Since Julia had her degree already, she would be in charge of the financial division. Christy would work alongside Jace to find the space and get all permits. She would be responsible for hiring the remaining staff that was necessary and for doing unseen task like setting a dress code and creating the employee handbook.

This was a purposeful step from Jace. He didn't think he could work day to day in constant contact with Julia and continue to keep it on a professional level. He knew she was young though and fresh out of college, so he didn't want to take advantage of her. His feelings would have to be set aside.

Julia's responsibilities would include filing for estate status as well as handling higher end real estate. The two girls worked together like they had known one another for years. They had very similar ideas on what they felt was needed in office design. Julia had a younger sister who was studying Interior Decorating. It was a great opportunity for her to design the office space as her term paper, for her final grade and it also placed a large feather in her cap as a client.

Within four weeks, the offices were picked out, furniture and décor ordered, and the remaining staff was hired. Logo business cards and forms were printed. It was all coming together just as Jace, Jr. planned.

That was the start of how they'd come to be the team that was before them today. After sixteen years of building, scratching, expanding, and challenges met and conquered, they were like a well-oiled machine.

Then the news that Jace, Sr. had passed from a stroke hit them. He was just 72 years old and it was such a shock as he was in excellent shape. They had not expected their day to day operations to be greatly affected as Jace, Jr. was the only living heir to the fortune. They were meeting with the corporate attorneys the night before to form a plan for changing things over when yet another bomb had been dropped.

Carol was just as shocked as anyone else in the room. Jace, Jr. had walked in the meeting in jeans and a dress shirt. His blackish brown locks reached just below his collar giving him that last little bit of rebellion against the system. However, jeans at a formal, legal meeting was just not like him. It seemed a bit too casual and didn't show the seriousness Carol felt he should give at a meeting of such importance. She made a note to speak with him about his attire later when it was over.

Everyone seemed to have arrived and was sitting around the massive boardroom with legal pads and pens to take notes when the doors opened one last time.

As they all turned their attention to the door, in came the of those needed to begin the meeting. When Carol heard the gasp, she turned around and her mouth was on the floor with shock, along with everyone else in the room. The only ones who weren't in a state of shock were the newcomers, Angela and Jason, as well as the lead attorney.

"What the hell? You have some nerve! How could you betray me like this? You signed a contract. Jace would not approve of you showing up now and bringing this shame to his family," Carol seethed with her upper lip all but curling up in rage.

"Family is precisely the reason I'm here," Angela began softly. "It was strictly Jace's wishes that our other son, Jason, be given the same privileges as his brother, Jace, Jr. I was not then, nor am I comfortable now with wealth. I specifically asked not to be left any money. I only requested that the home I purchased years ago with my own money, be left outside of these proceedings. I didn't know if it would affect things because Jace had lived in it for the past 42 years," Angela replied tearfully reaching into her bag for a Kleenex to wipe her eyes.

"Well this just takes the cake," Carol spat. "I gave you a chance to turn your life around and you were paid rather handsomely for your contribution. Not to mention the contract you signed and agreed to, said you would no longer have contact with my family." She stared at Jason with rage and awe.

Angela smiled and looked over at Jason. "I have not had contact with your family, Carol. I have raised *my* child away from the spotlight and your realm of life. We simply went about living our life. Jace chose to come to the island where my property was and spend time with me and his first born, Jason."

"First born? Oh, you've got to be kidding me!" she screeched. "You decide to keep a child that was conceived under contract for a surrogate pregnancy, to carry *my* child to term. You have no legal right to that child for one thing, he should have been given to us along with Jace, Jr. Not only that, but apparently you broke the contract by not following the agreed upon terms. You were to abort any other fetus than the one that you would carry to term for us." She paused and looked over at Jace, Jr. her pride showing in her child. "We told you we wanted Jace, Jr. to have the most optimal conditions during the pregnancy. So you not only broke the laws of the agreement, but you have a second child and decide to keep the first born for yourself. You can't possibly believe this is going to work. What were you expecting to gain?" She glanced over at Angela with a sneer. She was so angry it was surprising that steam wasn't coming from her mouth.

"If you had been listening to what I said, Carol, you would have heard me say that Jace chose to come to the island where my property is located and spend time with our son. Yes, *our* son." Holding her head high, she refused to be bullied. She had dreaded this day ever coming, but the time was now and she would stand up for her child. "It was Jace who made the decision for Jason to go with me and he took the smaller of the twins, Jace, Jr. home with him. He specifically said that if one of the children were to have health issues, he felt that child should be with him so he could receive state of the art, medical care," she huffed out. "So, you see it was Jace who made that decision, not myself. Just as it was Jace's decision not to let you know about the second child. He loved spending time away from your real world as you so amply call it, to get away to the island and enjoy life and his other son." She said at a much higher octave so that everyone knew she was following Jace's wishes. "Jace wanted it this way, he said that Jace Jr. would have everything money could buy, but that his first born, would be raised like a regular person and not be arrogant or self-entitled. After reading the papers and being told over the years of Jace, Jr.'s actions, I see what he was talking about."

Jace, Jr. spoke up in defense of his mother and himself. "Now wait just a minute here. I have been clean and sober for almost seventeen years now. I agree I made mistakes when I was younger, but I am not that same person anymore and it's not my mother's fault. That was my doing."

"I am aware of your turn around," Angela said with a smile of pride on her face for her youngest child. "I only ever wanted the best for you, Jace. I'm truly happy you turned it around."

"So, let's back up and explain to me how this started," Jace, Jr. questioned.

Angela began the story of how she had met Carol who was looking for a surrogate mother. "Carol didn't want her husband to know she no longer had viable eggs, so she agreed to pay a half million dollars if I would donate my eggs in secret. She wanted her husband to think the baby was theirs. A few months before you were born, your mother sent me off to a spa until delivery and it was then, your father and I became close. He came each and every day to check on me and the status of the babies. He knew almost from the moment I did that it was twins. After fertilization and implantation, one of the eggs split and became twins. My early test had shown there was only one viable pregnancy. Your father and I spent so much time together that we grew to care for one another. After you boys were born, I moved just as I had agreed to under the terms of the contract. Who was I to say that Jace could not come and see his other son?" She gave a deep sigh and wiped fresh tears from her face. "Jace and I eventually fell deeply in love and raising our child together was very special for all of us, your father chose to split his time between the two homes and two sons. He didn't want to show any difference with you boys and so he was adamant about equal time. He was also very strict to maintain exactly six months to the day in both homes, so that residence could be proven. He owned the plantation adjacent to mine so there would be property in his name. He never lived in it, however, and let the plantation manager and his family live there as part of his salary."

It was then that Jason chose to speak. "I grew up an only child of a couple that was truly and deeply in love. I was not aware that I had a twin brother until I was fifteen years old and saw your picture when he asked me to pay the gardener with cash from his wallet and I saw the pictures. I wonder at times if he didn't know how to tell me so he had done this on purpose to get it over with." He paused and looked at Jace, Jr. "You need to know it was not mine or our mother's idea to fight for any inheritance for me. Our father felt that if he passed, he wanted both of his sons to be a part of his legacy." Jason looked over at his mother seeking approval over his confession.

The two were extremely close and had a bond that was not often seen in this generation.

After hours of back and forth discussions and mediation, the case was settled out of court. Jace, Jr. had convinced Carol it would be best for the company as a whole, and to be honest, he wanted to learn more about Angela and Jason, both. He reminded her that since

Angela owned her own estate, that if Jason were to get half of the inheritance, it would actually leave him with a larger share as he would inherit his mother's estate as well. Carol fumed, cried, and pouted, all to no avail. The mediator was strictly business, and it didn't change his view one way or the other. The estate would be divided with Jace inheriting all the business that was controlled from the U.S. and Jason inheriting everything that was controlled elsewhere.

Carol knew that the majority of the Johnson estate was within the U.S. borders, so she was content. Angela, whom Carol insisted not speak during the negotiation part of the proceedings, never said a word, simply choosing to sit back and watch. Knowing that things owned in the states would not necessarily be controlled out of that portion of the estate, she felt safe and strong. It was true that as a "mistress," she wasn't entitled to any portion of the estate, where as Carol who was his wife should be.

Sadly, the estate was not split into thirds, but evenly between the two sons per Jace, Sr.'s will. Had Jace, Jr.'s attorney been on his toes, he would have researched where the home offices and funds came from, for each individual property. Choosing someone from his college fraternity had not been the best option in this case. Former jock turned attorney, Mr. Simpson had phoned in the majority of his cases and relied on his assistants to do most of the research. This time, research had not been completed, however good ole Jay Simpson felt so confident he could sway the negotiations in his favor, that he didn't let it delay the proceedings. That ended up being the proverbial straw that had broken the bank. After all the papers were signed and each party went their own ways, the papers were sent with exact figures. It was then that Carol and Jace got into a heated argument.

"How could you be so inept? You should have hired the best attorney in the field, but no, you chose to hire one of your fraternity brothers from college who did the same thing as you, and phoned it in. He was totally incompetent. He should have had all these facts on paper and charted so you could see exactly where each holding was funded and operated from. Not to mention that I was not even considered in these proceedings. I was married to that man for over fifty years and was left nothing. Not even a fund to take care of my personal expenses and household help. Although, I know you will not let your mother go hungry now will you Jace, my dear?"

"Mother, you have some nerve. You actually bashed me and kissed my ass in the same paragraph. I did do research and Simpson and Simpson have amazing stats winning cases like this. I have no idea what happened this time, he just dropped the ball. I am trying to see if we can get this thrown out of court so I can contest the ruling. Although the papers we signed did say we wouldn't fight any ruling from the moderation, this is not the normal outcome. Surely any judge who knew Daddy, will not let this stand. I'll have another firm get on things right away."

"Excuse me, Mr. Johnson. My name is Celeste and I am the paralegal for the Simpson firm. I just wanted to let you know that in this state there has never been a case won contesting the outcome from a case that has been through moderation. You, however, are more than welcome to try. I can have all the paperwork and today's transcripts delivered to your office later today if you would like."

Jace's face was a bright red as he turned to Celeste and ground out between gritted teeth, "That would be acceptable." Wishing he had allowed Julia to look over the paperwork, he tried to calm himself. She had a legal eye and would have caught all of the strange goings on. He had feared his feelings might be obvious if she were to spend any time with him around his mother, so he decided to leave her out of it. That was a whole box of worms he was not ready to purchase just yet. He was exerting all his effort into resisting an employee harassment suit as it was. He didn't know how much longer he could keep this in check.

6

All through the rest of the day and night, Jace and Carol had been on the phone with legal firms trying to find one that would even agree to represent them in court. No such luck. Moderation sealed the deal.

When Jace arrived at the office the following afternoon, his first move was to have his department heads in for a meeting. "Christy, I need to call an emergency meeting of the board. I want everyone in the conference room in an hour. That should give those who are working in the field ample time to make it in. Tell them this is absolutely mandatory and no excuses will be tolerated."

"You got it, Jace. I'll take care of everything." Which put Christy into rush mode making sure all needs would be met if the meeting should last any amount of time. There would be a meal catered if the meeting ran after 6:00pm. Two hours later fresh drinks would be brought in and refreshed along with a bit of a snack. When she got off the phone with the last of the preparations it was just moments away from time for the meeting to begin.

⁓

A few hours later...

"Wow Julia, can you believe this? What a turn, huh? I never would have anticipated this," Christy said with a face that was almost the color of a piece of paper.

"Do you want to get the memo typed up for the employees or would you like for me to take care of that?" Julia answered. She always found herself looking for more ways to spend time with Jace. She had been drooling after him for sixteen years now. If she had a bit of guts, she would have acted on it before now. However, being raised old-fashioned, there was no way she was going to make the first move. With how upset he looked, all she wanted to do was hug him and take away the stress.

"No, I have it. I feel like I owe it to them," Christy muttered, she still was totally blown away by the way things had worked out.

"Wow, what a day," Julia sighed.

"You can say that again. Did you have a single moment off your phone after the memo went out? I know my phone didn't stop until I turned off the ringer and sent all calls to voicemail," Julia sighed from exhaustion. "How did everyone on your end seem to take the news? Everyone I talked to was floored and beyond shocked. We all just expected everything to go to Jace, Jr. when that time came."

"Yeah, quite a switch up, isn't it?" Christy mused. "Can you believe we actually work for this secret twin now? And did you see him in that meeting? He is a dead ringer for Jace. Talk about a shocker. Finding out you don't really belong to your mother, you have an identical twin, and your father has been having an affair for over forty-three years all at once. That would have certainly turned my world upside down. I couldn't help but feel sorry for him," she lamented

"Yeah, it was certainly the turnaround of the century. I expect to see a story in the Wall Street Journal by tomorrow," Julia shook her head in amazement.

"I wonder what this Jason is like. Anything like Jace, you think?" Christy asked in a total state of confusion.

"Obviously in looks they couldn't be more alike. They even have a similar haircut and they had never seen one another before yesterday. However, in personality, I don't think they could be any more different. Jason seems to be so regular. He doesn't have Jace's light in his eyes. Have you ever noticed how they twinkle when the light hits them just right? This Jason is just one of the people, I guess. Plain."

"I have to agree with you there," Christy blurted out quickly. "Oh, excuse me, I didn't mean for that to come out that way. You know I have every respect for Jace. We have worked together for so long and I feel like I know everything about him. It's just that Jace could use a dose of manners with his wisdom at times, don't you think?"

"Who wouldn't agree with you there? It's obvious that Jace was brought up with privilege and standing. He has self esteem, where this Jason guy, was brought up as one of us regular folks. I think this will be a reality switch for Jace and I imagine for Jason, as well. For all intent and purposes, their lives are switching. The properties and businesses in the Bahama islands are controlled from the offices here in Atlanta. Then all the properties and businesses that are controlled in the States are controlled from the Bahama's. So I guess each of the brothers will see what it is like in the other's shoes, huh? Do you think old man Jace had this in mind all along?" Julia wondered aloud.

"I do believe exactly that. Each will grow to see what the other is like from his operations and choices," Christy smiled at the thought of old man Jace planning this in his head. Secretly wanting his twins to know one another, but not until he was away from the fallout. She chuckled at the thought.

"What a sneak. I totally would never have guessed this from him."

"Well, I think it was extremely mature for them to agree to this test. Each will be stepping into the life of the other for six months. Each will interact with a mother they never knew and learn a new side of the business, as well. They both might just learn something, especially if they take the time to ask the assistants. I mean we do the actual work anyway," Christy said, her voice sounding more melodic by the second. She was truly enjoying the change of events.

"Well, Christy, why don't you tell me what you really think?" Julia chuckled "Listen, I am a huge fan of Jace and I believe in him. Besides that, I have always had a bit of a crush on him." She finally expressed the feelings that had been simmering for sixteen years, to the day when they had met. It was a huge step for Julia who was all business and never showed her personal side.

"I admit he is exceptionally nice looking, but his attitude has always thrown me off. I mean he has never been anything but generous to me, or even us in general, but I have always known my place with him. I would never fit in his circle and I know Shelby wouldn't. I have to put my child first, because there is no one else in this world who will. I couldn't take a chance on falling for a guy who doesn't love children."

"Don't even pretend that is it. Christy, you know that your strict relationship with God would never allow you to fall for a man who didn't have the same feelings and goals as you do," Julia corrected.

"I admit it, my faith is all that has gotten me through these years of being a single mother. I really struggled doing it all by myself and my church is like my family. They support me and help me bring my child up the way I was, to put God first in everything."

"We all have different taste and beliefs, that's what makes the world interesting. It might be boring if we were all the same," Julia pointed out.

"That is one thing that we most certainly agree on." Christy looked over and again thanked God for Julia in her life. She had adored her the moment they met. She never made a commitment to God a requirement of her friends. She wouldn't isolate herself that way. She viewed Julia like a younger sister. She truly cared about her and wanted to share her greatest gift with her, but certainly wasn't going to force her to take it.

"Make sure you stay in contact with me over the next few months, okay? I know you will have your hands full helping Jace adjust to this major change. I will be praying for you. I'll be praying for myself as well. I admit, I am a bit scared too." Staying here and helping Jason learn how things were done in the states would be a challenge she hoped she was ready for. She would really miss seeing Julia every day, plus she had no idea what her new boss' attitude would be like. She just had to trust her faith to pull her through it.

7

Five months later...

"Hello? Yes, I'm calling for Julia is she in? Yes, I will hold."

"Christy, is that you? Please tell me that is you. I need you so bad," Julia gushed into the phone the moment she picked up the receiver.

"I would certainly hate to be in your shoes right now, if it weren't me," Christy laughed. "What do you need? I got your message and this is the first chance I have had to call. So spill."

"Oh, Christy, it happened. Finally! Can you believe it? I am just over the moon. It was more than I ever could have dreamed of and I just had to share it with my best friend."

"Apparently I need information here because if it's what I think it is, you've been holding out on me," Christy said, taking a seat to listen to her best friend gush.

"I was afraid to say anything till I knew it was real. I kept feeling like it was, but then thoughts would run through my head and tell me it was all my imagination. It couldn't be real. I mean I dreamed about it a million times, well I guess you could say I day dreamed it, cause I was awake most of the time. Then, last night we were closing up the office after the board meeting and when I was cleaning up and shutting everything down for the night, Jace came back in. I thought he was going to say that I had forgotten something or give me a list of things he needed done this morning, but I was wrong. He told me that he really appreciated how I have been here for him during this transition, how it was nice to have someone he could count on and knew had his back. Stepping into this side of things he didn't know the people and players and how they worked so it was like driving with a blindfold. He actually said he couldn't have done it without me. I mean I was totally blown away and thinking okay here it comes, I am going to get a good raise. I mean I did give up my apartment and move basically to the other side of the world to help him."

"Yeah, you most certainly did. Does this mean he gave you that raise you were hoping for?"

"No silly, it means that he admitted he can't do this without me by his side. We have been growing closer. We were both in a new country and didn't know anyone. We felt like outsiders for a bit, as if everyone was against us, so we basically only had one another to count on. We have put in a lot of long hours and worked through many meals. Then, the other night he kissed me."

"What? How could you not tell me this the moment you got to your room?" Christy screeched joyously.

"I wanted to, but I was scared he would tell me it was a mistake the next morning. We had worked like eighteen hours that day and had a few glasses of wine at dinner. I was scared he was going to say it was a mistake. I mean the way he looked afterward was one of fright. I was just hoping he wasn't going to fire me."

"As if! He isn't going to take a chance on losing the best thing that ever happened to him, well, besides me, that is," Christy said with such drama there was no way you could think she was doing anything but teasing her. "Okay, so go ahead, tell me the rest. I am dying here."

"Well, this morning he called me into his office the moment he got in. I grabbed my note pad and went in. I admit, I was very apprehensive. I sat down and then jumped right back up and asked him if he needed some coffee or anything before we got started. He actually laughed at me and said I just needed to calm down. I think my knees were quivering at this point. I sat back down for myself as well as for the humiliation level in the room. Grabbed my pen and stared at my pad waiting on him to start. I heard nothing, nothing, and more nothing. I finally looked up and he had his elbows on the desk with his hands tented together, and was looking straight at me. I couldn't help but giggle. I was so out of my depth here. How was I going to pay off my college loans if I was fired? My mind was racing over how much money I had in the bank and how many months I could survive before I would have to have another job. Then he cleared his throat and said he wanted to talk to me about last night. I could barely swallow, my throat was so dry. It felt like it was hours before he continued and I was still contemplating would my savings last longer here on the islands or should I fly back home. I mean, rent is low here, but if I was back home I could stay with my dad until I found a job, and I didn't know what I was gonna do. Then he said it." Julia hadn't taken a breath for what felt like an hour.

"Said what? If you don't tell me in the next five seconds, I might fly over there just to smack your bottom, now give!" Christy screeched, not caring if Julia needed air for the next part.

"Well, he said he was in love with me silly," Julia sighed. "It was just the most amazing moment in my entire life. He said that he had been trying to convince himself that it was because he was out of his element and I was the only thing left of his former life. He didn't want to make a step until he was sure it was for the right reasons. I mean, we both know he was no saint when he was in college and his reputation with the ladies had always been something for tabloid gossip. I truly just didn't know what to say. My mouth must have been in my lap because he said, well aren't you going to say anything? I just blurted it out, all of it. Every single time I had wanted to make a pass at him, every time I thought he was going to make a pass at me. Every idea for our future, that had crossed my mind. Why I had not dated anyone seriously since I had started working for Jayco. I was talking so fast, it's amazing he even understood what I was saying. He pushed his chair back and came around his desk and stood there just inches away from my face. We were both staring at one another. Not sure who should make the first move. I know he had to be as scared as I was. I mean, I know I was shaking all over. I almost wanted to stop to pinch myself to see if this was a dream. Then he did it, he leaned in and that was all the invitation I needed. I all but attacked the man. We were groping one another like teenagers. I couldn't get enough of his taste or smell, I just wanted to be consumed with him in every sense of the word. That's when he did it."

"What! What did he do?" Christy blurted out.

"He pulled back and pinched himself. He actually pinched himself. Just as he started to explain he wanted to see if he was dreaming. I couldn't help but giggle. I mean school girl giggle. It's so embarrassing when I look back on it now. I just couldn't help myself. He had been dreaming about me, too. Then he did one of those deep sexy chuckles that he does. You know the one I mean. He just stood there looking deep in my eyes and smiling that so sexy smile of his, you know what I'm talking about, I know you've seen it. Then he kissed me again. It felt like we were lost in one another and neither wanted to find the way out. We started talking about our feelings for one another. Can you believe it? He actually said he had been wanting to ask me out for over sixteen years now. I just can't believe it. He sat down in the chair next to mine in front of his desk and we just talked. We talked for over four hours straight. Every doubt we had about one another was erased. We talked about what we wanted, for the next six months, what we wanted for the future, what we thought everyone was going to say or think. We each talked about how many kids we wanted to have one day. He told me the song he wanted sung at our wedding. I jerked back and said wha, what? And he said, well you can't think I am going to let you go after all of this can you? It has been the absolute best day of my life. Which brings me to why I am calling."

"Okay, you are gonna have to slow down just a little bit here, Julia. You're talking so fast my brain is having trouble keeping up with you. Do you mean you weren't calling to tell me you were getting married?"

"Actually no, I was calling to ask you to be my Maid of Honor. Please say you wouldn't mind flying out this weekend. I know it's short notice, but you can bring Shelby with you. The island is so amazing. Shelby would love it and I could show you the sights here. The people are so nice. They really had to have resented us at first, but in no time at all, they saw that we weren't there as the evil villain. Then, we started really working together and we have achieved so much in such a short time." She paused for a second and then added, " Anyway, I am letting my excitement get the best of me. Please say that you can come. Oh please, please? I just can't imagine getting married and you not being here. What do you say?"

"Yes, well of course, I say yes. I can't wait to get there and fill you in on what's going on here in the states."

The end.

Time is on Their Side
D.E. Roraff

Timothy Edwards met Theia Roberts in kindergarten, but it wasn't love at first sight. Well, that's the story for Theia, but for Timothy, he knew she would always be the one. Many might say that's way too young to understand the concept of love, let alone feeling there will never be someone else for you. As unexplainable as that might be coming from the mouth of a seven-year-old boy, Timothy just knew. He told his mother after that first day that he had met an angel. She laughed and most likely dismissed it, but that day would replay in his head till his dying day, without fail.

Sometimes, the simplest of memories defy the ravages of time, because it means more to us than we will ever truly know.

Timothy would spend the next two years trying anything he could to get the attention of Theia without much success. She was kind to him, but every other kid was vying for her attention as well, so time together was limited. He relished in their play time and she seemed to be okay with it, even occasionally smiling back at him for apparently no reason and talking to him as well. Those moments, few and far between, elevated his mood for days to come both in school and at home. He became brighter around her, even if just for a few minutes, and could take on anything life threw at him, even the sudden death of his mother.

Timothy had made friends in the past year and a half of school, but when his mother suddenly died one Sunday afternoon, he found himself alone in the world. Yes, his father, Walter, was still there, but when it came to people his age, there were no calls or people stopping by that week. Children that young typically didn't understand such a thing.

~

At the funeral that Thursday afternoon, not even his teacher was in attendance. Just as loneliness was truly surrounding him, Theia's face stood out in the crowd, lifting his spirits just enough to keep him from falling apart. During the somber events of the day, she was almost always within eyesight, not quite smiling but rather showing a level of respect that kept Timothy from crying so much. Timothy didn't know it yet, but her presence that day meant the world to him.

After the service, there was a luncheon where they finally had a moment to chat, even though there wasn't much to talk about. Theia was quiet and respectful as Timothy didn't have much to say besides to thank her for her kind words and for showing up. During their chat, they discovered that their mothers had worked together. While that was the real reason Theia was there, Timothy was still pleased to see her. It might have been too early in his life to learn the harsh lesson, but it was on some of the worst days that a person learns who their friends truly are, and Theia seemed to be his only true friend at that moment.

Timothy tried to be friendly to others the following week at school, but knowing that none of them cared enough to show up, he quickly became distant to them. A few at least tried to give their condolences, but to him it was too little, too late. He would retain one close friend, Theia, the rest of that year until their induction into the second grade, which would open up the floodgates when it came to their peers.

They had a summer before them to explore and grow together.

Walter would almost always have a weekly visit from Theia's parents, Alice and Edmund. While Alice and Clara weren't that close, her death prompted the Robert's family to look in on Walter and young

Timothy out of respect and concern. Walter, a former military man, was terribly shielded from his emotions, but deep down welcomed the company as it distracted him from his own pain. Timothy also was happy to see these regular visits as it allowed him to see Theia more often as well.

Walter would often host some sort of cookout that lasted a few hours on the weekends. Those gatherings eventually turned into the entire afternoon that drifted into the evening as the adults played cards, talked, and generally did everything they could to have a good time. Timothy and Theia became closer over the course of those weekend gatherings.

Timothy was unsure how Theia felt about any of it, particularly the future, but then again what do seven-year-old kids know about love beyond their family?

Timothy and Theia met up the first day of school that fall in the hallway, but they had different homeroom classes. Despite their separation, they would still have lunch together and would often hang out before and after class. Their parents continued their weekend visits, bringing the families quite close that fall. With the holiday's only months away as well as the anniversary of Clara's death, there was talk of the families celebrating the holidays together. It made sense to the adults as Walter and Timothy were still adjusting to life without Clara.

~

Timothy and Theia also liked the idea and they each set about thinking of the perfect gifts for one another. Without having their own money, two seven-year-old kids had to think of some wonderful things to give to one another that required effort instead.

Timothy used what he knew about Theia; ponies, the color green, and an admiration for rainbows to make a large picture for her, complete with cotton ball clouds, glitter, and several ponies of various colors. He spent several weeks on the picture just before the holidays, making sure it was as perfect as possible. He worked from the time he arrived home from school till bedtime each night and kept it hidden away from sight when Theia and her family came over to visit. Proud of his work, he finished it off with a bow and his initials in the bottom corner. He anxiously awaited the holiday to come so he could show her the picture and couldn't wait to see what she had for him.

With the holiday celebration in full swing, there was a feeling of looming remembrance of Clara. Especially Walter, who was letting his emotions show more as the night went on, which left the kids to their own devices a fair amount of the night while Alice and Edmund did their best to calm Walter and keep him in better spirits. It was during one of those times where Walter was sitting in the kitchen flanked by Alice and Edmund that Theia decided to give Timothy his gift.

With a smile Timothy had grown accustomed to, she said, "Here Tim, why don't you open this? It's from me to you and your dad."

Timothy was intrigued by her gift, but had an idea what it related to when she said it was for both him and his father. Crudely wrapped by Theia herself, it was heavy and awkward, but beautiful already because she did it herself. Tearing through the paper, he found a candle, adorned with fake pearls and other knick-knacks that served as a reminder of his mother. There was lace that was strikingly similar to that of Clara's wedding dress, a red crayon because of her obsession with the color, and even a pair of sunglasses that looked amazingly like the ones she always used to wear despite being a facsimile. Timothy felt like crying, not out of pain, but for the joy and consideration Theia put into the gift.

Before he said anything, he ran off, leaving her confused until he came back with her gift trailing behind him. Wiping away his residual tears, he presented his picture to Theia and watched as her face lit up. She scanned over the picture with great care, taking in every detail as if her very existence required her to do so. Timothy occasionally glanced down to his candle. They both failed to realize that their parents had crept into the room and were watching the two of them with adoration. Theia finally put her picture aside and crawled towards Timothy, giving him a big hug and a kiss on the cheek. Timothy blushed and thoroughly enjoyed the moment far more than he ever let on. For the rest of that night, the two kids would be inseparable, even falling asleep next to one another when the hour got late.

For the rest of the year and into the next, the two young souls would grow together, meeting up more often than once a week, doing homework together, sharing their day over lunch and even playing together at the park both after school and on the weekends. Kismet is what some might call this, friends through thick and thin that could not be shaken. Then during their third year of elementary school, Walter was offered a new job over a thousand miles away.

Walter didn't want to uproot Timothy, but with the death of Clara still hanging onto him and job prospects locally coming up short, he had to do what was necessary for them to survive. With a heavy heart, Walter knew he needed to do what he could for not just himself, but also Timothy. He discussed the issue with Timothy at length, but got little in the way of support.

Timothy didn't want a new house, a new neighborhood, a new school, new friends, but most of all, when it came down to it, not having Theia close by was the worst. He felt heartbroken almost as bad as the day his mother died. While he didn't hate his father, he made it known this change didn't sit well with him.

Timothy found himself torn away from everything he knew and loved beside his father. They were moving halfway across the country to parts unknown. Walter promised Timothy that he and Theia would have regular contact because he wanted to keep in touch with Alice and Edmund, also. While letter writing, phone calls, and even email to keep in touch would be at least something, nothing would beat playing and laughing together.

Timothy spent most of the trip writing down his travel details across the country so he could share it with Theia as soon as possible. Even after they arrived at their new home, the first thing Timothy did was get the address down and ask for a stamp. Walter obliged him, knowing deep down how much Theia meant to his son.

While Timothy was slow to make any new friends, he religiously wrote and called Theia without fail. The first six months were a bit of a blur until the holidays as he adjusted to the new town and school. Theia kept Timothy up to date about what was going on at their school and, for the time, it was enough for the two of them. With middle school around the corner, that following summer is when the test started to happen again and the distance started to get to both of them.

Timothy had a few friends after some time at his new school, but none of them held a candle to Theia. That only meant he spent most of his time trying to contact her in one way or another rather than going out with people around him. Theia on the other hand, while not happy with their separation, still had other friends around her and didn't want to be tied to the phone or computer all day long instead of going out with her friends. Eventually, it turned into missed calls, emails that weren't responded to until days later, and letters that sat unopened until it was brought up again weeks later. Timothy understood the best he could for a ten-year-old, but there was also a limit to his understanding, so the message of his care and concern got lost in the ignorance of youth.

When they did talk, the fervor to share so much often took over for rational control, leading to hurt feelings when one dominated the conversation from the other. Still, the two plowed forward, doing their best to keep in touch as they both grew apart, not just with distance, but as individuals as well. Neither of them could say for certain that they would have remained as close as they were had Timothy not moved, but both were getting old enough to understand that the exuberance of youth was fading in time as they tried to live their lives over a thousand miles apart. Yet they tried to remain those two kids back in their earlier years. Something had to give, but the question was: which would be the one to not so much pull the plug, as slowly tug on it and test the waters afterwards?

Theia would be the one to start to pull away, not out of desire for distance so much as to not be tied to Timothy's whims alone. Granted, it didn't start till her fifth grade year, but Timothy wasn't as willing to let go so quickly. It was not that he needed Theia in his life to survive, it was the feeling he got from talking to her. No one else was able to make him feel like that. It scared him to lose her, even in a small way. As the year dragged on, the distance grew between them inexorably. Timothy shut down, his grades slipped, and life as a whole took on a bleak, colorless pallor that no one was able to pull him out of. That was, until his birthday when a package arrived from Theia. While the box wasn't huge, it was painstakingly wrapped in comic strip clippings of his favorite comic. Not only must it have taken her some time to collect them all, but none of them were overlapped; each one was there to read, in full without any missing context.

Timothy's mood flipped as if it were a coin, trading all his negativity into positivity upon seeing just the package alone.

Walter watched Timothy carefully look for a place to open the package without damaging the work Theia put into it. After several complete turns and viewings from almost every conceivable angle, Timothy walked into the kitchen and came back with a knife. Carefully inserting the blade at a seam, he cut around several comics that were folded neatly at the peak before turning the corner and doing the same. After several tense cuts that one might mistake for the precision of a surgeon, Timothy had the box out of the detailed wrapping without damaging a single comic pane.

Walter nodded several times to display his pride in Timothy's patience before speaking up, "So Timothy, what do you think it is?"

"I'm not sure dad, but if this wrapping is any sign of the thought she put into it, I'm sure I will love it."

Walter watched as Timothy tore into the box, caution no longer an issue as pieces of cardboard and packing flew about the kitchen table. After digging, two more wrapped packages were left; a rectangular package slightly larger than the average book and a smaller yet more bulbous package, each wrapped in simple blue paper. Timothy opened the smaller package first, finding inside an interesting looking timepiece with two independent analog clocks. With the clocks both running at different times, Timothy glanced to the clock on the wall and saw that the right side was matched up almost perfectly to the current time, but the one on the left was set two hours earlier. Timothy began to look for a way to adjust the left side, confusion on his face before Walter spoke up again.

"Timothy, I believe Theia has the left side set to her local time, so I don't feel it needs to be adjusted, unless you want to that is."

Timothy immediately could feel the tears forming behind his eyes but held them back, "That is so awesome of her; I wonder what else she sent me."

Timothy carefully opened the next package to find not only a sealed envelope but also a leather-bound book, a bookmark, and a fancy pen. Timothy thumbed through the book to find it blank. As he opened the envelope, Walter walked over and thumbed through the book himself and nodded quietly. As he did, Timothy unfolded the paper inside and began to read what Theia wrote.

Timothy,

I wanted to send you something for your birthday to maybe make up for being so busy that we haven't talked much lately. The clock should serve to connect us at least through the implied time travel every time we do talk and so we might better schedule times to talk. The book will serve two purposes as I bought two of them. I sent you one along with the bookmark and pen, so you can write about what is going on in your days when you feel the need. The other one I kept, I will do the same, and the next time we are able to meet up (hopefully soon) we can exchange them so we can see what the other has been thinking as well as what has been going on in our lives. I know you didn't want to move, and now we can still keep in touch when time permits until we can get together to visit.

With affection,
Theia

Timothy could not hold back the tears any more as Walter stepped behind him to comfort him. After some time to collect himself, Timothy took his presents up to his room, drafted a thank you letter to Theia and wrote in his journal for the first time. He was unable to get ahold of Theia that night, but the gift alone dragged him out of his self-pity. With hard work, he managed to turn his grades around and began a new outlook on life.

Sadly, it would be four years before they would have the chance to meet up face to face again. Naturally, they both changed drastically over the years.

Winter holiday break during their freshman year of high school, Alice and Edmund surprised Theia with a trip out to visit Walter and Timothy. Walter was informed of the trip some time before, but kept his lips sealed about it.

There was nothing out of the ordinary to see the guest room prepared nor the extra food in the house because his father often had company over for his business, often working from home and saving clients the burden of having to book a hotel room. So, while the holidays were just around the corner, the preparations by Walter did not raise the suspicions of Timothy that anything was up. Three days into his winter break, early on Monday morning around the time he would already be in class, the doorbell rang.

"Dad, your guests are here," Timothy exclaimed while still lying in bed.

Walter shouted from his office down the hall, "Could you get it please, Timothy? I'm trying to finish up this last piece of work."

Timothy had become a bit of recluse in the past four years, not to mention becoming more opinionated and obstinate in his teenage years. Shambling to the front door, he didn't even glance to see who it was. He unlocked the door and turned towards the kitchen while attempting a full-body yawn. Then, just as he got his bearings, he was nearly tackled from behind as Theia bear-hugged him. Timothy almost jumped out of his own skin as he turned around to see who it was, only to hold her tight, lift her off her feet and spun her around. Alice, Edmund, and even Walter looked on with smiles as the two stayed as one for several minutes. Both let go of their inhibitions and cried, not out of pain, but the joy brought by the company of the other once again, after so many years apart.

When they finally pulled away, they spent the rest of the day hovering as close to each other as possible. Neither of them could get enough of the other as they went through the day catching up as well as sharing how their first half of their freshman year of high school was going. Later that night, as their parents started to wind down and get ready for bed, they retreat to Timothy's room and quickly, without discussion, exchanged journals.

For the next few hours, they were in different rooms, getting four years of backstory from the perspective of the other. Timothy graciously left Theia in his room and moved to the living room to read. Each of them took their time, soaking in the information; some already shared at least on the surface and other entries coming as a complete surprise to the other. As the clock moved past midnight, Timothy was just a few pages from finishing up when a whisper from above him pulled him away from his reading.

Theia's voice softly filled the air around him, "Timothy, are you done by chance?"

Leaning his head back, he could see Theia overlooking the banister in a t-shirt and pajama pants. Looking back to the book and thumbing through it he looks back up to respond to her.

"I have maybe ten pages left, but if you want to talk, it can wait."

Theia bit her thumb as she started to fidget about, "It might be better if you finish first."

Timothy was puzzled at her response as well as her sudden actions, "What's on your mind, Theia? If it's important, we can talk about it now and I can finish this later. Are you already done reading mine?"

"I did… I want to discuss some things, but I figure I should let you finish first."

As she moved away towards Timothy's room, he closed her journal and dashed upstairs behind her. Following her into the room, she spun around, embraced him, and then without warning planted a soft kiss on his lips. Timothy, while in shock, took her cue and went along with it, resting his hands on the small of her back as he pulled her in tightly. As the two young teenagers continue to lock lips and press their bodies together, they instinctively moved over to the bed and fell onto it. A brief chuckle from Theia and a breath of air for both of them, they returned to making out beside one another, their hands boldly exploring one another.

As the time passed, hands found bare flesh and the temperature in the room rose, the sound of someone walking in the hall threw the two of them apart, Timothy found himself on the floor with a thud. Theia didn't laugh, but rather rolled off the bed to check on him only to fall atop him instead, impacting Timothy just as he got his breath back. After both the teenagers got over their respective falls and physical impacts, they both looked into the hallway to see Walter staring blankly at them from just outside the bathroom door. For what felt like several minutes, all three stayed perfectly still, barely even blinking due to the awkwardness of the situation.

Finally, to break the tension free from them all, Walter took a few short backpedaled steps towards the stairs. As he was about to disappear, he mouths the word "behave" to Theia and Timothy. The two look at one another in silence, Timothy gently stroking her hair as Theia ran her hand across him to check for any sore spots. They stayed there, occasionally kissing softly until Timothy's back started to hurt. When they got up and moved to the bed though, Theia sighed in such a way that it drew Timothy's attention.

"Theia, is something on your mind?"

She looked away before snapping her attention back to him, "I really should have let you finish reading my journal before things happened. I'm so sorry."

"Sorry? Sorry for what exactly?"

Theia got off the bed, grabbed her journal and handed it to Timothy, opening it up to the place he marked. Theia walked across the room, sat in a ball in the corner and started to anxiously bite at her thumb. Timothy was perplexed, but figured that the answer to that feeling was in the journal parts that he had not read. Theia watched on with cautious anticipation while Timothy carefully read the last few pages. The silence was thick, the air so tense someone could have hung laundry by simply drawing a line between the two as they sat there for several minutes. Finally, as Timothy read over the last page, he closed the book, letting it fall to the bed beside him as he put his head into his hands.

"Theia, why did you start something with me without saying something about this first?"

Theia spoke with a cracked voice from behind her now wrinkled thumb, "Nothing I can say will make it right, but I felt conflicted and needed to see what I might be missing back home. I never intended to hurt you with any of this."

Timothy looked up, the redness around his eyes a telltale sign of his distress, "But if you feel you are in love with someone else, why start to makeout with me?"

"Well, I…"

Timothy snapped as softly as his mood would allow, "Don't."

"But, I do Timothy. It might not seem like it, but I am deeply in…"

Timothy raised his voice a bit more that time, "I said don't… please."

Theia stood up and walked over to the bed, still keeping her distance from Timothy.

"Can we at least talk about this? I know things will never be the same, but I don't want us to be something less than friends because of this. I just needed to know if the feelings I have for you were just not an absence. We have had years apart, but every day, no matter how it might appear, you have been one of my first thoughts every morning, way too often the last thought I have before I go to sleep and constantly on my mind the rest of the day. I see something and I wonder what you would think about it. Or I hear a joke and immediately want to tell you, but we're not that close any more. This distance might have changed us both, but my feelings only became deeper, as if a part of my very being. Yes, I have a boyfriend back home, but to be fair, you still cross my mind more often than he does."

Timothy did his best to not sound snappy, but he had difficulty keeping his emotions in check, "So, why date him in the first place if you have these feelings for me?"

Theia started to cry, but kept herself poised high. "Because he reminds me of you."

Timothy laughed halfheartedly, "I'm not sure who should be more insulted by that comment… me or him."

Theia was unable to snap back despite being hurt by Timothy's words, "His name is James, but I guess I can understand why you are so upset. My feelings for you remain unchanged, frustration and all. I know this doesn't make it any easier, but I just needed to know and I do now. That might not make it easier for you to accept, but know that with all that I know now, I would change things for the both of us if I were capable."

Timothy calmed down a bit but still spoke with sharp punctuations, "So, I am just supposed to wait for you and hope in the future we can move closer to one another? I should just go on hoping that several years from now we'll do this right rather than as a way for you to test the waters?"

Theia reached out to put her hand on Timothy's shoulder, but he immediately recoiled. "I never asked you to wait for me, but in all fairness, am I not worth waiting for? I had a moment of weakness and sought comfort in another. I can't change that, but I can decide to do things differently in the future. That is, if we have any sort of a future."

Timothy looked up, stretching out from his ball like form, "I need to think about this."

"Of course. Take all the time you need, I'll just go now."

"No."

Theia stopped dead in her tracks just inside the doorframe, spinning around cautiously, "What do you mean when you say no?"

"I'm upset, but I don't want to kick you out of my room. Just as you have feelings you are dealing with, I too have to get through this. I know I can get through it on my own, but I would rather have you close because it feels like I'm home again."

Theia dropped to her knees, her hand quickly covering her face as she started to sob. Timothy, still unable to quell his own tears scooted to the end of the bed and cautiously put his hand on her shoulder.

"I feel like such an ass for making you cry."

Theia moved closer to the bed and kisses the back of Timothy's hand, "I'm not sad, Timothy. No, I'm actually quite happy right now."

"You have a strange way of showing you're happy. Last I checked, people generally only cry when they're sad or in pain."

Theia laughed as she stroked the side of her face with Timothy's hand, "Tears of joy are rare, but often mistaken for sadness or pain. You telling me you still want me near gives me hope and tells me you're not angry with me."

"I might be frustrated, confused and a little hurt, but what reason would I have to be angry with you?"

"I can't imagine how difficult this all is for you. Yet you still want me around. Does that make sense to you now that I've explained it more?"

Timothy started to gently tug on Theia, "Come here, please."

Perplexed, she looked up at him, "What?"

Timothy smiled in contrast to his red ringed eyes, "Come up here on the bed with me, please, Theia."

Theia took his hand and immediately found herself swept to the other side of the bed and under the covers before she could say a word. Timothy curled up behind her after flicking the light switch off and closing the door.

"Timothy, you don't need to do this. I'm sure I have you all twisted up inside."

"Hush now."

"But I don't..."

"Hush, please. We can sleep on it and see what tomorrow brings. Right now, I'm at peace."

Theia knew that Timothy had a point. For all the pain she caused with her revelation, there was an intangible connection that sprang to life because of it. The truth can be liberating just as much as it can hurt at times, and this was no exception.

Theia rolled over to face Timothy, putting her forehead softly against his. Within no time, their breathing matched up as they each wrapped their arms around the other, their pulses also synching up their rhythms. Then, just before Theia was about to give in and sleep, she leaned in to kiss Timothy, believing he was fast asleep. But just as her lips were about to touch his, he spoke.

"Not right now, please. I'm still confused about all of this."

Pulling back sheepishly, "Okay, I'm sorry about that."

"No need to apologize for it. You're entitled to feel how you do just as I am. How about a rain check on it?"

Theia giggled softly, "Sure thing Timothy. I'll keep that in mind for the future."

With the two of them cuddled up close, they fell asleep within minutes of one another without another word spoken. Both of them slept soundly without the slightest need to adjust their position or move from their spot. Over the course of the night, instinctively and without rousing the other, they further entwined their bodies closer to one another. For all they had dealt with the night before, a casual observer might not believe these were the two teenagers who had fought over one of them dating back home, but there it was.

Then again, there is ignorance in youth and it would be years before either of them would come to terms with the significance of that night.

The next morning, the two woke to the sound of hushed whispers coming from the doorway. Neither of them stirred immediately as they woke, realizing that their parents were most likely talking quietly amongst themselves near the bedroom door. Slightly embarrassed, Timothy finally rolled over to look at who he knew was already there. Alice, Edmund, and Walter were all there, coffee cups in hand looking down at them with a mix of emotions on their faces.

Walter was almost giddy when Alice and Edmund were not looking, somber when they looked his way.

Alice was trying her best to look a bit flustered, but showed her approval when not observed by the two men standing beside her.

Edmund was in no mood for games though, but kept his cool even though he was beginning to look quite heated about the situation.

Edmund finally could not contain himself any longer, "Theia, what exactly is going on here? What would James have to say about this were he to find out about it?"

Theia sprung up, shook to her core both by her father's voice and the audience that had gathered around the head of the bed. While she still had her pajama pants and a t-shirt on, her chest showing that the room was more than just cool. Crossing her arms in an attempt to hide the evidence, she attempted her best innocent face and started to explain things to her father.

"Daddy, we were just talking and fell asleep next to one another. Nothing happened the way you're imagining it so, please don't make this bigger than it actually is."

Theia did not realize her choice of words were in poor taste as Timothy threw the covers off in his groggy state to show he was pitching a tent in his pants. Timothy grabbed the covers to hide the sign of his morning wood, but everyone already saw it.

Angrily, Edmund spoke again as Alice attempted to calm him down, "So, nothing happened you say? Do I look like I was born yesterday?"

Theia got out of bed, careful not slide over or get too near to Timothy after her father blew up about the situation. After her feet hit the floor, Theia took it a step further to quell her father's anger.

"Dad, we never discussed where I was supposed to sleep since you and mom were in the guest room. Also, if this is a question about my virginity, I still am your little girl. We just slept next to one another, okay?"

Edmund was immediately disarmed, right around the point when Theia dropped the word virginity into the mix. Walter does his best not burst out laughing, quickly turning and walking away before he did. After several more minutes of peaceful conversation, Theia departed from Timothy's room to give him some time to think about their situation. After racking his brain a bit, he dressed and headed downstairs for breakfast. It was a quiet affair as was to be expected. Edmund, while calm, kept eyeballing Timothy, especially when either of the two teenagers so much as glanced at the other. This mood persisted the next few days until Christmas Eve night after everyone started heading to bed.

Timothy was just about done getting ready for bed when he heard a whisper from the hall.

"Timothy, can we talk please?"

Timothy scooted out of the restroom and into the hallway, dragging Theia with him quietly as his head darted around like he's looking for an attacker.

Quietly, but with strain in his voice, "Theia, I have no problem talking, but what about your father? He's barely let us be in the same room the last few days, let alone close to one another like this."

Theia glanced out of the door and down the hall to the guest room, "He drank enough tonight to keep him out till morning, but just to be sure I stuffed some spare pillows underneath my sheets to make him believe I was fast asleep."

Timothy strained and stretched, looking down the hall towards the far door, "That's great, but why are you here right now… in the middle of the night?"

Theia started to slide into bed beside Timothy as he attempted to protest halfheartedly, "Theia, your dad is still not happy with me… this isn't a good idea."

Theia frowned as she continued on, "Timothy, I want one last chance at this. I want to feel you beside me again, unless you are uncomfortable with that."

Timothy let his head hit the pillow as he surrendered to her request, "Okay, but you need to be out of here before your father discovers you here and I get buried in a shallow grave out back."

Theia was already snuggled in, almost half asleep already, "He wouldn't do that to you, because I wouldn't let him."

"You say it like you can stop him."

But Theia was already asleep, comfortably smiling all nuzzled in close. Timothy did his best to not let her warm breath on his neck cause him any sort of discomfort and closed his eyes as well. In the morning, he woke to find Theia was already gone. She had slipped out without disturbing him. He could hear everyone else downstairs happily talking and decided to join them. Theia was quiet, she kept shooting him glances layered with timid smiles the rest of the day. They didn't get a chance to speak again till later that night when she and her parents were getting ready to head back home.

Standing by the door as she was about to walk out to the car, Theia hugged Timothy and put her mouth by his ear, "Check under your pillow after I leave, please."

They both stood there staring into one another's eyes until Edmund called for Theia to get going. Pulling apart, they didn't separate until their hands fell loose from one another. Timothy watched from the doorway as they drove away before retreating to his room to check under his pillow. Beneath his pillow that still smelled of Theia's hair, he found the note she had left for him. Opening up the envelope, he read the note several times before putting it down.

Timothy,

I know it won't make it easier to understand, but my short time with James I realize was just to fill the void of you not being in my life as I had grown accustomed to. You were right saying it was unfair, but it wasn't just unfair to you… but all of us. It was unfair to put that on you knowing I had started a relationship back home. For James, it was unfair of me to use him to fill that void and then turn around and cheat on him. Last, I was unfair to myself because I let myself do this to two great guys because I could not deny my feelings once I saw you again.

I hope you know I would never hurt you, and I understand if there is no amount of apologies I can make. Just know I think the world of you and mistakes are made with the best intentions, even if they don't feel like it. I hope that we are still okay as friends, but no matter how things go, I wish you the best in life, always and in all ways.

With affection,
Theia

Timothy read over the note for the fifth time when his father walked up to the doorway, "So, my son, interesting couple of days we just had. Want to talk about what when on, particularly between you, Theia and her family?"

Timothy put the note down beside him and looked up to his father, attempting to keep the signs of melancholy off his face, "Nothing happened between us dad. We just slept next to one another... and kissed a bit, to be honest."

"I know, son. You two look at one another just like your mother and I did when we were younger."

"Well dad, she has a boyfriend back home, so it's not the same as you and mom."

Walter took a seat next to Timothy and put his hand on his shoulder, "Son, if you believe that your mother and I didn't have our moments where we are about to strangle one another, let me set the record straight. There are always rocky times that will test you no matter who you're with, but it's the process of working through it together, that is love."

"Who said anything about either of us loving the other dad? Sure, we care, but love might be a stretch."

"Please son, I have a few more years on me than you. I know it when I see it."

"Thanks dad, but this is not something that can happen easily. It is best I just move on and hope she is happy doing the same."

"There it is, my boy. Don't you ever forget that feeling."

~

Theia and Timothy wouldn't see each other again for the reminder of their high school years. Both would keep in contact and both would eventually find someone they truly had feelings for during their senior years. They remained in contact, not daily, but at least once a week without fail. The two talked about everything, becoming closer to one another in ways they weren't with their significant others. While this situation caused some strain in their respective relationships, they both were invested in their significant other enough to assure them that they were only friends and respected the other like family.

Both moved on to college, keeping in contact still at least once a week, no matter how strenuous their dorm life got. Through the years, Timothy became single for the better part of a year before he met Sally during one of his math classes. What started out as doing homework together turned into a romance as things moved forward with comforting grace. Theia too moved on, twice, yet when she started to date Alex her junior year, things got quite serious. Throughout it all though, Theia and Timothy never missed a week until halfway through their senior year.

Neither would admit to it, but their busy schedules and relationships were taking up most of their time. While they remained close, their lives were moving in different directions. One week went by without either reaching out to the other, and then another. After a month, they each felt the absence and felt they were responsible for the lack of communication, but neither wanted to make the first move back into the life of the other.

Theia was just weeks from graduating when she and Alex had a huge fight, resulting in throwing things to punctuate their shouting. Sitting outside their apartment shaking, Theia dialed Timothy's number as she tried to stop crying.

"Theia, could you give me one second, please?"

Theia chokes back her tears, "Sure."

After a few seconds of strange noises, a door shuts and Timothy came back to the phone, "Theia, what is going on? It's what, almost three in the morning here and even earlier there."

Theia could not hold back the tears anymore, "Alex and I had a fight and I needed to hear your voice. It… it calms me."

Timothy, still oblivious to how serious the argument was, "That's nice to hear, but I haven't heard from you in months. What would you all of a sudden contact me now? I realize I am as guilty as you, but we can't keep coming back to one another only when the chips are down. I've been concerned about you these past few months and should have reached out, but why now? What changed that you needed my voice tonight?"

Theia did her best to not feel offended by his inquiry. "I needed a stability that I don't have here right now, but if it is a problem I can talk to you another time."

"No, I don't want to let you go right now, but I would like you to answer my question. As your friend, I believe I have the right to know, even if it's not the best time for you. Why don't we shelf it for now and get back to it another time? So, tell me about this fight."

Theia paused, Timothy's words rattling around in her head before she finally formulated what she wanted to say, "No, you are right Timothy. I owe you from that time in high school and should answer your question before getting into my problems. I guess I had too much on my plate and figured you would call. I put my expectations on you and that was unfair of me on so many levels. I'm not sure where to start apologizing."

Timothy let out a soft laugh. "I believe you just apologized and I did the same. I got busy and expected you to call as well. We need to move past that though and get to the heart of the matter. So, tell me about this fight and then we can get to what you two can do to mend this break."

"You don't need to do that Timothy. It's not your fight."

"You're right, it's your fight, but I won't let you go through it alone. The floor is yours, Theia."

Theia sighed and started in, explaining the last few months in explicit detail. All the stress of school for her and Alex, the time apart due to schedules and even the added changes caused by moving in together. Timothy spoke little, letting her vent for over two hours before speaking again.

"Okay, Theia, now the tough question: what can I do to help you with this?"

Theia knew it wasn't a rhetorical question, "I'm not sure, Timothy. I just needed to vent and I believe I know what I need to do now. You are something else, Timothy. I don't know many people who would do what you just did after such an absence."

"Anytime, Theia, as long as the distance doesn't grow again, okay?"

"I'll keep that in mind, Timothy and thank you, even though I feel like I should say so much more."

"You just take care and I'll talk to you later, Theia."

"Of course... you too."

Timothy put his phone down and crept back into bed quietly. Sally rolled over half asleep and put her arm over him.

"Who called you at this hour, Timmy?"

"An old friend had a fight with her significant other and needed an ear."

"That's nice of you, but I don't remember any of your guy friends being that forthcoming about their relationships or their problems."

"That's because it was Theia and not one of the guys."

Sally's tone screamed of dismissiveness, "Oh, her."

"Please don't; we're just friends."

"So, that night in high school meant nothing to you? Odd since you can't seem to let go of it."

"Sally, you confuse nostalgia with something more. I'm with you, not her."

"Let's just sleep and talk about this tomorrow."

Sally and Timothy didn't get much sleep and Sally was still upset the following morning. Timothy did everything he could to smooth it over repeatedly to no avail. When Sally left for work after several hours of drilling him, he was left confused and frustrated.

~

Over a thousand miles away, Theia lay next to Alex after they had a long chat, and stared at the ceiling. She wondered what happened to bring her to this moment and if she actually got over her feelings for Timothy. Even after the mutual gap in communication, there was something about talking to him that no one else came close to replicating on any level.

Theia fought with herself well into the morning hours, contemplating where her heart lay and made a decision. She was with

Alex and unless everything in her life changed that would be the end of it. She still enjoyed talking to Timothy, but she had to put some of her feelings away, lest it would destroy what she had now and in the future.

Timothy was beginning to contemplate where he was too, but he was looking in different directions. Thousands of miles away and yet their thoughts both hovered around someone they hadn't seen since High school. It was a catch-twenty-two neither of them liked to be a part of yet could not deny.

For the rest of their school year, the two stayed in contact, but not weekly as they were before. Each smoothed over things with their significant others, growing closer to them as their college years came to an end. Once again, schedules as well as after college plans left the two of them unable to communicate with one another easily unless it was in passing. Adjusting to life, they start leaving messages for one another, even resorting to standard mail, writing letters and sending pictures as they would have done when they were kids. With careers on the horizon, their lives again took a turn towards significant changes.

Timothy got offered a job on the other side of the country, while Theia had an offer further south than she expected. Sally's career took her in a different direction and after serious discussion with Timothy, they decided to call it quits. Timothy didn't bring it up to Theia, but she figured it out less than a week after he moved. Theia and Alex manage to work things out and he found a position where she needed to move for her job offer. Timothy, of course, expressed his congratulations to them and life continued forward for them all unabated.

Years passed, until one day, Theia shared a picture of her with a ring on her finger. Timothy again expressed his happiness for Theia, asking for details about when they're getting married, leading to an intense conversation.

"Timothy, we're looking at a summer wedding. Does that work for you? You'll be there, right?"

Timothy waited several seconds before responding, "You two want me there?"

"Of course silly; you are my best friend after all."

"I'll see if I can get vacation around that time, but I'll make no promises."

Theia's voice dropped to almost a whisper, "If you want to come that is... I guess."

"It's not that, Theia. Work is just crazy right now with no clear sign it might lighten before then. I will do my absolute best to make it. Send me an invite and I will show my boss."

"Timothy, are you okay with me marrying Alex?"

"Two things; one, why wouldn't I be? And two, it's not my decision to judge."

"But you have an opinion about it, right?"

"A better question is, if you want to hear what I have to say about it in the first place?"

"Yes, if you would, please. Your opinion matters to me."

Timothy again took his time to speak, "Are you happy, Theia?"

"With my life as a whole, or are you talking about something more specific?"

"Whatever way suits you."

"Are you referring to Alex? Is that what this is about, Timothy?"

"If it were about that alone, would it matter? I figured asking that question as your best friend wasn't subject to gender or the past. This is your future we're talking about, after all."

"Yes, I am happy. We have our moments, but yes, overall, I am without any major complaints."

"That is all I needed to hear, then. I have to get back to work, but send out that invite and I will do my best to be there for you."

"Promise?"

"You know I can't do that, Theia. If I can't make it there I will make sure to get ahold of you after the honeymoon."

"After?"

"I doubt you want me interrupting your wedded bliss at that time. We'll see come summer."

As the year came full swing to the summer, it was clear to Theia that Timothy might not make it to her wedding. Doing her best to not be distraught, something snapped inside of her. In no time, she started to dismiss his calls and rarely responded to his messages. She never grasped why she felt so hurt by it, and looked only forward with hope and love. Alex was not perfect, but he had made great strides to change without her having to complain or prompt his changes. She was ready to settle down with him, hopefully growing old together.

When the wedding day finally came, Theia found herself peeking about looking for Timothy despite all her attempts to get him out of her mind. Chalking it up to cold feet, she did her best to put herself back into the situation and marry the man she had loved for so many years. It was just before the music started and her father was about to give her away that her phone buzzed to let her know she got a text. With only a few seconds to spare, she grabbed her phone and took a look at the message.

Timothy: Sorry for the late notice, but I just wanted you to know you look beyond beautiful as well as happy. I wish you both the very best.

Theia stared at the screen until her attendant brought her back into the present and sent her out the door to get married. She did her best to be proper and stick to the practiced behavior, but she couldn't help her eyes from scanning the crowd for Timothy. She came up empty as she reached the altar and faced Alex. Swallowing hard, she made up her mind and went through with marrying Alex without another stray thought.

After they were pronounced husband and wife, she was able to look at the crowd again, her eyes resuming her search for Timothy before she realized it. As the newlyweds walk down the aisle and out of the church, she didn't see Timothy at all. She began to question his text and if he just sent it in lieu of joining them instead. With some effort, she put the thought away and got back to her reception.

Theia soon took her new and upcoming life with ease as she danced, talked, and rubbed elbows with all their guests. As the night went on, a few start to depart and she found her new husband going off to do his own thing more and more, leaving her to her thoughts from time to time. As a wave of melancholy was about to wash over her when she heard a voice from behind her, a voice she hadn't heard much in the last year or so.

"Theia, would it be terrible of me to ask you for a dance?"

Timothy, all dressed to the hilt in a suit, stood there as she came to terms with the fact it has been many years since she had last seen him face-to-face. Without words, they fell gracefully into one another's arms and started dancing, making their way to the dance floor. As they dance, everyone watched the two of them, Alex included with silent reverence. They passed one song into the next before yet another, Alex walked over to them as the third song came to an end.

Alex did little to hide his disapproval, "Theia, who is this you're dancing with while your husband stands alone?"

Theia didn't look away from Timothy as the two men lock their gaze on one another, "An old friend that moved away when I was still in school, back home and he made it in at the last minute."

"That's great, but my parents would like to talk to us, if you don't mind."

Timothy stepped back and motioned for both of them to step away, "Don't let me intrude; my apologies for monopolizing her time."

Theia continued to look towards Timothy until she lost him while weaving through the crowd. Theia wanted to talk; she wanted to catch up with Timothy in so many ways, but never got the chance that night. While they would continue to contact one another on a semi-regular basis, it would be three kids, fifteen years, and a divorce before they would meet one another face-to-face again.

With several bags and three kids in tow, Theia was on her way back to her hometown to get on her feet again after losing her job and home. Alex had left her for another woman he met at work without warning, or cause. Stressed out, heartbroken, and generally not in the mood for anyone other than her parents, she once again heard a voice she didn't expect and was immediately uplifted by it.

"Theia, is that you?"

She paused to see Timothy there, a few bags of his own walking across the concourse perpendicular to Theia and her kids.

Theia exclaimed, "Timothy, what are you doing here?"

"I'm on a business trip actually and about to head back home. Are you and your family going on a trip?"

Theia bit her lip as she motioned for her kids to take a seat nearby. "Actually, Alex and I are getting a divorce after he decided the yoga instructor was working better for him than I was. So, I'm moving back in with my parents until I figure things out."

"I'm sorry, Theia."

"I'm not."

"Theia, do you love him?"

Theia stood frozen, dumbfounded by Timothy's comment, "What do you mean do I love him? He cheated on me!"

"I meant no offense, but my question stands all the same."

Theia wanted to punch him until she realized that his question was not implying anything so much as bringing a level of clarity to her mind. She let her guard down, started to cry, and fell into Timothy's arms. Timothy caught her, letting his bags fall to the ground with a shattering sound.

"What was that? Did something break?"

"Maybe, but it's just an object and can be replaced. I apologize for pouring salt in your wound."

Theia didn't take her tear-soaked eyes off of his bag, "Yes."

"Yes?"

"I still love him, even if I want to castrate him."

"Then you had something real, even if he wasn't able to see it or appreciate it properly."

"I could have had it better though."

Timothy put his hands around her face and gently pulled her gaze to meet his, "And you could have had it worse."

Timothy then leaned in and kissed her on the forehead as she immediately blushed. Theia looked up with a smile as Timothy looked towards his watch with a frown.

"I have to get going or I'll miss my flight, but I have something for you with me actually."

He digs through his pocket as Theia wiped away her dwindling tears, "Here you go."

Timothy handed her a plain white envelope that has most likely been in his pocket for a great deal of time. Before Theia could ask any questions, Timothy had already picked up his things and headed off to his flight, waving and shouting back to her as he rounded the bend towards his terminal. Theia put away the envelope and continued on with her kids to her parent's home. She almost forgot the envelope until she got everyone settled in later that night and her parents were already in bed.

Opening it up carefully, she found two pieces of folded paper inside; one quite old from the looks of it and one fairly new. Opening the old one first, she found the letter she wrote to him that night back over the winter holiday season after they made out and she implied her feelings for him. He had kept it all this time, possibly on his person or nearby over all the years since. On the verge of crying, she unfolded the newer note and lost control of her tears.

Inside is a handwritten note, complete with a crudely drawn pony and rainbow at the top. The whole note is written in green ink and appeared to be a bit older than it first appeared due to the date written in the upper corner; the day after she got married to Alex over fifteen years ago.

Theia,

It was good to see you today and dance with you one last time before I figure we will both have to let our lives take other paths. I wouldn't apologize for my actions before Alex came over as I feel I did nothing wrong. I just wanted one dance with you so I could say I had the honor, on that day of all days none the less. You looked happy and I didn't want to spoil anything for you so I left after you and Alex went to talk to his parents. We have never discussed that day and I feel I know why in some small way. I just hope that your life was not deterred by my actions that day or that I have harmed our friendship in any way.

I will hold onto this letter until we meet again, whenever that may be. If you continue to smile like you did that day, we might never meet again, but we did and I am grateful for that. I got to know you, I got to hold you, I slept next to you, I danced with you, and even managed to get an unexpected kiss from you. While it's not the culmination of my life, it completed me in some way to at least get a taste of what could have been.

I never said anything that night back in high school, but I'm sure it is obvious what I wanted to say as well as what I stopped you from doing. It wasn't that I didn't want to hear it, but I was not the man I am today and didn't realize just how much you truly mean to me. Maybe that's why I have always done what I can to be there for you, no matter how distant the role. I just want to know you're happy and I'll continue to live a happy life as well.

Part of me hopes this note never makes it to you, because that means your love and life was complete. If it does though, know that I am always here for you, back were when our paths began to diverge down one of two paths. Just because it has been what I imagine to be many, many years, that path never closed completely in my mind.

With admiration and respect,
Timothy

Theia took her time, crying a bit before she looked over the note again. She was stuck on what he meant near the end of it, until she realized that he might be referring to his new home after he moved back in grad school. She had never really asked him where he was even though she knew he moved several times since college. The question plaguing her was whether or not this was an invite or just his way of saying where he was. She was not going to take any chances though when it came to her kids and once again put that thought on the back burner until she was ready to face the situation with a level head.

Several years passed and while Theia and Timothy continued to talk, neither mentioned their meeting that one day nor the envelope. Finally comfortable in her own place and her kids old enough to understand, she talked to her kids as well as her parents for several months before buying a plane ticket. Packed, ready to go, and a hotel room already lined up, Theia traveled halfway across the country to see what, if anything, there still was for her with the boy she didn't grab ahold of over half her life ago. Pit in her stomach, she landed, and took a cab directly to Walter's old house.

The place looked much like it used too with additional plants and landscaping strewn about. Several deep breaths and a heavy sigh, she walked up to the door to find a note taped to the doorbell. Taking a peek, she realizes it was for her right away.

Theia,

If you are reading this, I am out back. Come find me there.

After putting her bags down, she moved past the porch and made her way around the house to the back gate. Stepping into the backyard, she walked into the garden and saw Timothy near the back of the lot tending to the plants. Walking up slowly, as well as quietly, she cleared her throat to get his attention.

Timothy turns to her and grins from ear to ear. "You came. I take it you read my note."

"Yes, but you didn't need to wait for me or anything like that."

"Who says I waited for you. It's not as if I've not tried dating since Sally."

"I know, but still, why me of all people?"

"What do you mean why you? Why not you would be a better question."

Theia stepped closer to Timothy, but kept her hands to herself, "I was happy with Alex, there was no doubt about that, but every time we talked, or the rare time I saw you, I went back to that night back here. I did everything I could and yet I could never shake the feeling inside of me."

"I know. That's why I kept myself away as best I could."

"But now I'm divorced, have three kids, and am not really in the right mindset for anything. Yet, you are standing here making me feel just like I did that night all over again. It's not fair to you."

"This has nothing to do with me, Theia. I'm not asking you to move in or do anything you don't want to. I only want things to change if it's mutual. If it isn't mutual, I'll gladly let it stay right where it is."

Theia took her hand and started to wrap hers around his. Timothy attempted to pull his hand away citing they were dirty, but she didn't care. He gave in finally and stood there watching her in the afternoon sun for several minutes before she finally spoke again.

"I'm not sure just yet, but taking me on is getting an instant family and that is a lot for anyone."

Timothy raised one of her hands to his lips and kissed the back of it before speaking, "Theia, if we move forward, I take all that comes with you. I know you're a package deal and I'm ready to move at any pace you deem appropriate, if at all. If not though, I need you to say something right now."

"I thought you weren't waiting for me, though."

"I never was waiting as I said before, but I've yet to meet anyone that compares to you. We would never be perfect together, but are we going to keep denying ourselves how we feel for one another?"

Theia stood silent as she looked into Timothy's eyes, as enough time passed for the shadows in the yard to change shape. Then, as if something sparked her, she moved forward and kissed Timothy, wrapping her arms around him tightly.

"Thank you, and yes, I want to see where we can go together."

Timothy smiled, but pulled away as he walks to a nearby table. Turning back around, he starts to fiddle with the very same clock she gave him so many years ago with the two independent faces.

Theia's eyes widen, "You kept that old thing?"

Timothy continued to fiddle with it before setting it down with both faces matching time, "I did; even had it repaired, twice over the years."

"Why would you keep it all these years, not to mention spend money to keep it running?"

"I repaired it because it reminded me of you. Some things you just can't throw away, so you fix them instead. Kind of like you and I over all these years. We're old friends that might not be those young kids, but we work well next to one another."

"I suppose I could say that you've always made time for me then, when it comes right down to it."

"I have, but I've also made mistakes with that as well. I just want to do right by you for your sake, your kids, and myself also."

"Where would we live though? I have my children to think of, too, not to mention a place of my own and a job I can't just leave."

"Theia, we can ease into this over time. I travel for work, so I really can live anywhere I choose. While I'm glad this is moving forward, I don't need everything to change by tomorrow. I've been patient about this for decades, so if we have to wait until things are better suited for a chance, I will understand."

"But having you wait isn't what I want for you. It's not fair."

"Life isn't fair, but what is time but the passage of moments. I'd rather have a few short years of grand moments with you than twenty years of moments I can't stand."

"But it could be years before we could really be together, Timothy."

"I should have said something over twenty years ago, but I choked. After that mistake, I have all the time in the world for this to be right for both of us."

"So, you'll wait? You'll adjust to me and my kids?"

"All I have is time and I give it all to you."

Under the Carousel
A.B. Martin

The sun was shining brightly through the window when Kristal awoke. She rolled over away from the blinding light and saw her two-month-old son looking at her. Jordan was her world. She had never thought she would be able to have children. After the years of physical and sexual abuse throughout her childhood at the hands of her mother's boyfriends, the doctors said she would never be able to have a full-term pregnancy. But Jordan was her miracle.

James was terrified when they had learned she was pregnant. He, too, had grown up in an abusive home. His father regularly used him as a punching bag. It was one of the things that had bonded them throughout their relationship. They had helped each other start to heal, but learning that Kristal was pregnant was too much for James. He was positive that the genes he carried would make him abuse his child just like his father had abused him. She had tried her best to reassure him, but in the end her love wasn't enough to heal the deep wounds within him and they split up when she was six months pregnant with Jordan.

After the break up, Kristal moved in with her cousin Elsie. Thank God for Elsie! She had been Kristal's best friend while growing up. They confided in each other, consoled and comforted each other as if they had been born twin sisters instead of cousins six months apart in age.

Kristal lay gazing at her son's big blue eyes as he played with his own fingers in his crib. It was amazing to try to see the world through the eyes of a child. Everything takes on so much more magic and mystery when it's fresh and new. Watching him, she imagined not knowing what your fingers are, or even that they are attached to your body. Even something as mundane as looking at your fingers holds new discoveries to a baby.

As her alarm clock went off, Kristal got out of the bed to shut it off. She scooped up little Jordan, smiling down into his angelic face. She felt like her heart would burst with love every time she looked at him. It made her a little sad that James couldn't feel the joy that being a parent brought to her. She wished she could wave a magic wand and fix the damage to his psyche so they could experience parenthood together. She missed making his meals, helping him with his college classes, driving him to work, and holding his hand. Having Jordan more than made up for it, but she was still heartbroken. She had thought she and James would be married about this time and have their entire lives ahead of them. Instead, she was a single mom and James had disappeared from their tiny hometown. He had told his brother that he needed a fresh start and had been in contact with him at fairly regular intervals. She wished for him to find peace and healing.

Kristal was working part-time to save for her own apartment while attending the local community college. After the heartache of breaking up with James, she decided to focus on making a good life for herself and her son independent of another man in her life.

After changing Jordan, Kristal walked out of her bedroom into the kitchen and started to sing to him as she poured her coffee. Thank God he was such a good-natured baby and let her wake up before demanding to be fed. He continued to play with his fingers while she sipped and contemplated what she was going to have for breakfast, wondering if she would be able to squeeze in the time to cook an omelet for herself and Elsie before Jordan demanded his own breakfast.

Elsie wandered into the kitchen disheveled from her sleep and poured her own coffee. Without looking at Kristal and Jordan, she shuffled back out of the kitchen to have her coffee alone. As Kristal heard Elsie's bedroom door shut Jordan started to fuss.

So much for Mommy's breakfast before Jordan's, she thought. She headed back to her bedroom to nurse the baby while she finished her coffee. He was a big boy, born just under ten pounds and nursed for more than half an hour before he was done. Kristal laid him back down in his bassinet while she showered and dressed for the day.

Today would be fun, she mused in the shower. It was opening day of the county fair. She and Elsie had made plans to go together. Elsie's boyfriend, Kevin, was working at the fair again this year so it would be just Kristal and Elsie wandering the midway with Jordan. Getting out of the shower, she dressed in a pretty blue and white sun dress and put Jordan in little blue shorts with a white t-shirt. The day was going to be sunny and hot with projected highs in the upper 80's. The nighttime low was only going down into the upper 70's so even if they stayed late, Jordan would be warm enough.

Just in case, Kristal packed a little hoodie and jeans set into Jordan's diaper bag. When both were dressed and the diaper bag packed Kristal joined Elsie in the kitchen for breakfast which turned out to be omelets that Elsie cooked while Kristal had been caring for Jordan. Elsie and Kristal decided to walk to the fair after Jordan had his morning nap and lunchtime feeding.

~

Kaleb awakened to pitch black in the camper. He hated being on the road working for his father. The spot wasn't far from home, but far enough that he wasn't going to drive each night after work. He long ago lost the disillusionment that most people had with carnivals and fairs. After all, he had seen the seedy underside of the midway since he was a toddler when his father bought the show.

Growing up the boss's eldest son was not all sunshine and roses. He couldn't remember a summer that he didn't work 14-16 hour days on the weekends starting in May. Then going into seven days a week from the day school let out straight until the day it started again. Every year, his friends would tell stories of camping, fishing, hiking, riding bikes, going to the beach, and playing all summer long. Kaleb never experienced the joys of summer break for himself, yet all his friends were envious of him.

On the flip side of things, he always had all the cool toys as soon as they came out. At 16, he had bought himself a brand new Monte Carlo SS and had all the girls in his class begging for a ride. He was the epitome of "tall, dark, and handsome" with his wavy dark brown shoulder length hair, eyes the color of warm caramel along with a six-foot-tall athletic frame.He was naturally athletic, but all the summers of setting up, tearing down, stocking, and working on the rides and game trailers had given his muscles definition.

Add his looks to the money always in his pocket from the long summer hours and he was never short of female company, but none had ever touched his heart. It wasn't that he was cold or uninterested, it just seemed like none of the girls he met were attractive after the first few days. He didn't want to spend his time with someone who couldn't hold an intelligent conversation. He had no interest in spending hours wandering a mall or shopping for clothes. He wanted a woman who was his equal. Someone who would disagree with him and have lively debates with him. Someone who he could share his dreams of family and home. A woman, not a girl, who made his pulse quicken and gave him butterflies in his stomach every time their eyes met.

At 22-years-old he considered himself past the age where he should have found such a female if she existed. Kaleb didn't hold out much hope of meeting his dream wife and so he was coasting through this summer on autopilot trying to decide what he would do after this season. He knew he didn't want to work for his father next year or any after that.

Dragging himself out of the stiff, narrow bunk bed, Kaleb pulled on a pair of shorts and clean shirt. He didn't need to pay attention to what he grabbed, all his shorts were black and all his t-shirts bore the emblem of his father's company. As long as the clothes were clean, they did the job. He fumbled around in the dim kitchen of the trailer and made himself coffee. Scrubbing the grit from his eyes he looked at his watch. It was 9:00 am and his father expected all the rides inspected before they opened at noon. Considering that they had finished setting up around 3 am, Kaleb thought he was doing remarkably well just being conscious at this hour. Luckily, he had showered before falling onto his bunk last night so he grabbed a bagel on his way out of the trailer, lowering his sunglasses against the blazing sun.

Respect from his father's other employees had been hard-earned by Kaleb. He worked the hardest and the longest hours of any of the crew. His father was rarely on site the last few years. So the majority of the responsibility fell to him even though most of the crew was not the type to take orders from such a young boss. It had been an uphill battle every year with each new crew.

At least at this spot, he had his cousin Kevin with him. Kevin would make sure all the games were stocked and the crew was ready to open. That cut his workload in half. They had worked together a lot while growing up and he knew he could trust him. He walked out of his trailer to begin the ride inspections less than fifteen minutes after opening his eyes.

~

Kristal and Elsie arrived at the fairgrounds just before noon. Little Jordan had eaten two more times and gotten in a good two-hour nap. Elsie was anxious to see her boyfriend, Kevin. After dating for the last three years they were normally glued together, but Kevin's work schedule over the last week had meant they hadn't seen each other since the prior week.

As they headed through the gates, they set out to find Kevin amongst the midway games. Walking by the rides, Kristal noticed a man walking the I-beam of the big wheel. The height was terrifying to her. She couldn't imagine being that high up and considered that it must take a lot of practice and bravery to do such a job.

Lost staring at the brave stranger, Kristal almost bumped into Elsie when she spotted Kevin next to the big wheel. Elsie and Kevin shared a passionate kiss while Kristal remained focused on the man working on the ride. He was climbing down through the crisscrossing metal beams of the ride as if he was walking down a smooth sidewalk. When he reached the bottom, he came over to the threesome.

"Thanks for noticing that Kev, I got a new clip in place so she's good to go," he said when he arrived next to Kevin.

"No Problem, Kaleb. This is my girlfriend, Elsie, and her cousin, Kristal. Girls, this is my cousin, Kaleb," Kevin made introductions.

Looking at him up close, Kristal felt like she was the one that had just climbed 70 feet in the air with no safety line. Her stomach somersaulted and her heartbeat raced. She had never had such a reaction, even from James who she thought she would marry. Every aspect of him physically was the opposite of James. Where James had been rail thin, Kaleb had a powerful looking body. Where James had been pale-skinned, Kaleb's skin was tanned a golden brown. She could see his chest hair curling at the collar of his shirt, James had been smooth chested; the hair looked soft and her hand itched to run her fingers through it. She couldn't see his eyes because of his sunglasses, but she would bet they were just as stunning as the rest of him. She was so lost in her attraction to him she didn't realize that Kaleb was speaking.

"...then we should all have an early lunch together tomorrow before we open." Was all she caught. It was too late though because Elsie was already saying they would both love to go. The fair was opening so Kevin and Kaleb left the girls to enjoy being spectators while they regaled the other fair-goers from the opposite side of the rides and games.

"What did you get me into Elsie?" Kristal asked as soon as the guys were out of hearing range.

"Nothing much, just lunch at the park with Kaleb and Kevin."

"I'm not going on a double date! I have a two-month-old baby, I'm not ready to go on a date!" Kristal protested.

"It's not like that, calm down. Kaleb is tired of the fair scene and just wants to spend some time with normal people. He obviously saw you have Jordan since he's right there in the stroller. I'm sure Kevin mentioned it to him before, that my cousin has a son. It's not a double date, I swear... even if you were almost drooling."

Kristal blushed, but didn't deny her attraction to Kaleb. How could she? She had no choice now anyway since Elsie had already accepted for both of them.

Kaleb didn't know what the hell was wrong with him. He swore he was done picking up girls, but when he looked at Elsie's cousin, it was like he suddenly had a fever. Goosebumps rose on his arms and he was slightly dizzy. If he hadn't climbed the wheel hundreds of times, he would have written it off to having just climbed down, but he had never had a problem with heights. It had to be this Kristal.

She wasn't his typical type. He liked brunettes, curvy with a big chest and a little waist. She was blond with blue eyes the color of denim, definitely curvy though. Nothing Kevin had told him about his girlfriend's cousin sounded like she was looking for someone like him. She had a baby. She was in college for computer programming and he had dropped out of high school in the tenth grade to work for his father. She liked being a country girl and he liked being in the city. Asking the three of them to go to lunch in the nearby park was a stupid idea he didn't have time for. But it had come out of his mouth before he even knew he was saying it.

He shook his head resolving to forget about it, and her, for the rest of the day. Maybe it would be nice to spend some time with people off the lot, but getting ahead of himself was pointless.

He continued his supervision of the rides in a better mood than he'd been in, since longer than he could remember. Every few minutes, Kristal's sad eyes found their way into his thoughts. They had been sad. Each time they recurred to him he wanted to see them smile, to take away the sadness he had seen.

When the tilt-a-whirl broke down, it didn't darken his mood as it normally would have. He went about fixing it with a smile in his face. Some of the crew noticed the difference in his demeanor, but nobody wanted it to change, so nothing was said to him. Opening day flew by with small problems here and there and occasionally, while dealing with them, Kaleb caught a glimpse of Kristal, Elsie and Jordan as the enjoyed the fair. Kristal's blond hair blew in the breeze as she laughed making her even prettier than he'd first thought. From a distance, he couldn't see the sadness in her eyes and he caught tiny glimpses of how beautiful her smile was without her being aware.

As the sun was setting Kaleb's stomach started to rumble, reminding him that he'd only eaten a bagel all day. Making sure his two-way radio was turned up he headed to the firemen's tent to get some late dinner hoping he'd have time to sit and eat before the next ride needed his attention. Standing in line, he heard the sweetest laugh he'd ever heard. He looked around the crowded space to find the source and wasn't surprised to see Kristal and Elsie in the corner playing with the baby. After getting his food. he found himself walking over to their table.

"Mind if I join the fun?" Kaleb asked.

"Actually, you can take my place while I spend Kevin's dinner break with him," said Elsie as she quickly made her exit.

Having found himself unexpectedly alone with Kristal and her tiny son, Kaleb was at a loss for words. He searched his mind for something to say that wouldn't make him sound like an idiot. Finally, he realized that the baby would be a safe subject.

"How old is he?" he heard himself ask.

"Two months and two days," she replied. He had taken his sunglasses off and Kristal found it difficult to look away from his eyes. They were the most hypnotic brown, pulling her in, making her feel warm and comfortable.

"Have you taken him on any of the rides?" Kaleb suddenly wanted to make the day memorable for her even if the baby was too young to remember.

"No, he's too little for any of them."

"I wouldn't suggest taking him on the Ranger, but he could go on the big wheel or the carrousel, I could go with you. I should have another half hour free."

Kristal considered his offer. Just sitting with him, hearing his voice was relaxing. She felt safe and cared for even though she had just met him. Jordan wouldn't remember if she said yes or no. He was too little. She acknowledged that if she said yes it would be only for herself. She wanted to be close to Kaleb. What harm could it do to take her baby on a few rides with him?

"Ok, but you didn't eat your sausage," she replied, pointing to his dinner.

Kaleb laughed, sending shivers down Kristal's spine. He picked up his sausage and finished it in three bites. He was anxious to make her smile and hear her laughter. Never had he wanted to make a woman happy as much as he wanted to make her happy. He didn't care if his father would get angry that he spent time with her instead of continually checking on the crew and equipment.

Leaving the food tent together, Kaleb led her first to the carousel. It was his father's pride and joy. He had searched for years for just the right pieces. There were beautifully painted tigers, lions, horses, and seals adorning the benches. Each animal on the carousel was painstakingly detailed and had cost his father more than any single ride in the show. Kaleb sidestepped the line and motioned Kristal to bring the baby's stroller inside the barricade. Show guests were not normally allowed to bring possessions inside the barricade but right now she was Kaleb's guest, not just any show guest. He wanted to make her feel special and safe, even if it was a tiny gesture. He didn't want her to worry about someone stealing the stroller or diaper bag hanging off of it.

When the ride came to a stop Kaleb led Kristal to his favorite bench, after she picked Jordan up out of his stroller. His father had it made when he first bought the show. It was handmade and had his parent's initials carved in a heart along the backrest. It was the only romantic gesture he had ever known his father to make in all the years his parents had been married. He offered her a hand as she stepped up onto the surface of the carousel.

As soon as she put her hand in his, he knew he would do anything for her. He felt more connected to her just from their hands touching than anyone he had ever met. If he hadn't felt the attraction before now, there was no denying it any longer. It was more than attraction though. He wanted to hold her, smooth her hair away from her brow, wake up to her, and go to sleep feeling her heartbeat against his skin. He had never believed in love at first sight. Now he knew it could happen.

He knew even before they sat down that he would make her his wife regardless of what it took. He held her hand throughout the length of the ride and played with the baby hoping to distract her from pulling her hand away from his.

When the ride came to a stop, he reluctantly let her hand go and led her to the big wheel after exiting the carrousel. She kept Jordan in her arms and he pushed the stroller. This morning he hadn't contemplated having children of his own, but now he found he enjoyed pushing the stroller next to Kristal. He enjoyed their conversation about nothing in particular. When they arrived at the big wheel, he again sidestepped the line and claimed the next empty car. He settled Kristal in the car and pulled the safety bar down after sitting and securing the safety belt across them both. Kristal had put Jordan in his carrier so he was securely snuggled against her. As soon as the ride started moving, Kaleb picked up Kristal's hand in his.

With his heart beating wildly in his chest he quickly looked up at her to see if she would be upset. As their eyes met, she smiled and continued their conversation as if nothing had changed. As their car approached the bottom, he motioned to the operator to send the wheel through another cycle so he could have more time with her. They made another three circles while she pointed out the high school she went to. The house she lived in with Elsie, and her grandparent's house. Each time they came to the top, he learned something new about her hometown. He listened intently, wanting to know every detail of her life.

The ride came to a stop and Kaleb knew he would have to go back to work. He dreaded parting with her. After she settled the baby into the stroller, they walked over to Kevin's game where they found Elsie waiting for her.

"I figured Kaleb had kidnapped you and you would show up here eventually," Elsie said good-naturedly.

Kristal turned to Kaleb and thanked him for taking the time to ride the carousel and big wheel with them. She seemed to want to say more, but bit her lower lip instead of releasing the words.

The couples said their goodnights, and then Elsie and Kristal started their walk home.

~

"I noticed you holding hands with Kaleb when you came over to Kevin's game," Elsie chided playfully as soon as they were outside the fair gates. "I thought you weren't ready to date." She wiggled her eyebrows so Kristal would know she was picking on her.

"I'm not, but it felt so natural when he held my hand. I couldn't pull away. I'm sure he's looking for a one night stand. Isn't that the way Kevin always says Kaleb is? Never stays with a girl more than a few days? I'll go to lunch tomorrow, but I can't let myself fall for him. I can't handle a one night stand. I want marriage, a good father figure for Jordan, stability… a home to raise a family in," Kristal answered, fading out as she finished her small tirade.

"Yeah, Kevin's always said what a player Kaleb is. Maybe he's changed his mind. Maybe *you* changed his mind."

"Maybe," Kristal answered, falling into silence as she remembered how it felt to have Kaleb touch her. Nothing prepared her for the feeling of safety, comfort, and longing holding his hand gave her. Even during her relationship, knowing how much she thought she loved James, his touch only elicited feelings of protectiveness and mothering within her. When Kaleb touched her, she felt her body awaken like never before. Her entire body tingled even at the sound of his voice. She felt wanted, perfect, and completely beyond any harm. Her attraction to him was intense and scary, yet she wanted to see him again. Her brain said she should avoid him; he was going to hurt her. But her body and her heart were telling her that he was different from anyone she had met. He was the one.

When they reached the house, Kristal and Elsie said goodnight to each other and went off to their own bedrooms. Kristal continued to think about her attraction to Kaleb. She missed him already. It was crazy! She had gone weeks with James out of town and it never bothered her. She had been away from Kaleb for a few hours after barely meeting him and she missed him. She knew she would quickly become addicted to his touch.

Then the realization hit her that Grandma Abby was right; what she had had with James wasn't true love. It was a shadow compared to the feelings already stirring within her for Kaleb. She could see a future with him, even teaching Jordan to ride a bike years down the road. She could even see wanting more children with this man. But she didn't even know him really. They had only met ten hours ago and spent less than two hours together. She couldn't be in love with him already. She needed to put an end to this attraction before she got her heart trampled. She crawled into bed resolving to never see him again after lunch tomorrow. After all, he would be moving onto the next town, the next fair, and more than likely the next girl.

~

Kaleb spent the night alone in the narrow bunk, laying wide awake. He tossed and turned thinking about Kristal. He wanted her badly. His body had been wound tightly since he first touched her.

After closing down, he had briefly considered seeking relief with one of the many willing groupies that always hung around, but found the idea repugnant. Just a few weeks ago he would have been delighted to spend the small hours with any of them. As he looked at them tonight he compared them all to Kristal and found they all fell short. He was in deep after no more than a few hours. He tried to sleep, but the feeling of her body next to his on the big wheel kept coming back to him. The sound of her voice whispered in his ear. He couldn't wait until 11 am so he could see her again.

~

Kristal awoke to a cloudy day. Jordan was still sleeping and the birds were chirping softly outside her window. She had tossed and turned for hours, only falling asleep around 4 a.m. and looking at her alarm clock told her that she had slept about four hours. She was going to be exhausted all day.

She quickly showered, listening for Jordan with the bathroom door open. Her mind drifted back to Kaleb. She would see him in just three hours. She reminded herself that she wasn't going to fall for him and purposefully started mentally quizzing herself on the programming material she would have to know when classes resumed next week. By then, Kaleb would be a memory. Her studies were her priority. Her college degree was the security she and Jordan needed.

Jordan was awake, playing with his toes this time when she came back into the bedroom. She threw on her robe, picked him up out of his crib and changed him. He would never pass as Kaleb's child. His coloring was too close to her own, and a mirror of James'.

Where had that thought come from? She chided herself for even considering Kaleb being a father figure to Jordan as she began nursing him. Clearing her mind while the baby ate, she again started quizzing herself on her programming knowledge.

When Jordan finished, she dressed him and headed out to the kitchen. She wasn't hungry this morning, but reminded herself she had to eat so her body would have the nutrients to nurse her son. She placed Jordan into his baby seat and poured herself a bowl of cereal and sliced banana into the bowl. Elsie must have been up for a while because she heard the vacuum going in the living room. Elsie came into the kitchen as Kristal was washing her cereal bowl.

"Do you want me to watch Jordan while you get sexy for lunch?" she asked.

"Haha, I told you I don't want a one-night stand and I'm sure Kaleb doesn't want a marriage."

"So what, go get dolled up! It'll make you feel wonderful at the very least!"

"Okay, but I'm not going to see him after today, so there won't be anything more than maybe flirting."

Kristal went back to her bedroom and carefully applied some blush, eyeliner, and mascara. Then she braided her hair and admired the finished product. She did look cute. Too bad Kaleb wasn't the one.

She left her bedroom and found Elsie already had Jordan in his stroller. Grandma Abby would be watching him while they met Kevin and Kaleb for lunch. They walked the few blocks together, discussing the neighborhood flower gardens and anything else that wasn't Kaleb. Grandma Abby met them at the door.

"Give me that sweet boy! Come to Grandma Abby, precious!" she cooed as soon as they turned down her walkway.

She met them halfway saying. "You girls don't hurry back. Me and this little man are going to have a grand date today." Without giving them a chance to respond she took the stroller and turned back to the house, obviously dismissing them.

They both started laughing and headed to the park.

Kristal saw Kaleb sitting at the picnic table from across the park and the butterflies started flying around in her stomach. She was tempted to make an excuse to Elsie and go back to Grandma Abby's, but she had never been a coward. They walked up to the table to find a feast for a crowd. The guys had brought grilled chicken, macaroni salad, potato salad, potato chips, grapes, cookies, even a pie.

"Kaleb bought out the whole store this morning," reported Kevin. "He wanted to make sure he got enough to feed us for the next week, I swear it. Along with all this food we have water, Pepsi, Coke, Sprite, and Dr. Pepper."

"Wow, I never get a spread like this. Kev, take me for a walk before we eat," Elsie said. It was obvious to both of them that Kristal and Kaleb were strongly attracted to each other and they were eager to help them along to happiness.

Kevin held out his hand for Elsie and they walked off down the forest path next to the picnic table leaving Kristal and Kaleb alone.

"Hungry?" asked Kaleb.

"No, not really, sorry. Look, about yesterday. I find you very attractive, but I'm not interested in a one-night stand. I know you aren't into long term relationships and I'm not into short term. I shouldn't have held your hand and flirted with you. I'm sorry I led you on," Kristal spit out before she lost her conviction and courage. It was awkward to blurt it out like that, but she couldn't help it.

"Sit down, please, I promise I'm not going to bite you," Kaleb responded calmly. He took her hands and led her to the picnic bench. Sliding his hands up to her elbows he said, "I'm not looking for a one night stand. I'm done with that. If that's what I wanted, I could have had it last night, from multiple willing parties. It's not and I didn't. All I could think about last night was you. I couldn't sleep. I smelled you, I felt you, I missed you, and I wanted you all night. I know we only met yesterday, but I feel like I've known you my whole life. I know I've waited my whole life to meet you. I want to get to know what makes you smile and do that every day. I want to help you take care of Jordan. I want to be there when he learns to talk and when he goes to kindergarten. I want to hold you and watch sappy movies and scary movies together. I want to go to sleep next to you and wake up with you. You'll think I'm crazy, but I want to marry you."

Sucking in an astonished breath, Kristal was nearly in tears and replied, "You don't know anything about me. You don't know how damaged I am."

"I don't see you as damaged. I know you didn't have it easy. Kevin doesn't know much, but he told me you had been abused. I want to strangle anyone that could hurt you, but it doesn't change how I feel about you. Kristal, I know it's fast. I don't expect you to say you'll marry me right now, but give me a chance, please. I spoke to my father this morning. I resigned from the show. I have an appointment this afternoon to look at houses and commercial properties. I'm staying here in town, opening my own business. What I'm asking is for you to give us a chance." He leaned in and kissed her forehead, her cheek and finally her mouth. Kristal didn't have the willpower not to kiss him back. The world faded away and the earth stood still. Neither knew, nor cared, how long the kiss lasted. Kaleb knew he'd found forever with Kristal and was determined to show her how much he already loved her, that he would provide for her and Jordan, and be the husband and step-father they deserved. Kristal felt promise, safety, hope, and home instantly.

Over the next several weeks, they were together from morning until late each night. Kaleb never pushed her. They spent hours curled up on Elsie's couch watching movies with Jordan sitting between them or in his swing. Kristal went with Kaleb to look at houses and he asked her opinion frequently during the walk-throughs.

About a month after they met, Kaleb closed on a three-bedroom house between Elsie's and Grandma Abby's as well as a garage property on Main Street. They went to dinner to celebrate, leaving Jordan with Grandma Abby.

"I'm so excited for you Kaleb, your own home," Kristal beamed at him while they waited for their entrees.

"It'll only be a real home, when you and Jordan move in with me. All you have to do is tell me when you're ready. You know I love you both. This is for when you're ready," he replied, handing her a jeweler's box.

"Marry me Kristal; let me be Jordan's daddy."

"Yes, I'm ready. I love you Kaleb, I can think of no better daddy for Jordan, or husband for me."

RECKLESS
Elle Vaughn

CHAPTER ONE

"Mae! Mae! You get your stupid, fat ass back here right now!"

Gasping for air, I stumbled down the hillside, dirt and loose gravel filling my tennis shoes as I slid, making me grimace. By the time I reached the main road, I could hear his footsteps only a few feet behind me. My face ached where his fist had collided with it and I put my hand over it as I ran. Where I was going, I didn't really know, but I was going as fast as I could.

"God damn you, you stupid whore, get back here!"

"Just leave me alone, Tim!" I yelled over my shoulder. "Just leave me alone!"

"You. Get. Back. Here," he said between his yellowed, clenched teeth.

"No!" I cried as I felt him finally grasp the hem of my t-shirt and yank me to a halt.

I awoke with a start, clawing at the covers around me. I felt nauseated and hot as my eyes searched the darkness around me. Alone. I was alone. Just like I'd been for the past six months. Nevertheless, every now and again, another one of those nightmares would come back to remind me of a time when I wasn't so alone.

Wiping my damp forehead with the back of my hand, I climbed out of bed and tiptoed to the window of my little house to get a look at the front yard. It was darkened, of course, the only light coming from the streetlamp across the street, which was half-heartedly illuminating the doctor's office that where I worked. Everything was the way it should be.

Letting the curtain fall closed once again, I sauntered off to the kitchen to pour myself a glass of water and reveled in the sensation of the cool liquid gliding down my dry throat.

"Fuck," I scolded quietly. "It's time to get yourself under control. You can't keep doing this."

Silently agreeing with myself, I began to make my way back to bed when I heard the unmistakable sound of a motorcycle engine outside. Shoving my water glass onto the counter, I hurried back to the front window and pushed the curtain aside again. A motorcycle was driving recklessly fast down the little street in front of my house.

I craned my neck, pressing my face against the cool glass as I tried to keep it in sight, but it just kept going. Probably headed into town. There was a popular motorcycle bar downtown, he was no doubt headed to. It was the only exciting thing we had going in our little town. Sighing, I let the curtain fall again and hurried back to the bed. Sleep. All I needed was a little bit of sleep. Just a few hours of uninterrupted bliss without any nightmares. That wasn't too much to ask for, was it?

"Good morning, Mae," Dr. Ainsley said with a yawn just before he lifted his mug to his lips and took a long sip.

"Good morning." Walking into the office, I felt flustered this morning already. I pulled anxiously at my hem of my dowdy flowered skirt.

"Sleep well?"

"Just fine, Dr. Ainsley."

"You know," he said, leaning his backside against my desk. "That heater has been known to go out from time to time. The nights are starting to get cooler, don't hesitate to let me know if it seems like it's not working right. I'll get someone in there to take a look at it right away." I hated asking Dr. Ainsley for anything. He was already being so generous by letting me live in his rental and work off part of the rent. It didn't feel right asking for more.

I smiled at the man. He was so handsome and kind. Soft hazel eyes and unruly brown hair. His wife was a lucky woman. "Thank you very much. I will."

He yawned again and then shuffled over to the coffee pot to pour himself another cup.

"Dr. Ainsley, you look like you haven't gotten much sleep."

He grimaced. "That's something I wanted to talk to you about."

"Yes?"

"Look, you're such a nice girl. I would never put you in a bad position."

I suddenly got a bad feeling in my stomach and I unconsciously placed my hand over it. "What is it?"

"Well, my brother came into town last night."

"Oh, I didn't know you had a brother."

He grimaced again. "I don't talk about him much."

I stood still perfectly still, unsure of what this had to do with me.

"He was pretty wasted when he showed up at my doorstep last night and he's sleeping it off now. But his life is a pretty big mess right now and he's going to need a place to stay for a while."

"Oh," I said suddenly with understanding. "Oh, I see. I can be moved out pretty fast. I don't have many things to pack."

He pulled his brows together. "What are you talking about, Mae?"

"He needs a place to stay. You need your house back so he can stay there right? I understand and I can be out of there by tomorrow."

"Oh, Mae, that's not what I'm saying at all. No, he's going to be staying in our basement over at our house for a while. You can keep living in your house. I keep telling you, that's your house. You signed a twelve-month lease. It's your place, I'm only your landlord. It's not going anywhere."

I felt tears of relief spring into my eyes, but I fought them back. "Oh, that's good. Then what is it?"

"Um, I'm going to have to bring him into the office tonight for some medical treatment, but I'm going to have to do it after hours. And I'm going to need your help."

"My help? I haven't even started my CNA training yet. I won't know what to do."

"I'll tell you what to do, you'll be fine."

Suddenly, my eyes flitted to his as I recalled something he had said. "What do you mean after hours?"

He hesitated for a moment before responding. "He's sort of in a bit of trouble right now and I don't want to draw attention to him being here."

"Oh," I said, biting my lip. "What kind of trouble?"

"I'm not entirely sure. But that doesn't matter right now. Mae, will you come back here tonight? Around nine? I'm really going to need your help."

Squaring my shoulders, I nodded. "Of course."

CHAPTER TWO

"God damn it, Kyle," an unfamiliar voice barked from the back exam room, making me jump.

Taking a deep breath, I locked the front door to the office and began making my way quietly down the hall towards the exam room.

"Are you trying to fucking kill me?" the voice said again.

"Stop your complaining, Ethan. You're acting like a Goddamned baby."

Taking a deep breath as I approached the closed door, I raised my hand and knocked quietly.

"Oh, thank God," I heard Dr. Ainsley mutter. "Come in, Mae."

"Who the fuck is Mae—God damn, that fucking hurts!"

I gasped, slapping my hand over my mouth as I entered the room. I found a man sprawled across the exam table. His shirt was off and there was blood everywhere; some dried and some fresh. His arms were covered in colorful tattoos, and as he rolled briefly onto his side, I caught a glimpse of a large piece on his back. Dr. Ainsley had his head bent as he worked on a wound in the man's stomach.

"Mae, put on some gloves and then take this," Dr. Ainsley snapped, waving a bloody pair of forceps in the air.

Blanching, I hurried to the box of sterile gloves and pulled them on as fast I could with quaking hands.

"Here," he urged as I hesitantly approached the table. "Help me keep the flesh apart."

"What?" I said, shaking my head. "I don't know how—"

"Just do it," he said with urgency.

I glanced at Dr. Ainsley briefly as I took the forceps from him, he was pale and his forehead was peppered with tiny beads of sweat.

"Okay," I whispered. Following his lead, I spread the wound apart as far as I could, willing myself not to gag from the sight.

"More, more," he snapped.

I pulled the flesh apart further and couldn't stop the heaving sound that erupted from my mouth as I watched him shove another set of forceps down into the wound, fishing around for I didn't know what.

"Keep it together, Mae," Dr. Ainsley muttered under his breath.

"Fuck!" the man screamed, arching his back. "No more!"

"Hold the fuck still, Ethan," Dr. Ainsley said between clenched teeth. "You got yourself into this mess. Man up for once."

I was shocked to hear Dr. Ainsley talk so sharply to anyone. He was usually so evenly mannered.

"I've almost got it," Dr. Ainsley said.

I heaved again, as I fought to remain upright and keep a steady hold of the flesh I was keeping pried apart and started to wonder if nursing was my true calling.

"Almost done, Mae," he said. "Keep it together. Just a couple more minutes."

The man moaned and I tore my eyes away from the wound to look at his face though I couldn't get my eyes to focus on him.

"There!" Dr. Ainsley said with triumph. "Got it."

Dr. Ainsley jerked his head back towards the counter. "Grab the sutchering kit."

"Got it," I replied as I shoved it in his hands, mine still quaking wildly.

"Good girl," he murmured. "Hold the wound closed just like this, please," he said so softly I had to strain to hear him.

"Yes, Dr. Ainsley," I said. I did as instructed, keeping my breathing even as I watched with both disgust and intrigue as he neatly sutured the wound closed.

"There," he said finally, snipping the thread. He straightening and pulled his gloves off as he admired his work. "Finished."

I slowly straightened, too, nodding. Suddenly the world began to spin and fade simultaneously and then I felt my knees buckle.

"Mae, Mae." From somewhere far away I heard someone calling my name. "Come on, Mae. Come back now."

I realized it was Dr. Ainsley calling my name and began to struggle frantically to wake up.

"Oh," I gasped as I opened my eyes again, looking up into Dr. Ainsley's face. "I'm so sorry. I passed out."

"I noticed," he said with a chuckle, helping me to my feet. "Here, take a seat here and sip some water."

I felt my face burning with embarrassment and I kept my eyes glued to the floor.

"That's the first time you've ever seen anything like that, isn't it?"

I nodded. "It was a bit shocking."

"You handled it like a champ, I couldn't have done it without you," Dr. Ainsley said with a grin.

"What about me? I think I deserve a fucking cookie, too. For, you know, letting you dig that bullet out?"

I startled at the voice behind me. I slowly turned to face the man lying on the exam table. My breath caught. He looked just like Dr. Ainsley, but a bit younger. Less composed and more rugged. Wild maybe. His hair was darker and longer, and he had a thick five o'clock shadow covering his face. His body was rock solid, and his tattoos made him look dangerous. He was watching me steadily, his dark eyes never breaking away from mine.

"Miss Parker," Dr. Ainsley said, snapping me back to reality. "I'd like to introduce you to my little brother, Ethan."

"How do you do?" I whispered.

"Not too well, as you might have noticed," he said thickly, making me shiver as his eyes roamed my body unapologetically.

"You alright, Mae?" Dr. Ainsley touched my arm. "You still look pale."

"I'm alright. I'm sorry, I should have handled that better."

"Just the opposite, I'm very impressed with how you handled yourself. You're going to make an excellent nurse one day, Mae."

"Thank you, Dr. Ainsley."

Ethan laughed, throwing his head back. "Do you make Heather call you Dr. Ainsley, too, or just your staff? My big brother thinks pretty highly of himself, doesn't he, Miss Parker?"

I sucked in a breath. I didn't know how to respond to that.

"Don't mind him, Mae," Dr. Ainsley said. "He's always like this. Always trying to get under people's skin."

I nodded and tried to feign a convincing smile, but avoided looking in Ethan's direction again.

"Mae, thank you again for helping. Please go home and rest, and I'll see you in the morning."

"Okay, if you're sure. Good night, Dr. Ainsley." I quickly stood to make my escape.

"Good night, Mae."

I wrapped my arms around myself as I hurried back through the office and out the front door, shutting it quietly behind myself again. I had never experienced anything like what had just happened. But that wasn't the part I found so unsettling. It was Ethan.

CHAPTER THREE

When I woke up, my face was wet. With the back of my hand I clumsily wiped my tears away and climbed out of bed. Another nightmare.

Glancing at the clock on my nightstand, I realized I was going to be late for work. Hurriedly, I got dressed and did the best that I could with my hair before grabbing my purse and keys and leaving the house.

Reaching the door to the office, it flew open before I had the chance to grasp the handle.

"You know what, Kyle? You can go fuck yourself if you think I'm going to stand here to listen to you lecture me about my life!" Ethan towered in the doorway with his back to me as he held the door open, his eyes fixed on Dr. Ainsley who coughed and nodded in my direction.

Ethan's head whipped around to face me. His jaw set and he looked me up and down. "Back so soon?"

I swallowed hard. "I-It's time for me to clock in for the day...sir..."

Ethan smiled down at me, but it wasn't the same kind smile I was accustomed to receiving from Dr. Ainsley. It was...alarming. "Sir, huh? Wow Kyle, you really have this one trained well."

"Shut up, Ethan. Come on in Mae, and get settled in. My brother was just leaving."

Keeping my head down, I skirted around Ethan and darted to the back office to clock in and deposit my purse in my locker. I decided I didn't like this Ethan one bit. He wasn't anything like his brother and I silently prayed that he would be leaving soon. Taking one quick look in the mirror that hung above Dr. Ainsley's desk, I licked my fingertips and smoothed a few stray hairs and then patted my red cheeks that betrayed my embarrassment.

"I'm sorry about him." Dr. Ainsley said as I entered the room again and went to my desk.

"That's alright," I said with a smile.

"I guess you could say he's not a people person."

"It's really fine, Dr. Ainsley."

"Mae, thank you so much for your help last night. It wasn't right asking that of you. Thank you for coming through for me. You deserve a raise."

My cheeks burned again and I didn't know what to say. "Thank you, sir."

"I'm going to go work in my office for a bit. When is my first appointment?"

"Your eight o'clock canceled yesterday, your first appointment is at eight-thirty," I answered, automatically.

With a nod, he turned and headed toward his office, shutting the door behind himself.

"What kind of name is 'Mae' anyway, Miss Parker?"

Jumping out of my skin, I clutched my hand over my savagely beating heart and spun around to face Ethan who was leaning against the big oak tree in my front yard. I wondered how long he'd been watching me as I fumbled with the door lock. It was always jamming.

With an uncomfortable shrug, I replied, "I don't know, it's just my name."

"Why hasn't Kyle gotten that door fixed for you?"

"I haven't mentioned anything about the door. There's nothing wrong with it."

With a little grunt, I jiggled the key back and forth as I pressed my shoulder against the door.

"Step aside, Miss Parker," Ethan said softly, standing so closely I could almost feel him touching me. "Let me give it a try."

Tucking a strand of hair behind my ear nervously, I sidestepped Ethan and wrapped my arms around myself. After a few attempts to unlock my door, he was finally successful and it swung open with a creak.

"Thank you," I said before hurrying through the doorway.

"Hey," he said, sticking his hand out to stop the door from shutting. "Aren't you going to invite me in to say thank you for helping you with the door?"

"No," I blurted out. "That wouldn't be very proper, would it?"

It wasn't fair how beautiful Ethan looked when he grinned. "Just exactly what century did you fall out of, Miss Parker?"

I blushed and looked down at my feet. "It's getting late."

"Well, aren't you at least going to ask me how I'm feeling after our little impromptu surgery last night?"

I eyed him cautiously. "How are you feeling?"

"Better than I expected," he said.

"I'm glad. Goodnight, Mr. Ainsley."

Then I shut the door, quickly flipping the deadbolt and leaned my forehead against it.

Oh, hell.

Giving my shoulders a quick shake, I turned and headed for my kitchen to make myself something to eat—even though my stomach churned at the mere thought of food. And just then my heart lurched when I heard a knock at my door. Damn it. Why wouldn't that man take no for an answer? Marching over to the front door, I flipped the deadbolt unlocked and swung the door open but it wasn't Ethan standing on the other side. It was Dr. Ainsley's wife.

"Hello, Mae," Heather said, her short blond bob meticulously styled as always.

"Hello, Mrs. Ainsley."

"Kyle told me about what happened last night."

"Oh?"

She pursed her lips. "I told him he was a selfish ass for putting you in that position. Are you alright?"

"Oh, Mrs. Ainsley, it wasn't a big deal. I was happy to help."

"You're too sweet." She reached forward and touched my arm. "He shouldn't have taken advantage of your kindness. His lowlife brother is always turning our world upside down and I've had about enough of it."

My heart went pitter-patter inside my chest at the thought of Ethan, but I did my best to keep my face neutral. "I see."

"Anyway, I just wanted to tell you that I was sorry for that. And if the cops catch wind of any of this, your name will never be mentioned, okay?"

"Mrs. Ainsley, why exactly is Eth—Dr. Ainsley's brother in trouble?"

She hesitated, biting her lip. "Well," she said with a whisper. "I don't know for sure. But I think he got into a lot of trouble with that motorcycle club he's in."

"Motorcycle club?"

"Shhh," she said, putting her hand up and lowering her voice to whisper. "Yeah. But I'm really not sure what happened. Or why he got shot. And to be perfectly honest, I don't much care. I just want that man out of my house. "

My eyes darted around the front yard as I looked for any sign of Ethan lurking around. "I don't blame you."

"I'd better get going. Goodnight, Mae."

"Goodnight, Mrs. Ainsley."

After Heather left, I worried about Ethan. I wondered what he had done to get himself into so much trouble. And I worried about myself, too. How could I be so attracted to such an insufferable individual?

CHAPTER FOUR

I hated how much I hoped to see Ethan again. The rest of the week had gone by and I hadn't seen him even one time since our encounter outside my house when I practically shut the door in his face. I began to wonder if he left town. After spending the morning speculating, I finally decided to brave the question while Dr. Ainsley was looking for a file in the cabinet.

"Dr. Ainsley," I started.

"What is it?"

I suddenly felt embarrassed to ask, but I wanted to know. "Did your brother leave?"

Dr. Ainsley smiled and shook his head, his eyes returning to the file he was holding. "No, Mae, he's just been—"

"I've just been laying low and letting this pesky flesh wound heal," Ethan said as he strode through the door. "Why, Miss Parker, I didn't know you cared."

I blushed. "I was just wondering," I said sheepishly.

"So," Dr. Ainsley drawled out. "How is your wound feeling? Have you been caring for it like I told you to?"

"Yes, doctor," Ethan said with an eye roll. "It's feeling much better."

"Even still, it's going to take a few weeks to heal. Then I'll remove those sutures."

"If I'm still around by then," Ethan said.

Now it was Dr. Ainsley's turn to roll his eyes. "Of course."

My eyes darted back to Ethan and I found him watching me carefully. When we made eye contact, he smiled and rubbed his chin.

"Miss Parker, I never properly thanked you for helping me."

"Oh, stop it, Ethan," Dr. Ainsley said.

"Stop what?" Ethan grinned broadly. "I can't thank her?"

"Mae, it's a slow day today and I'm just going to be working on paperwork most of the day. Heather can help keep an eye on the phones today if you would like to leave a bit early?"

My mouth hung open for a moment as I wondered if I had done something wrong, but then I snapped it shut and nodded. "Of course."

"Have a good weekend and I'll see you on Monday, Mae," Dr. Ainsley called as I left.

I took a few cautious steps down the front steps when I heard the two of them yelling. Quietly, I snuck back to the door and pressed my ear against it.

"I swear to God, Ethan, you had better leave that girl alone."

"Stay out of my business," Ethan snapped back.

"I would love to stay out of your business, but somehow you keep ending up on my doorstep and putting me right back in the middle of it again. And now you're trying to drag Mae into it, too."

"I'm not dragging her anywhere, she's just a nice girl," Ethan said so quietly, I had to strain to hear him.

"Exactly. She's a nice girl. She's not your type. She's not like the painted up whores you keep around to fuck. She's decent and I get the feeling she's had her fair share of rough rows to hoe, so please, just leave her alone."

I heard the shuffling of feet and then, "Okay, fine, I promise I'll leave Mae alone, alright, big brother? Jesus fucking Christ."

Gasping, I sprinted as silently as I could away from the door, stumbling as I got to the concrete path and then proceeded to dart across the street to my house, only halfway looking for cars as I did so. Reaching my hand up to tame my hair, I hurried up the path to my house only to hear a set of footsteps behind me.

"You weren't listening to our conversation, were you, Miss Parker?"

"Why do you keep calling me that?" I whipped around to face Ethan.

"Does it bother you?"

"It feels like you're making fun of me," I said.

After a few beats, he asked, "Why were you listening?"

"I wasn't."

He grinned. "If you say so."

"I need to go home," I said, turning and walking briskly towards my front door.

"I'll help you with the lock."

"I've got it."

"I'll help you," he said more firmly, grabbing my house keys and stepping around me. "I'll rummage through Kyle and Heather's garage and see if I can find some tools to fix this door for you."

My body was buzzing as I watched him fiddle with the lock. He was so close and smelled so good. I had to fight the urge to reach my hand out and touch him. Just to run my fingers along his skin—

"There you go," he said, interrupting my thoughts.

I had to blink myself back into the present and realized my face felt flushed. I was sure he noticed it, too. Then I felt myself blush from the embarrassment of it.

"Thank you, Mr. Ainsley." Then I thought about how silly it really was that I was calling him that. "Ethan."

"Mae," he said thickly, shoving his hands in the front pockets of his jeans.

"Goodbye," I said after a few moments of awkward tension. Then I slipped around his towering form and stepped inside my house only to feel him following close behind me. Kicking the door shut, Ethan grabbed my arm gently and spun me around to face him.

"What are you—" my words were cut off as his mouth descended onto mine. I moaned into his mouth, my lips parting without resistance to his tongue.

He pushed me backwards roughly until my behind collided with my small kitchen table. His hands were at my sides, touching and exploring my hips and waist. I gasped for air when his mouth finally relinquished control over mine, his lips moving to my throat. Tasting me. My heart was hammering in my chest and my ears roared. I knew I had to get my wits about me. I knew I had to stop what was happening. But I didn't want to.

"Ethan, stop," I whispered between breaths.

Ethan stilled and stiffened, pulling away. "I can't say I'm sorry."

I looked up into his eyes. They were dark and cloudy, and his lips parted slightly. Feeling bold, I reached up and cupped his face before I pressed my lips to his one last time.

"I can't," I said finally.

"You can't because of what you heard my brother say. He made me sound like a bad guy. I'm not."

"That's not it, Ethan."

He ignored me and continued. "But he was right about one thing: you're a good woman. I knew that from the first moment I met you. It was clear as day that you were frightened by what you saw when I was laying there on that table. But you dug deep and did what you had to do."

"It's not that…"

"I was jealous my brother got to catch you as you fainted. I thought you looked like an angel that night. It seemed like you came out of nowhere. Your gorgeous curly hair and exquisite body. Even though you keep it covered up under all these clothes," he said, running his fingers down my thighs.

Blushing, I shook my head frantically. "It's not that, Ethan. I mean, no, it's true that I'm not the right kind of girl for you. But that's not the problem."

"But you are the right kind of girl for me. That's what I've been realizing. I've spent my life hanging around the wrong kind of people and maybe I'm starting to grow up for once—"

"Ethan, I'm married," I blurted out.

Straightening completely, Ethan took a few steps backwards, rubbing the stubble on his chin. "You're married?"

"I am. Which is why you need to leave."

Blinking a few times, he looked to me, then around the house, then back to me again. "You don't look like you live with anyone. I've…never seen a man around here. Kyle never mentioned you had a husband." Then he grabbed my left hand and inspected it, holding on longer than necessary. "You're not wearing a ring."

Pulling my hand away, I said, "No. I left him six months ago back in Tennessee. But I'm still married."

"Why did you leave?"

"That's none of your business. You need to go."

Hesitantly, he backed up a few steps before turning around to reach for the door handle. Then he took one last glance at me and left.

CHAPTER FIVE

I was so embarrassed for how I acted with Ethan. Like a slut. Grimacing in the mirror, I wondered what I would do when I walked into work Monday morning. I wondered if Dr. Ainsley watched Ethan follow me into the house. What did he think of me now? I couldn't risk losing my job.

I secretly hoped that Ethan would be leaving town soon. I didn't need that kind of distraction, and he was so distracting. Just all wrong for me. Even if I was available.

Swallowing hard, my eyes moved to the stack of papers on my nightstand. Divorce papers to be exact. I hadn't been able to work up the courage to send them to Tim, but I knew I had to do. I couldn't hide forever. As soon as he received these papers, he'd know where I lived. He could find me. But…maybe everything would be okay. It'd been so long since we'd last spoken. Since I snuck out of the house in the middle of the night while he was passed out drunk. Since I had taken the bus all the way to this small New Mexico town, maybe he'd be willing to sign the papers and let me go.

One could hope anyway.

He wasn't going to run my life anymore. That was the whole point of me getting away from him. As long as I was still married to him, he would continue to control me. Fuck it.

Grabbing my cell off the dresser, I dialed my attorney's number.

"Swanson and Associates," the receptionist said into the line.

"Is Deborah in please?"

"She was just about to leave for the day, let me see if I can catch her. May I tell her who's calling?"

"Mae Parker."

I listened to hold music for a good five minutes before Deborah picked up.

"Mae, so good to hear from you."

"It's good to talk to you, too."

"What can I do for you?"

Placing a hand over my hammering heart, I said, "I'm ready to have him served."

She was quiet for a moment before she replied, "I'm so happy to hear that, Mae."

After I got off the phone with Deborah, I took a deep breath. This was happening. It was really happening. I couldn't believe it. I was finally going to be free from him.

"Mae, could you come in here for a moment?" Dr. Ainsley called from his office.

I looked up from the patient invoice I was working on. "Of course."

Standing, I smoothed out my skirt and walked to Dr. Ainsley's office. "Yes?"

Looking up at me in silence for a moment, he finally said, "Mae, I know this is none of my business. I know that I shouldn't ask you this, but I honestly care about you and your well-being so I want to make sure that you're okay."

My heart dropped. I knew what he wanted to talk to me about. "I don't know what you mean."

Dr. Ainsley steepled his fingers and placed them beneath his chin. "Mae." Clearing his throat, he continued. "Are you married?"

Looking down at my hands, I weighed my words. I wasn't sure what I should say or what would bring this conversation to the end. But finally, "Yes."

He nodded. "Like I said, it's absolutely none of my business. I just wanted to make sure that you were alright."

"I'm fine, why wouldn't I be?"

He sighed. "Good. I just wanted to make sure."

I tried to flash him a convincing smile and turned to leave.

"And Mae?"

"Yes?" I stopped.

"Stay away from Ethan, alright?"

My heart began to hammer and I felt a deep blush creep over my cheeks, so I kept my back turned to him. "Of course, Dr. Ainsley. I'm not interested in him."

He let out a hearty sigh. "Good." Then I heard him mutter under his breath, "Because he's interested in you."

I almost choked, but I just walked back to my desk and pretended I hadn't heard him say that. I couldn't wait for Ethan Ainsley to leave town and go back to wherever he came from. I didn't want him here screwing up the new life I was creating. I had a good job. A good place to live. Things were looking up for me for the first time in a long time. Falling in love with a man like him couldn't possibly end in anything but a disaster. I couldn't put myself in a position where Dr. Ainsley would fire me and kick me out of the house I was renting from him. I couldn't do anything to make things bad for myself again. I couldn't fall in love with Ethan Ainsley.

On cue, Ethan walked into the office, the little jingle of the bell and the creak of the door alerting me to his presence.

"Hey, Mae," he said lightly, pulling his baseball cap off and holding it between his hands.

"Hello."

"I just came to have my brother look at my stitches. I think I might have pulled one...the other day..."

Shaking my head frantically, my eyes flew to Dr. Ainsley's office, but from what I could tell, he was too focused on what he was working on to notice anything. I knew my face was a thousand different shades of red, so I kept my eyes averted.

"Mae," he whispered. Suddenly he was leaning over my desk. "I can't stop thinking about you."

Looking up into his eyes, I felt shaken by what I saw. There was something in his eyes, something I wanted.

"You shouldn't be thinking about me," I whispered back, my eyes periodically flicking over to Dr. Ainsley's office to make sure he was still distracted.

"I know you're married," he said, drawing in a breath. "But I don't care. Obviously you weren't happy with him or else you wouldn't have run away."

"Ethan—"

"Mae," he said hoarsely. "I just... I can't leave you alone."

Something inexplicable came over me. Something very unlike myself.

"Come over tonight," I whispered.

His eyes widened briefly before he swallowed hard and nodded, stepping away from my desk.

"What's going on?" Dr. Ainsley said, breaking Ethan and I out of... whatever had just happened.

Ethan didn't miss a beat and began to clutch his side. "Fuck, Kyle, these stitches are killing me. I think one came out."

Dr. Ainsley rolled his eyes. "Come on back, I'm between patients right now."

"Thanks, doc," Ethan said, falling behind his brother, but looked over his shoulder to flash me a smile and wink.

Shit.

CHAPTER SIX

Standing in front of my bedroom mirror, brushing my hair, I wondered who I'd turned into. I was acting like a different person. I left my door unlocked when I got home. Why? So that Ethan could let himself in when and if he showed up. I guess it'd been so long since I'd had that kind of attention from a man that I was desperate for it. Desperation for a man like Ethan Ainsley. I knew I should put a stop to this. Put a stop to what was about to happen, but I didn't want it to stop. Maybe I was enjoying being reckless just a little bit too much.

Then suddenly, I wondered if he was still planning on coming. Glancing at the clock, I realized it was almost nine. Maybe he changed his mind—but just then I heard the soft creak of the front door swinging open. My heart lurched and then began to pound wildly against my ribs. I sucked in a breath of air when his large form appeared in my bedroom doorway. Suddenly my mouth went dry and I wrapped my arms around my middle.

"I'm sorry I didn't get here sooner. I was waiting until Kyle and Heather were settled in for the night before I snuck out."

"A man your age has to sneak out?" I asked, flashing him a smart smile.

"I do when I'm being hounded by my overbearing older brother about a particular girl."

Taking a step forward, I started to speak, but he cut me off.

"Enough fucking small talk," he said gruffly, closing the distance between us and kissing me hard. He shoved his fingers through my hair, holding my face to his firmly as his lips pushed mine apart.

Moaning, I lifted my arms and encircled them around his neck. His hands moved lower as they explored my body without hesitation. He kneaded and groped my ass, pulling my skirt restlessly upwards until it was bunched around my waist. Then he pushed my panties down my thighs until my bare flesh was exposed. I gasped as my panties fell around my ankles and Ethan's mouth traveled down my neck. My entire body was buzzing and everything felt frenzied. Without thinking, I grabbed his shirt by the hem and pulled it roughly over his head. Just as I was taking in the glorious sight of his bare chest, I noticed him wince slightly and I suddenly remembered his sutures.

"I'm so sorry," I whispered.

He shook his head. "Please don't be. I would endure anything to be right here with you. A few stitches won't stop me."

Then he stared unabashedly down at me as he slowly unbuttoned my top before sliding it off my shoulders and down my arms. His lips found my neck again and he kissed and nipped at my skin while his hands worked on unhooking my bra. After my bra had been cast aside, Ethan hurriedly shoved my skirt all the way down until it hit the floor. With his hands at my hips, he guided me slowly to my bed as he kicked off his shoes, socks, and pants until we were both completely bare to one another.

"Mae," he whispered as his lips closed over mine again.

Pushing me back onto the bed, I felt his hand appear between my legs.

"Fuck, you're so wet already."

I moaned and arched my back as his finger delved deep inside me, his thumb gently rubbing my sensitive clit in tiny circles. I gasped as his mouth closed over my nipple, his tongue flicking it teasingly. I felt overloaded with sensation as I gasped for breath. I felt a warm stirring form between my legs as his fingers fucked me hard.

"Ethan," I cried out.

I looked up and found him watching me with hunger in his eyes. I also noticed that he kept wincing as he tried to keep himself propped on his elbow above me.

"Ethan," I whispered, pushing his skillful hand away. "Lay down."

"What?"

"You're hurt. I don't want you pulling any of your sutures. Lay down."

Hesitantly, he did as I said and I couldn't stop myself from looking at the generous cock that was laying rigid against his stomach.

"Did you bring any…" I blushed. "You know…"

Grinning devilishly, he nodded. "In the front pocket of my jeans."

After I found the condom, I crawled back onto the bed and opened it. Ethan grabbed me gently by the back of my head and kissed me deeply as I rolled the condom down over his cock. Then, I carefully straddled him.

"Tell me if I hurt you," I whispered.

He nodded jerkily, and gripped my hips tightly as I slowly slid him inside, throwing my head back as I took him, in his entirety.

"Oh, fuck," he said as I began to ride him, rocking my hips back and forth. "Yes. Fuck yes."

I sucked in a breath when he began to tease me with the pad of his thumb. Letting my head fall back, I rode him up and down. He moved in time with me, lifting his hips to meet mine. He was far more vocal than Tim had ever been with me. Ethan grunted and cussed and said dirty, wonderful things to me as we fucked.

"Enough," Ethan snapped. Reaching for me, he pulled me down against him and then rolled me onto my back so that he was pinning me to the bed.

"Ethan," I gasped. "You'll hurt yourself."

Leaning down, he caught my lip between his teeth and sucked hard on it before replying, "I can't take it just laying there while you're grinding on me like that. God, do you know how fucking sexy you are?"

Nuzzling my neck, Ethan began to thrust in and out of me, softly at first, but then he picked up pace. That deep stirring returned; a tingling heat swirling in my groin. I held on to Ethan's big shoulders, my nails digging into his flesh as he fucked me.

"Come for me, Mae, I need to feel you," he said, his lips pressed to my ear.

That was my undoing. Crying out, I threw my head back and writhed beneath him as he reached his own climax. I delighted as he grunted and shook before collapsing beside me with his arm draped over my middle.

"Thank God," Ethan murmured, his eyes still closed.

"What?"

"I didn't know how much longer I could take imaging what you looked like naked."

I giggled, slapping his shoulder. "Oh stop. Well, now you know and you can stop wondering."

His eyes opened and smiled softly at me. "You are even more beautiful than I imagined."

My heart skipped a beat and I didn't know how to respond.

"Goodnight, Mae."

"Goodnight, Ethan," I whispered.

"By the way," he said sleepily. "What time do you have to be at work tomorrow?"

"About eight. Why?"

"I wanted to know what time I needed to wake up so I could make you come again before you left for the office," he said simply before fading into sleep.

CHAPTER SEVEN

The next morning, I felt terribly guilty as I sat down at my desk and started my day. I was quite positive that Dr. Ainsley knew what I had done last night. Every time he said my name, I almost jumped out of my skin. Thank goodness we had a full day of patients booked to keep us busy so he wouldn't ask me any questions. Also… keep my mind off of Ethan.

I could get used to him, and that frightened me. He was fun and handsome and charismatic. He had made me feel more special in the short time I'd known him than any other guy ever had before as a whole. I blushed as I thought about the things that we did together this morning. He wasn't lying last night when he said he was going to make me come again before work. He was bringing out a wild side of me that I'd never known before. I felt so wicked. Ethan woke me slowly and sensually this morning as he gently placed kisses over my body, eventually finding himself between my legs.

I shivered at the memory.

I was becoming too attached to a man that would be leaving soon. He'd be wanting to go back to his life again soon and not one I could join. If Heather was right about him belonging to a motorcycle club, that wasn't a life I wanted to be a part of. And I wanted to know why he'd been shot. I'd been afraid to ask, but I had to know.

"Mae!" Dr. Ainsley snapped impatiently, bringing me out of my thoughts.

"Sorry," I said, jumping to my feet.

"When's my next appointment?"

I glanced at the schedule. "You have Mrs. Harris at 10:45."

"Alright, I'm going to go work on some paperwork in my office until then. Let me know when she's checked in."

"Yes, Dr. Ainsley."

God, I felt so guilty. Why? I had nothing to hide. I was a grown woman. And Ethan was a grown man. There was no reason why we couldn't do what we wanted in private.

Except that I was still married. My stomach turned. He had to have received the papers by now. What was Tim thinking? Was he furious? Relieved? I prayed that he was more than happy to sign them and be done with me for good. With a heavy sigh, I pushed from the desk and stood, stretching. Then I went to the filing cabinet to pull Mrs. Harris' folder. Just then, I felt someone gently brush my hair over my shoulder to expose the back of my neck. Then I felt his lips press small kisses there. Smiling, I leaned back against him.

"Stop, Ethan, you're going to get me in trouble," I whispered as I tried to suppress a giggle.

"Guess again."

My blood went cold and I whipped around only to have Tim slap his hand over my mouth. "Hey there, wife. So this is where you've been. I've been looking for you," he said quietly, a disgusting grin spread across his face.

Whimpering, I tried to push him away, but he held me fast, his fingers digging into my cheeks. "Would you like to come with me now, or do you want to make a scene?"

After he ever so slightly moved his hand so I could talk, I whispered, "Please don't make a scene. I'll come with you."

"Good girl," he said, brushing a strand of hair from my face. "Let's go."

He took my hand, painfully tight and began yanking me towards the door.

"Mae?" Dr. Ainsley appeared in the doorway of his office. "Introduce me to your friend."

Tim was crushing my hand inside his. "I'm Mae's husband."

"Is that so?" Dr. Ainsley pulled his glasses off and his eyes kept jumping between Tim and I. "Are you going somewhere, Mae?"

My head was spinning and I was in full-blown panic mode. I had no idea what to do or what to say. Dread filled every cell of my body and I could hardly force my legs to keep me upright. I opened my mouth to speak but no words would come out.

"We were just leaving, weren't we, Mae?" Tim said, gripping my bicep so hard that I knew he was going to leave my skin bruised. "I think you've had enough fun on your little adventure and now it's time to go home, right?"

Fuck, I didn't want to go with him. But I didn't know what to do. He was just as mad as I had feared he would be—maybe even more. In that moment, I knew I was trapped; He would never let me go. I had to figure out some other way to get away from him.

"Come on, sweetie, let's go now. We need to go home," Tim said.

Then Tim whipped us around, yanked the door open and pulled me outside with him. Looking over my shoulder, I made eye contact with Dr. Ainsley and I mouthed I'm sorry. As I stumbled along beside Tim to the car, anxiety coursed through my bloodstream. I knew the moment I was in that car, it wouldn't be so easy to get away again.

"Who the fuck is Ethan, Mae?" he asked between clenched teeth. "Just who the fuck is he?"

Then something snapped inside me. Digging my heels into the ground, I yanked myself backwards, making him lose his grip.

"God damn it," he muttered, reaching for me again, but I backed away.

"I want a divorce, Tim."

"You don't know what you want, Mae. You're a stupid woman and you need to come home with me now. You're damned lucky I'm willing to take you back."

"Give me a divorce," I said, squaring my shoulders.

"Get in the fucking car, Mae!" Tim yelled, reaching for me again.

"Mae," Dr. Ainsley called calmly from the front steps of the office. "Why don't you come back in and we can all talk about this."

I watched Tim's face get redder and knew he was about to explode.

"Is this Ethan, Mae?" he said so quietly that only I could hear. "Is this the piece of shit you've been fucking?"

Tim was quaking with rage. I wouldn't go with him. I couldn't take it. Without thinking, I lunged forward and grabbed him hard by the shoulders, kneeing him hard in the groin. Tim coughed and groaned, falling to the ground. While he was down I kicked him soundly in the stomach. Then I reached inside his front right pocket, the pocket he always kept his keys in, and made a run for the car.

"You fucking whore!" he yelled as he staggered to his feet and started to give chase. By the time he was on his feet, I had the car in gear and had stomped my feet on the gas, leaving a cloud of dust behind me.

My heart was racing. I kept glancing in the rearview mirror to see if anyone was following, but as far as I could tell, I was alone. I didn't know what to do so I just kept driving. I just had to keep driving. Then I realized that I had nothing. I didn't have my purse. I didn't have clothes. And I certainly didn't have anywhere to go. And there was that pesky detail about how I stole Tim's car.

"Fuck me," I muttered to myself, pulling over. I was almost to the outskirts of town, but I realized that I couldn't use Tim's car to escape. That would only made things worse for me.

Leaving the keys in the ignition, I climbed out and looked around. Still, no one seemed to be following me. So I ran across the street into an alleyway and began the journey back to my house again. I hoped that by the time I made it back, Tim would be long gone searching for me. I could get into my house, get my things, and then be on a bus before nightfall.

CHAPTER EIGHT

I took my time getting back to the house. The longer I stayed away, the more hope I had that Tim would be gone. When I got to my backyard, I crouched down by some bushes and looked around. No one. It was quiet, save for the rain that had begun to fall heavily from the darkened sky.

I began to weigh my options. My purse was still in Dr. Ainsley's office. I couldn't go back for it now. I couldn't get them involved. I'd have to leave it. But I had some cash stashed in my house. It wasn't a lot but it would be enough to get me out of this town and someplace far away from here. My chest tightened. And away from Tim.

Straightening, I jogged across the backyard to my bedroom window. Of course, it was locked; I religiously checked all the windows daily. Looking around at the ground around my feet, I spotted a fist-sized rock and picked it up. Then covering my face with my arm, I smashed the window and then hoisted myself inside the house, managing to receive only minor cuts from the broken glass.

Brushing my wet hair from my face, I began to make my way to the front of the house. As I went, I began to notice that things seemed out of place. When I got to the living room, I found the place in complete disarray. My things had been knocked to the floor. Broken. I found the kitchen in even worse shape. The jar I kept on the counter was now lying shattered on the floor, money gone. My heart fell to the floor.

Looking over my shoulder when I felt a breeze, I noticed the broken window just above the kitchen sink. Fuck. Tim broke in after I left. Of course he did. My new address was on the divorce papers. He knew exactly where I lived and he wasted no time stealing from me before he left. Asshole.

Backing away, my shoes crunched over broken glass. Now what was I going to do? I had no money to leave town now. It was only a matter of time before Tim decided to come back here to look for me. I had no choice but to leave anyway. I'd make it work somehow. Fuck it. Turning around to leave, I ended up face-to-face with Tim. Gasping, I stumbled backwards, falling onto the broken glass on the kitchen floor.

"Do you have any idea what you got yourself into?" Tim raised his hand and let it fly across my face, leaving a mighty sting on my cheek. "Just how stupid do you think I am?"

Shit, I was in trouble. I was so stupid for coming back here. Scrambling to my feet, I backed away from Tim until my back was pressed up against the refrigerator. His eyes were filled with rage I knew I had to think fast or things would get even worse.

"Tim, just calm down and let's talk about this."

"What do you want to talk about? How you ran away from our home? How you ended up in New Mexico? How you've been fucking other men? How many, Mae? How many men have you fucked?"

"I haven't slept with anyone else, Tim, I swear!"

"What about this Ethan guy?"

My heart lurched. I didn't want him to know anything about Ethan. I would never be able to forgive myself if something happened to Ethan.

"There is no Ethan," I whispered, a sob tearing from my throat as his hand closed painfully around it.

"I would have to disagree with that statement."

I gasped and looked to my right to find Ethan standing in the doorway. He had murder in his eyes. He looked menacing as he stood with the moonlight and pouring rain at his back, holding a large wrench in his hands. His eyes flicked to mine once, but then stayed locked on Tim.

"Back the fuck away from her," he said, stepping into the room.

"Ethan, don't!" I cried. "He's dangerous. Just leave. I'll be fine."

I grimaced as Ethan let out humorless chuckle. "I think I'd rather stay and meet your friend here."

"So you're Ethan, huh?" Tim said. "You're the loser who's been fucking my wife. I'm glad to meet you.".

Ethan grinned, taking a step closer. "And why is that?"

"So I can kick the shit out of you for sleeping with my wife, you piece of shit."

Ethan rocked back on his heels, looking thoughtful. "So, Tim, is it? I have a question for you, Tim. Have you ever heard of the Heaven's Reapers?"

Tim stopped, looking surprised by the question. "I...don't think so. What the fuck does that have to do with anything?"

"Oh, nothing really. It's just a little club I'm a member of."

"What the hell are you talking about?" Tim asked impatiently.

Ethan lunged forward, grabbing Tim by the throat and pinning him up against the kitchen wall. "I just want you to know that I've done some bad things in my life. Taking your life right here, right now wouldn't make me lose a minute of sleep. I've lived a life that you couldn't even imagine. I've seen things that would make you piss yourself like the pussy you are. Do you know what the members of my club do to guys like you? Guys who beat their wives?"

Tim clawed at Ethan's hand, coughing, eyes bulging. He shook his head frantically.

"Want me to tell you? Or do you want me to let it be a surprise?" Ethan asked, his face inches from Tim's.

Just then, Dr. Ainsley stepped into the room, his white dress shirt soaked and plastered to his body, a dark look in his eyes that I'd never seen before. Slowly, almost ominously, he undid the buttons of his shirt and pulled it off, revealing a torso that was covered in tattoos. He began to rub the knuckles of one hand into the palm of his other hand as he looked at Tim with disgust.

"I'm sorry," Tim choked out.

"Sorry?" Ethan asked, releasing Tim and letting him fall to the floor, coughing and wheezing.

"I'm sorry, I'm sorry, okay? I'll leave."

Ethan grinned. "Yes, you will. But before you do you're going to make sure your divorce is finalized, right?"

Tim nodded.

Ethan looked over at me. "Wait here, baby, I'll be back as soon as I can."

Then I watched in shock as Ethan grabbed Tim by the throat again and drug him out of my house and into the night, Dr. Ainsley following closely behind

CHAPTER NINE

After staring at the open door in shock for a few moments, I gathered up my wits enough to shut and lock the front door. Then I grabbed towels and hung them over the broken windows to keep out some of the rain. After that was done, I spent the rest of my time cleaning up the broken glass off the floor and trying to clean the place up again. I couldn't stop shaking and felt like I was in shock after the events that had just taken place.

So it was true, Ethan was a member of a motorcycle club. Why did he get shot? What happened?

And Dr. Ainsley. That look in his eyes was terrifying. And he had the same tattoos as Ethan. He was part of the club, too?

Shivering, I turned off the light in the kitchen and headed for bed. I jumped as a loud bang came from the front door.

"Mae, it's just me, let me in." Ethan.

I sprinted to the door, unlocking it and thrusting it open wide in one movement. "Ethan."

Taking two quick strides towards me, Ethan cupped my face and kissed me soundly. "It's over now."

My breath caught in my chest and I took a couple steps back to get a good look at him. He was covered in blood. "What does that mean? What did you do, Ethan?"

His jaw set and he said, "I didn't kill him, if that's what you're wondering."

"Dr. Ainsley, he…he has tattoos just like you…is he…?"

"I used to be," Dr. Ainsley said, stepping around Ethan. "Not anymore. Not for a long time." His bare torso was splattered with blood as well and his slacks were torn and dirty.

Ethan chuckled. "Kyle was the reason I joined the club in the first place. I wanted to be like my big brother."

"I got out of it when I met Heather. I decided I didn't want that life anymore, so I finished medical school."

I looked up at Ethan. "But you're still in it? Even after you got shot?"

Ethan brushed a strand of hair from my face before rubbing his thumb along my cheekbone. "I am. They're my brothers. My getting shot was just the result of a…misunderstanding."

I caught Dr. Ainsley rolling his eyes. "Misunderstanding my ass," he muttered under his breath.

"I have so many questions. This has all been so much."

Dr. Ainsley coughed. "I should go home now. Heather is probably out of her mind worrying about me. And pissed," he added with a wink.

"Thank you for everything, Dr. Ainsley. I'm sorry for this."

"Call me Kyle, Mae," he said with a smile, and then disappeared into the night.

I turned back to Ethan. "Ethan, you risked your life for me. You and Dr. Ains—Kyle. I don't know what to say." I shook my head, trying to make sense of it all. "Am I really, truly free from Tim? Could it be possible?"

"First of all, I didn't exactly risk my life. I've been in much more dangerous situations before. Just last month I was in a fight with four guys who were all about twice the size as Tim. All Kyle and I did tonight was beat the shit out of the sorry excuse for a man." He smiled, "And yes, you're free from that fuck face."

"Now what?" I asked softly. "What do we do now?"

"Mae, I like you. I really like you. I could see myself falling hard for you. Tonight when Kyle told me what happened with your ex, I lost it. I couldn't think straight. When he told me you took the car and I couldn't find you… I thought I was going to go out of my mind with worry. All I could think about was finding you so that I could protect you and make sure that you're safe. All I want… is you."

"You want me?"

Kissing me again, he pressed his hard body against mine. Eventually, he broke the kiss and whispered, "You're everything I want."

"Ethan, I want you, too. I've never met anyone like you. But I don't think I'd fit in your life."

"I know, I know. I've lived a dangerous and pretty stupid life. But I'll slow down for you. I can slow down. Please. I can't let go of you."

"You can't slow down your life for me. That wouldn't be right of me. And I'm building my own life here."

Kissing my forehead, Ethan drew in a shaking breath and said, "I don't want to control you. I don't want you to give up the life you've been working so hard at creating since you left Tim. That's one of the reasons I find you so Goddamn amazing. I just want to be a part of your life. Please, just give me a chance to be the man in your life. If you were my girl, I would make sure you were always happy. I would make sure you always felt cherished and cared for. Mae," he whispered before placing small kisses along the side of my face.

"I care about you, too, Ethan. I don't want to let you go, either."

He grinned, pulling away to look down into my eyes. "So, can we do this? Can I call you my girl, Miss Parker?"

I smiled back, tears in my eyes. "Yes, but soon you're going to have to start calling me Miss Hudson. I'm about to be an old, divorced bitty."

"I can't wait," he said with a grin, pulling me into his arms for a kiss.

Coming soon from Elle Vaughn…

The Reckless Series

Poisonous Frogs and a Prince
Sharon E. Foster

It was the winter of 2010 when her world began to crumble. If she was being brutally honest, it was already crumbling long before her three-year marriage, but up to that point, she felt she was keeping a decent enough hold on things, considering all she'd already dealt with.

Elizabeth was a small-town country girl, who moved from an awful past in the south, to the north, to be with the part of her family that actually loved her. She brought who she thought was the *"man of her dreams"* with her. At the time, she had no idea that he was the total opposite of what he led her to believe.

As a child, she suffered mental and physical abuse from her mother regularly. At one point in her life, she felt as if she wasn't going to survive what she was enduring. Living in fear of a parent who didn't want her, wasn't easy by any means. A true believer from a very young age, she prayed to God for strength to make it through the life she had been given. She sought out strangers in her community for shoulders to cry on. They taught her the way life should be lived; how someone with a loving heart acts. They helped further her education with school lessons, and taught her all they could about life so she would be prepared for adulthood. Although she was going through a lot, she was smart enough to know she needed help to keep going, and be productive as she grew older. She was blessed to find people that cared. Though it would have been easier to just give up, she never did.

Her father was her best friend, and was there with her through it all. Unfortunately, he endured the same pain at the hands of her mother, and became frail over the years. The more fragile he became, the rougher the abuse was. Her dad stayed around and endured the abuse so she wouldn't be left alone. Because he never left Elizabeth, and shared so much of his wisdom, she became stronger and very loving. When he passed away, she immediately sought a new path away from her wretched mother.

Elizabeth moved up north in 2006. She had met her soon to be husband randomly one day on a phone chat line she joined after a nasty break up. Being hurt and vulnerable, she craved companionship and fell for the first one that seemed to fit her view, not realizing he was a rebound relationship. Though, the man and his friend were actually playing around on the phone to waste time, after they spent time talking, for so long, he seemed truly interested.

They talked day in and day out. Nicholas lived two hours away in a city nearby, but it felt as if they were neighbors or rather good friends. They became close quickly, and spent hours getting to know one another. Even when Nicholas was at work, he would sneak in the bathroom and call. She would always ask him, "How much are you really working?" They would laugh about it.

She had a nice apartment, where she and her former boyfriend had lived together. She had been heartbroken discovering he wasn't being faithful. Trying to give back, she let one of her friends stay over from time to time when she needed a place to crash. The problem was she helped herself to more than just the apartment and had ended up in the sack with her boyfriend. Furious, she had nowhere to go on the spur of the moment, and didn't want to get into any trouble, so she was without any other options and that left her forced to call her mother to come pick her up. Unfortunately, that meant she would have to stay with her mother once again and that would put the burden on him as the only thing to brighten her day. He, too, was not in an ideal situation. With an eviction from his current living situation looming, he seemed to crave a change just as she did. They passed the hours together and shared their woes while bonding over their shared struggles in life.

Nicholas would always tell her how his parents only wanted his money, but would never do anything for him in return. He had suffered with Cerebral Palsy since he was a child, so his main income came from a government check for his disability. Though it was his disability, his parents would often take his money for their own needs, leaving him with nothing. The two had a lot in common when it came to feeling unloved, which only bonded them further.

While toughing it out at her mom's house, and making sure her siblings were eating properly, and making sure that the house was clean. She also protected the kids from their mother and perverted stepfather, both of which were menaces and unfit to be parents. She was living in constant fear and yet had to keep a close eye on her stepfather because he was always trying to take advantage of her sexually, she found herself in the position of needing to protect the younger girls as well. This has been an ongoing battle ever since she was sixteen, but she somehow managed to keep him off. Unfortunately, her mother married him anyway, even after Elizabeth told her what was going on. She was stuck fighting him off constantly until she turned twenty-five and, even then, his own children weren't safe from his lechery.

Meanwhile, Nicholas was trying to get away from his parents because they were trying to force him to come back home after his eviction. His mother came to his apartment with boxes and started packing his things without even asking him, forcing him to do as she said. They were on the phone at the time. It tore at her heart to hear him crying to her.

"I don't want to go with them. They just want my money and I'll be trapped in my room, with no life," he lamented.

After enduring all this along side him, she felt so bad for him. She began to see that she was already falling for Nicholas, so hearing him this upset was a new sort of pain for her. She asked her mother if it would be okay for Nicholas to come for a short time and stay, provided he paid his way. She quickly agreed to the situation and looked forward to the additional income. As he planned to make his way to Elizabeth.

With only one more night to live in his apartment, he became frenzied. His mother would be there the next day to move him out of his own place of freedom and into her house. His first thought was to catch the bus to her mother's home, but he would have to wait for the correct bus at the station, and his parents would surely find him there. He quickly realized he needed another plan.

He asked a friend if she could drive him over. After little goading, she quickly agreed. She needed to pay her credit card bill and Nicholas offered to pay her, so it was a *"no brainer"*. She also knew the hell Nicholas went through, so she was happy to try and aid his escape.

Nicholas made it a little bit after midnight the next day. They were so happy to see one another. It was like they were one another's saving grace. Life was finally turning around for the good. A bit of balance crept into their lives for the moment.

A couple of weeks after Nicholas had moved in the electricity was shut off. He had paid her the rent upon moving in, but they were left in the house while her mother and step-father went to a hotel. Even though the money he paid in rent was supposed to go towards keeping the bills paid, and her mother had known the bill was due, she blew the money on herself and left them in the dark, literally.

Luckily, one of her cousin came for a visit and paid to rent a room. So, they would no longer be in a hot, dark house in the south and summer time. Above being hot and frustrated, they also felt hurt and abandoned.

He just didn't understand how the electricity was shut off after he had given her money for it. She quickly explained to him how things worked, and how her mother typically handled her life in more detail, then he understood all too well. Elizabeth had been waiting for her last paycheck from a former employer, then they would be able to afford to leave. When neither were able to find any work, suddenly they were homeless.

Elizabeth was finally able to get a phone number for her family that lived up north, and they made a plan together to get them away from her mother's house immediately. Her brother and his family were happy to take her in. Since he was married to her best friend, it would also give her a female she could trust to talk to, and she would be able to see her nephew while starting over in a new place.

Even before she could enact her plan, she had to stop her mother from assaulting her younger brother with a deadly weapon on the next visit to the house when she went to gather her belongings. She held her mother down as best she could, so her little brother could run away. She finally let her mother go, after begging her not to hurt her little brother, thinking that would be the end of it, but her mother turned around and hit her in the face. Elizabeth vowed to her that day, she would leave when her money came and never return.

Everyone was always so scared of her mother because they never knew what was going to happen next. She was a volatile, angry spirit with no account for others. When she walked in the door, everyone became a block of ice, frozen in fear. Luckily, they didn't have to wait long for Elizabeth's money to arrive so they could escape.

She gave her mother a substantial amount of money, put food in the house, and bought her siblings some things they needed to settle what she felt was a debt to them and take care of her siblings at least a bit longer. She did more than her fair share and left knowing she did the right thing. Of course, that wasn't good enough for her mother. She wanted Elizabeth to move her and her step-father into a house, paying all of the bills and she actually wanted them to move in as well and to stay in that house with her step-father.

Unsure of what to do she called her cousin over to "visit". While she was talking to Elizabeth's mother, the others were sneaking as much of Elizabeth's belongings out of the house as they could. Unfortunately, they had to leave some things behind, but she quickly realized they were just things and could be purchased again. Nothing was worth more than freedom.

When she finally got away, she was so scared that her mother would look for her that she was a mess the rest of the night. She was crying and shaking, and watching over her shoulder for hours. They went to the bus station to get tickets, but they couldn't leave until the next morning. They had to check into a hotel and wait all night. she was so scared that her mother was going to burst through the door at any moment, that she started having anxiety attacks. Her mother was calling her phone repeatedly and leaving terrible messages. They couldn't wait until the morning came.

When it finally arrived, they said their goodbyes to her cousin and got on a bus heading north. Even fighting it she wasn't able to stop the crying. She didn't want to leave her siblings, but she had to get out. She wasn't going to make it if she stayed there, and she knew it.

The day trip on the bus was hard. Still receiving phone calls and messages from her mother, she was shaken up, but the calls from her best friend on the way up north kept her calm, along with Nicholas beside her. She knew her life was about to change, and she was ready for it. It was a fresh start and she had to make a better life for herself, and now she had a partner by her side. Everything was going to be okay now.

They finally arrived at their new home up north and immediately felt safe and welcomed. It was so cool to both of them to see all of the tall buildings. There were so many people in the city, buzzing around doing their things. There were tons of bridges, rivers, and museums. It was a whole new experience and place to be.

To Elizabeth and Nicholas, nothing was bad about being away from the situation they were in. She hugged her best friend so tight she thought she was glued to her. Honestly, she was a wreck and just so hurt. She had needed this break and was very happy to see her family there and, for the first time in a long time, she saw a glimmer of hope.

Nicholas contacted his family and they had nothing nice to say about the situation. There was nothing he could say to make them understand, so he just didn't talk to them for a while. Elizabeth didn't talk to her mother for a while either, even though she called being really nice on the phone after she cooled down from her anger. That was her usual pattern, in order to keep her thumb on Elizabeth to use her for whatever she needed. As much as Elizabeth loved her mother, she could not take it anymore. She was already sick and the stress from her mother was making things worse, so she decided to take a hiatus from that contact.

Elizabeth and Nicholas got settled into their new life up north, but that didn't mean things were perfect. At first, they were getting along just fine and they married in 2007. Of course neither of their families attended the wedding. A little while after that, things went downhill.

Both sets of parents claimed distance and mistakes, saying they didn't want to waste their time attending something that wouldn't work out anyway. Negativity surrounded the couple at every turn.

Even though they were together for some time before their marriage, it was only after the wedding that they truly started to find out things about each other that had been hidden. They began to clash, a lot. Elizabeth also started to grow tired of Nicholas' parents calling saying mean things about her. He would just walk around with the phone and let them vent, not saying anything to defend her. He was scared of them still and would look at Elizabeth and shrug, figuring she understood. She did not understand and she was furious and hurt that her own husband wasn't willing to defend her.

If anyone said anything about Nicholas in a negative way, Elizabeth would lose her cool and put that person in their place immediately. She thought couples were supposed to put the other first in everything, but it was becoming more and more obvious that they didn't have the same Priorities. With anyone else besides his parents, he would defend Elizabeth. However, that still didn't make the hurt any better. Nicholas was a hard worker, and a great provider, however money couldn't fix hurt or change differences.

Time sputtered along and argument after argument arose, things fell apart, and after too many negative things happened in their marriage, Elizabeth asked for a divorce. She felt so hurt because their marriage didn't work, but all she knew was she had to go because he wasn't the right person for her. No matter how hard either of them tried, it always seemed to fall apart over and over. When neither of them were willing to fight anymore, they ended their marriage.

During the three years of their marriage, Elizabeth was rather ill and in a wheelchair. After some time, she had a major surgery and was able to walk and work again. By the time the divorce was final, Elizabeth was able to support herself and regain her freedom. At every turn in her life, she had been through the wringer. Though her heart was still tender, she knew she was a good woman and hadn't given up yet in life, so she pushed through like she always did.

After her divorce, she lived with her best friend, Lynn. She'd seen all of the good and bad and understood what was happening. She had cried on her shoulder many days, until it was all over. Lynn encouraged her daily, to keep her head up and think positive. She always said, "The best is yet to come."

She began working and tried to heal from her divorce when she met the first of a few of the frogs she would kiss.

She met Anthony in the little town where she lived, not far from where she worked. He and his family members often came into the store where she worked. She had never gone on looks alone, but to her, Anthony was the best looking man she had ever known. He quickly became the wind in her sails. She wanted nothing more than to speak to him every hour of the day, nothing would sway her attention from him, even adamant pleas from her best friend.

Anthony had just moved back into town and was living with his brother. He had been living in a nearby town dating a girl who decided she wanted to go back to her child's father. She immediately felt bad for him and his heartache.

They started spending time together and Elizabeth told him everything up front that she was going through, from her family woes, ex-lovers, and life. She was honest to a fault with him. To her, that was the best way to be. After all she had been through in her life, there was nothing anyone else could do to break her down, so she thought. Anthony changed that whole thought around.

Within the first month of dating, Anthony had already slammed her against a wall in her apartment, picked her up and slammed her into the floor, and punched her in her lower back, knowing she had a back disease. He had a very bad temper. He felt that due to his past, he didn't need to truly care about anyone. He didn't know how to show any affection or communicate.

Elizabeth felt bad for him and she continued to talk to him, even after he'd already shown who he was. She didn't want to believe what her own eyes were showing her and continued to constantly search for the good in him. He was there every day when she couldn't sleep at night due to crying and not feeling well. To her, that meant everything.

To him, it was his usual way of getting a woman to cling to him, so he could get what he wanted. He wasn't there for her, he was there for a free place to sleep and eat. He wouldn't need to find a job or a place of his own if she was taking care of things. Elizabeth didn't realize that yet, but when her eyes opened, she would see it all.

After a couple of months, Elizabeth let him move in as a "roommate." He briefly had a job when he moved in, but he wasn't making much money. She understood and gave him a chance. Within a short time, he had a surgery on his arm and was down for a while. At one point, she gave up her bed for him and slept on the pallet in his room so he could be comfortable. She took care of him when she was home. She also did all of the cooking and cleaning and catered to his every need, while hers were forever ignored.

When he was healed, he never went back to work. She was now supporting her "boyfriend" while he was still in the other room as a roommate. When she would go to work, he would be under the influence of narcotics. He would order inappropriate movies on her cable account. She didn't find out until the bill came that it was over seven hundred dollars and the company was disconnecting her service. Elizabeth was furious, but she still let him stay there. He apologized and, somehow, all was well in her mind.

As the months went on, he continued to abuse her. Everyone else could see what was going on, where she remained blind. She went to work with sunglasses on to hide her swollen eyes. It got to the point where he choked her until she passed out, smacked her around for anything, while he abused narcotics on a regular basis. He began stealing from her, and took every dime she had.

She was in and out of the hospital so regularly, but with different excuses that one of the doctors finally said to her, "I know you are being abused and if you come in here again like this, I will have to call the police." Elizabeth was scared because she didn't want anything to happen to Anthony or herself, so she just stayed home and dealt with things from there on out.

She began moving from place to place because there was so much arguing and fighting. She feared being thrown out by her landlord, because he said he couldn't know the abuse was going on and keep her there. The neighbors were complaining about her boyfriend and he would not renew her lease. Elizabeth had to move. Anthony didn't help her at all. He just didn't care.

When they moved to the next place, things worsened. Even though the place was her favorite style townhouse and a bit more expensive, it was located in a bad area and he knew lots of people that were into drugs there. He was in heaven and Elizabeth was in hell.

She worked hard to pay her bills and support both of them. She couldn't afford to get a good car, so he ran every one she got into the ground. Being financially on her own, meant she could barely afford the basic things she needed, because she was constantly taking care of his needs.

Soon he started cheating with a girl around the corner from where they lived, and he even tried to seduce girls who were not eighteen. He claimed to be younger than he was and admitted he beat his girlfriend. Apparently to that crowd, something like that was interesting or alluring.

Anthony had been in trouble with some people years before he met Elizabeth, and they wanted revenge. There were rumors that her place was going to be shot up by gang members. Fortunately, her neighbors knew them and said she had nothing to do with it so they didn't hurt her. However, they were driving back home one day and the car window was shot out. She thought they were dead. She was so scared, instead of calling the police first, she called her best friend. She didn't know what to think at the moment. Later they found out who had done it, but without proof there was nothing that could be done about it. Elizabeth gave Anthony the money to get her window replaced by a mechanic. He spent the money on drugs and tried to fix the window himself. It never worked properly again. She eventually had to get another car.

One day when he began asking her for money, and she said no. An argument started because he was calling her names. She couldn't afford to give him money because she was paying all of the bills, buying food, and such. He started choking her and saying that he would kill her, and finally Elizabeth blacked out.

When she came to, he was gone. She called the neighbor to ask for help, but her neighbor didn't want anything to do with it. Anthony had said he wasn't doing anything wrong but said Elizabeth was crazy. He'd starting turning everyone against her. The abuse continued, but not as regularly.

When she finally reached her breaking point, they split up and Anthony left to go to a rehabilitation center. Elizabeth moved into her own place.

It wasn't long till Anthony was released early, he had been swearing at the patients and nurses alike. He called Elizabeth and, true to history, she went to pick him up and they got back together. The abuse had become more mental than physical by the this point. There was very little physical abuse. Some days she felt like she would rather take a punch to the face than listen to the things he said to her. She tried to talk to him because she felt he was very mean to her for no reason. Then she found out he was still abusing drugs, but was lying to everyone about it.

Everyone that knew him had been telling her for years she needed to leave him. He had always been like this with women. She knew she should listen, but she heard his pleas to give him just one more chance, that he was trying to change for her. Listening to her heart instead of her head was the only thing she seemed to be able to do.

She soon learned he was cheating on her again. A couple of his family members felt she should know, and she was so hurt. She had enough, she threw him out. He started living with a family member that was about five minutes away. Even after all he'd done, she continued to give him chances. He would come to her house and get money, food, and other things from her. He would take food out of her freezer every time he came, without her permission.

Weeks later, Elizabeth decided to let him come back because she was lonely and knew she really loved him. He would take off for weeks at a time. When he came back one night, she told him how she felt about him never coming home and that she had feelings and needs. Physically, she wanted the man she loved to show her affection. She knew she wasn't treated right and she figured maybe he would be better to her somehow. Of course that didn't happen.

That night, he put his arms around her chest and squeezed it tight. She could barely breathe. Then he threw her down and grabbed her by the throat. She was begging him to stop, but he wouldn't. He forced himself on her and while she was crying, begging him to stop, he was asking, "Is this what you want? I bet now you will shut your damn mouth and learn how to talk to me."

She was so scared and continuously crying. She pulled herself together and ran out of the room screaming, "I told you no! Why did you do that to me?"

He started laughing and said, "What are you going to do? Call the police? Go ahead bitch. You can't rape the willing."

He kept laughing telling her to shut up. He left and stayed gone for weeks. Elizabeth was so afraid. She told her best friend she feared for her life and she came there, packed up Elizabeth's things, and drove her to another friend's house four hours away. In desperation, Elizabeth gave all of her things away, except for her clothing. She planned on starting a new life in the new place and simply ran.

The new place turned out to be just as bad, the friend she thought she had, turned out not to be her friend at all. So after one month, she returned to live with her best friend once again. Elizabeth felt safe, but she also felt like a failure. She had wound up right back where she had begun.

Anthony was calling Elizabeth even when she left town trying to use her and get her to come back. When she was with her family he couldn't get to her because he knew better than to attempt to find out where her family lived and show up there. They loathed Anthony, but refused to do anything about him because they knew she would go right back to him. Doing something wouldn't help anyone, until she was truly finished with him in her heart. She loved him and didn't want to see anything happen to him, even though he was ruining her life and mind one day at a time.

After a few months, Elizabeth was able to get back into her own place. She was very lonely and kissed a couple of other frogs that just weren't right. Finally, she just said, "Forget it. I'm going to focus on me." And that's what she did.

Elizabeth had so much to work to do on the inside; from the trauma of her childhood, all the way through what happened in her life as an adult. She was determined to change her life around. She started at a community college in 2014 to study criminal justice. She decided she wanted to be a Victim's Advocate and start her own foundation to help others find their way through life. She ended up finding a great job after her second semester of school. This allowed her to support other people in achieving their goals. She was able to relate very well to them due to her past experiences. While doing her job, she was also able to understand more and more about herself. Elizabeth was on her way to a bright future that she so deserved.

On the day of graduation from school, Elizabeth met a nice gentleman by the name of Brandon. She was hesitant about talking to Brandon or anyone because at this point, she had enough trust issues to fill a castle. However, Brandon was determined to be in Elizabeth's life and kept on talking to her after that day.

They exchanged numbers and Brandon started sending Elizabeth little cute text messages to encourage her in everything she was trying to do. He knew she worked, but he also knew she was trying to start her own advocacy foundation. He was so proud of her and was her greatest supporter, cheering her on at every turn.

She finally started to realize that Brandon was genuinely a nice person and he really liked her, for her. That summer, he was finally able to get her to accept him taking her on their first date. She happily accepted.

As soon as she accepted, Brandon explained that she needed to move things around for the date. Though confused, they started to plan and mess with her schedule until she was free for a few weeks. Brandon announced that he, too, took a few weeks off from work. Confused, Elizabeth questioned why the mystery and insane amount of time off and effort in a little date.

He simply smiled and announced that he was taking her to Tuscany, Italy. She was in total shock because it was the one place in the entire world she had always dreamed of going.

She told him "This is not a date, honey. It's a vacation!" Happy she didn't put up too much of a struggle to reconfigure her schedule, she started packing her bags.

Elizabeth had never been on a vacation before, so she was very excited. Though she was still a little hesitant because they had just met recently, she decided to at least give things a shot. She wasn't sure if things would work out because she just wasn't a girl who took such expensive trips, but any man that was willing to put forth such effort and basically make her relax and appreciate life while doing something unbelievable was worth notice. She was going to just have to suck up her nervousness.

Elizabeth looked at herself in the mirror for a moment and grinned. In that moment, she realized that all of the bad she had endured was so she could truly enjoy the good things when they came. If nothing else, Brandon was a blessing and this trip was going to be the adventure of a lifetime.

"I deserve good things and I'm worth the effort," she said to herself with pride in her voice. "He's a good person and we're going to have an amazing time. Even if it sucks, I will be in Tuscany! That's never happened before." Almost wanting to make a complete fool of herself and yelling "YOLO" through her apartment, she tried to get a grip before finishing her packing.

Brandon and Elizabeth went on several scenic tours in Tuscany. Brandon had done his research and found many places he thought Elizabeth would love to see.

One afternoon, he took her to *Montecatini Terme*, a spa known for its thermal waters. They went to a classic spa called *Terme Tettuccio* where there was live music daily and they were able to get wellness treatments. She was in awe of the beautiful town and all it had to offer. She could honestly say that was the best day of her entire life.

She hugged Brandon so tight that he could probably feel the warmth in her heart. No one had ever done anything so awesome for her ever.

They traveled around Italy for two weeks. By the time they were done, they had seen more beauty than ever before. The night tours were the absolute best and the most romantic.

Finally, though neither of them wanted it to end, they had to go back home.

They continued to date for another year and a half while learning about each other. One big thing both of them slowly realized was that they loved each other and simply couldn't live without each other. They did everything together, while still managing to keep some personal space. Where she liked to do her own things, he did his and then they would meet in the middle for their time together where they enjoyed life to the fullest, every day. It was completely obvious to everyone around them that they were soulmates.

On Elizabeth's birthday that year, Brandon took her out for a nice dinner and proposed to her in a crowded restaurant full of strangers. She accepted his proposal with eyes full of tears. She was in total shock as she never truly expected him to want forever with her, but she was happier than she'd ever been.

He'd bought her the most simple, sweet engagement ring. She loved it. She was always a simple girl at heart who didn't like flashy things.

Elizabeth asked, "Why did you propose to me in a restaurant with lots of people we don't know, instead of calling everyone?"

"I wanted to show you that I would confess my love for you in front of the entire world without hesitation," he said simply.

Elizabeth hugged Brandon and started to cry again. She was really beside herself with joy. This man tried so hard at every turn to make sure she felt loved, even when she never thought she was worth even a moment of his effort. It was in that moment, something in her mind clicked and she simply smiled at him. He was worthy of her love, so she must be worthy of his in return. Soulmate wasn't a one-sided deal.

Right after that, he called up a few connections of his own and found a sponsor for her advocacy foundation and it was up and running in no time. He was a businessman, so he already knew what to do to help her achieve success and was willing to do anything to make her smile and succeed with him. They were a true team.

Elizabeth realized that she had enabled Anthony to treat her the way he did, because she accepted it every time. She knew he didn't love her, but she had given him chance after chance through all of the abuse and manipulation. Looking back, she felt that because of how her mother treated her, and the way she was brought up, that it was the kind of treatment she deserved. Elizabeth was a very bright young woman with a lot of love to spread around. She was the total opposite of her mother and just like her kind and caring father. He taught her so much, but she had felt weak later in life, after his death.

She had to go through a lot of unfortunate things in order to learn some very powerful lessons, before she could get to the light at the end of her once dark, dreary tunnel. She started taking care of her own wellness and building a life for herself. She was no longer a victim, but a strong survivor. She knew she didn't deserve what her mother, or especially Anthony had done to her, or any other funky frog in her path. She was heartbroken for most of her life, living on pain and scraps of dreams. But she turned all of those negative experiences into positive ones to help other people. That had always been her dream; to give back and help others so no one had to ever feel the way she once did.

Brandon and Elizabeth moved into their home shortly after he proposed so they could start their life together. He knew everything Elizabeth wanted in life and he supported her every step of the way. He played an active role in her foundation, along with her best friend, Lynn, who was there from day one and did so much to help her get started. She never left Elizabeth's side.

Elizabeth continues being an advocate for many, and is very happy with her fiancé, Brandon. She let him know that she wanted to be engaged for at least a year because that's something she always wanted and he had no problem with that. She had finally found a way to slow life down and enjoy the journey instead of forcing a happy ending. Brandon agreed to her terms, but admitted that he was ready to marry her the day after he proposed to her.

They have set a date to be married and are currently planning their dream wedding together.

She finally knows what real love feels like and she is grateful. She now knows her own worth. Elizabeth and Brandon are building a wonderful life together. After all of those frogs, she finally found her prince.

About the Authors

C.L. Foster

CL is eclectic, geeky, positive, nature-loving and completely non-"normal" (just the way she likes to be). She has been a fan of literature since she was a small child and finally decided to take her dreams (both waking and sleeping!) and do something positive with them.

CL has lived all over the world and has a Bachelor's degree in Criminal Justice, minoring in Psychology and Forensics. Which means you don't want to cross her because she knows how and where to hide a body so it's never found! She proudly admits to hearing voices in her head, but at times, her characters' impromptu visits can be rude and annoying. Thankfully, she has adequate patience for their shenanigans and can out ninja them any day of the week.

CL can be stalked at:
www.facebook.com/authorclfoster
https://www.instagram.com/clfoster1/

Jessica Surgett

Jessica has been madly in love with the written word since her days as a fetus. In childhood, she drew sustenance from the writings of Tolkien, Ingalls-Wilder, and Silverstein. Her appetite increased as she grew, and soon she was devouring literature of all flavors. Sweet love stories, savory epics of fantasy, and even the bitter taste of horror. Now in adulthood, Jessica finds herself full to the brim with words and phrases. She writes them down as best she can in hopes they will nourish someone else the way they have nourished her.

Jennifer Rose

Jennifer Rose lives the glamorous life in Canada working as a part-time office clerk/manager. A mother of three grown boys, she decided to give up cleaning, cooking and day to day household chores in favor of sitting with a favorite beverage, be it coffee or wine and her trusty laptop, after a friend and author convinced her that she had what it took to write romance novels, so she took a creative writing course and finally started writing.

Facebook fan page:
https://www.facebook.com/pages/Author-Jennifer-Rose/231674010318730
Twitter: @JenniferRose62
Website: www.jenniferroseauthor.wix.com/jennifer-rose

Hannah Thorley

When she's not being a superhero, salsa-dancing, face-painting, cake-making beacon of amazingness. Hannah also likes to scribble a blog or two. Safe Haven is her first published work.

Stina Rubio

Stina Rubio's love of books runs deep. After being an avid reader for longer than she can remember, she turned her love of books into more and became a cover artists and a writer. As a mother of three boys and two pups, she tries not to melt in the California heat while wrestling with her muse and penning her tales.

You can find Stina at:

Facebook fan page: https://www.facebook.com/Stina-Rubio-Author-138662976280463/

Twitter: @Stinarubio

Karla Bostic

Karla Bostic is a mother to four grown children and when her chicks left the nest she began to look for other things to do to contribute to the world. Dealing with several health issues left her bed-bound disabled but that doesn't slow her down at all. Having been an avid reader for many years, she slowly moved into editing books for her favorite authors and things began to take off.

Change of Station is her debut short story.

She also runs a charity called Covers for Comfort where people make and donate items to babies in the NICU at a hospital that is local to them.

You can find Karla's ninja-lurking across the interwebs:

Facebook fan page:https://www.facebook.com/karla.bostic

Twitter: https://twitter.com/KarlaMBostic

David Roraff

David, also known as Grunge, Wynter or even Nefarious de Wit, is a chaotic mess that has a particular knack for the written word and getting into people's heads. Trespassing aside, he currently works as a security officer, is father to two wonderful kids, and has multiple projects on the burner, stirred frequently.

Residing in the land of cheese, beer, brats and lawless weather that is Wisconsin, this winter-loving poet and author has only recently forayed into the world of writing as a true passion. Like madness, gravity, or a neglected '67 Shelby, it took this joker a little shove to get him started, but hopefully the push will maintain this knight's strength and words to keep him going for years to come.

A criminal justice major by trade, mathematical-minded, role-playing enthusiast, music lover and movie-fanatic, David is hard to pin to a particular genre or style. Then again, that might be part of his charm.

You can find David lurking about at:
https://www.Facebook.com/DERoraff or @WynterIgnatius

A.B. Martin

A.B. Martin has had a pen in one hand and pencil in the other for over 30 years. Only recently has she decided to share her musings with the world.

She grew up in Western New York and has been an avid outdoorswoman her entire life. She enjoys fishing and hunting alongside her husband of more than 20 years. She is also the proud mother of two grown children and one step-child.

https://www.facebook.com/AB-Martin-1678163522452218/

Elle Vaughn

Elle Vaughn is an avid book lover - especially romance novels. She's the author of the Anna and Quinton novella series and is always working on a new story project. When she's not lost in her character creations she can be found chasing around her toddler, being outside in the Colorado outdoors, gardening and attempting to cook for her family!

Facebook fan page:www.facebook.com/ElleVaughnAuthor
Twitter: @_ellevaughn
Website: www.ellevaughn.com

Sharon E. Foster

Sharon is spiritual soul with hopes and dreams that could fill a stadium. Though she never set out to be a writer, she is making her debut in this short story collection. She also plans to write her own self-help book in the future and continues to advocate for those who need a voice.

She's a sister, friend, student, and so much more. She loves music, movies, art, life, nature, and anything that can make her soul feel balanced.

To keep up with Sharon, you can follow her:
https://www.facebook.com/SE-Foster-637453376353435

15166614R00169

Printed in Great Britain
by Amazon.co.uk, Ltd.,
Marston Gate.